THE
TRUTH
OF IT ALL

THE
TRUTH
OF IT ALL

A NOVEL

GWEN FLORIO

CROOKED
LANE

NEW YORK

Copyright © 2021 by Gwen Florio

Published in the United States by Crooked Lane Books, an imprint of The Quick Brown Fox & Company LLC.

Crooked Lane Books and its logo are trademarks of The Quick Brown Fox & Company LLC.

Library of Congress Catalog-in-Publication data available upon request.

ISBN (hardcover): 978-1-64385-857-9
ISBN (ebook): 978-1-64385-858-6

Cover design by Kelly Martin

Printed in the United States.

www.crookedlanebooks.com

Crooked Lane Books
34 West 27th St., 10th Floor
New York, NY 10001

First Edition: August 2021

10 9 8 7 6 5 4 3 2 1

To Scott, who I met when he was pushing
a story about public defenders.
Fifteen years later, here it is.

1

JULIA GEARY—FIVE FOOT nothing, hardly a hundred pounds, freckled head to toe and red hair a fright—neared her thirtieth year mad as a feral cat, all hiss and spit just below the surface. She had reason, God knows, life gone to hell four years earlier and never finding its way back, everything wrong all the time ever since.

On this particular morning as the year hurtled toward its close, wrong started with sleeping late, the whole day off kilter from the start. Julia tried to slide unnoticed into the kitchen, her mother-in-law at the stove, back to her.

Failure.

"I made you eggs. But you took too long. They're ruined." Stink of sulfur rising from the pan.

Julia hated eggs. She smiled. Too soon.

"So I made more."

Looking at Beverly—the careful gray coif, the faded blue eyes behind round glasses, the knee-length skirts and hose, worn even around the house—people might guess librarian. Or store clerk, the helpful sort. A nice lady. They'd be wrong.

Julia thought of her mother-in-law as a human switchblade, all spring-loaded lethality, razoring steel ready to leap forward, draw blood, Jabberwocky's vorpal blade rendered unfunny.

"No time." Julia dodged around the kitchen island toward the breakfast nook, where her son perched on his booster seat.

Beverly stepped in front of her, plate in hand, blocking her escape route. Two eggs aimed a jiggly yellow glare at Julia. Melted fat pooled beneath the bacon, congealing apace with Beverly's tone. "You need a good breakfast. Working as hard as you do."

Repeat those words to anyone—say, to Claudette Greene, Julia's officemate in the Public Defender's Division—and they'd sound innocuous—caring, even. Julia could just hear Claudette's reply: "Wish someone would make me breakfast. Can't remember the last time I ate sitting down." Claudette juggled three kids, a spouse, and a sixty-hour-a-week job dealing with people who made excuses for their misdeeds all day long. Claudette was disinclined to sympathy, even toward Julia, who held the widow card.

Defeated, Julia joined Calvin in the breakfast nook. The murmur of public radio flowed through the silence, the announcer's voice soothing, words barely distinguishable as she ran through a routine story—the latest polling data on the coming mayoral election. Julia poked a fork in her eggs. Yolk ran everywhere. She stood. "I'll just make some toast." Something to sop up that damn mess on her plate. Beverly put a hand to Julia's shoulder, the barest touch. Julia's butt smacked back down onto the bench. "Carbs, dear. Nothing but unnecessary calories."

"And yet." Julia nudged the bacon with her fork.

Beverly affected not to hear, as did Calvin, happily attacking his own bacon, precut into small pieces, an egg—and toast!—at the far end of the table. Just four, too young for the truth, he loved the old bitch. "Gamma." He summoned her, arms up, angling his face for a kiss. Beverly touched her cheek to his, powder flaking from the fine creases laid down by too many decades on a dairy farm in the state's wide southern valleys before she fled the punishing sun and scouring wind, trading the ammoniac reek of cows for the cool shelter of Duck Creek, a pine-scented mining town turned ski resort within shouting distance of the Canadian border.

Julia disentangled herself from Calvin's grasp and turned back to the pressing matter of Julia's faults.

"Is that what you're going to wear?" Seven in the morning and Beverly was decked out in tweed skirt, boiled wool jacket, and for

God's sake, pearls. It was bridge club day, competitive in ways that went beyond the game. Julia often wondered at Beverly's enthusiasm for a pastime that, despite the alacrity with which she'd adopted the mufti of a town dowager, required such an unsparing display of her hands. The nails might have been expertly manicured, but the sophistication ended there.

Her fingers were knotted as old rope, betraying their competence, hands that could work their way inside a bellowing cow and hook a calving chain around tiny hooves, and then, after a rough scrubbing with grainy soap, rub lard into flour for a pie crust of surpassing flakiness.

Julia suspected Beverly's resentment of her was twofold. Not only did her mother-in-law blame Julia for her son's death—if she hadn't gotten herself pregnant (as though Michael had nothing to do with it), he'd never have felt obligated to join the army, dangling the signing bonus as a someday down payment on a house of their own. But Julia also remembered the Beverly of old, who'd sold the farm the day after she buried her own husband and moved to Duck Creek, abandoning along the way her muck boots in favor of a collection of slipper-soft pumps from the Little Heel Shop. A pair, dove-gray to match her jacket, waited by the front door, ready for their final few outings before winter swept in and demanded Sorels.

The only holdover from that former life was Lyle, a bobtailed barn cat grown fat in his retirement from rodent patrol. He sauntered across the kitchen and positioned himself beside Julia's chair, lifting a paw and dragging his rough tongue across it, pretending indifference, aware that if Beverly turned her back, some eggs were bound to slide his way.

Julia offered what she knew would be an unacceptable explanation for her attire.

"I've got jail."

It was her turn in the public defenders' rotation to interview the miscreants who'd been booked into the county jail overnight or early that morning, in preparation for their court appearances the next day. She wore a formless, below-the-knee dress, dark tights, and clogs, the defense against the inevitability that her clients would see her as a woman first, their lawyer later. She couldn't keep track of how many times they'd hit on her.

"What have you got in mind?" she'd snapped at one early on. "Candlelight dinner in the interview room?"

A mistake. He'd told her exactly what he had in mind.

The radio's somnolent recitation went shrill with a sound bite from Duck Creek's leading mayoral candidate, volume rising, the campaign at a fever pitch in these final weeks before the election. The Candidate's voice was high and hoarse, with a hint of a lisp, oddly unsuited to his penchant for diatribes. He railed against immigrants, the perfect segue into a local spot about the town's refugee program. "Send 'em back. End this bull—" the Candidate blustered, the word cut off just in time.

Beverly glanced toward Calvin, killed the radio, and moved to distract. "Time, dear. You don't want to be late for your important job." A scalpel slipped deftly between Julia's ribs, twisted with a verbal flick of the wrist. Julia's clients were nobody's idea of important. Nor did her job command the kind of salary that merited the word. Even living with Beverly, it would take her years to pay off her law school loans, a span Julia had calculated to the day, a weekly notation of the time remaining typed into the calendar on her phone. The minute that number hit zero, she'd kiss Duck Creek goodbye.

Julia rose and grabbed Calvin's hand with relief, so happy at her daily escape that she let the gibe slide.

Beverly called her routine farewell. "Kiss Daddy goodbye." She stood in the kitchen doorway as they donned their coats, watching to make sure.

A photo of Michael in his service uniform hung between the front door and the stately front stairwell that no one used, above the glass-enclosed folded American flag presented to Julia at his funeral, the flag that Beverly had tugged from her hands a moment later.

"For better or worse," he'd promised her. But this was the worst, and he was supposed to have been beside her for it, not have caused it. Light through the stained-glass transom splashed purple and gold bars across his face. Julia suspected Beverly had positioned the photo there for that very reason, the shimmering hues underscoring the saintliness she'd ascribed to her son even before his untimely death.

Julia opened the front door, mandating a quick getaway. Cold gusted in, wrapping her ankles, fall barely begun but winter already a promise. The wind lofted the long light hair of a girl walking past, heading coatless for the nearby high school, quick-stepping in the cold, arms wrapped around her thin body, lips moving as though in incantation. The girl glanced her way. Their eyes met, the girl's full of an anguish that mirrored Julia's own. Probably mooning over some boy. Julia directed an unspoken warning her way: It won't end well.

Beverly lingered, immobile, impervious. Julia boosted Calvin up. He kissed the picture of the father he didn't remember, leaving a smear that Beverly would remove with her daily polishing. "Bye, Daddy."

Michael gazed from the photo with all the solemnity mandated for these dress portraits, a corner of his mouth nonetheless quirked toward a grin. Even now, dead nearly as long as they'd been together, that damned grin got her. Someday she'd forgive herself for falling for it, right before she forgave him for going off to Iraq and getting killed. That day hadn't come yet.

She pursed her lips against the cool, cool glass, and whispered below her breath, as she did every morning to the man whose death had bound her life in limitations.

"Goodbye, you son of a bitch."

CHAPTER

2

CHIEF PUBLIC DEFENDER Bill Decker thumped his elbows onto his desk and steepled his fingers before his face, which had the unfortunate effect of making his index fingers look as though they were about to disappear up his nose.

"Geary. Sorry about the short notice."

Her phone had shrilled as she walked into her office, heralding an immediate meeting with her boss. It wasn't a request.

Julia looked away. Decker's office was barely larger than her shared one, although at least the polished desk looked like real wood, not the scratched cheap veneer of her own, which gave every appearance of having come from a surplus closet.

And, unlike her desk, its surface obscured by her impossible caseload's ever-higher stacks of files, Decker's was free of everything but a blotter, a phone, and a lone file. Likewise, the shelves held only law books; the walls, the usual framed diplomas. Julia's diplomas also hung on her office walls, but hers displayed the names of the state university and law school.

Decker's boasted Harvard undergrad and Yale law, silently underscoring his status as part of a new class of lawyers who'd followed the ski money to Duck Creek after the resort's transformation from a mom-and-pop operation into one the Chamber of Commerce touted as the Vail of the North. A third framed certificate proclaimed his long-ago—very long-ago—argument before the U.S. Supreme Court, a typically tangled water rights case that, as Julia and everyone else in the office knew because Decker mentioned it on every flimsiest excuse, he'd won.

"How long have you been with us now, Geary?"

Forever. "A few years."

"Minus a break."

A break. He made it sound like a vacation, the extended leave she'd taken after Calvin's birth and not a year later Michael's death, career seemingly irrevocably stalled ever since, even though she hadn't missed a day of work since returning. Which he knew, just as well as she knew this particular tactic: lob softballs first, so that it would feel like a regular chat rather than the interrogation it was. What was Decker working up to?

Whatever it was, she'd be well advised to stick to yes or no answers. As she repeatedly reminded her clients, volunteering information always got people in trouble.

"And your little . . . boy, is it?"

"Yes."

"How is he? He must be getting big now."

"Yes."

Red alert now. Federal rules about personal questions be damned; Julia was achingly, painfully aware of every professional woman's reality: a child was a liability. Somehow the men in the office were presumed—even though the public defenders' salaries hardly allowed for it—to have wives who stayed at home and took care of all of life's inconveniences. Like children. As for single mothers, forget it. The condescending assumptions layered onto them were enough to flatten even the most modest ambitions.

Except for Susan Parrish, the county's first woman chief prosecutor, the blazing exception to the rule. Julia studied Susan furtively whenever she saw her in the hallway, always perfectly turned out in the sort of severely tailored business suits that Julia assumed involved extended shopping trips to Seattle. Duck Creek had its share of high-end boutiques, but they mostly offered apres-ski togs. Mink-topped snow boots had yet to become standard court attire.

Debra, the office receptionist, was a brazen gossip. The junior attorneys believed her unprofessionalism was tolerated only because she served as an interoffice spy for Decker. As she told it, Susan—with the help of a teacher husband who took on most of the childcare duties—had advanced methodically up the ladder when her daughter was young, ditching the husband as soon as the girl hit a more self-sufficient age. At which point, having reduced her personal obligations by half, Susan's career took off.

Julia wrenched her thoughts back to the matter at hand. She must have done something wrong to receive a summons from Decker as soon as she arrived at work, especially given these desultory questions designed to ease her into complacency. She sieved through her memory.

"You're the one who's been whining about wanting bigger cases," he'd said when he rang her extension. She was sure she'd never said as much directly to him. Debra must have passed along an overheard snippet. Julia made a note to herself: no Christmas cookies for Deb. Except that would only make things worse.

And just like that, with her momentary lapse into resentment, Decker caught her off guard.

"So." He spoke into his hands. "Tell me about your husband."

Julia's throat closed. Sonofabitch. She should have seen something like this coming. She'd sat through too many trials watching Decker's specialty move, turning his back on the poor schmuck on the witness stand as though he were done with his cross-examination, speaking over his shoulder, almost as an afterthought. "So. Tell me . . ." About the one thing the witness hadn't figured on him knowing.

Julia stalled, a yes or no answer insufficient for this one. "What about him?" And why the hell was he asking?

Decker's smile peeped out from either side of his hands, all benevolence. As if. "Whatever you want me to know."

Julia gave the biographical version of name, rank, and serial number. "Grew up on a dairy farm in the southern part of the state. Landed here after college like every other wannabe ski bum. Joined the military not quite five years ago. Caught an IED after seven months in country. End of story."

Davis lowered his hands and cocked his head. Almost too big for his gym-toned body, that head, made larger still by the shock of snowy hair, looking nearly natural in its sweep and wave over his forehead. "Senatorial hair," Julia had observed when she first met him.

"Senate, hell," Claudette Greene, Julia's office mate, had snorted. "All that campaigning? And the fundraising? That's not our Li'l Pecker's style."

Decker's name lent itself to the unfortunate nickname, made more unfortunate still by the fact that his father had been a judge—not just any judge, but on the federal bench—and thus accorded Big Pecker status.

"No, he's holding out for a judgeship," Claudette said. "He'll still have to campaign, but judicial races are pretty low-key. Looked like things were going his way, too, until Susan Parrish came along. He's just hoping Judge Baker retires so that he can get the spot before she wins a big enough case to knock him out of contention."

Disappointment leaked from Claudette's words. She was Decker's obvious heir apparent, but obviously stacked up against black and woman was nobody's idea of a guarantee. The longer Judge Baker waited to retire, the more chance Susan had to make a name for herself and present a serious challenge to Decker. Judges were elected in their state, and the public generally favored crime-fighting prosecutors over public defenders. If Susan beat Li'l Pecker to a judge's job, Claudette could be stuck as a deputy forever. "She needs to lose a case," Claudette often muttered. "A big one."

Meanwhile, Decker waited, avuncular, beaming, seemingly oblivious to the seething ambition all around him, just as he was now to the warning tone in Julia's voice.

"A ski bum . . . and a reporter, too, if I remember correctly?"

Of course he remembered correctly. Not long after starting her job at the Public Defender's Office, Julia had had to stand in his office like a misbehaving pupil before a principal and remind him that her new boyfriend didn't cover the courts; swear she never, ever discussed cases with him; and nod her understanding that should Decker ever have cause to as much as suspect otherwise, she'd be out on her ass. Until he died a hero, Michael had been the second-biggest liability to Julia's career—later surpassed, of course, by Calvin—and now she had to live with the fact that the searing thread of resentment running through their marriage had likely factored into his fleeing into the army.

"Iraq, yes?" Decker's voice crept into the lengthening silence, so intimate it was barely audible.

It reminded her of something, that silky, insinuating tone, inviting confidences in return. What was it? She closed her eyes and let it come to her. The mingled scents of oiled wood, incense, and musty upholstery. A sliding sound. A screen. That was it. The confessional. "Bless me, Father, for I have sinned."

Well, she had sinned, plenty, starting with a party where she somehow ended up kissing the hostess's date, which saw the end of that friendship but the beginning of some of the most enthusiastic and unrepentant sinning of her life, not one goddamn bit of it deserving of the eternity of penance that had been inflicted upon her.

Decker waited, every pore oozing empathy.

"Yes, Iraq." She sank her teeth into her lower lip. Whenever someone or other breezily opined that it was time for the United States to bring its troops home, she had to stop herself from adding, "Not before we've bombed the shit out of Iraq," along with an equally silent prayer that said bombing would obliterate the person responsible for ruining her life.

"Not Afghanistan."

"No." What was he up to? Any idiot could look this stuff up on Google. Type in Michael's name, and story after story scrolled past. He'd only lived in Duck Creek a few years, but you'd have thought he'd been the mayor, the way the town had carried on when he died. No, not died. Was killed. Murdered, probably by some teenager who'd paid attention in whatever passed for chemistry class in that godforsaken country. There'd been the black-bordered photo on the front page of *The Bulletin*. A parade of sorts, people lining the streets to watch the hearse carrying his too-light casket pass. Kids, uncomprehending, waving little American flags as though it really were a parade, some sort of cause for celebration. Julia stared dully at them through the limo's dark-tinted windows, wondering at their smiles, fighting an inexplicable impulse to raise her hand, wave back, every action in these early days after Michael's death rote, automatic.

"I'm so sorry for your loss."

How many times had she heard that? "It's been four years. A little more. I've had time to get used to it." Except that she hadn't, the passing years simultaneously a blink and an eternity.

"Geary."

She knew that tone. Goodbye, wise priest; hello, boss. She was finally going to find out what this was all about.

"You've been asking for more responsibility for quite a while. Par for the course for young attorneys. They want to put all those years of law school to work, strut their newly acquired stuff."

Julia inched forward in her chair. Was it her imagination, or had Decker stocked his office with oversized furniture? She'd heard of attorneys pulling stunts like that, anything for an advantage. In a regular chair, her feet barely touched the floor. In this one, they dangled with a couple of inches of clearance, no way to reach the carpet without perching on the very edge of the seat, dangerously prone to pitching forward. She gripped the arms.

"I've been out of school a few years now."

"Yes, yes. And you've done yeoman work. You've managed to get decent plea agreements for some of our most difficult clients."

Julia held herself rigid, awaiting a lecture on the virtues of patience.

Decker picked up a file from his desk and rifled through it. "Yes, I think it's time. How do you feel about sex offenses?"

CHAPTER

3

J ULIA'S BREATH CAUGHT. Advantage: Decker.

"How do I feel about them? That's not really the issue, is it?"

Buying time by daring a bit of defiance, knowing the crap assumption behind the question. Men, even one as studied as Decker, went all crawly on the subject, because everybody knew the stats, one in five women groped, fondled, abused, raped, and therefore—naturally, right?—prone to be a little unreliable. So, always the sideways question; in this case, her take on sex crimes.

When in reality he wanted to ask: Has it ever happened to you? Can I trust you to handle this kind of case without falling apart on me? As if men never got into fistfights and then went on to handle assault cases without anyone raising an eyebrow.

Hence her response, a tactful pushback, no way to say that she'd been one of the lucky ones without coming across as defensive or even lying.

Decker smiled without showing his teeth. "Good. Because I think you're the perfect person for this case. It hasn't hit the news yet, but it will any minute. Apparently, it's already flying around social media."

Julia slid to the edge of the chair and planted her feet firmly on the floor, no need to worry about toppling now. If anything, she feared the opposite, floating ceilingward like a released balloon, suddenly buoyant with relief and nearly forgotten ambition, along with the added fillip of change.

A sex offense that would bring in the press? That meant somebody prominent: a public official maybe, or an athlete. She mentally sifted through the possibilities, and the attendant pros and cons, "publicity" being inadequate to describe the media feeding frenzy that usually accompanied such cases. Not to mention the difficulty of the cases themselves, sex offenses being notoriously troublesome, especially when the accused was someone well known, the sort of person who, in the court of public opinion, could never ever.

And if you successfully secured a precious not-guilty verdict for your prominent client? Something that saw your name in the newspapers and, far more important, circulating in the legal community, something that could finally bring that job offer from a firm? No more Mother Sullivan and her goddamn runny eggs. Julia's free-floating daydream bumped up against a hard reality. Why would someone prominent have a public defender?

But he'd said it was a big case. The victim must have the high profile, then, something that changed the equation entirely. Because even though a sexual assault victim never would be publicly identified, in a town of Duck Creek, most people would have a good idea who she was.

Tricky, tricky. If there'd been the least deviance from the stranger-in-the-bushes scenario, Julia's task would be immeasurably easier. Because nearly all victims knew their assailants, making a defense attorney's job so, so much easier. A girl who willingly went over to a boy's house to play video games as she had ever since they were little kids? A woman who willingly had a drink with a coworker at day's end? Or one who accepted a ride home from the nice guy with whom she'd shared a couple of tipsy kisses?

Forget #MeToo. Unless the offenses were ongoing and egregious, unless the disparity between assailant and victim gaped wide, it was almost laughably easy to sway a jury away from unanimity, if not complete agreement on a not-guilty verdict.

"And remember," a law school professor had warned a class full of first-year women resistant to the idea of defending the same sorts of creeps with whom they'd dealt for years, "not guilty doesn't mean innocent." As if that was supposed to make anyone feel better.

On the other hand. Things could go south fast for the defense if the victim, not the accused, were the kind of person who could never. An elderly woman. A little girl—or boy—although those cases could be problematic, depending on how well the child in question could articulate the abuse. Or the rare assault by a stranger. And even then, the woman had better have fought back, a few bruises a boon to the prosecution, broken limbs so much the better.

Decker, bastard that he was, probably had one of those impossible cases in mind. The prosecutor's office preferred not to chase sex crimes unless they were slam dunks. This way, Decker could say he'd given Julia the big case she'd wanted and use the fact that she'd lost it as an excuse to stick her with drunk and disorderlies for the foreseeable, interminable future.

Julia's hopeful balloon deflated. Just get it over with, she silently urged Decker. Her grip on the chair's arms tightened against the impulse to snatch the file from his hands. She held her breath until he bestowed it upon her with an odd look, the smile still hovering on his lips, but his eyes cold, assessing.

She flipped through the paucity of pages within, a few words jumping out at her from the terse phrasing of the police report. Duck Creek High School. A locker room. A soccer player and a girl. Other soccer players. A witness's name stood out. Cody Landers. She did some quick mental math. Too young to be the son, but possibly the grandson of the contractor who'd built half the ski resort.

"But these are kids!" Juvenile cases were a whole different ball game, usually handled by another attorney in the office.

"Check the birthdate."

Julia did some quick math. Indeed, the accused youth was eighteen, just, but fully qualified as an adult for the purposes of the legal system. Just as important, his age qualified the crime as a felony, given the three-year difference between him and the victim, a sophomore at the high school. That would see him, if convicted, housed in the state prison with men decades his senior. She digested the unusual name as she studied the mugshot, shock of dark hair above large panicked eyes in a narrow face, mouth tight with fear. Brown skin.

Realization dawned. "He's one of the refugees."

This would be the polar opposite of the usual high-profile rape trials, where public opinion nearly always leaned in favor of the man—or, in this case, boy—and held the woman in question to be a lying, conniving slut out to destroy his reputation.

Julia checked the victim's name again. Ana Olsen. Norwegian, then, likely a descendant of the Scandinavians who'd given up on the dusty prairies to the south and traded their view of endless sky for the reliable paycheck of the mines' round-the-clock darkness; people who'd long ago transcended the early, dismissive Squarehead label and, in rose-hued retrospect, merited adjectives like "hard-working" and "thrifty." The right kind of immigrant. Duck Creek's considerable anti-refugee contingent would paint Ana as the flower of white womanhood, beset by a member of a rampaging dark horde.

Why not Claudette? She'd handled any number of sex crimes. Julia stopped herself before asking the question, the answer too obvious. The optics were awful. Julia could already hear the whispers—of course Claudette would defend one of them. Brown skin, black skin, the shades of cultural difference discounted. They always stick together, don't they?

So, a white lawyer. Not just white, but a woman. Always better, in such cases, to have a woman defender. Because surely a woman wouldn't stand up for someone accused of something so heinous unless she truly believed him innocent. Still, Claudette wasn't the only one in the office who'd taken such cases.

Julia couldn't help herself. It slipped out. "Why me?"

"Because you're perfect for this particular defendant."

Julia's mind sifted through the possibilities. Snagged on one. Shied away. Impossible. Even Decker, blandly conniving Decker, wasn't capable of this sort of cruelty. But—

"Where's he from?"

Decker waited.

"No."

Of course. Who better than to defend the predatory foreigner accused of assaulting a white girl than the woman whose husband had been killed by one of the suspect's countrymen? She choked back a cry of rage, managing to force only a whisper past it.

"Iraq. Right? He's from Iraq."

4

L OOK PAST THE orange jumpsuit.

That's what Julia learned in law school. A successful defense meant helping people get past the initial impression—"the prisoner"—and see the human being. Call him—or her, the renewed crackdown on drugs leading to an increasing number of women—by first name. In court, use that name as often as possible, starting with the very first appearance, months before the case goes to trial, if it ever does. Especially persuade the judge, who will decide bail. Stand close to your client. Touch him—a hand on the arm, or the shoulder. Let the judge know with your body language as well as your words that he couldn't possibly present a danger to society.

That initial court appearance was still a day away. Julia didn't have to worry about standing close to Sami Mohammed, or—she shuddered—touching him. Bad enough she had to sit across from him at one of the steel tables in the jail's interview room. She'd focus on the easiest thing, seeing past the jumpsuit that nearly swallowed up his lanky body.

Despite the cheap jeans and knockoff college hoodie that, according to his file, he'd worn when booked into the jail that morning, she couldn't help but imagine him in some sort of baggy, pajama-type get-up. A rifle slung over his shoulder, fingers poised above the detonator in his hand.

He jumped from a chair and held out his hand, the gesture of a well-brought-up child, and she took it, her response as automatic as his offer, something odd about the brief grasp before both jerked their hands away, her touch seemingly as abhorrent to him as his to her. She motioned for him to sit.

He balanced crookedly on the edge of his chair, his weight on one hip, quivering, silent. A first-timer. The frequent fliers slouched in their chairs, relaxing to the extent possible when surrounded by metal and concrete, yammering as soon as she walked into the room. Anything to draw out the precious time away from the cellblock. Attitude abounded. And, if she'd represented them before, unwelcome familiarity.

"Hey, hey, it's my lucky day," one crowed. "Got Thumbelina for my lawyer. Outta here!" A fluttering motion with his hands toward the wire-reinforced window, image of a bird flying free, a backhanded compliment to her success at wangling reasonable bail amounts.

The nickname was bestowed by one of the older guys on his umpteenth DUI and smart enough not to blow when presented with the Breathalyzer, betting on the longest of shots that he'd get a public defender skilled enough to get him off with a six-month license suspension. Which she'd done. He'd turned to her in surprise as the judge dismissed them with a bored tap of his gavel.

"Be damned. Didn't think you had it in you. Little thing like you. Thanks, Thumbelina."

Snickers from the next guy on the docket and a grin from Claudette, so confident of her case that she was comfortable in flats. Her client must have passed it on when the van took the lot of them back to jail that day, and she'd been Thumbelina ever since. She'd thought about taking Claudette's route, getting some heels, twisting her undisciplined hair high on her head, in hopes of reaching the lofty height of, say, five foot three. Maybe even five foot four. Which still would leave her shoulder height at best for a lot of her clients. Like this one.

Get this over with, she lectured herself. She opened his file and matched the mugshot within to the youth sitting across from her. Handsome—beautiful, more like—even in the unforgiving mug. Maybe he'd counted on his looks to win the girl over, and when that hadn't worked . . . no. That line of thinking belonged to whomever

Susan Parrish assigned to prosecute the case. Which, from a prosecutor's point of view, was at this point a gimme. The file informed
her that another boy had reported seeing Sami assaulting a girl in a
school locker room. Neither Sami nor his victim was talking, but
then again neither had denied the incident.

"Sami Mohammed." Ice crystallizing on every syllable. She
spelled it, enunciating carefully, even though she'd been told his
English was good enough that she wouldn't need a translator. "Is
that correct?"

He dipped his chin in what she took for assent.

"Eighteen years old?"

Another chin bob, eyes fixed on the floor, avoiding hers.

Obviously guilty. Except, she knew better. Some of her guiltiest
clients looked her straight in the eye while they lied and lied and lied.

Maybe this one wasn't looking at her because he wasn't allowed
to look at women. Expected them to be cringing, deferential, faces
wound in disguising scarves. She'd turn the tables, force him to see
her, to acknowledge what he—his people—had done.

She glanced down at the police report, reminding herself. He
was a member of the soccer team. She had a vague impression—
headlines glimpsed on the sports pages she never read; snippets from
the nightly news—that the team routinely bagged championships.
Sometimes girls threw themselves at athletes. At least, that's how the
athletes told it, and juries tended to believe them, something that
could work to her advantage.

She retrieved the pen hooked on the neckline of her dress—no
purses allowed in the jail—and slapped the file down on the desk.
He didn't even flinch.

She raised her voice. "Why don't you tell me what—"

She stopped herself just before saying, "what you did." Cleared
her throat. "Tell me what happened."

Sami raised his eyes at last. Met hers. His were a startling hazel,
not the brown she'd expected. She braced for defensiveness, hostility;
fear, even. But his eyes were drained of all hope, his voice as flat as his
gaze when he finally spoke.

"Nothing."

And for just an eye-blink, an indrawn breath before common sense prevailed, "what if?" wriggled within Julia.

* * *

She squelched it fast, her retort more challenge than question.

"That's not what the boys said."

"Boys?" His gaze had wandered off again. Not back to the floor, but over her shoulder. She fought an impulse to turn, knowing she'd see only a blank cinderblock wall.

"Your teammates. They said they saw you in the locker room. The girls' locker room. Were you there?"

A beat. "Yes."

"Was Ana Olsen there?"

A longer beat. "Yes."

"Were your teammates there?"

She looked again at her file, at the account Cody Landers, the soccer team captain, had given police. He'd apparently gone in first, catching Sami in the act, his teammates following. But Sami's silence went on so long she glanced up, wondering if he'd dozed off as her clients sometimes did, so drunk or exhausted after a night in jail or both that the quiet of the interview room lulled them into slumber.

But Sami was wide awake, gaze boring a hole in that concrete wall, and the "yes" that finally emerged through clenched teeth was more hiss than articulated word, such fury contained in the single syllable that she flinched. She knew a guard hovered just outside the door; had availed herself of that protection more than once when an interview went sideways. She'd been reluctant on those first frankly terrifying occasions, an inmate on his feet, yelling, fist raised, until Claudette had assured her it had happened to all the public defenders, the guys too, including one who'd waited too long and ended up with a dislocated shoulder when he'd been the subject of a tug-of-war between guard and inmate.

Time to dial it down. "When did this happen? What time of day?"

She'd come to expect the pause. But when he replied, his voice edged back toward normal. "Morning. Early. Before first class."

"Can you remember the exact time?"

He shook his head.

"Maybe this will help. What time do you usually get to school?"

"Six thirty. To practice football." *Fute-bole*, he said it, still hesitating over the switch to the American soccer.

She attempted what she hoped would be seen as an encouraging smile. "You see? You do remember a time." Thinking to herself that, at this time of year, it would be just beginning to get light at six thirty. Could the players see well enough to practice on the field then? Maybe there were lights? She made a note to check.

"What do you do in the morning? Do you play practice games?"

"We do this first." He raised his arms and lowered them, pantomiming lifting weights. "Then we run. Do drills. After school, we play the game."

That made sense. She crossed out her note and doodled in the blank spot below it, killing a moment or two before she got back to what really mattered.

"Why were you in the girls' locker room?"

A shrug, duly noted.

"Did you know Ana was there?"

"No!"

A shadow crossed the small square window in the door. The guard, attentive as always to a change in volume.

"Was she undressed except for a towel?"

If he so much as twitched, she was going to yell for help. But he pressed his lips in a thin, bloodless line, and remained mute.

"Did you," she checked the file, "force her down onto a bench?"

Nothing.

"Did you lie on top of her?"

Nothing.

"Were your pants down?"

Nothing.

"Sami Mohamed, did you rape—or were you trying to rape—Ana Olsen? If there was no"—she hesitated, wondering if he'd understand a word like "penetration"—"if you were trying, but didn't actually, uh, manage to, I can help you."

Claudette, who'd defended her share of sex offenders over the years, often expressed exasperation at the embarrassment of guys who refused to admit they'd gone soft at the crucial moment, preferring a felony conviction to a public revelation of impotence. The medical report noted no semen on or in Ana's body. Which didn't necessarily mean anything. "You'd be amazed," Claudette told her once, "how many rapists wear condoms. Especially the serial ones."

"I said before. Nothing."

He rose. She opened her mouth to scream. But he merely walked to the door and rapped on it, wordlessly signaling to both the jailer and to Julia that they were done.

*   *   *

Julia started running before the jail's front door closed behind her, stumbling into the parking lot, throwing up just before she got to her car.

She doubled over, gagging, yanking her hair out of the way with one hand, swiping the back of the other across her mouth. The way the boy had looked at her, through her, as though she weren't even there. The kind of look someone gave you if you'd ceased to exist in any meaningful way, so that it wouldn't matter if you were erased from the earth. With an IED, for instance. He hadn't killed her husband; she knew that. She'd read his file, done the math, calculated that he was in a refugee settlement in Germany when one of his countrymen exploded the crude bomb beneath Michael's feet. But the emptiness in those eyes—given the right set of circumstances, he could have. And if he could have done that, what might he have done to that girl?

Soon she'd have to see him again, stand beside him in court at his initial appearance, and tell a justice of the peace why he should be allowed to be free on his own recognizance while awaiting further proceedings, rather than face the hefty bail the prosecution would request. Bile again climbed into her throat. Her shoulders heaved.

"Miss? Are you all right?"

She whirled, choking back the sick.

A man stood a few feet away, thin in a too-big blazer, concern tensing his features, along with a dawning recognition.

"Mrs. Sullivan?"

Even now, four years after Michael's death, people looked twice when they saw Julia, trying to place her. She'd watch it come to them—the newspaper photos, the television spots—and brace herself. She was The Widow. But this man's face underwent a different sort of transformation, from puzzlement to a quick smile. That was new.

She gaped, trying to place him. Medium height, loose curls going gray and in need of a cut, eyes tired behind wire-rimmed glasses, deep grooves etching parentheses on either side of his mouth.

"Geary," she said finally. "I kept my name." Another of the many things for which her mother-in-law would never forgive her. "And you are . . ."

"You probably know me—or know of me—better as Elena's dad. My daughter babysits your little boy once in a while. I've picked her up at your house."

"Of course. And you're the principal over at the high school."

He held out his hand. "Dom Parrish." Julia underwent her own deductive process. As in Parrish, the prosecutor. Susan's husband. She glanced at his bare left hand. Ex-husband. She remembered Debra's breathless revelations about the divorce, the sniggering remarks that Susan had ditched her starter husband.

She took a step back. "I don't think you want to shake my hand just now. I—I think maybe I'm coming down with something. Nice to meet you again, Don."

"Dom. Short for Domenico. But I've been Donned my whole life."

"I know the feeling. I get Sullivaned all the time."

His smile returned, transforming his face so completely, the grooves receding into mere dents, that Julia nearly smiled herself in response to the sudden brightness. When was the last time anyone had appreciated a single thing she'd said?

He dropped his hand but lingered. "What brings you here? Surely your son isn't acting up at kindergarten?"

A clumsy attempt at a joke, but it had the effect of anchoring her in reality. "Preschool." She took a breath, and slotted Sami into a dark, cold space in her brain. "A client. I'm a public defender. What about you? Surely one of your students isn't acting up at school?" Her own gibe as awkward as his.

The smile fled his face, and he looked nearly as sick as she'd just felt.

"As a matter of fact—" He spread his hands. "That's exactly why I'm here, if they'll let me see him. Not something I've ever had to deal with before. But I thought I should at least try. They arrested him this morning."

Julia shook her head. "You won't be able to see him this quickly. Is he still a juvie?"

"No. Is that good or bad?"

Bad, but he didn't need to know that. "If they arrested him today, he'll be in court tomorrow. They do the initial appearances at three, in Justice Court on the first floor. You can see him then—or just wait until it's over. Kids, they usually walk. He might be back in class in a couple of days."

Probably a DUI, she thought. Or some other alcohol-related offense, partying in the canyons outside town, or getting drunk and stupid in public. More than run-of-the-mill stupid, though; otherwise, the case would have been handled in municipal court, if it even made it that far. New money had sloshed through Duck Creek with the development of the ski resort, bringing people whose sense of privilege didn't hold with court appearances for normal teenage hijinks, along with a raft of attorneys at their service—for a pretty price—to protect that privilege.

"Like I said, they'll probably release him. Unless it's something super-serious."

She waited for that smile again, but if anything, he looked worse, practically folding into himself as he turned away.

"I'm afraid it's super-serious. Nice to meet you, Mrs.—Ms.— Geary. I hope you feel better." He turned back and, despite her previous protestation, enfolded her hand in his. "Thank you for your help. I'm afraid I find myself in uncharted waters. I don't envy your job."

His hand was large and warm and reassuring and she clung to it a second longer than necessary.

"Honestly, given the nature of most of my clients' offenses, it's probably not much different than yours."

She hoped for that smile again, but he merely gave her hand a sad squeeze and trudged away, Julia realizing too late that his troublesome student was almost certainly her new client.

5

LIVING WITH BEVERLY had the lone benefit of location. Julia's supposed-to-be-temporary neighborhood was just a few blocks from the county courthouse where she spent most of her time. Even better, Calvin's preschool was on the way.

If Julia had gotten up a few minutes earlier, she and Calvin could have taken their preferred detour, on the walking path along the stream that gave the town its name. Duck Creek barreled out of the mountains, only to flatten and deepen when it hit the valley. There it burbled pretty and picturesque, a welcome distraction from the low surrounding foothills that in the coming winter would trap clouds in days-long inversions, wrapping the town in a cottony gray blanket of damp. Hills and clouds combined for a claustrophobic feel, bearing down upon Duck Creek the way the implacable eons had ground away at the once-wild lesser peaks, slowly and imperceptibly turning them into tame round humps crouching low on rocky knees.

Beyond the foothills loomed the mountain, host to the ski resort that saved Duck Creek from oblivion after the mines had been dug dry, and then the fallback—timber—went bust when the recession killed the housing market. Through it all the mountain stood impervious, its peak lofty, arrogant, still striving—as Julia herself once had been. On clear days, it demanded attention, all snowcap against brilliant blue, and she'd remember that former self, wisps of ambition floating evanescent before her, too insubstantial to grasp, vanishing in the face of the realities of these last years.

Then the clouds would roll in again, blotting the view with its hint of possibilities, reminding her that for the foreseeable future, she was trapped, the opportunity Decker had so gleefully handed her providing no escape at all.

* * *

"About time." Claudette cut her eyes to the clock, which stood at an accusing ten minutes past eight, and went back to her coffee and the newspaper.

Julia dropped her briefcase on the desk shoved up against Claudette's. "Let me guess. You were here at seven."

Claudette raised her mug in a toast to her own efficiency, reminding Julia of what she already knew. "Every morning. Gives me time to get organized before the madness starts, and read my paper in peace, which is something I can't do at home. Here, it's just me and Pavarotti."

A canary in a corner cage, far from the drafty window, obliged with a warble. The courthouse had the requisite quotient of signs forbidding all animals with the exception of guide dogs, but no one had the nerve to take on Claudette when it came to Pavarotti.

"I'll trade your kids for my mother-in-law. She forced breakfast on me again. And I had to walk through another demonstration to get into the building, people all up in arms about the refugees again. Those refugees have been here for months. What's got the whackjob contingent going now?"

The protesters had swarmed her as she approached the building, eager for a fresh audience in a town grown accustomed to their antics. A couple of cops on the corner raised their heads, ascertained she was fine, and gazed heavy-lidded back off into space. They wore helmets and flak vests, tricked out for the sort of attack that had never happened in Duck Creek's history, not even in the days of union-busting at the mine. But ever since 9/11, police departments had been the beneficiary of federal largesse in the form of riot gear and bomb-destroying robots and armored vehicles, and on the reliable occasions when the demonstrators clustered in front of the courthouse with their insulated coffee mugs and bubba chairs, Duck Creek's streets hummed an incongruous undertone of menace.

Claudette waved the newspaper. She liked her information old-school, mocking Julia's habit of peering into her phone during rare breaks. "Our would-be mayor went on another tear about immigrants. That always stirs people up. And according to this, I'm about to get company. That probably explains the demonstration."

"How's that?" Julia reached for the half-full coffee press on Claudette's desk and poured herself a cup.

"Thanks, Claudette, for making coffee," Claudette prompted.

"Thanks, Claudette, for making coffee." Julia took a long, grateful swallow and blew her a kiss. "I think you've saved both our lives." Even by the standards of the public defender's office, so impoverished that the threat of layoffs hovered omnipresent, the office coffee was vile. Claudette kept an electric kettle and the press in the office as a survival mechanism. Julia rolled the taste around on her tongue, bent her head to her mug and sniffed. "Cardamom?"

Claudette nodded. "A little something extra to start the day off right."

"I keep waiting for the day you decide to add whiskey." Julia leaned across the desk and tapped the newspaper. "What do you mean, you're about to get company?"

"The refugee program is bringing in a new batch, with some Africans this time. Real Africans, not like those washed-out Ethiopians who came with the first bunch. There's some people from the Middle East, too. People are going to lose their shit, worse than before, especially when that new case of yours hits the press."

Julia nodded understanding. The refugee resettlement program launched in their town the previous year had spurred an agitated series of community meetings, with some attendees blatantly sporting the holstered handguns allowed by the state's open-carry law. There'd been demonstrations. Threats to withdraw kids from the public schools that the refugees' children would attend. Letters to the editor filled with warnings of impending Sharia law—all of it propelling the Candidate into his frontrunner status,

The town's liberal residents responded with counter-protests, festooning trees and fences with the yellow ribbons symbolizing welcome, handing out premade signs to any business that wanted to proclaim itself a "safe space" for the newcomers, which of course risked a boycott by those on the other side. Some hapless store owners tried to play it both ways—succeeding only in angering both sides—by tucking a discreet yellow ribbon here and there, while also offering for sale the black bandanas favored by the Candidate in lieu of a tie.

"This is exhausting," Beverly exclaimed one day, a rare sentiment with which Julia agreed. "I was tempted to drive to the supermarket in the next county so as not to worry about offending anyone. Why does everybody have to pick a side? We need a Switzerland. Or three."

Julia was just glad her favorite coffee shop was yellow ribbon territory. Claudette made the coffee every morning, but it was Julia's job to supply it, and Colombia was the best coffee roaster in Duck Creek. She took the newspaper from Claudette and checked the byline on the refugee story.

Chance Larsen. He and Michael had been friends in a beers-after-work sort of way when Michael worked at the paper. After the most recent round of layoffs at *The Bulletin*, he'd added coverage of the refugees to his regular courthouse beat. Julia saw him frequently in the halls, heading toward whatever courtroom featured the most interesting case. Never any of her cases, which was just as well.

Four years after Michael's death, and people still didn't know how to act around Julia, an awkwardness heightened for the few people in town—Chance among them—who'd known them both. How long did they have to offer sympathy for his death whenever they saw her? Should they mention him at all? When was it safe to talk about normal topics—the weather, say, or mildly delicious water cooler gossip?

Most people were savvy enough to avoid the most offensive platitudes: "God doesn't give you a heavier burden than you can carry." (Really? Would you like to try and carry it?) "He's gone to a better place." (Actually, the bomb that hit him sent him to about two hundred places, and those are just the pieces they could find.) "I know how you feel." (Trust me. You so fucking don't.)

Many, like Chance, took the easy way out, reaching for their phones and pretending an urgent call at her approach, dodging in another direction, or simply tossing a mumbled "hey" as they rushed past. She was inordinately grateful to Claudette, who'd offered her a simple "I'm sorry about your husband," and had slipped Julia a bottle of tequila when she'd dropped by the house with a covered dish in those first unimaginable weeks afterward. "How many lasagnas do you have in your freezer?"

Julia eyed the foiled-wrapped container with something close to hatred. "A least a dozen."

"I figured as much. My husband is from New Mexico. The only thing that man ever demanded of me was that I learn how to make chili verde. This'll wake your taste buds right up. Don't share it with your mother-in-law."

At the time, Julia couldn't imagine ever being hungry again. But the first fiery-smoky bite of the green chili had kicked her taste buds back to wakefulness. She'd tucked the pan in the back of the fridge and eaten chili verde morning, noon, and night until it was gone. Claudette had been right, as—she often liked to remind Julia—she usually was.

"You know the minute this new bunch shows up, everybody's going to start asking me again where I'm from," Claudette said. "Like they can't tell me from an actual African. These new people, they're going to be a kind of black no one here has ever seen before."

When Julia first met her office partner, she'd thought of how black people's skin color always seemed to be described in food terms: Caramel. Café au lait. Butterscotch. Soft, gooey things, unthreatening.

Claudette made her think of teak, a wood so hard it would send an ax bouncing back if you went up against it the wrong way. Claudette especially liked striding into court and confronting a new prosecutor, so as to watch the series of shocks—at her blackness, at her heft, and at the great height from which she glared down at him, daring him to seek an impossible bail for her clients.

BSBW, she called herself. Big Scary Black Woman, pre-empting the Angry Black Woman label inevitably thrown her way, black a rarity in their mountain town, and brown only barely more of a presence. The ski resort just outside town had its contingent of Hispanic maids and maintenance crews, so poorly paid that even Duck Creek's more marginal neighborhoods remained beyond their means. They slipped through town on their way to and from work, riding buses provided by the resort to the clusters of down-valley trailer parks that housed them, nearly invisible in town but for a beefed-up selection of mass-market prepackaged tortillas and canned refritos in the super-markets and convenience stores.

In her early years in the public defender's office, Claudette had favored colorful ankara headwraps that added even more inches to her height, but soon tired of being asked about her home country.

"Omaha," she'd snapped. Repeatedly. Now the headwraps only came out on special occasions.

"Are more Iraqis coming?" The question was out of Julia's mouth before she could stop it. There'd been a single Iraqi family among the first arrivals—a family that, she knew now, included her new client.

The equation seemed so imbalanced. Duck Creek had sent a single soldier to Iraq, and he'd paid with his life. But Duck Creek granted safety to an entire Iraqi family. She knew that wasn't how it worked. And she knew her resentment wasn't fair. But there it was, whenever she thought of this new family, so safe, so alive, an ember still smoldering from the conflagration that had consumed her upon Michael's death.

When the refugees first arrived it had taken Julia, with her access to all sorts of otherwise-private databases, about a minute to find the address of the repurposed motel on the outskirts of town where they'd been settled. She'd resisted the impulse to drive to that address, to park her car, to walk up to the door and knock and—then what? To pose the question that rightfully would have labeled her a crazy woman: "Excuse me, does the person who killed my hus-band live here?"

Michael was still over there, bits and pieces of him, anyway, whatever the medics hadn't been able to scrape up after the IED hit his convoy. Whoever had assembled that lethal contraption buried it along the edge of the road frequented by the American patrols, arranged for the diversion that caused the convoy to swerve to the far side of the road and then thumbed the detonator as the trucks passed, had deprived Calvin of a father and Julia of a husband, and sentenced her to this half-life of indentured gratitude to her mother-in-law. The coffee went sour in her throat. The only person she hated more than Michael for doing this to her was the person who'd done this to him.

And now she was expected to defend one of his countrymen.

6

IN CASUAL CONVERSATION, Claudette's voice filled the room. Anger made the rafters quake. Now she dropped it to a low rumble, drawing Julia's attention to the window.

"They're gone. The protesters." She scooted her chair to the window and rubbed her sleeve against it, a futile effort given the decades of grime deposited on the other side. "All except for Krazy Karl."

"Who?" Julia stooped beside the window and peered through it. A lone man in a green-and-black buffalo-check jacket paced the sidewalk, shaking a sign at approaching passersby, who crossed the street to avoid him. The hand-lettered sign showed the word "refugees" in a circle with a slash through it, with the message "They rape, kill, destroy."

"Carl Smith, though he styles himself as Karl Schmidt these days. Claims somebody at Ellis Island robbed his family of their true name. Try not to gag on the irony."

Julia put her hands to the window and pressed her face against it, straining to see more clearly. Karl paced the sidewalk in a bowlegged roll that didn't quite succeed in disguising a limp. A spade-shaped gray beard curled up at the sides, as did his extravagant mustache. A bit of a dandy, then. He had the hawk nose, sunken cheeks, and glittering glare of a prophet, a look that not a few of Julia's clients shared; the wife-beaters, usually, quivering with intensity as they insisted that their women had driven them to it.

"What's his deal?"

"He showed up here a few years back, bought a bunch of land up in the forest when the timber industry went bust, called it Real Amerika and went on neo-Nazi and white-supremacist websites calling for settlers for his new white homeland. As far as I can tell, his white paradise is just his family and a few others. Once people figure out the snow piles up eight feet deep in those canyons, they realize that they're better off mingling with the masses back in civilization."

"How do you know all this?"

A long look. "Because I have to. This whole area is lousy with these types."

Julia was vaguely aware that just as the craggy forested beauty of the Northwest beguiled those with the money and time to fly in, develop ski resorts and guest ranches, and build the log mansions they insisted upon calling cabins, its relative isolation and sparse population and even the interminable winters also lent themselves to those enamored of rugged individualism, attracting its share of separatist groups. She shrugged. "They're just a bunch of bozos running around in the woods, playing with their guns, waiting for Armageddon. They're harmless."

"That's what people said about the likes of Tim McVeigh, back before he decided to turn a rental truck into a bomb and drive it to the federal building in Oklahoma City. A hundred sixty-eight dead people. Not exactly harmless. What happens once Karl and his crew decide to come down out of the woods and goose Armageddon along? Regular Aryan princess like you, you'll be able to blend in. Me, not so much."

Julia waited for the eye roll, the barking laugh of sarcasm. In vain.

"Oh, come on, Claudette. They're pathetic. Seems like they just want attention. I mean, look out there. Everybody went off and left him. Ignoring them is the best thing to do."

Claudette slid her chair back to her desk. Her gaze, longer this time, raked Julia with disdain, mixed with just enough pity to spur a hot burst of shame. "Easy for you to say."

On the sidewalk below, Karl Schmidt tucked his sign under his arm and lurched on his bandy legs toward a Bondo-plastered pickup

of indeterminate color. He slid a parking ticket from beneath the
wiper blade and let it flutter to the street.

Julia turned away and started to apologize—she wasn't entirely
sure what for, but one seemed in order—but Claudette's voice
boomed again, kicking the brief bad feeling in the room to the
curb.

"What's your day like?"

"Jail again this morning." A relief to return to her mind-numbing
routine after the intensity of the previous day, put her new case out
of her mind, if only for a few more hours, when Sami Mohammed
would have his first court appearance. "And Dan Tibbits has a trial.
I'm going to try to sit in, at least for opening statements."

When it came to defense attorneys, Tibbits was the biggest name
in the biggest firm in their part of the state, the joke among the
courthouse denizens being, "If you did it, better call Tibbits."

"Is that the guy on his seventh DUI? The contractor who built
the stands and that fancy electronic scoreboard at the high school
playing field? What's his name—Anders? No, Landers."

"And who ran his Bimmer off the street, across the lawn, and up
a porch, nearly taking out an old lady sitting in the swing with her
knitting? Nelson Landers. That's the one."

"Time Tibbits is finished with the jury, he'll have them believing
she lured him up onto that porch on account of she wanted a ride in
that pretty car." Claudette raised her mug.

Julia clinked hers against it and sketched out the rest of the scenario. "And that she was an alcoholic who spilled her third Arnold
Palmer all over poor Mr. Landers's nice suit and didn't even offer to
pick up the dry-cleaning bill, thus accounting—ladies and gentle-
man of the jury—for the smell of alcohol noted in the police report
and sadly attributed to my client."

Something like that, anyhow. This not being the contractor's
first rodeo, he'd been smart enough not to blow, and despite all the
obvious signs—the inability to stand without staggering, let alone
walk heel to toe; speech so slurred it fortunately obscured most of the
insults he directed at the cop—there was no blood-alcohol reading
offering incontrovertible proof.

Julia did her best to be in the courtroom whenever Tibbits tried a case, sure that if she watched hard enough, sat close enough, took enough notes, she'd start to acquire similar skills, propelling her up and out of the public defender's office and into private practice.

"Tibbits'll be able to buy another slopeside condo when he's done billing the hours for this one," Claudette said. "Who's on your jail list today?"

Julia logged onto her computer, clicked a few keys, and sighed.

"Ray Belmar." One of the system's frequent fliers.

"What is it this time? Wait, let me guess. Drunk and disorderly?"

"Duh." Julia scrolled through the document on her screen. "Bar fight at the Bum Steer—at least he's expanding his range. Let's see . . . two AM . . . clearly inebriated. That's the bartender's fault for overserving." She made a notation on a legal pad and kept scrolling. "Took it outside . . . oops."

"Oops?"

Julia chortled, a sound so rare that Claudette put down her newspaper. "There was—oh, Lord. Hold on." She whooped aloud, laughter withheld for months, years, exulting in its unexpected freedom. Claudette, who officially wasn't afraid of anything, rolled her chair back from her desk. Pavarotti let loose an unmelodic cheep.

"When the cops came in to break up the fight, somehow Ray slipped past them. Their car was sitting outside. They'd left a window open. Ray had to pee. But it's against the law to pee on the street."

"Oh, no. He didn't."

"Oh, yes, he did. Right through the window. Cop's partner had to ride in the back seat with Ray. Public lewdness—oh, for God's sake. That should've been disorderly conduct and they know it. Damage to public property. He's in a world of hurt this time. But you've got to admire his style."

Julia existed within a dark, roiling cloud of insults, the ongoing accumulation of small wounds from the coldly cordial swordplay with Beverly; the crushing drudgery of her job, defending the indefensible small stupidities of her revolving door of clients, arguing against the outsize penalties imposed upon them; the only standout her simmering fury at Michael for getting killed and her full-blown rage at those responsible for his death. And now, this case that Li'l Pecker had dumped in her lap.

So when a shaft of sunlight peeked through, even if only in the form of Ray Belmar's truly monumental idiocy, her laughter was as much relief as amusement.

"It's not that funny. Messing with cops—he won't get out on bail this time." Claudette underscored the rebuke by claiming the last of the good coffee.

"It's not. I know that." Julia wiped her eyes. "It's just . . . different. God. I didn't realize how much I needed something, anything, to be different."

"Speaking of sameness." Claudette moved quickly to cut off any impulse toward self-pity. She scooped up a stack of case files. "Jail for you, court for me. Judge Baker." She kicked off her flats and retrieved the four-inch scarlet heels she kept in her lower desk drawer for the days she felt she needed an extra advantage. Judge Roy Baker's penchant for rambling, colorful asides and utterly unpredictable rulings had become so pronounced recently that he generally was considered to be on the edge of senility, forcing her to deploy the full Claudette in order to keep his attention. Almost, Julia felt sorry for him.

"Isn't he supposed to retire soon?"

"About five years ago. Poor Li'l Pecker. He's been waiting half his life for that job." She wedged her feet into the heels.

"When he called me yesterday, I thought he was going to lay me off. Instead . . ." Julia tried to push away the thought that she'd have preferred no job at all rather than the case she'd been dealt.

"Julia Geary, oh so dreary. Why do you always look on the dark side? For one thing, our Li'l Pecker is way too image-savvy to lay off the war widow."

Claudette was the only one who came right out and called her what she was. Everyone else treated her almost as though her status was too terrible to name aloud, as though it were something to be ashamed of. Claudette stood and found her balance in the heels, shoulders back, ass in, ready to do battle on behalf of the unwashed and unlovable.

"Watch out," Claudette said, stepping aside to let Julia go before her into the hallway.

Julia walked with her through the office vestibule, giving a wide berth to both the regular coffee machine and Debra, not speaking again until they were safely in the courthouse rotunda.

"For what? Debra's coffee?"

"For what you call 'those people.' Calling them the whackjob contingent. It's fine in the office, but out here, you never know who's listening, what they think. Those damn black bandanas are everywhere."

Defense attorneys and prosecutors alike were publicly apolitical, but many of their clients were not, as well as an untold number of the courthouse clerks, along with the cops and corrections officers whose jobs required frequent appearances in the building. Black bandanas were knotted around a fair number of necks in the courthouse, oddly jaunty proclamations of the wearers' unforgiving intentions. People who'd commingled for years without incident became quick to take offense. A judge who'd asked her staff to refrain, for the sake of maintaining the peace, from wearing anything with a political meaning found herself the target of a Human Rights Bureau complaint, with concurrent mutterings about the First Amendment. Thin ice crackled everywhere underfoot.

"Remember what you said?" Claudette called over her shoulder as she and Julia headed off to their separate tasks. "About wanting things to change? You know what they say—be careful what you wish for. Guess you learned your lesson."

CHAPTER

7

THE BAILIFF'S VOICE rang through the courtroom. "All rise!"

Julia stood, taking the opportunity to move a step away from Sami, tensing against the unwanted proximity, humanizing strategy be damned.

Behind her, a prolonged susurration rustled through the gallery. She chanced a quick glance, recognizing only the principal she'd seen in the jail parking lot, and Claudette, there to lend support on the first court hearing of Julia's first big case. A middle-aged couple, faces seamed with worry, the woman in a headscarf, stood flanked by two older white women who stood close in solidarity. Sami's parents, Julia guessed, with volunteers from the refugee center.

She searched the crowd for their counterpart and found them fast, a well-tended white couple, their suits worn with everyday comfort, not dragged from the back of the closet where they awaited job interviews and funerals, acquiring stiffness, wrinkles. The kind of people with the stature to ensure an attentive prosecution for their daughter's assailant.

Teenagers packed most of the rows, fingers flying over their muted phones, transmitting to the world the most exciting thing to happen in Duck Creek High in recent memory. Half the high school must have rushed to the courthouse after the final bell, abandoning extracurricular activities, Julia thought. A group of boys, clean-cut and smooth-skinned in letter jackets, took up a whole row. Sami's soccer teammates, she surmised. There in support, or out of the same lurid curiosity as their classmates? Given that they'd reported him, she guessed the latter. A few of the adults wore the Candidate's black bandana, courtroom protocol dispensed with in the interest of maintaining the peace. Easier to let standards slide than deal with the inevitable protests. Julia spotted Karl Schmidt in his green-and-black coat. She wondered how hard it had been for him to leave his gun in his truck.

A cold rain lashed the tall, arched windows. The room smelled of something indefinable that seemed to permeate the very walls, a decades-old mixture of sweat and shredded nerves. Justice Court was the first step of the process, and for some defendants, the last. Many came straight from jail after hours-earlier arrests, the first-timers sleepless and disoriented and afraid. Those lucky enough to have private lawyers who'd arranged for bail and fetched them immediately after their arrests showed up in well-pressed street clothes, freshly showered and shaved. More often than not their time in the courthouse ended there, their lawyers filing various motions resulting in the dropped charges that would allow them to resume their lives with minimal disruption.

People fidgeted as they stood, calves pressing against the gallery's high-backed benches, carved in a century that viewed comfort as a temptation to indolence. The courthouse, a ponderous limestone building in the center of town, stood as testament to Duck Creek's heritage, when the town fathers—anxious to establish it as more than just another ephemeral mining camp—successfully lobbied the legislature to establish it as the county seat. The courthouse followed, for more than a century the town's tallest structure, rising triumphant from the valley floor, its copper dome slowly greening against the mountain's backdrop. In its infancy, its lawn witnessed hangings, crowds gathering with picnic baskets, kids underfoot, but these were civilized times and now the bloodlust played out online.

A door opened in the courtroom's paneled rear wall and the justice of the peace made her appearance, the Scottish terrier trotting by her side nearly blending into the folds of her black robe. The JP loved her dog MacArthur almost as much as she loved the law, and that— along with MacArthur's impeccable behavior—meant his presence, like Pavarotti's, was tolerated.

The judge climbed up onto her perch behind the bench, and MacArthur settled himself at her feet, out of sight of the rest of the courtroom, although Julia had heard the occasional low growl during especially fraught court proceedings.

The judge rapped her gavel once. "Be seated."

Julia stared unseeing at the file before her during the hearing's routine proceedings. Susan Parrish had grabbed this one for herself, confirming Li'l Pecker's intuition that this would be a very high-profile case indeed. She'd even assigned one of the deputy prosecutors to work with her, proactively playing defense against any conflict of interest, given that her ex-husband was the principal of the defendant's—and the victim's—school. Susan was in full regalia, a nipped-waist scarlet blazer over a bias-cut black skirt that swirled around her legs as she paced before the bench, outlining all the reasons Sami Mohammed should be held on fifty thousand dollars' bond.

A low feminine moan sounded from the gallery, a mother's anguish, inadequately suppressed.

Susan ignored it, chopping at the air with her hands, pointing out that a foreigner was always a flight risk, that the events in question, although the details remained hazy—"Your honor, the victim is severely traumatized"—were of an especially heinous sort. "A clear danger to the community."

She finally sat, the flush of accomplishment pinking her cheeks, a smile forbidden to her lips but gleaming in her eyes.

The judge turned to Julia. She half-rose in her seat, self-conscious in her jail day attire, no way to compete with Susan's reliable perfection, anyway. "The defense has no objections, your honor."

The loud throat-clearing behind her could only have come from Claudette.

The judge's gaze swept the room, wordlessly commanding Julia to see the obvious: the fact of Sami's youth, the fact that his school principal was there in support—and unseen but equally obvious, that despite being the foreigner of Susan's disdainful description, Sami held legal refugee status—all of which should have been presented by Julia in an impassioned argument on behalf of her client's release on his own recognizance.

"Ms. Geary. Are you sure?" The judge's words were more warning than question.

A canine muttering, barely audible, came from the base of the bench.

Susan leaned forward in her seat, a twitch of the lips the only betrayal of a snag in her seamless control, signaling her thoughts as though she'd shouted them to the room. *Oh, this is going to be so easy.*

Julia made a lightning calculation: defending this repugnant client versus her soaring fantasy of that job with a private firm, loans paid off, a home of her own in a different town, far from Duck Creek's entrapments.

"Your honor. What I mean to say is . . ." Julia forced the words from her throat, reciting the rest by rote: the supportive family and friends, the lack of any prior offenses, his tender age. She did not gag. She did not scream. She did not turn to Sami and strike at him with her voice, her fists. Her voice droned on and on, as though a stranger were reading from a first-year law student's textbook on criminal procedure.

The muttering from beneath the bench subsided. Susan rolled her eyes and sat back.

The judge nodded. "I'll release him on his own recognizance"— she rapped her gavel three times to quell the outrage from the gallery—"but he'll have to wear an electronic monitor." She raced through the standard conditions: no alcohol, Sami was to stay a certain distance from his presumed accuser, and if they had any classes together, the school was to arrange a tutor for one or both of them, and so forth—and slammed the gavel a final time, in seeming relief. "Dismissed."

A bailiff stepped across the room and took Sami by the arm. Julia sensed the youth looking an unspoken question toward her: What now?

For now, she was done with him. Thank God. She turned away as the bailiff led him from the room.

The principal who'd seen her throwing up in the parking lot approached the rail. "Ms. Geary? Are you feeling better?"

She gave a quick nod and tried to turn her back on him, too, but he was still talking. "I just wanted to thank you for what you did for Sami."

The judge, gathering her robes to step down from the bench, paused, all alertness.

"It's nothing. It's my job." Julia spoke fast and low, hoping the judge wouldn't hear her. A snort attested to her failure.

Dom Parrish persisted. "What happened to An—" He cut himself off, belatedly mindful of the need for anonymity. "To the girl. Who's also one of my students. It's awful, and someone needs to be held accountable. But Sami. He shouldn't be in jail. It's right that he's being released. He's had his share of trouble, sure, but something like this—I just can't imagine he did it."

Trouble?

A word encompassing everything from shooting spitballs to a few minutes of terror in a locker room, more likely to interest a prosecutor than a defense attorney but containing about a hundred percent more information on Sami than was in the file. She searched her briefcase for the business cards she only used a couple of times a year, at conferences and seminars, and finally found one, battered and smudged. "Why don't you come see me? Just call the number here and they'll put you through. I'd love to hear more about this."

The judge stepped down, but Julia sensed her continued attention. She added quickly, "Anything that might help him."

Dom brightened. The judge sighed.

"Ms. Geary. A word." The judge stood beside the bench, MacArthur a small fierce presence beside her, eager for the treat that awaited him at the end of each court session.

Together they waited until Dom left the courtroom, clutching Julia's card as though it contained the answer to a prayer.

"I won't see you again on this case." A justice of the peace only handled a defendant's initial appearance. Further proceedings moved to the county court. "But I gave you a break. That's not likely to happen when you go before Judge Baker. I hope he won't see the sort of behavior that you exhibited today."

Julia shook her head, not trusting her voice.

"See that he doesn't." The door closed behind her.

Julia faced an empty gallery. Even Claudette had decamped, no doubt waiting back in their shared quarters, readying a piece of her mind. Julia allowed herself the pleasure of swearing out loud.

"Hell and goddamnation."

How was she going to do this?

You know this drill. Fake it till you make it.

Michael's voice, arising whenever she least expected it, though more and more infrequently as the months passed. The same message he'd given her through those brutal early days in the public defender's office, when late at night she'd finally close the last file and drag herself from the kitchen table to bed, protesting to Michael— only half-awake himself except for the part of him that was wide awake—that she was too tired even to make love. "My alarm's going off in, oh, Jesus, five hours. I thought law school would be the worst of it. But this . . ."

"Tell you what, darlin'." Affecting a lazy flatland drawl. Even though she couldn't see his grin for the darkness, she heard it in his voice. "You just lie back and fake it."

But, no matter how late the hour, no matter how utterly complete her exhaustion, she'd never had to. Not once.

CHAPTER

8

SAMI'S INITIAL COURT appearance was the final item on the day's docket and by the time Julia left the courtroom, the hallways had gone dark and echoey. She hurried for the door, eager to get home to Calvin and even Beverly, whose chilly disregard at least afforded her some quiet.

She pushed open the heavy brass door and stepped into bedlam.

"Ms. Geary, Ms. Geary!" A mob surged toward her, television reporters at the forefront, thrusting microphones her way with one hand, balancing heavy cameras on shoulders with the other. Duck Creek's television stations were staffed with rookies, paid so poorly that one reporter had complained to Julia she qualified for food stamps. Most moved on as soon as possible, to higher-profile jobs in the state capital or neighboring states, but some stayed, scenting opportunity in the town's growth spurt and acquiring some chops in the process. One positioned herself at the front of the pack, elbows akimbo to deflect her compatriots, determined to be the first with a question. She planted her feet, pushed her fuzzy mic so close that she effectively pinned Julia against the door, and delivered her question in her most accusatory tone:

"Ms. Geary. How do you feel about defending someone from the country where your husband died?"

Julia barely stopped herself from delivering a bleep-worthy retort. Just her luck to get the one television reporter who'd spent more than five minutes in Duck Creek and thus knew about Michael.

"Julia. Care to offer any comment about today's proceedings?" A familiar voice. Chance Larsen, the reporter who'd worked with her husband before Michael had opted for patriotism, throwing her a lifeline, knowing all the public defenders adhered to an unwritten code of not talking about cases in progress.

"No," she managed. "No comment."

The TV reporter held her ground a moment more, then huffed and lowered her mic, shooting Chance a look that vowed retribution. Julia braced herself to wade through the scrum when the courthouse door gave way behind her and someone edged out past her, or tried to.

The crowd swung like a school of predatory fish flowing toward a more toothsome prey, Chance shouting his questions—real ones, this time, not softballs—along with the rest of them, surrounding the high school principal before he had time to escape.

This time, the civilians who'd been in the courtroom beat the reporters to the punch.

"What are you going to do about that rapist in our school? Just because the court let him out doesn't mean you'll let him back in the school, does it? Does it?"

The parents congealed in a single quivering mass, their faces contorted with all the fear and fury any reasonable person might expect if a rapist were indeed prowling the hallways of Duck Creek High at that very minute. Which he wasn't, as the hapless principal tried to point out. "No one's been convicted of anything yet."

Julia slid to the edges of the crowd but paused there, nearly as curious as the teenagers who pushed past her, phones held high, jostling for position with the reporters trying vainly to gain the upper hand from a man who'd bulldozed past them all. Karl Schmidt, with another one of his signs, "Justice for White Womanhood." His presence created a momentary dilemma for the parents in the crowd, pushing to get as close as possible to the principal but not necessarily wanting to be associated with the likes of Schmidt.

"He does not set one foot in that school. Understood?"

Dilemma resolved. They were all on the same page. The parents closed in.

Dom Parrish held up his hands. Even the reporters fell silent. Better to take any quote they could get, rather than risk another "no comment" response.

"We'll comply with the judge's order to keep them apart . . ." Which was all it took to set the parents off again, their voices bouncing off the walls of the courthouse, echoing along the street, and banging at Julia's eardrums.

"She's not the judge of this school!"

"She doesn't even have kids. If she did, she'd understand. All she has is that stupid little dog."

"If that boy so much as looks crosswise at any of our girls, we'll file a lawsuit that will put the whole school district into bankruptcy."

The principal held his hands higher, looking for all the world like someone confronted with a loaded gun. Which, in a sense, he was.

"I think we're all forgetting something very important here." Julia noticed that "we," a feeble attempt to put them all on the same side, and felt sorry for him. She could have told him that, with emotions running this high, it wouldn't work. She winced at his next words.

"That the student in question is innocent until proven guilty. And he's not charged with rape." True enough. Susan Parrish had left herself plenty of wiggle room by charging Sami Mohammed with the vagueness of sexual assault, an offense encompassing anything from a hallway titty grab to just shy of penetration.

Julia thought the crowd had reached maximum volume. She'd been wrong.

A sound rose, louder even than the parents' shouted epithets, riding higher and sharper, drowning them out. Sirens. The sheriff's office occupied the rear of the courthouse, and now three black-and-whites screamed around the corner, lights washing red and blue across the throng before receding along with the sound. The kids figured it out first, alerts likely setting their phones throbbing in their hands. "Somebody vandalized the refugee center," one shouted. Within moments the mob, scenting fresh blood, was gone.

The principal slumped against the door, then noticed Julia across the broad width of the steps.

"I deal with all sorts of crap every day at school. But this is a first. How'd I do?"

Julia figured Dom Parrish had had enough bullshit for one day.

"You sucked."

He nodded.

"Agreed. Guess I'd better go home and work on some talking points. Because the one thing I have learned is that they"—he lifted his chin toward the blessedly empty space only minutes before occupied Schmidt and the parents—"won't quit. There's no more formidable creature on earth than the pissed-off parent of a high school student."

He walked halfway down the stairs, then stopped and gave Julia a long, searching look.

"I hope you don't suck, Ms. Geary. Because you're that kid's only hope."

9

Sami's only hope sat at the kitchen table at two in the morning, sobbing into a paper towel.

"I can't do it."

Lyle, divining her distress, butted his head against her calf and uttered a querulous meow. Julia dropped a hand to his fur and worked it along his back. He purred beneath her touch. "I can't."

She'd clicked off her cell phone after leaving the courthouse, picked up Calvin from his preschool, and took him to a park, nearly deserted in the fast-lowering twilight. She sensed his scrutiny, her poor boy, trying to decide if the change in routine was a delightful surprise or something ominous.

The former, she tried to assure him, pointing out he had the slide, the monkey bars, the swings all to himself. He ran to them, hesitantly at first, glancing back at her for reassurance, and so she dutifully caught him as he rocketed down the slide; stood arms outstretched beside him as he swung beneath the monkey bars, cheering him on as he reached the end, pumped up and proud and ready for more.

"Swings?" He'd lost his cap in the effort, and his sandy hair stood up in cowlicks and despite the fact that his grin was still more winsome than cocky, he was so much his father at that moment that her breath caught.

He refused what he called the "baby" swing, a plastic bucket-like contraption with holes for chubby toddler legs, and so she fitted him instead into a canvas sling and began to push, sending him soaring into the pale circle cast by the streetlight, and back down into darkness for another shove skyward. This is fun, she told herself, trying to paper over her curdled anger with an acceptable emotion. I should do this more often.

So what if she lost the case? So what if she never got another big one? What if she was stuck with the small stuff for the rest of her working life? There'd be time for more days like this, heading home early, spending goddamn quality time with her son.

Each time he returned, she pushed him harder and higher, until his ecstatic shrieks took on a sharper pitch.

"Ma'am? Ma'am!"

A woman tugged at her arm, raised to give Calvin another shove.

Julia stepped back, blinking until the woman's face came into focus. Older, tired, her thin body wrapped in a cheap coat, fingers wrapped around the handle of one of those expensive strollers nearly as big as herself. A sitter then, not a mother.

"Does he like going so high?" Even as the woman posed the question, the swing slowed, a little lower with each back-and-forth, Calvin silent now, catching his breath, face as white as the knuckles on the small hands gripping the chains.

Julia caught at them as the swing came back to her, stopping it, and helped Calvin from the seat.

"We were just leaving," she told the woman. Everything under control. Until this dark-of-night moment, when she'd crept downstairs, blindly clutching the bannister, gulping tears, fearful of waking Calvin or, worse, Beverly.

She mopped at her face with the shreds of the paper towel. Lyle arched beneath her hand and hissed. Light flooded the kitchen and Julia looked down the yawning bore of a shotgun barrel.

*   *   *

Julia pinched one of Beverly's Waterford cordial glasses between her shaking fingers; the crystal, like the bridge club, the house in the right neighborhood, the kitten-heel pumps that would never see a crust of cowshit, all part of Beverly's rigorous transformation from farm wife to town dowager.

Beverly stood at the sideboard, somehow perfectly turned out for her presumed confrontation with a burglar, steel-gray hair brushed away from her face, bathrobe pulled high around her neck, its belt knotted tight around her pointedly slim waist. Beverly did not do carbs. She padded soundlessly in her shearling slippers to join Julia at the dining room table.

Julia lifted the glass to her lips for another sip of something orange, sweet and bitter all at once, and eyeballed the shotgun lying on the table between them, its blued barrel longer than she would have thought. She resisted the urge to poke it with her finger, slide it farther away from her.

"How long has that thing been in the house? Where does it live? In your bedroom?" The room where Calvin sometimes frolicked with his toys.

"It was my husband's, and his father's before that. He kept it by the back door. We shot rattlesnakes with it—a waste of such a beautiful piece. I wanted to give it to Michael but he insisted I keep it. Especially when he left for Iraq, he was worried about all of us here without him. He wanted us to have protection, you know."

No. She hadn't known. What did it mean that when it came to protection, Michael counted on his mother, not on her? And if he wanted to protect them, why hadn't he just stayed home with them instead of running away to Iraq and stashing her and Calvin with his mother and a bullshit excuse about saving money? An arrangement that suited neither woman, but who was going to argue with a man going off to war? She derailed her thoughts from their familiar track and focused on the present.

"But Calvin. A loaded gun. Why didn't you just call 911?"

"Don't be ridiculous. I didn't want to bother them if it turned out Lyle had just knocked something off the counter." She lifted the gun, broke the barrel, and tilted two shells into her hand.

They rolled from her outstretched fingers across the table, their ridged scarlet hulls and gleaming brass caps almost festive against the polished oak.

"There. Now it's not loaded anymore. I keep it on a high shelf in my closet, and the shells in a drawer across the room. Calvin can't reach it. By the time he can, he'll have taken his hunter education classes and he'll know all about gun safety. Look. Even though I've unloaded it, the safety's on." She showed Julia the button, the way it slid to "off," then put it back on again.

Julia decided the argument about whether Calvin would learn to hunt was best saved for another day. She took another sip, more of a gulp. "What is this stuff?"

"Cointreau. Would you like more?"

Anyone else just would have poured. Leave it to Beverly to force her into politesse.

"Yes, please." She touched a fingertip to her nose, blotting the moisture there. Beverly reached into her pocket. A lace-edged handkerchief emerged, so blindingly white it fairly glowed in the dim light, Beverly's initials embroidered into one corner with white silk thread. Julia ran the cloth between her fingers and rubbed her thumb over the monogram. "You actually blow your nose on something this pretty?"

Beverly's smile came and went so fast that Julia wasn't sure she'd seen it. "Just because something is useful doesn't mean it can't be beautiful. For example." She pointed to the shotgun, the gleaming walnut stock, its plate embossed with whorls and flowers, then lifted her own glass, facets refracting the warm glow of the liqueur within. At the farm, Michael had told Julia, Sunday dinners featured a table set as though for Thanksgiving—cloth napkins, an array of cutlery, his father teasing Beverly by purposely taking the salad fork to the roast. "Even back then," he'd said, "she was planning for a different life."

Julia's mind snagged on the thought. Had Beverly as a young woman spent teeth-grinding nights at the thought of one morning milking after another and on into infinity, dreaming of a future where the orderly rows of waxed supermarket cartons were the closest she came to a cow? She narrowed her eyes and tried to see something of herself in Beverly, who finally topped off her Cointreau.

"Now. What is so distressing that it caused you to disturb my sleep?"

Julia hiccupped and downed the Cointreau in a single swallow, ignoring Beverly's wince. Probably best not to say, "My husband—your son—is dead." Because it all came back to that.

"This case," she finally managed. "I can't."

Beverly sat back. "Because?"

Rage bubbled to the surface and burst free in a shout. "Because of who he is!"

They both looked toward the ceiling, silent for a moment, alert to any rustling from above indicating she'd woken Calvin. She lowered her voice, lending a flat finality to her words. "I can't."

Beverly delivered a smile. No warmth in it, though, and certainly no sympathy. It presented only challenge.

"Can't," Beverly mused. "Oh, my. What would Michael say to that?"

How dare she? In this one thing—and maybe this only thing—Beverly should be on her side. Instead, she had the gall to evoke Michael, and even worse, she appeared aware that Julia knew good and well exactly what Michael would say.

He'd come back at her with the same thing he always said whenever he found her kneeling before the toilet with early-pregnancy nausea and vowing to call in sick; or slapping a file shut, saying it was high time Ray Belmar sat on his ass in jail instead of wasting her time defending him every few weeks; or declaring she'd rather be a greeter at Walmart rather than have her ass kicked all around the courtroom again by that bitch Susan Parrish.

Michael would give her that grin. "So be the bigger bitch."

"That's impossible."

"Oh, I don't know. I'll bet you've got it in you. You've just got to give it some try." Michael then just like his mother now, his smile all challenge

"He'd say . . ." Beverly urged in a whisper.

And despite herself, Julia whispered back:

"Give it some try."

She gathered herself to say more, that a simple farm-boy slogan wasn't going to cut it against the enormity of what she faced, when Lyle, who'd settled himself in the chair beside Julia, scrambled to his feet, hissing and yowling. A quick rap rattled the front door.

"What the—?" Julia scooped up the cat, who rewarded her with long gouges on her forearm as he scratched himself free.

The shotgun shells rattled as Beverly dropped them back into the chamber. She held the gun one-handed, safety off, finger on the trigger guard. With her other hand, she reached for the door.

"Beverly, wait," Julia gasped as the door swung open. What if her mother-in-law actually shot someone? Her mind raced through legal scenarios.

"Oh, for heaven's sake." Beverly clicked the safety back on and looked up and down the street before returning her exasperated gaze to the burning paper bag at her feet.

Her foot went up—"Beverly, no!" Julia cried again—but it was too late to stop Beverly Sullivan's snowy shearling slipper from splatting straight down into the dogshit within.

*　*　*

It was Julia's turn to splash the cordial into glasses, albeit with a heavier hand than Beverly's.

This time, her mother-in-law dispensed with the ritual of holding the glass to the light, imbibing in delicate sips. Her hand darted quick as a striking snake. She wrapped it around the dainty cordial glass and knocked back the contents as efficiently as a rummy on the end stool in a corner taproom. Julia raised an eyebrow and poured again.

"I can't believe you've never heard of the dogshit trick. I thought it was part of every high school handbook."

"I never had time for that sort of nonsense." Beverly's voice, so shaky moments before, flattened, tinged with the bitterness that arose at even the most glancing reference to the farm, the bawling cows demanding attention every twelve hours, no allowances made for sleepovers with friends, or proms, or spring break getaways. Somehow, she'd escaped to college, only to fall in love with . . . a dairy farmer. Who'd promised her things would be different. Which they were, but only after he died twenty-some years into the marriage.

Julia reached for the phone.

"Who are you calling?"

"The police. This time, there really was someone there."

Beverly shook her head so emphatically that Julia hung up. "For a kids' prank? Why waste their time?"

"What if it wasn't a kids' prank?"

"What else would it be?" Beverly didn't wait for an answer. She carried the two glasses to the sink, rinsed them, and dried them with a tea towel before returning them to the sideboard. She scooped the shotgun shells from the table, dropped them into the pocket of her robe. She turned to Julia. An uncharacteristically plaintive note tinged her words.

"Calvin and I are going to the cemetery tomorrow."

Beverly, Calvin in tow, visited Michael's grave in the town's cemetery weekly, a production that involved a stop at a florist for three long-stemmed roses, one from each of the people he'd left behind. Even if one of them had refused to return to the cemetery after his burial.

Beverly told Calvin stories about his father on the way to and from the cemetery, so many that Julia had the uncomfortable feeling Calvin now knew more about Michael than she ever had. She imagined the grave, when she allowed herself to think about it, smothered beneath a ziggurat of withered roses, the stone long since obscured by the weekly offerings.

Even though she knew better. There must be someone who took care of the place, who rinsed the stones of summer's dust, who brushed snow from Michael's name in the winter . . . at which point, she would force herself to think of something else.

She sat wordless until Beverly sighed and made her way barefoot up the stairs with the shotgun. Lyle materialized from wherever he'd been and wound himself around Julia's ankles before running lightly to the first step and looking back at her. Her bedtime, too.

Julia lingered, running a finger up and down the phone receiver, fighting the urge to pick it up.

A kids' prank.

But when she'd cleaned the mess from the step, an indistinct object at the end of the walk, just beyond the glow of the porch light, caught her eye. Something there, maybe another bag, dropped in haste. She gave thanks for her heavy rubber kitchen gloves and went to retrieve it.

And stopped.

What lay before her could have been dropped by anyone, at any time. So she told herself as she knelt on the sidewalk, damning the porch lamp that lit her up like a spotlight, a target for anyone who might be lurking in the shadows. She held her breath, listening for a telltale rustle, a cough. A curse. Nothing. Julia picked up the black bandana with the tips of her gloved finger, rose and carried it back to the trash can along the side of the house, dropping it atop the shit-smeared slipper.

10

THE GOOD THING about the dogshit debacle, as Julia mentally labeled it, was that for the first time she could remember, Beverly was not waiting to ambush her with eggs in the morning.

The kitchen was dark, the silence broken only by Lyle's demanding meows as she dished out his kibble.

She hurried Calvin through a breakfast of cereal and a banana, one eye on the stairs, expecting a wrathful Beverly to materialize at any minute, wielding a spatula and a lecture about the necessity of protein. She didn't breathe easy until they'd made it out the door, giving Michael's portrait a triumphant cold shoulder as she brushed past. She dropped Calvin at his preschool and then, with twenty minutes to spare, succumbed to the blinking neon come-on of the café across the street from the courthouse.

She settled into a booth and waved away the menu. "French toast. Oh, and a biscuit." Hello, heavenly carbs.

And fat and sugar, too, she thought, as she slathered the French toast and the biscuit with butter when they arrived, upending the syrup container so liberally that she nearly set the toast afloat in a puddle of sweetness.

"Busted," a voice boomed above her head.

"Busted yourself." Julia waved a forkful of dripping French toast at Claudette, urging her into the seat across from her. "What are you doing here? I thought you went straight to the office before the sun rose."

"Oh, I did. Got in at six. Taking a break. Just coffee, black," Claudette said to the server, nonetheless reaching for Julia's biscuit.

Julia grabbed her wrist. "Get your own biscuit. Do you know how long it's going to be before I see one of these again?"

"You'd better bring me a biscuit," Claudette said when the server returned with her coffee. "Otherwise, my esteemed colleague might stab me with her fork."

The café boasted a cook from Georgia whose buttermilk biscuits rose high and feather-light, the perfect butter delivery device. Claudette tested the coffee, nodded her approval to the anxious server familiar with her exacting standards, and turned back to Julia. "Why are we carb-loading this morning? Let me guess—" Julia readied the story of the flaming dogshit. "It's because of this case."

Julia shoved a final piece of limp French toast through syrup gone cold, bits of butter congealing like gelatinous islands atop it.

"What was that nonsense in court yesterday, anyway? You're lucky Judge French didn't slap you with a fine."

Julia glanced up, met Claudette's accusing eye, and looked away. "He needs to plead guilty. Given his age, and that it might not have been rape, I bet I can get a minimal sentence."

Claudette's lips tightened as summoned the server. "Another biscuit. Going to need my strength if I've got to listen to any more of this crap."

"Oh, come on. There were witnesses."

"One. Boy says he saw the two of them in the locker room, her with her titties out. Doesn't mean a damn thing."

Of course Claudette had read the probable cause affidavit. Just as Julia would have done if Claudette had snagged a big case, eager to help her strategize, play devil's advocate, as Claudette was doing now. So why did she feel so defensive?

"She was crying." Claudette had conveniently skipped that detail.

"Spare me. Boo-hooing because she got caught."

"Claudette! You of all people, victim-blaming."

Claudette broke her biscuit apart and applied butter with small, precise movements. She took a bite and chewed very slowly. She raised her napkin to her lips and blotted away a crumb. "What do you mean, me of all people?"

Julia signaled for the check. "And can you please add on a go-cup of coffee?" Maybe best not to count on the usual office largesse from Claudette. Who, face frozen, awaited an answer.

"It's obvious."

"Obvious."

Julia counted out cash and stumbled on. "I mean, I'm sure people have blamed you for, you know, getting jobs and stuff. So I'd have thought you'd be more sensitive to people falling back on stereotypes . . ." Her voice trailed off.

"Is that so?"

Julia thought of the previous night, the way Beverly had cursed quickly, effectively, as she examined the reeking, ineradicable stain on her slipper, and contemplated the fact that she herself had apparently just stepped in shit far more thoroughly than Beverly.

Claudette's next words removed any doubt.

"Because I'm black? Because my whole life, people, some people"—and Julia knew herself now included in this damning category—"have assumed I've gotten where I am because of that? And that makes me some sort of a victim?"

"I'm sorry. I didn't mean . . ."

"What did you mean, Julia? Because it sounds like you're making assumptions about me, the same way you're making assumptions about that boy. You want an assumption? Here's one you can take to the bank."

The server approached with care, aware of their tone, if not their actual words.

Julia reached for both checks. "I've got this."

Claudette snatched hers away. "I can buy my own damn breakfast, thank you very much." She slapped a bill down on the table. "The only reason you got this case? The last thing Decker needs is to win this one. Successfully defending a foreign sex offender is not going to get him that judgeship that gives him wet dreams every night. So he hands it to little inexperienced you. You lose, he gets his judgeship, I get his job, and nobody thinks worse of you because nobody expected you to win it, anyway. Let's call it a win-win-win. For everybody except that poor goddamn kid."

She rose and stalked from the booth. She wasn't wearing her heels. But she might as well have been.

* * *

The café was across the street from the courthouse, in the middle of the block, and Julia usually jaywalked back to her job, barely suppressing the impulse to flip off anyone who honked. On this day she took the long way around, heading for the end of the block, waiting for the light, and once across circling the block around the courthouse, giving herself time, stepping cautiously on legs shaking with anger and humiliation.

That fucker Decker. "You've done yeoman work." Buttering her up with flattery just as she'd slathered her French toast a little while earlier. And she'd lapped it up, practically drooling, believing he actually thought her deserving, when she knew full well Decker didn't make a move unless it benefited him in some way. Oh, he'd played her just right, discerning the flicker of ambition that would draw her attention away from the impossibility of the case.

"Bastard."

"Geez, lady. What'd I ever do to you?"

Julia didn't realize her thoughts had turned vocal. The courthouse lawn, edged with aging oaks that provided summer shade and winter shelter, was a favorite gathering place for Duck Creek's small but persistent transient community. One of them had made himself as comfortable as possible for someone sleeping on the grass, head pillowed on a backpack, stained coat pulled tight around his neck, hands drawn up into his sleeves, his life already one of humiliation, and now a stranger apparently was adding more.

"Not you," she said. "Sorry."

The moment jolted her out of her thoughts. She stopped, drew in a breath, and blew it out. Again. The man rolled onto his side and propped himself on an elbow, watching her.

"Here." Julia thrust her coffee at him in inadequate apology. "It's just black but it's still hot."

He reached up and took it with a grave nod. "Hope your day gets better."

Doubtful. But this time, she kept her thoughts to herself.

* * *

The problem with her little detour, she realized as she headed into the warren of offices that housed the public defenders, was that she'd given Claudette time to get back ahead of her.

Debra let her know she didn't have to worry about it just yet.

"What's going on with Claudette?" the receptionist chirped.

"What do you mean?" Julia cast a glance at the coffeepot next to Debra's desk. There'd be no coffee, fragrant with cinnamon or cardamom or whatever Claudette had chosen to add, waiting for her in their office today. But the stuff in the stained pot was nearly translucent. She dug her nails into a palm still warm from the handed-off go-cup, another in a fast-accumulating pile of mistakes.

"She got in early like she always does"—Julia read the subtext: *not like you*—"went out to get some breakfast, came back in a huff and slammed on out of here again. And what's wrong with you, Julia Geary, oh, so dreary? You look like somebody went and died on you."

Julia allowed herself the small satisfaction of watching the eager curiosity leach from Debra's eyes as she realized her gaffe. "Julia, I'm so sorry."

Julia drew herself up and assumed the air of wounded dignity that was her right as a widow. "I know. You didn't mean it. And yet." Letting the barb linger, hoping it might fend off Debra's prying for, oh, maybe half a day. Because, given the case she'd been handed, Debra would be after her for every little detail, despite repeated warnings about workplace confidentiality.

The office somehow seemed smaller without Claudette's outsize presence. She'd left the newspaper, though. Julia scanned it, giving thanks that Chance Larsen must have thought the judge's implied rebuke too inside-baseball to include in his story about the court hearing. The vandalism at the refugee center got nearly as much ink, along with a splashy photo of two workers scrubbing away a painted message: "Rapist go home." Plywood covered a broken window.

A few seeds pattered onto the page. Behind her, Pavarotti hopped from perch to perch, occasionally letting loose with mixed-up fragments of opera's greatest hits—a bit of "Quando me'n vo'" followed by a snatch of "Nessun dorma," echoing whatever Claudette listened to on her computer when she was alone in the office. Julia's fingers quivered as she turned the pages, no way to fool herself into thinking Claudette's revelation was of no consequence. Just as she'd never been able to fool herself into a calm acceptance of Michael's decision to go to Iraq. The bird let loose with a soaring snatch from *Carmen*.

"Shut up, Pavarotti." Said with such vehemence that he tried to escape, banging into the bars of the cage, sending a couple of feathers flying. Great. Now she had to apologize to a bird.

Sami's file sat in silent rebuke. Nothing in it would help her—or him. It wasn't that she was incompetent—a quick gnaw of doubt: Did Decker truly think that? The case was truly indefensible. She opened the file, marshaling talking points to make her case, when Claudette returned. The narrative, as reconstructed by the officer who'd interviewed the few people willing to talk, was thin unto the point of vanishing.

At around 7:15 AM, Rina Jackson, the school nurse, had passed Ana Olsen in the hallway of Duck Creek High, looking wan and disheveled, and asked her whether everything was all right, at which point Ana burst into uncontrollable tears. But even after Mrs. Jackson had pulled the girl into the privacy of her office and assured her of confidentiality, Ana refused to say what was wrong.

At 7:25 AM, Cody Landers and three of his teammates walked into the Duck Creek Police Department and asked to speak to someone about an incident at the school. They were referred to a detective, telling her that they'd come upon Sami Mohammed the previous morning assaulting Ana in the girls' locker room. As to what they were all doing in the girls' locker room, the boys said they'd seen Sami duck in as they were headed to their own locker room following a workout. After a few minutes of joshing about the refugee not understanding the difference between the boys' and girls' lockers even after all this time, they became concerned one of the girls would catch him in there and he'd get in trouble. So Cody poked his head in, calling to Sami about his mistake.

Instead, he saw Ana struggling naked beneath Sami, his pants down. He yelled for the other boys, but by the time they gathered their wits, Sami had fled, disappearing until the police arrived at his home the next morning. Why had they waited until the next day to tell anyone? And why the police, rather than a coach or principal?

"Witnesses reported being upset and confused and worried about getting their teammate in trouble. But finally decided it was the right thing and contacted police upon urging from a parent."

Julia studied the medical report again. Ana's parents brought her straight to a clinic after getting the school nurse's call. Although the exam couldn't verify penetration, photos showed fingerprint bruises on the girl's arms. Someone's hands had dug in deep to keep her from escaping his grip. Just as she had in the nurse's office, Ana refused to say anything at the exam, other than brief nods for the consent demanded at each step in the excruciating procedure, or in the subsequent interview with a specially trained female detective. "Re-interview at a later date," the detective had typed at the end of her report. Standard procedure in dealing with assault victims, often so traumatized that their memories began to coalesce only after a few days.

Sami likewise remained mute during his questioning by the police, saying nothing beyond confirming that he was indeed Sami Mohammed, born 1998 in Baghdad, left with his family when he was seven, two years after the American invasion and, after more than a year of following refugee routes through Central Asia and the Peloponnese into Eastern Europe, finally arrived in Germany, where the family lived in a refugee resettlement center outside Berlin before arriving in Duck Creek nine months earlier. So much detail about his early years, none at all about three minutes in that locker room.

"Uncooperative," the detective unnecessarily noted.

How was Julia supposed to help Sami if he wouldn't even help himself? No one could blame her if he ended up being convicted. She wondered how long it would take her to convince him to plead guilty rather than face a jury trial. She'd have to get him past that "I didn't do it" stage that they all adopted at first.

"Hell," she said to herself, just as Claudette walked in.

"Hell, what?" The ice in Claudette's voice would have set a polar bear to shivering. Still, it was an opening.

"There's not a single thing in here that helps me. Not one. This is useless." She closed the file, slapped it against the desk, and took a breath. "Claudette, I'm sorry about what happened in the café. That was an asshole thing to say."

"Yes, it was. Give me that."

Julia knew better than to say anything as Claudette read through the file's negligible contents once, then twice. Claudette set it down without a word and busied herself heating water in the hot pot and measuring coffee into the press. She opened a tin beside the press, releasing the scent of chocolate, and rubbed cocoa nibs between her fingers, letting the flakes fall onto the grounds.

Julia closed her eyes and inhaled as the combined aromas filled the small office, but didn't truly allow herself to hope until Claudette had poured her own cup and then held up the press in her direction.

Forgiven? Maybe.

Tolerated, more likely, which was more than she deserved. She scrambled for her mug, sipping in grateful silence until Claudette deigned to speak.

"You're right."

Julia choked. "I am?"

"There's nothing in here that helps him. But there's something else."

"What's that?"

"The only description we have of what happened comes from that one boy. The others didn't see anything. There's not a single thing in here that warrants filing charges, at least not at this point. They rushed their case."

"But why?"

Claudette's lips twisted. "You tell me, whitegirl. Tell me how you're going to win this one over a pro like Susan Parrish."

Julia nodded acknowledgment that she had it coming, hoping to somehow convey her understanding that her own heedless insult exceeded Claudette's intentional one by several degrees of offensiveness, even if Claudette had underscored it by reminding her that, when it came to Susan the alpha bitch, she was outmatched. Michael's words came back to her.

So be the bigger bitch.

"Give me back that file." Whatever was—or wasn't—in there that was so obvious to Claudette, she was going to find it.

And when she did? The possibility flickered, an ember fanned by Claudette's gauntlet. "Tell me how you're going to win this one over Susan Parrish."

Time to give it some try.

11

Duck Creek's library was on her way home from Calvin's day care center, a location that made it a frequent delaying tactic for Julia on days when the job had rubbed her edges too rough and bloodied for immediate exposure to Beverly, waiting with a shaker full of metaphorical salt.

The town had been one of the lucky ones, acquiring in its early days a Carnegie library as part of its push to transform itself from a muddy miners' redoubt to respectability. It occupied the center of a downtown block, with a small park on either side, the better to set off its importance. Brick walls further underscored that fact, standing in haughty rebuke to most of Duck Creek's buildings, which relied on the seemingly inexhaustible supply of pine boards from the surrounding forests. Even the courthouse and city hall, the only two other edifices of distinction in Duck Creek's early days, were built of limestone dug from the mountain.

Library patrons mounted the library's broad marble steps, daily scrubbed white, and passed between soaring Ionic columns with their ram's-horn curls to enter the hushed, high-ceilinged rooms within. Julia didn't go to church—a rare line she'd drawn with Beverly—but to step through its doors was to briefly feel that same sense of awe, the presence of holiness. Calvin darted into the children's room as Julia indulged in a ritual as sacred as communion, selecting a book at random from the stacks, bowing her head to breathe in the scent of paper and glue and dust, closing her eyes to acknowledge the benediction of books.

"Hey, Julia."

So much for sacrament. She slotted the book back and turned to see Chance Larsen.

"So you're on the Mohammed case. How'd you score this one?" Never one to beat around the bush, Chance.

"You know I can't talk about ongoing cases."

"On background? Does he have a prayer? Blink once if yes, twice if no. Or maybe it's the other way around."

She thought of the principal and his clumsy gibe about Calvin and jail. Why did people feel compelled to make stupid jokes in her presence? Maybe they thought it would ease the tension, but really, wasn't her tension justified?

Chance's smile slid from his face once he realized Julia wasn't going to answer. "Seriously, Julia, I don't envy you this one. It's going to be a shit show." Leaving it like that, open-ended, an invitation for her to chime in on the shit-showness of it all.

"Nice try, Chance."

He shrugged and turned to leave. "Worth a shot."

"What are you doing in the library, anyway? Shouldn't you be writing one of your stories?" She glanced through the soaring window. The mountain loomed black against a sky gone gray with just a few streaks of orange, shreds of a sun already set. "Aren't you on deadline?"

She'd learned early never to call Michael at the office in the late afternoon, when he'd be in a panicked rush to collect the last bits of information he needed for his stories as deadlines bore down.

"Already filed for today. After yesterday, things were pretty quiet. Just doing research for a weekend story."

He ran a hand through thick, dark hair, shorter than he'd worn it when she'd first met him. A wedding band indicated he must have finally married the woman he'd been living with forever. Julia hadn't been invited. Not surprising. Who on their wedding day would want a visible reminder of the very worst way a marriage could go south?

Chance and Michael were the same age; had started work at *The Bulletin* the same year. If Michael were still alive, would he, too, have trimmed his hair to suburban-dad length? Would he, like Chance,

have added a few pounds around the middle? Adopted the bland uniform of chinos and Oxford-cloth shirts, tie optional? She thought of
Michael in his jeans, specifically of Michael's ass in his jeans. That's
how it was these days, lust—usually the gauziest of memories—
hitting her at odd moments, derailing her thoughts, just when she
most needed to focus. Like now, with a reporter hovering, suddenly
gone as cagey as herself.

"Research on what?"

"You know I can't comment on ongoing stories."

Tou-freaking-*ché*, she thought as Chance waved goodbye. She
shook off the discomfort that any encounter with a reporter engen-
dered, and turned back to the task at hand. Usually, she lingered in
the fiction section, novels a relief after her days of dealing with inconvenient and unyielding facts. But on this day, she was on a mission.
She asked one of the librarians where to find what she was seeking,
still vaguely resentful of the computerized card catalog that denied
her the childhood pleasure of flipping through physical cards, running her fingers over the barely detectable impressions left by actual
typewriters. A sentimentalist, Michael had teased her. As though it
were something to be ashamed of.

"You're the second person to ask about that today," the librarian
said, which told Julia exactly what Chance had been up to.

She found the shelf the librarian had indicated, pulled the book
from the shelf and claimed an unoccupied desk. At least yearbooks
hadn't gone digital. It was far too soon to be thinking in terms of a
trial, but if that's where the case took her, Julia would need to know
everything she could about her client, even—and especially—the
things he didn't want to tell her. Which, in this case, appeared to be
everything. Claudette had turned her onto the yearbook trick, which
Chance apparently also knew.

"You'll be able to tell a jury that the person accused of chopping
his vics into little tiny pieces and putting them in trash bags and tossing them into Duck Creek, only to be uncovered by an elementary
school class on its annual river cleanup day, was actually captain of
the chess team, Le Président of the French club, and voted nicest kid
ever in the history of Duck Creek High. And even if they spent most

of their high school years in juvie, never underestimate the value of a freshman-year class portrait. Those baby faces get 'em every time, give them pause. Sometimes that pause is all you need for a hung jury."

Unfortunately, Sami had started at Duck Creek in his junior year, so his class photo didn't look that much different from his mug shot. No help there. Julia turned the heavy, slick pages to the photos of school activities. Sami stood in the back row of the soccer team's group shot, partially obscured by the taller youth in front of him. The other players clowned around for the photo, throwing white-boy versions of what they imagined to be gang signs. Cody Landers, as team captain, stood in the middle of the front row, black-and-white windowpaned ball tucked against his side. Square shoulders, square jaw, his hair like most of his teammates' cut high and tight on the sides, long and swept back on top in a style Julia prayed would have passed by the time Calvin hit high school. A single photo, black-bordered, on the opposite page diverted her attention. "Rusty Tibbits."

As in son of Dan, the defense attorney whose near-hundred-percent prowess made prosecutors rue the day they'd decided upon a career of fighting crime. Julia remembered the guilty relief that had swept the courthouse with the news that Rusty Tibbits had been driving alone, only managing to kill himself the night he wrapped the classic Firebird his parents had bought him around a tree. No one would have wanted the task of prosecuting Rusty had he survived, or taken anyone else out with him.

Julia scanned the yearbook's pages again, but saw no other photos of Sami. She started to close the book, then thought of something. She opened it to the sophomore class photos, page after page of the baby faces Claudette found so useful. Ana Olsen was in the middle, a round-cheeked girl whose dark eyes stood startling in contrast to her pale straight hair and pale skin. With a start, Julia recognized the girl she'd seen from her porch a few mornings earlier, heading to school on the day after whatever happened in that locker room, trying to pretend everything was normal.

Julia wondered what had made Ana fall apart only minutes after walking into Duck Creek High that morning. A sidelong glance, a whispered comment? The boys had waited overnight before saying anything to the principal. Who had they talked to in the meantime? "It's already flying around social media," Decker had warned. Or maybe it was just the simple act of returning to the scene of the crime. If there'd been one, Julia reminded herself.

And why hadn't Ana, whom she'd seen marching so determinedly toward school that morning, contacted police herself? She already knew the answer to that one: Most girls didn't, knowing that unless they'd been injured unto the point of death, somehow the blame would come back on them. Unless Ana was that one case in thousands of false accusation. Julia banished the thought as quickly as it crossed her mind. Despite Herculean training efforts aimed at law enforcement, too often a sneaking sort of suspicion against the girl still permeated such cases. If the police thought Ana's case was worth kicking up to the prosecutor's office, there was probably a there there. The girl stared unsmiling back at her. Apparently she'd been no more helpful with police and medical personnel than this silent photo.

Back to the activities pages, where, as with Sami, Ana's only presence was in athletics. She stood with the cross-country team—varsity, despite only being a sophomore—a step to the side of her teammates, head tilted downward. But the team's page also contained a shot of her crossing the finish line in full stride, head thrown back, ponytail streaming behind her, faced filled with such joy and triumph that Julia barely recognized her as the same girl. She took out her phone and snapped a photo, then for good measure, also shot the team photos and class pictures for both Sami and Ana.

She set the yearbook aside and turned to the computer. The library offered free access to the newspaper's online archives. She clicked through the handful of stories noting the refugees' arrival and the controversy that accompanied it. Again, not much information about Sami specifically, although Chance had detailed the family's journey after fleeing Iraq. First Turkey, then—Julia began counting countries on her fingers—Greece, Macedonia, Serbia. Cutting across a corner of Bosnia. Through Croatia. Slovenia. Austria. Eight countries over the course of nearly three years, with harrowing

delays in refugee camps whose very mention drew tears from Sami's
mother—duly noted in Chance's story—before arriving in Germany.
There they lived in two rooms in a repurposed candy factory outside
Berlin, where one day a miracle arrived in the form of a new program
for refugees in a part of America none of them had ever heard of.

Julia stared unseeing into the screen, placing herself in the details
Chance's story had described. She tried to imagine setting out with
Calvin and a single suitcase, catching taxis and buses on good days,
crammed with strangers in the back of fetid trucks or even walking on the bad. The ever-present fear of violence, rape. What did
people do when the money ran out, as surely it must have at some
point? How did they feed their children, keep them clean? Where
did they get diapers for the babies? Sanitary products for themselves?
She'd gotten her period early once while five miles into a hike with
Michael. He'd been unperturbed, offering his bandana, but Julia was
both mortified and excruciatingly uncomfortable, the inadequate
bandana shifting and bunching during the interminable walk back.
What if that same experience had confronted her every month for
three years?

A portrait of Sami's parents, the couple she'd seen in the courtroom, accompanied the story. They stared unsmiling as if from an
old daguerreotype, the woman's eyes darkly pouched, the husband
bald, long-jawed, exuding weariness. And yet their words to Chance
were hopeful. "Our dream," the mother said. "Everything is possible
here."

"Anything can happen," her husband echoed.

Unfortunately, they'd been right.

The streetlights came on outside. It was time to go. Julia signed
off the computer and picked up the yearbook, flipping a few more
pages, pretending to herself that she'd ended up on the yearbook's
administration page by accident. Dom Parrish leaned a hip against
his desk, arms folded, his for-the-camera smile holding no hint of
the genuine warmth that had so changed his face when Julia had met
him in the parking lot. So different from the grin that had sparked
an instant flame when she'd first met Michael; still, she'd felt . . .
something.

"Mommy." Calvin materialized beside her, arms full of picture books, every last one with a dinosaur on the cover. He was only just learning his ABCs yet could twist his tongue around ichthyosaurs and archaeopteryx with the aplomb of a paleontologist. He'd early learned to count to seven, the library's weekly limit of books he was permitted. "Hungry."

She looked at her phone. Nearly six. Beverly would reheat Calvin's dinner, but maybe not hers. She started to close the yearbook, then lifted her phone and clicked the camera at the principal's page, smiling at her own foolishness as she slid the book back onto the shelf.

CHAPTER

12

Usually Julia walked to work, grudgingly giving Beverly credit for buying a home in Duck Creek's oldest neighborhood, with its deep-porched Craftsman homes interspersed with rambling Victorians that once housed the town's founding fathers.

Built to impress and also for convenience, they were close enough to the downtown businesses and banks and law offices that their owners could stroll home for the lunches their wives prepared for them, and return to their busy days refreshed from a postprandial forty winks in a soft chair as the rest of the household tiptoed around them.

On this day, though, she drove. When she'd called the school to ask about a good time to re-interview Sami, the principal told her Sami was absent, and likely to remain so. "I'm just collecting his homework, and Ana's, too, to send to their houses," he told her. "Ana's a good student. She'll be fine, at least as far as her grades are concerned, but the last thing Sami needs is to fall behind in his classes. He's doing better than expected—he's making Cs, and believe me, they're not mercy Cs—but he struggles for each one."

Julia made a snap decision. "Let me take them to him."

Going to a client's house would be a first, so unorthodox that she decided not to ask about its advisability. Another of Michael's favorite sayings: Never ask permission. He had a trove of tactics from his days as a reporter, and at the time Julia had thought them sneaky and underhanded. Now she was beginning to appreciate them.

The school sat on the bank of the creek, an inconvenience in so many ways, according to Claudette, who because her kids were fast approaching high school age was hurriedly acquainting herself with all the kinds of mischief possible in teenage minds. According to other parents in the office, kids smoked—regular cigarettes and otherwise—under cover of the bank's bushy willows, quaffed schoolday beers, and fornicated, their discarded condoms provoking horrified merriment on cleanup days.

In winter, the ice proved a deadly temptation, the current murderous beneath its too-thin surface. Over the years, the creek had claimed more than one wintry adventurer, though thankfully not—yet—anyone from Duck Creek High. "I'd drain that damn thing tomorrow if I could," Claudette had been heard to mutter of the town's eponymous attraction.

Julia appreciated the dangers posed by the creek—she clasped Calvin's hand tightly whenever they took the walking path along it, tugging back against his impulse to play at the edge—but still she loved its soothing gurgle, the mists that curled sinuously above it early in the morning and, once the sun rose, the way the wavelets caught the light and scattered it skyward in extravagant jeweled handfuls.

Its waters moved languid and deep through town and the valley beyond in a miles-long breather after its headlong rush out of the mountains. On her worst days, Julia imagined launching a small boat, nothing fancy like the trout-fishing outfits that plied the creek in summer, their occupants swishing whippy fly rods in ten-two patterns. A kayak would suffice, a cut above the inner tubes deployed in flotillas by students, just enough to take her bobbing away from reality.

Her arrival at the school told her there'd be no avoiding reality on this day.

A police car sat at the parking lot entrance, and Julia felt sure some sort of dash cam recorded her presence as her car rolled slowly past, toward the crowd at the door that seemed to materialize wherever they thought the latest development in the case might be occurring. This one was larger than usual, several dozen people, an impressive size for a town still coming to terms with its resort-fueled growth spurt.

There was Karl Schmidt, albeit with a new sign—"Send him home"—there were the parents, moms mostly but a few dads, too; there were the kids with their phones, Snapchatting or whatever it was they did like mad. Didn't they have classes?

Julia, head down and hands shoved into her pockets, got halfway through the throng before she moved out of the shadows and into the sun, which caught her hair and lit its copper strands like a semaphore, signaling her presence to the world. A whisper at first, an elbow to ribs, then a shout: "Hey. It's that lawyer!" She sprinted up the steps, breathlessly explained her mission to the woman standing there, arms folded across her chest, and was admitted to cries of protest from those behind her.

Dom Parrish was waiting just inside the door. "Celia Walks On," he introduced the woman at the door. "School secretary and bouncer."

"We'll take you out a back way," Celia said.

"But my car."

They looked at each other, then through the glass doors at the people milling at the entrance. One man put a booted foot to the bottom stair, a bull pawing his defiance.

Celia rapped at the window. He jumped back. "They know that the minute they come up those steps, it's trespassing. But they can't seem to stop themselves from trying."

"I've got an idea." Dom opened the door and called out to the crowd. "Any parents here?"

"For Chrissakes, Parrish. You know who we are."

Julia recognized the voice before Dan Tibbits emerged from the throng, leading a contingent of women who looked equal parts worried and pissed off.

"PTA moms," Celia told Julia. "Or, as I like to call them, the Reign of Terror."

"But why's he here? His son . . ." Julia didn't know how to say tactfully that, given his son's death, Tibbits no longer had status as a Duck Creek High parent.

"He's their lawyer."

Julia turned in surprise. "Why? Are they suing?" And over what? So far as she knew, everything had been handled by the book. She wondered if Tibbits's eagerness to rush to Ana's defense had anything to do with his inability to protect his own son.

"Not yet." Celia gave the words a wry twist. "They just want us to know they might. But that's pretty much their default position on anything." She jutted her chin at Dom. "I don't know how he stands it."

"My massive salary makes it easier." He attempted a small, tight smile at the obvious joke. "I'll go get Sami's schoolwork."

Julia watched his progress down the hall, past an arrow that indicated a gym and the restrooms. She shifted from one foot to the other, pantomiming need. "Mind if I duck into the bathroom? Way too much coffee already."

She headed toward the sign, forestalling any attempt Celia might make to direct her to another bathroom. No harm, no foul if she'd guessed wrong. But she hadn't. Because of course, where there's a gym, there are locker rooms. Which, hallelujah, were just past the restrooms. She looked over her shoulder to ensure that Celia's focus was once again outward, and ducked into the girls' locker room, only to be assailed by a time-travel sensation so strong it left her dizzy. Scent of baby powder and sweaty clothes and fruity hair product. Rows of narrow benches; the lockers festooned with images of favorite bands. Julia read unfamiliar names and stepped closer, the better to see the images in the dim light. In her day, it had been boy bands, their photos torn from magazines. Now the images were computer printouts, and girl groups, fierce and unsmiling, competed for space with baby-faced boys. Good for them, Julia thought, wondering if this new generation would be the one that finally threw off all the old limitations. But no. She brought herself back to reality. Ana hadn't dared to go to police, not even with a complaint—given the suspect—sure to be believed. The old goddamn rules still applied.

She made a quick circuit of the room, looking for security cameras, and saw none. She glanced into the alcove that housed the toilets and showers, the latter with the same inadequate curtains she remembered from her own school years, permitting the quick,

embarrassed glimpses of one another's bodies, the inevitable comparisons with girls whose breasts were bigger, stomachs smaller, and oh, God, let's not even think about the mortification of pubic hair and social signifier of waxing.

She hurried back into the hallway, a shoal of safety after the flood of memory, and accepted a bundle of books and papers from Dom, then stood aside with Celia as he held the door open, beckoning toward the group.

"I'll meet with the parents in my office now. The rest of you can stay here if you like—it's your right—or go home. I just ask that you don't interfere with our students during school hours or cause any sort of disruption that would interfere with classes."

The volume of the resulting outrage would surely count as interference, Julia thought. Celia gave her a shove so sharp she nearly stumbled. "Hurry up. They're so busy going all First Amendment they won't notice you for a few minutes. But for God's sake, take this." She snatched a Duck Creek High baseball cap from the display of school merchandise just inside the door. "Cover your hair."

Julia tucked it up inside the cap, gave Celia's arm a grateful squeeze, and forced herself across the lot at a leisurely stroll, expecting any moment to hear a roar of discovery, hot breath on her neck, the predator realizing its prey was escaping. To her mind, the chunk of her car's door locks, the stutter of the accelerator catching, outranked the sweetest aria Pavarotti had ever warbled in their office.

She didn't look in the rearview mirror as she left. She didn't want to know.

13

B UT FOR HER own neighborhood—Beverly's, not hers, she reminded herself—Julia rarely turned off Duck Creek's main thoroughfares, never realized that tucked in among the concrete plants and storage units and construction companies on the outskirts of town were dreary trailer parks and two-story apartment complexes with rows of doors along outside promenades, looking like so many rundown motels. Which some of them surely had been before finding new life as permanent dwellings for the sorts of people Julia found herself representing in court.

Her phone dictated directions. She turned, passed a small quarry, a yawning rocky pit that took up an entire city block. Machinery clanked and groaned, raising gritty dust that filmed Julia's windshield. She'd thought Duck Creek's industrial era had ended when the mines closed; that these days, it was more of a bedroom community for the ski hill. Another thing she'd been wrong about.

A strip joint, its name familiar from regular appearances in the daily newspaper's police blotter, confronted her. Trucks, both the region's ubiquitous pickups and detached semi-cabs, filled the lot. It was nine in the morning. According to her phone, Sami's home was only a couple of blocks away. She wondered if Sami walked past the place every day heading to or from school. Whether he was repelled by it or drawn to it. Whether the daily reminder of readily available female flesh just on the other side of the door might have festered in

his imagination, leading him, upon seeing a girl in a deserted hallway, to follow her into a locker room . . .

Julia tried to put a stop to such thoughts. This was her client,
whom she was bound to defend, whose principal couldn't imagine
he'd done anything wrong.

As if that meant Sami could somehow banish lust. Julia thought
it a cruel trick that her grief, which had so casually defeated joy and
curiosity and but for the fact of Calvin nearly all desire to live, had
proved powerless in the face of lust. She still awoke mornings craving
Michael with a fierceness that shocked her. It had been their favorite time—"Let's get you ready for court," he'd say—intensity compounded by the ticking clock, Julia still pink-cheeked and breathless
as she rushed from their apartment, the day's pending indignities
reduced to triviality.

In her long, long list of Reasons to be Mad at Michael for Dying,
a list charred and smoking from the heat of her anger, carefully
curated and updated on a regular basis, his leaving her celibate in her
prime hovered near the top.

She'd been mortified, upon meeting the principal, at the way her
gaze had slipped to his left hand, noting the lack of a ring. Pretty
much the only single men she met were her clients. Claudette had
urged her to date in typical blunt fashion—"You carry on like this
much longer, you'll dry up. Get out there."—but whenever Julia
thought about it for more than two minutes it seemed so impossible
that she relapsed into the familiarity of rage.

Her phone chirped a welcome distraction: "You have arrived at
your destination."

Sami lived in an apartment building on the very edge of town, at
the mouth of a canyon whose steep sides kept the neighborhood in
shadow most of the day, its rocky walls awaiting winter's softening
mantle of snow. Duck Creek's winds were infamous, gathering speed
as they coursed through the canyon walls and barreled through the
town's streets.

Julia thought about how they'd slam past the apartment building,
rattling the single-pane windows in their cracked and peeling frames.
The day was chilly but not yet cold; still, she shivered at the thought

of spending a winter in such inadequate shelter. She reminded herself that Sami and his family likely had endured far worse.

She pulled into a parking space and sat a few moments in her serviceable Subaru, which stood out among the beaters in the lot like a Caddy in a junkyard. "You have arrived at your destination," the phone said again.

No, she hadn't. There was still the climb up the metal staircase at one end of the building, the long walk down the hall to confront people who, with the exception of Sami, she'd never met.

She gathered the schoolbooks and assignments, and banished all thoughts of gyrating dancers, barely remembered sex, and a weeping schoolgirl.

* * *

Julia put her knuckles to the door, more tap than knock, and yet it flew open as though she'd pounded upon it.

A woman in a headscarf, finger to lips in the universal sign for silence, blocked her way. Behind her, Julia glimpsed a darkened living room, a pull-out sofa, a form curled upon it, pillow wrapped around head.

The woman's eyes widened in recognition, then narrowed in a diviner's comprehending scan. She drew herself up, nostrils flaring.

Julia felt herself read, judged, improbably dismissed as a fraud. *She knows.* Then rebuked herself for insomnia-induced silliness.

The woman stood aside. "My husband," she said, so softly the words barely registered. "He works nights, sleeps days."

Julia nodded and tiptoed in, nearly stumbling over a pile of shoes. The woman closed the door silently behind her, then went to the sofa and pulled the pillow away, murmuring into the man's ear. He startled upright and Julia turned away to give him some privacy, reflexively kicking off her clogs and adding them to the collection of shoes beside the door, not turning back until she heard another door close.

Sami's mother snapped up the shades, yanked the covers tight over the sofa-bed, flipped it back into a couch, and scooped a baby from a blanket from the floor, her movements rough, abrupt. She waved a hand toward a small table, set with four chairs. "Sit."

Julia sat, inhaling the yeasty scent of fresh bread, along with indefinable spices, unfamiliar but good. The apartment's main room combined a living room, dining area, and kitchen. Julia assumed one of the doors led to a bedroom. Water gurgling behind the other indicated a bathroom.

Sami's mother cocked a hip and balanced the child against it as she filled a teapot and set it on the stove.

Julia put the books and papers on the table. "You don't have to do that. At least let me hold him—her?—for you."

"Her." The woman brushed her hand over the little girl's fuzz of hair and touched her cheek to her face before handing her to Julia. The baby settled readily into her lap, giving her a four-toothed grin before reaching for Julia's hair, pulling it across her face. Through its curtain, Julia studied the room, nearly bare of furnishings but for the sofa, a pre–flat screen television on an overturned milk crate, a folding chair at a card table holding a computer of a vintage barely more recent than the television's. The carpet was frayed and faded, but clean, as was every surface in the place. Still, Sami's mother brushed an imaginary speck from the table before she slammed down two mugs of tea so hard that their steaming contents performed miniature tsunamis within.

The bathroom door opened and a man emerged, dressed in an off-brand polo shirt and chinos too light for the weather, hair and face still damp, the shadows under his eyes far darker than that of his beard, voice hoarse with exhaustion. He bowed toward her. "I am Moheb."

Julia held out her hand and after a moment he took it, his own quivering so violently she quickly dropped it.

"Julia Geary," she said. Then, trying to lighten the moment, she gave the baby a bounce. "And who is this?"

The man's stricken expression softened. "This Zuleikah. But we call her Mishmish for . . . for . . ."

"Apricot," his wife said from the kitchen, in a voice whose chill stood at odds with the sunny climes the fruit evoked.

"Apricot," the man repeated. "For"—he touched his fingers to his own gaunt cheeks, then pointed to the baby's, indeed as plump and tan as apricots.

"Mishmish," Julia repeated. The baby crowed at the sound of her name, and tried to clap her hands, now thoroughly tangled in Julia's hair.

Sami's mother returned with another slam, this time a dish of almonds and dates and still-warm flatbread. She took a chair beside her husband and together they stared at Julia, who in turn stared into her tea, trying not to look at the closed bedroom door, behind which Sami surely lurked.

"I brought his work from school," she said finally. They continued staring, wordless, anguish etched in the grooves of the father's face, the mother's set in the hard planes of anger.

Julia shifted in her chair. "Do you understand . . . your English . . .?"

"We understand," Sami's mother said, biting off the words. "We were teachers in Iraq. Professional people. Here, I clean motel rooms. My husband bundles the newspaper for delivery. He comes home smelling of ink."

Julia glanced at Moheb's hands, black lines highlighting their wrinkles and whorls. "I'm sorry." Even as she spoke Julia wondered what, exactly, she was apologizing for. A country that offered safety, but demanded a groveling sort of gratitude in exchange? "That must be very difficult."

"Difficult? The work is fine. It is a small price to pay. I no longer worry about someone killing my children if they set foot outside our home. Sami can play football all day long here and the worst that will happen is a bump on his head, a . . ." She shoved the fingers of one hand hard against the table. "What do you call this?"

"Jammed." Julia winced at the imagery.

"These boys here, these fortunate children, they do not understand when he insists to keep playing. They do not know that such things are nothing.

"What is difficult is this . . . this thing that has happened to my son."

"Yes." Julia seized upon the opening. "Which is why I hope to talk with Sami. I cannot help him unless . . ."

"You can help him. But you will not," his mother broke in. "You hate him. It is in your eyes."

"Jamilah!" Moheb rebuked his wife, speaking low and quickly in Arabic. She retorted in English. "It's true. You saw her that day. In the court. And we know why."

She knows. Julia's first reaction had been correct.

The morning newspaper lay on the table with its stories about the refugee center, the hearing. The damning information Chance Larsen had seen fit to include—"public defender Julia Geary, whose husband Michael Sullivan was killed in Iraq . . ."

But maybe the woman only spoke English, couldn't read it?

Jamilah's next word destroyed Julia's last hope.

"You think you're the only one who lost anyone in that war?"

Shame cut through her, a hot knife parting viscera.

The baby chose the moment to draw her hands apart, pulling aside Julia's disguising veil, nothing to hide the emotions that must be clear on her face, including the realization that of all the mistakes she'd made in her life, coming to this home on this day to meet these people ranked near the top. She compounded the error by falling back on platitudes.

"I take my job very seriously. I do the best for my clients."

"Your job, your job." Jamilah's scorn filled the room. Next to this woman, Beverly was an amateur. Mishmish tensed in Julia's arms. Julia automatically held her closer, rubbing a hand against her back as though to compensate for the harshness of her mother's words.

"It is what is in your heart that matters. You hate my son for something he didn't do. He didn't kill your husband. Just as he didn't do this thing." Pain finally triumphed over scorn. Jamilah's face crumpled. Her voice broke. "Do you have children?"

"A son," Julia barely managed.

"Then you know. You know." She turned her face away and wept.

Julia indulged in brief, bitter longing for the impersonal concrete grimness of the interview room and its defiant clients. She cursed herself for coming. She cursed herself for taking the case. She had moved on to cursing the universe when the bedroom door opened, framing Sami.

14

A T HOME, IN a sweatshirt and the kind of acid-washed jeans
found only in thrift stores, Sami seemed younger and more
vulnerable than the tense, closed-off youth she'd encountered in the
jail and courtroom.

Mishmish squealed so loudly at his appearance that he crossed
the room to her. Julia held the baby up to him, their fingers briefly
touching as she unraveled her hair from the baby's grasp, each of
them flinching at the touch.

Sami backed away fast, nearly tripping over three smaller boys
who'd emerged from the bedroom. Julia glimpsed twin beds and did
the math—two boys per bed. The pull-out sofa for the parents, the
pallet on the floor for the baby.

In Beverly's home, the house she so loathed, she had a room to
herself with a bay window and a cushioned window seat, the mirror
image of Beverly's own; Calvin's room down the hall big enough to
accommodate the looping S-curves of the train set that had once been
his father's. A fourth bedroom served as Beverly's sewing room, the
skirted machine table set up beside the bed for guests who never came.
Beverly's bedroom had its own bathroom, while Julia and Calvin
shared one off the hallway, and on the first floor a powder room nestled
beneath the stairs, all of them hung with thick towels of Turkish cotton, vanities stocked with lotion and shampoo and extra bars of soap
and stacked rolls of triple-ply toilet paper. Meanwhile—Julia counted
twice to make sure—seven people made do with the apartment's lone

bathroom. And the table, with only four chairs. They must eat in shifts. Or maybe the kids sat on the sofa, balancing plates on their laps.

Julia caught Jamilah's bitter, bemused expression and tried to paper over the transparency of her thoughts by shoving Sami's schoolbooks across the table, past the untouched plate of dates and almonds. "I brought your work from school."

Sami nodded, waiting.

She'd come here, puffed up with Claudette's challenge, breaking protocol to talk with him on his own turf, determined to ferret out the set of facts that would either allow her to prove his innocence, or—in what she still believed the far more likely scenario—persuade him to plead guilty to a lesser charge and take the penalty that would allow him to begin the long grind of putting whatever had happened in that locker room in his past.

But there'd be no talking to him under these conditions. Not with his parents who—his mother's spot-on suspicion notwithstanding—stared at her as though she held the answer to their most desperate prayers, not with her lap still warm from the sweet weight of the baby who'd wrapped her fists in her hair and rubbed its silkiness against her apricot cheeks, not with the three wide-eyed, half-grown boys pressing against their big brother as though they were the ones in danger, not him.

"Sami. Go back in your room. You have brought enough trouble on this family."

At the edge in Moheb's voice, such a lightning change from the diffidence of moments before, the younger boys eased away from their brother, their fearful gazes now alternating between their father and the stranger in their midst.

Jamilah leapt to her feet and braced her hands against the table. "I have told you and told you. Our son did not do this!"

Julia, too, stood. What would allow a graceful escape?

But as one they turned away, toward the window, the boys moving slowly to it, faces alight with apprehension, yet drawn by the taut invisible string of curiosity. Jamilah and Moheb exchanged the sort of to-be-continued glances that Julia remembered from her own brief marriage, then rose and followed their sons.

Julia stood forgotten and later would be ashamed of the sharp relief that propelled her to the door, stepping into her clogs, reaching for the knob until she, too, heard the commotion tugging the family's attention away from her.

She knew that sound. Rejected the knowledge. Had to see, reassure herself that this was just one more mistake in a day full of them. Forgot to take off her clogs as she crossed the room to stand beside Sami's parents, so close she could feel Jamilah trembling as together they beheld the mob Julia had led to their home.

*   *   *

One of the dubious benefits of Julia's job was that she'd gotten to know a number of the beat cops and sheriff's deputies over the years. Some gave every sign of despising her, viewing her as someone attempting to free the very people they'd worked so hard to arrest (although, privately, Julia thought most of her clients didn't require much effort to arrest, their offenses so blatant, verging on ludicrous in their bravado or stupidity). Other officers, especially the ones who'd been on the job a few years, acknowledged they were all part of the same imperfect system, their roles intersecting and overlapping, not quite colleagues, but far from mortal foes. She called dispatch and was patched through to a deputy sheriff.

"Hey, Wayne. We've got a situation over here."

The sigh told her she was out of line. Which she knew. As long as the protesters stayed in the parking lot, they could jump up and down and hoot and holler outside Sami's apartment all day long, or at least until the television cameras—which, sharks to chum, had showed up shortly after their arrival—went off in pursuit of the next story.

Nonetheless, the black SUV with its sheriff's-star decal on the side rolled into the lot a few minutes later. Julia started to say goodbye to the family Mohammed, but they had retreated to various corners of the apartment, all the boys behind the bedroom's decisively closed door, Moheb with a muttered apology to the couch, which he didn't bother to unfold, merely stretching himself along its length and wrapping the pillow around his head again, and Jamilah to the kitchen with the baby, her back resolutely to Julia.

She slipped out of the apartment. Deputy Sheriff Wayne Peterson awaited on the second-floor walkway. Normally he patrolled the farthest reaches of the county, up into the canyons, dark unknowable places touched by the sun only a few hours a day, its rays further foiled by the near-impenetrable canopy of pines. Dark places bred dark crimes, wives beaten, kids raped. The public defenders laid bets on which canyon tallied the most incest cases. When it came to the folks Wayne brought into court, Julia was a little less inclined to feel bad when a judge denied her request for lower bail, glad that an OR was out of the question.

"What are you doing in town? County's your turf."

The people below had gone silent at Wayne's arrival, alert to the possibility of some new development. When Julia emerged from the apartment, a chant arose, a mimicry of one of the Candidate's campaign slogans. "Lock him up! Lock him up!" A contingent led by Karl Schmidt matched the rhythm, their words different. "Hang him high!"

Wayne talked fast as they descended the steps. "Got called in to help cover things here. City cops are still over at the school. I was about to head back out when I got your call. Tell you what. Days like this, I prefer my regular job. At least I know my perps; can sometimes talk sense into them before things get out of hand. This crowd—they don't seem inclined to listen to anyone. Get your keys out. Ready?"

He took her elbow and they plunged in. The local photographers and TV reporters had been joined by journalists from some of the national outlets, drawn by a story that played into the national debate over immigration. For all their blow-dried, wool-topcoated insouciance, they wielded sharp elbows, shouting their who-what-when-where-whys with aplomb. A woman about Julia's own age deployed her own elbows, wedging her way past even the reporters.

"That's right, call the cops. Something that poor girl didn't have time to do. And maybe the next one won't either, now that you've let that rapist loose. Maybe the next one will be you." She drew back, worked her mouth. A viscous gob landed on Julia's shoulder. Cameras whirred and clicked.

"Jesus!"

"Keys." Wayne grabbed them from her, wrestled the car door open, shoved her in, slammed it shut. Julia twisted to look back at the woman.

A fur collar framed her face. She wore high boots, soft leather gloves. Encounter her anywhere else—in line at the coffee shop, or on the next pump at a gas station, and Julia would likely nod and smile, maybe offer a comment about the coming cold—the common courtesies afforded someone like herself.

Nowhere in her playbook, even with a few years under her belt of dealing with angry or disappointed clients, was a response to a well-dressed woman who cursed and spat, who wished her violated, heedless of the presence of a sheriff's deputy. He tapped at the window. Julia rolled it down a crack. He cocked a thumb at the wobbly, glistening blob on her jacket. "Put some dishwashing liquid on that. That's what my wife does, and you can imagine what I come home with on my clothes. Works every time."

The crowd, restless and unfulfilled, turned away, resuming the chanting for the benefit of the cameras. Julia started the car.

"Oh, and Julia. This was a favor, just because I was in town. I won't be around next time and city's got better things to do than babysit you. You're going to have to figure out how to deal with this stuff on your own."

He slapped the hood in farewell and she drove away, thinking about the people in the apartment behind her, no sheriff's deputy or police officer to escort them from the apartment to their jobs, to school, or just outdoors for the simple breath of free air—something afforded even to prisoners. Which, by default, they now were.

* * *

She drove home to leave the car there. Parking near the courthouse was impossible and the state didn't see fit to fund free spaces for the public defenders. But instead of walking directly to work, she went indoors for a few minutes.

She paused a moment on the porch that wrapped the house on three sides and thought of the summer weekends she spent in its welcome cool, swaying in the porch swing as she worked through her files and Calvin zoomed his Matchbox cars across the satisfyingly noisy bumps in the floorboards.

Inside, she lingered again, Michael regarding her from behind glass as she caressed the polished newel post, the light from the stained-glass transom rainbowing across her hand. She trailed her fingers along the hallway wainscoting and collapsed onto the bench in the breakfast nook. Turn her head left and she'd see into the dining room and the long table set with eight chairs; right, and the view took in the windows that ran the width of the room, the expanse of deck and yard beyond it, the thick grass so soft beneath summer-bare soles only now beginning to brown.

"Julia? What are you doing home in the middle of the day?"

Beverly made her way down the back stairwell, a bit of sewing in hand, unable to completely escape the habits of a farm wife despite her best efforts. She held a small swatch of plaid flannel, probably something for Calvin.

"So much space," Julia murmured.

Beverly looked at her sharply. "Excuse me?"

"I went to his house. The boy's. Not a house, an apartment. One bedroom, seven people. All those crazy demonstrators. That woman—she has a little baby. How is she going to shop for groceries? You can't take a baby out into that."

Beverly went to the coffeemaker, the morning's remnants black and bitter within. She emptied them into a mug, nuked it, and gave it to Julia. "Here. It'll be awful, but that might be just what you need right now."

She was right on both counts.

Julia gulped it down, ignoring the taste, needing the caffeine to knock some sense into her. Beverly opened her mouth as though to ask a question, reconsidered, and closed it, shaking her head.

"Thanks," Julia said, as much for Beverly's silence as the coffee. "I'd better get back to work."

She rinsed the cup and put it in the dishwasher and left the house under Beverly's watchful gaze, not realizing until she was halfway to the courthouse that Beverly had not called her customary command to kiss Michael goodbye.

*   *   *

She lectured herself the rest of the day and into the night, well past the time when the hush throughout the house told her that Beverly and Calvin and even Lyle, curled and occasionally purring on the other pillow, were asleep.

A lot—most, probably—of her clients had awful lives. The police reports and prosecutors' affidavits in her files were full of descriptions of children alone for hours in squalor, heat turned off, every dish in the house crusted and stinking in the sink and on the counters, diapers not changed for days. But the children in the Mohammed apartment weren't neglected in any sense of the word. Julia turned over in her too-big bed and kicked the covers away, gasping for air. She got up and went to the window and parted the curtain. The moon slung a bright, shining banner across the lawn. Julia stared down unseeing, confronted yet again with the memory of the little boys clustered around their big brother, clutching at his clothing for safety. Mishmish's squeal of delight at the very sight of him. His mother's anguish, his father's despair.

So his family loved him. So what? Julia had seen that, too, a years-long parade of her clients' relatives through her office, insisting their loved ones were incapable of the charge against them.

Which the defendants usually insisted, too. Not always. Sometimes they shrugged and said yeah, maybe it went down that way (although, in the domestic cases, it was always *her* fault). Or even lifted their chins and puffed out their chests and damn near bragged about what they'd—almost—pulled off.

Never, though, had someone simply refused to talk.

Julia's hand dropped to her side. The curtains rejoined, throwing the room back into darkness. She felt her way back to bed and settled in for another night of no sleep.

She couldn't face that apartment again, the faces so full of hope and desperation. She'd schedule an appointment in the office with Sami, call in a chit with city cops and ask them to bring him to her.

At some point, he was going to have to say something.

15

B UT FIRST, SHE called the principal.

"You're in luck," Celia Walks On told her. "Things have calmed down, at least around here, now that Sami's not in school. Plus, it's an in-service day. No classes, and the teachers are meeting without him. Are you busy today? He could duck out for a while. Is there a good time?"

She was always busy. It had never occurred to her that the addition of a big case did not mean a corresponding lessening of the rest of her caseload. Geological strata of paper layered her desk.

"Now is good."

She had his statement to police. And because he wasn't a witness to the actual event, she wouldn't have to depose him, interviewing him with the prosecution team present. But she hoped to tease out more information, something that might aid the case—or a detail so damning that she could bring it up when she re-interviewed Sami and use it to nudge him toward that guilty plea, quick and clean, a move that in a case like this would count as a victory as opposed to the wreckage a trial could cause, give her a leg up on the next big case.

She'd push for a decent plea agreement, citing his youth, his unfamiliarity with American culture. Maybe the girl had said something, something that would be innocuous here, but seen as a come-on where he was from. Would Judge Baker look kindly on such an argument? Or did he secretly harbor some of the same attitudes expressed by the people organizing the demonstration—the same attitudes that she herself might acknowledge if the demonstrators had chosen to make their point differently—say, in a printable op-ed to the newspaper.

Even after reading Chance's stories about Sami's family, after meeting them, antipathy toward Iraq and by extension its people clung stubbornly within her. Surely it was naïve not to acknowledge that among the innocents lurked people whose main objective was to kill Americans. The kind of people who'd killed Michael.

She dropped her head to her desk, shifting the tectonic plates on its surface. Some papers seesawed toward the floor.

"Here. Let me help you with those."

Dom Parrish bent beside her, sweeping up the papers, so close she caught scents of soap and shaving cream.

She froze, breathing deep. She missed so many things about Michael—the companionship, the conversation, and for sure the sex. As much as any of those, though, she missed his simple physical presence; his smell, the warmth of him next to her as she rolled over at night, the feel of his muscles shifting beneath his skin when she placed her hand on his bare chest and slid it down over his stomach, and down farther still. Dom held the papers toward her. Julia snatched them away and spent longer than necessary rearranging them on her desk, waiting for the heat of embarrassment and maybe something else, too, to subside.

He rose. "I didn't mean to startle you. Are you all right?"

Which is what he'd asked her a few days earlier when they met in the jail parking lot, catching her in mid-hurl. What must he think of her?

"I think I'm just getting over whatever bug I had."

As before, he'd reached to shake her hand. He hesitated.

"Don't worry. Pretty sure I'm not contagious anymore." Not unless paranoia, free-ranging desire, and full-on weirdness were catching. "Have a seat."

"It was good to get your call," he said. "But I already talked to the police." He perched on Claudette's chair, his unease so obvious that Julia regained the slightest sense of control. She straightened.

"I read the police report. It was really thorough. You have a good eye for detail." Handing him a compliment, going through the well-worn motions of putting someone so at ease they'd offer up the one detail they'd unwittingly withheld. "But the police report was only concerned with the incident, and understandably so. That's their job. My job is"—she forced the words—"to defend Sami. Is there a favorite teacher, a best friend, someone who could give me an idea as to what kind of person he is? For that matter, what can you tell me?"

Dom shook his head slowly, mouth set in the not-quite grimace that Julia often saw on her own face when she glanced in a mirror. Whatever he was thinking, it wasn't good. Maybe Sami had some sort of history, some trouble either with this girl or another one.

"Something happened to Ana. In my school, on my watch." He looked as sick as she herself when he'd found her hurling in the jail parking lot. "And I want whoever's responsible out of our school even more than that PTA lynch mob does. But the only thing that would make this whole situation worse than it already is would be to go after the wrong person. If you asked me the least likely boy in the whole school to be involved in something like this, I'd have told you Sami."

Sah-mee, he said it. Not the Americanized *Sammy* that most people seemed to use. "He's almost painfully shy. A lot of that is probably the language barrier, although his English is better than I'd expected. And some of it's probably cultural, too. Somehow, I doubt that whatever sort of school he went to in Iraq, and certainly the schools in Germany, would stand for the sorts of things students get away with here. The teachers, most of them, love him."

Most of them.

"Who doesn't?"

A shrug. He looked at his hands. "Oh, you know how it is."

"I don't. It's been a while since high school."

His eyebrows shot up but he didn't say anything, for which Julia was grateful. People were forever downgrading her age to match her size. "But you look so much younger!" More than once, she'd stopped herself from responding, "And you look so much older."

"The soccer coach—Sami's one of his best players. Until this happened, I'd have said Sami and Cody Landers would probably lead the team to another championship next year. But Sami can't catch a break from Burkle—that's the coach. Guy's kind of a throwback, a walking stereotype, tiptoes right up to the edge of calling Sami a raghead. Writes him up for every infraction."

From his tone, his reddened face, Julia deduced that Burkle was as much a problem to Dom as to Sami. She made a mental note to double back on the subject of Sami's infractions.

"What about the girl?" She glanced at the file. "Ana. What's she like?"

Dom spread his hands. "I barely know her. Good student, so she doesn't come to my attention the way most kids do, by getting in trouble. She and my daughter run track. Elena's a year ahead of her. I wouldn't call them friends, though. Acquaintances, more like. She's not one of those girls you worry about, the drinkers, the risk-takers. You hear them talking on Friday about all the partying they plan to do on the weekend, and you hold your breath until they show up safe on Monday morning. But not Ana. She's the kind of kid who hangs around the edges of things, always watching but not really participating. Do you know what I mean?"

Julia knew exactly what he meant. She herself had been one of those kids. The fringes were safe. Until, for Ana, they hadn't been.

"She's not coming to school, either. And if this, whatever it is, happened to her—I feel sick just thinking about it. But if he'd done something to her, don't you think she'd say so?"

"Not necessarily." Striving for tactful, professional. But he'd caught the edge in her voice.

"That's what Celia said. Apparently, I'm clueless on this particular subject. Which my daughter also tells me. She's friends with Sami, too—knows him from volunteering from the refugee center. This one's tearing her apart. She wants to support them both, but one of them has to be in the wrong."

Julia wanted to tell him that all men were clueless on the subject of the things done to women but needed to keep the conversation on track. "One thing about this job, it teaches you that everybody's got their own version of the truth, especially in cases like this. People are surprisingly adept at convincing themselves of their version of things. Pretty sure that to this day, OJ Simpson doesn't really think he killed Nicole. You've heard the old saw—prisons are full of innocent people. Especially in cases like this, guys will swear on a stack of Bibles the woman was enjoying herself and God help me, some probably even believe it."

She'd gone off on a tangent despite herself, leaning forward, her voice rising. Dom Parrish looked at her with interest. "Sounds like what I deal with all day in the principal's office, only with higher stakes. Jail instead of detention." Inviting her to share, to come back at him with her own experiences.

Regret stabbed her. Why couldn't this have been a casual conversation, wandering where it might in furtherance of whatever incipient warmth underlay their brief encounters so far, instead of a fact-finding mission?

Time to reel things back in. "What about the students? How does Sami get along with kids in his classes?"

Julia tossed it out as a throwaway question, a distraction before pursuing whatever issue the coach had with Sami, but Dom crossed one leg over the other, his foot bouncing, fingers twisting a loose button on his shirt cuff.

"Mr. Parrish."

"Dom."

"Dom, sometimes things that seem negative can help paint a fuller picture. If there's something you might have forgotten to tell police, you're better off telling me now than having the prosecutor get to it on a witness stand."

His fingers froze on the button. His foot stilled.

"There have been some . . . disagreements."

"You mean, like arguments? Physical?"

"Sort of. He's pushed a couple of kids. Cussed out some others. As I said, his command of English can sometimes startle."

Julia jotted some notes. "Unprovoked?"

"That's what the other kids said. But then, they would. Apparently, there's been some bullying. Name-calling. Nothing I've been able to pin down enough to discipline anyone for it. It's really frustrating."

"What sort of name-calling?"

"I guess his teammates call him The Terrorist. You could argue that they mean it as a compliment."

"What does Sami"—she made sure to pronounce it correctly—"say?"

"I've tried asking him about it. He says nothing's happened."

"Same thing he said in this case." It wasn't as though she was sharing state secrets. The affidavit against Sami was a public document. The version with the girl's name redacted, provided by the court clerk's office to anyone who asked and posted on at least half a dozen websites, noted each party's refusal to talk about the incident.

Julia dropped the pen she'd poised over her legal pad. "Isn't there anything else? Anything sexual in the nature of any of these encounters?" Then, reminding herself that her job was to defend Sami, "Any indication the bullying had escalated beyond name-calling?"

"No." He shook his head more decisively than before. "As you might imagine, it's been a big topic of discussion in the teachers' lounge. Believe me, to a man and woman they can spot the kid who's going to be trouble the minute he walks through the door. But Sami wasn't that kid. That's good, right? Won't you need character witnesses?"

"Those don't come in until sentencing." Julia wondered, if and when the time came, how many people—no matter what they said about Sami in the safety of the teachers' lounge—would be willing to stand up for a convicted sex offender before a courtroom packed with their friends and neighbors, all of them panting for blood. "But the idea is to keep this from ever going to trial."

"Yes, yes!" Dom's smile erased the weariness from his face. He leaned forward, and again Julia caught the scent of clean, well-tended male, so different from her clients, who too often reeked of alcohol and cigarettes, unwashed flesh and clothing worn too long.

"The problem is, right now all we've got is one boy saying he saw something, and the two people involved not talking. If you know anything that could help, this is the time to speak up. Anything, no matter how trivial. You'd be surprised at the little details that can make or break a case."

She'd once watched a homicide trial in which a guy accused of killing his wife appeared poised to walk. He'd sworn that he'd woken early to an empty bed, found his wife's battered body in the driveway, covered it with a blanket, and immediately called police. Only after several days of testimony—including that of a police officer who described lifting the damp blanket to reveal the horror beneath—did the prosecution call to the stand a meteorologist, who produced dew-point records that showed the blanket must have lain atop the body for hours.

Dom's expression settled back into its creases of frustration and hopelessness. "Nothing. Not now, at least."

"Of course, if something proves useful, the information will be available to both sides as part of discovery. You could be called as a witness if this goes to trial."

"Understood. I'll keep thinking. And I'll call you if I do." He took a business card from the holder on her desk. "I misplaced your other one. Sorry."

Julia took it from him and wrote her number on the back. "This is my personal cell. Call anytime." She handed it off quickly, hoping he hadn't noticed the quiver in her fingers as memory assailed her, so hard and sharp she sank back into her chair.

Six years earlier, when she was fresh out of law school, Michael had filled in at the courthouse on a day when Chance was double-booked. She'd come upon him at one of the courthouse computers where the public could look up cases, hands hovering helplessly over the keyboard. The court clerk had posted instructions on the wall behind the computer, but Julia knew from her own early days that they were nearly incomprehensible—and she also knew the deputy clerks' trick of picking up their phones whenever a rookie wandered in, so as not to be bothered with annoying questions.

"Need help?"

He told her what he was looking for, moving his chair back to let her at the keyboard. She typed in the case number. Hit a few keys, aware of his eyes on her. "There. It gets easier after you do it a few times."

"Hope this is the only time. But just in case it's not, can I call you and have you walk me through it again? Hate to count on another good Samaritan coming through the door." He cracked a smile, simultaneously acknowledging the come-on and daring her to call him on it. He tore a piece of paper out of his notebook and handed it to her, along with his pen.

She noted the usual things, the fan of creases at the corners of his eyes and slightly roughened skin that betrayed him as one of Duck Creek's denizens of the slopes, accustomed to squinting into blinding white snowscapes. The bare left hand. The grin, the goddamned grin, slow and sure of itself.

She took him for a law clerk, maybe, or a paralegal, although a little older than usual in either case. "Won't you be in here a lot? You'll figure it out fast." Even as she scrawled her number and handed the paper back to him. Because why the hell not?

Then he told her about doing Chance's job for the day. He was a reporter. That was why not.

And when he called her a few weeks later, not to ask her to demystify the public login on the courthouse computers, but to invite her to a party on the ski hill—"at my girlfriend's place"—she tried to laugh at her droop of disappointment. She went anyway.

She'd barely known anyone and chugged two beers too fast, waving away shots, wondering how soon she could leave. After her third circuit of the crowded condo redolent of weed, she finally asked someone where he was, trying to sound casual and evidently failing, given the knowing look she got in return. The woman looked ceilingward. "Up there. They're either breaking up again or having make-up sex. Maybe both."

Julia stopped with one arm in her coat. "If you had to bet?"

"The former. Have another beer. He'll be down soon."

She did, and he was.

If the circumstances were different, would she be giving her phone number to Dom Parrish with the hopes of a similar outcome?

But the circumstances weren't different. He was there about Sami, lingering in the door, invoking the boy's name.

"I'll talk to people, see if I can find out anything. But I already know what anyone who knows Sami, really knows him, will say. He's one of the good ones."

CHAPTER

16

B ut Dom had let slip that not everybody thought Sami was one
of the good ones.

His teammates called him Terrorist—a joke, or something
darker? She'd love to talk with them, get the real story, but knew
that with teenagers it would be nearly impossible. Kids went all weird
and skittish and tribal when adults sniffed around at their business.
Prosecutors had a distinct advantage, able to wield the trump card
of filing charges, maybe scare them into something approaching the
truth. On the other hand, Julia could present herself as their teammate's defender, the thing standing between their friend and jail—if
they were truly friends. She didn't want to walk into those interviews
blind. She'd need more information before she tried to talk to any
of the kids.

Who was that coach? She flipped back through the pages of the
legal pad until she found the name she'd jotted. Bill Burkle. She
called his number at school and left a message and made a note on
her calendar for a follow-up call in a couple of days. She wondered
how many tries it would take, a lawyer the only caller less welcome
than a telemarketer.

But to her surprise, her message light blinked Burkle's response
when she returned from a bathroom break, saying he'd be free at two
the next day.

* * *

A throwback, Dom had called Burkle.

Was it the flattop, bristling like steel filings called to attention by an unseen magnet? The hard round shelf of gut? Or the hands, curled into fists, so obviously hovering at the ready that the gentleness of his handshake came as a surprise?

He sat without being asked, folded his arms atop the gut, and launched. "You want to talk about Sami."

So, no small talk. Fine.

"I hear he was a good student in his classes. What about his time on the team?"

"You mean, what kind of player was he? The best. Walked onto varsity. We needed him, too, after we lost Rusty Tibbits."

Julia waited during the obligatory moment of silence for Dan Tibbits's wayward son.

"Between him and Cody Landers, we've got a shot at another championship."

But Dom had said Burkle was always writing Sami up. "What about discipline?"

"Terrific. Showed up early for practice and stayed late with the guys, running hills. They'd hit the hills anyway, but they're going at it longer and harder than even I'd make them, and Sami went right along with them. They all want to be wildland firefighters when they turn eighteen, pull down those big bucks in the summer."

"Right." Whole patches of the mountain lay bare and charred, victim to the wildfires that swept through at the peak of summer's glory, filling the valleys with smoke and wreaking havoc with tourism. But the fires provided a reliable source of income for those who fought them, and to be on one of the crews was a badge of honor, proof that one had passed the rigorous physical tests required. As soon as the snow melted, runners with forty-five-pound firefighter packs labored up the foothills trails, getting in shape for summer's battles against flame and smoke. Michael had done his time on a hotshot crew and had the body to prove it.

So, in addition to being a good student, Sami was a helluva player and diligent in his workouts. Between them, Dom and Burkle were doing a pretty good job polishing a halo for Sami. She wondered if

Burkle had deliberately chosen to misinterpret her question about discipline.

Julia plucked a treat for Pavarotti from the bowl on Claudette's desk and turned to his cage, pushing it through the bars, asking over her shoulder as though distracted, "But he had some"—what had Dom called them—"infractions?"

"Oh. Those."

Yes, those.

Burkle stretched his arms before him, laced his fingers together and popped his knuckles. "Nothing big. Showing up late, stuff like that. I wanted to impress upon him how we did things here."

"But you just said he always showed up early."

"For workouts."

"Then . . ."

Burkle's chin came up. His eyes were blue and bright and met hers with an unmistakable message: This is how the rest of this little talk is going to go.

Julia spent far too much of every day dealing with people who viewed a woman as insignificant, especially one so young and small, their disappointment obvious at having drawn what they viewed as a short straw. Some, as Burkle was doing now, refused outright to deal with her.

"I see."

Burkle rose.

"Mr. Burkle."

He stopped in the doorway.

"If you had no intention of giving me any helpful information, why were you so prompt to answer my call?"

A flash of unseemly glee, the look of a teenager who'd just pulled a fast one, crossed his face. "Got me out of teaching social studies, my last class. It lasts forty minutes. This took—what, ten? Now I'm done for the day."

*   *   *

Back to the file. Julia had read and reread Sami's so often that she felt as though she could recite every single page by heart—the police report, Ana's medical file from the clinic, the interviews with the nurse and the principal and the soccer players.

She brought it with her to court and studied it while she waited for her own clients to be called before the judge. She shuffled pages, reread them, put them back in order, and read them a third time. A tenth. A fiftieth. Waiting for something to snag, for a phrase or even a single word to take on slap-the-head prominence. The police and medical reports weren't going to change.

Enough with pieces of paper, with secondary sources like Dom and Burkle. "I need to depose the boys." Whispering it under her breath, trying to convince herself, depositions not being a typical tactic in a criminal trial. But she was fresh out of tactics.

Armed with the necessary permission from Judge Baker for depositions, she looked up the number for the prosecutor's office.

Of course, Julia had the right to depose Cody Landers and the others, the cool voice on the other end of the line agreed. But the boys all had their own attorneys and it might take a while for Susan Parrish to coordinate things. Maybe—Julia heard the sound of pages swishing on an old-fashioned desk calendar—at least two weeks out, the receptionist said, her voice betraying none of the toxic mix of salacious curiosity and martyrdom that characterized every interaction with Debra in the public defender's office. "I'll have to call Mr. Tibbits and all the others."

No surprise that Cody Landers had lawyered up. But his parents had sprung for Tibbits, which made Julia all the more eager to talk with him, despite dreading the ordeal it would be with Tibbits riding herd on the conversation. Parents, if they had any disposable income at all, and even if they didn't, were smart enough these days to get a lawyer if their kids came in contact with the legal system. But one of Tibbits's caliber?

Julia hung up. The file sat innocuous and unhelpful on her desk, a manila-enclosed sheaf of uselessness. But what if Cody had misremembered some details? Or if there was someone else involved, someone Cody was trying to shield? Or what if the story was flipped; if Cody were the actual perpetrator, if blaming everything on Sami was part of the bullying Dom had mentioned? Far-fetched, but not beyond the bounds of probability.

A boy as popular as Cody could probably count on compliance from a girl like Ana, already shy and now traumatized. Julia thought back to her own high school years, imagining what Ana's life would be like if a girl like her accused a boy like Cody, the sort of misery inflicted upon a girl these days magnified a thousand-fold by social media. Kids sometimes killed themselves under that sort of pressure. She reined in her galloping thoughts and reminded herself of the first, second, and third rules of criminal law—the simplest explanation almost always was the right one.

Problem was, with neither Ana nor Sami talking, she'd be deposing Cody without the benefit of whatever information the supposed perpetrator and victim could offer.

And what of the other boys? Had they really lingered outside? The longer she had to wait before depositions, the more time they'd have to get their story together, if indeed there was a story to be concocted.

Julia stood, made fists of her hands, balled them against her hips, and moved her feet far apart. She sucked in air, held it, whooshed it out. She'd read somewhere that this particular stance raised levels of cortisol, whatever that was. Something crucial, making one confident and fierce. "The testosterone stance," Claudette called it. "Stand like you've got big brass balls swinging between your legs. Not brass. Titanium!" She held the pose for two interminable minutes, stomped her feet, shook out her arms, and jabbed the phone's redial button.

"Peak County Prosecutor's Office."

"This is Julia Geary. I just talked with you about scheduling a deposition with Cody Landers. I'm afraid a two-week wait won't do. We'll need something within the next couple of days." *We.* As though there were more than one of her.

"That won't be possible."

Julia put her hand across her mouth to enforce her own silence and waited.

The woman sighed. More page-flipping. "I'll see what we can do."

"Do that. And get back to me by the end of the day." Julia choked back her automatic "please" as she hung up.

She grabbed her coat. A small victory, but one deserving of celebration. Colombia made lattes with froth the consistency of whipped cream and baked a mean pie besides. It was midday, past the post-lunch caffeine rush. She'd take a chance that Colombia would be near-deserted and get a slice to bring back to the office with her.

She marched along, cortisol still sloshing through her veins, and nearly ran into Susan Parrish as she rounded a corner. Susan danced nimbly out of the way. "Julia! Nice to see you in court the other day." She showed her eyeteeth in a wolfish smile. The better to chew you up and spit you out, my dear.

"Mmm." Best to stick to noncommittal noises. Anything she said to this woman could and would be used against her.

"I hear you want a deposition from Cody Landers and the other boys. Unusual in a criminal case. But of course, this is your first big case. It'll be a good learning experience for you."

Damn the woman. Julia couldn't tear her eyes away from Susan's lips, the way they pursed in a perfect blood-red bow before delivering each verbal arrow.

Julia tried a subtle version of the power stance, sliding her feet a few inches farther apart, cocking a hand on her hip. "I'll want to talk with Ana, too, of course."

Susan made a sharp, shattering sound, like glass breaking. It took a moment for Julia to recognize it as a laugh. "So do we all, dear. So do we all."

Maybe it was the cortisol, just enough left in her system to make her reckless. Or maybe it was the half-assed power stance. Or maybe it was only that condescending "dear."

"She'll have to talk. They jail people for refusing to cooperate."

Susan's eyes widened in genuine shock. "Please tell me you're not threatening a victim."

"Good God, of course not—"

But Susan was already hustling away, the set of her shoulders telegraphing outrage even in retreat.

Julia continued on to the coffee shop, her celebratory mood deflating with each step, so much so that she ignored the pie and ordered a plain coffee that had gone cold and bitter by the time she got back to her office, where Li'l Pecker waited in the doorway, his voice echoing down a hallway lined with offices gone silent, the better to hear the lecture through doors cracked with studious carelessness.

"Have you lost your fucking mind?

CHAPTER

17

Beverly put the same question to her, albeit with far more delicacy, the next morning.

"Goodness. What were you thinking?"

She brandished the morning paper like a weapon. Had the newspaper upped its font size for the headline? Maybe it was just Julia's guilty conscience. She took the paper Beverly and turned it facedown so as not to see it again.

Prosecutor: Public defender threatens victim.

Calvin watched, bright-eyed with curiosity, his lips working at a question that his mind hadn't quite formed. Julia dropped a kiss on his head to distract him and reminded him to brush his teeth. To her surprise, he complied with alacrity, at four already adept at reading danger signs, the bathroom clearly safer than the kitchen on this morning.

Julia might have been done with the headline, but Beverly wasn't done with her. "You didn't even defend yourself."

Julia tackled her eggs without complaint, each bite sliding down her throat like a slippery rebuke. "What do you mean?"

"It says in here you didn't return calls seeking comment."

The red light on the office phone had blinked all afternoon, but Julia had avoided her messages, fearing a follow-up from Li'l Pecker. Claudette disappeared during the afternoon, and while her icy pained wrath following Julia's inexcusable comment in the café was nearly unbearable, the empty office was perhaps worse for its silent censure.

In Calvin's absence, Julia felt free to explain herself. "I didn't exactly say that. I just said the law allows it. Which it does. But I would never do that. No one would. Well. Some do. But I wouldn't."

"And yet." Beverly's fingernail, polished and filed to a pale pink point—she considered red vulgar—underscored the headline.

"She's just trying her case in the press." Julia suppressed a grudging admiration for Susan. It was a slick move, shitty but smart.

"And?"

Julia picked up a piece of bacon and bit off the end, ignoring Beverly's exaggerated flinch. Beverly would prefer she used a knife and fork. But the bacon, which Beverly inexplicably saw as protein, was her reward for struggling through the eggs, and she'd eat it any way she damn well chose.

"And what?"

"What are you going to do about it?"

Julia dropped the bacon. "What do you mean?"

Beverly rolled up the paper and tapped the table with it. "What am I going to read in the newspaper tomorrow?" She deposited Calvin's cereal bowl in the dishwasher, rinsed her hands beneath the faucet, and flapped the dish towel like a matador's red cape in Julia's direction. "How do you plan to try your own case in the press?" She left the room without another word.

The bacon grew cold. The wall clock ticked loud, seconds and then minutes passing as Julia's anger flared hot, then cooled, then reignited in a slow burn. Because Beverly, damn her, was exactly right. The only thing to do was punch back, hard. But how?

Calvin materialized by her side, baring his teeth to show their perfection.

"Great job, sweetie." She cut the bacon into bits, slipped it into the cat's dish, cleared the table, and helped him into his coat, still thinking.

"Mommy. Mommy." He tugged at her sleeve. "Mommy."

"Sorry." She twisted into her own coat. "What? Hold out your arms." She fitted his bookbag onto his back, and he dropped his arms.

"Mommy—wait, um—" He ran through a series of facial contortions as he struggled to say something just right. "See you next Tuesday!"

"*What?*" Maybe she'd misunderstood.

He said it again, more sure of himself this time. "See. You. Next. Tuesday."

"Where did you learn that?"

"The boys." Meaning the big boys at his preschool, the eight- and nine-year-olds who came to the preschool's after-school program for older kids.

Calvin pointed at her. "Mommy is See You Next Tuesday!" He doubled over with laughter, which ceased abruptly. "Mommy. Kiss Daddy."

Julia, rushing headlong toward the door in her fury, stopped, boosted Calvin, and absently pressed her lips to the glass over Michael's face without her usual parting shot.

"You stay away from those boys," she told Calvin. She left him at the door of the preschool, rather than accompanying him to his cubby as she usually did. Best to save a talk with the director for later in the day, when she'd cooled down. She'd learned her lesson, albeit belatedly, about shooting from the hip.

She strode the two blocks to the courthouse, as though smashing the boys' ugly taunt with each step. See. You. Next. Tuesday. C. U. N. T.

In her ears, Beverly's question murmured loud as Duck Creek in spring runoff.

What am I going to read in the newspaper tomorrow?

And Michael's urging.

Give it some try. Be the bigger bitch.

She had an idea.

CHAPTER

18

JULIA WAS A big fan of the snooze button, setting her alarm half an hour earlier than necessary so as to ease into her day with increasingly wakeful intervals between beeps.

But on this morning she shot upright with the first rude shrill, reaching for her phone, clicking on the local paper's website, praying that this would be one of the days a neighbor's unprotected Wi-Fi signal came in strong. Beverly regarded the internet as a necessary evil, but not so necessary that she'd seen fit to replace a recalcitrant router.

The wheel on the screen spun and spun, the paper's site refusing to load.

Julia leapt from bed, cursing the cold floor, and hurried straight downstairs rather than seeking the immediate steaming warmth of the shower. As usual, Calvin was up before her, warming his hands over the cup of cocoa. Beverly, despite her wariness of starches, saw no problem with starting a four-year-old's day with a dose of sugar.

"Why, Julia. What a surprise to see you this early," Beverly began.

Julia brushed past her to the front door, hesitating on the step. The rolled newspaper lay at the far end of the walk, nearly on the sidewalk. Julia cast a glance up and down the street. No neighbors in sight to see her in one of Michael's old T-shirts and his castoff boxers in which she slept. She dashed barefoot down the walk and sprinted back with the paper tucked against her side, her brief foray into the cold making even Beverly's kitchen seem warm by comparison.

She hopped on one foot, then the other as she shook the paper open.

A story ran down the single column on the right side of the page, with a terse stacked headline: *Defender: Stop Harassment.*

Below it, under Chance Larsen's byline:

"The public defender for Sami Mohammed, the Duck Creek High student accused of assaulting a classmate, said she and her client have been harassed ever since he was charged, and that she wants it to stop.

"'Expletives painted on the walls of the refugee center. Dog— on my doorstep. People seem to have forgotten the concept of innocent until proven guilty.

"'This case is in the very early stages,' Julia Geary continued. 'It's entirely possible more investigation will reveal other suspects. There were several people present around the time of the incident.'"

Julia smiled and nodded and kept reading. Chance had written the story exactly as she hoped.

"Geary pointed out that her client, a refugee from Iraq only recently arrived in this country, 'has already been through hell in his young life. What are these actions teaching him about democracy, about our legal system?'"

"Geary's husband, Michael Sullivan, a former reporter at this news-paper, left to join the Army in 2011, and was killed in Iraq by an IED later that same year."

"Dammit." Julia's throat closed up. Why the hell did he have to include that again?

"Language." Beverly leaned over her shoulder, reading the story along with her

Julia skimmed the next paragraph. "Hell."

"But prosecutor Susan Parrish said it's unlikely the case will involve another suspect or suspects. 'We have incontrovertible proof that none of the other people in proximity to the events of that morning were in any way involved in the assault. With all due respect, Ms. Geary might want to be wary of making such reckless statements. She's already threatened the victim in this case with jail.'"

"Incontrovertible proof, my ass. What a steaming crock of shit."

"Julia! I will not have this!"

Julia forced herself to keep reading. Chance had called her back about Susan's contention, and this time she'd taken the call, hoping her forceful response meant that he wouldn't include Susan's words in the story. At least he'd printed her retort.

"'I did no such thing,' Geary said when asked about Parrish's statement. 'I pointed out, as Ms. Parrish well knows, that such an option has been used—rarely—in these sorts of cases. I myself would never go that route, and I hope that Ms. Parrish treats my client with the same respect.'"

Not that it did any good. No one was going to read that far down in the story.

"Mommy," Calvin spoke up. "What's shit?"

* * *

Julia helped Calvin off with his coat and hung it in his cubby and deposited his lunch bag in the preschool's fridge before tapping at the director's door. She'd done the responsible thing and given herself a twenty-four-hour cooling-off period. She was ready.

"Mrs. Clyde? Do you have a moment?"

The woman sat at a desk cluttered with the crafts of the moment, tissue-wrapped lollipop ghosts in anticipation of Halloween. A macaroni necklace, no doubt presented with great solemnity by one of her charges, rattled as Jane Clyde raised her head. Something crossed her face, a quick tightness about the eyes and mouth, when she saw Julia. But it passed, and when she answered, it was in the smiling singsong italics adopted all too often by people who work with young children.

"Of *course*, Mrs. Sullivan. Come *in*."

Julia had given up reminding Jane Clyde that she used her own name. "But that's so *confusing* for the children, don't you think?" Mrs. Clyde had responded once.

"They're preschoolers. If they know my name at all, they think it's 'Calvin's mom.'" Which had gotten her nowhere. She satisfied herself by addressing the woman as "Mrs. Clyde," rather than Miss Janey, as the children called her.

Now she settled herself into the chair across from Mrs. Clyde's desk and shrugged out of her coat, trying not to see the way the woman's eyes swept her up and down, taking in her workday attire. For someone whose livelihood depended upon working parents, her disapproval was nonetheless evident.

"One of the kids said something, ah, unfortunate to Calvin yesterday. I thought you should know about it."

A practiced concern replaced disapproval. Kids probably said inappropriate things all the time. Nonetheless. "Our school is a *safe space*," Mrs. Clyde declared. She picked up a purple pen and pulled a notebook toward her. "What was said, please? And who said it?"

"I don't know who. Calvin said one of the big boys, so probably the kids who come in for the after-school program. Calvin could point him out to you."

"Well, now." Mrs. Clyde put the pen down, closed the notebook. "We don't want to put Calvin in the position of being a tattletale. Sometimes it's best to let children work these things out for themselves. I will, of course, instruct the aides to be vigilant, so that nothing gets out of hand."

"It's already out of hand."

Julia knew that look. *I'll be the judge of that.* She'd planned to soft-pedal the news, go with what the kid had actually said. See You Next Tuesday. But these extra few minutes in Mrs. Clyde's office were going to make her late again, and she was tired of the woman's—of everyone's—silent condescension.

"He told Calvin that I was a cunt."

Delivering the word like a slap, watching it register.

Mrs. Clyde reared back in her chair, face twisting. "Please don't use that language in this place!"

"I didn't use it. Your student did. To my son. Not the sort of thing a four-year-old should be expected to handle by himself."

Mrs. Clyde collected herself, the red flush that wrapped her neck like an itchy muffler slowly subsiding. Julia slipped back into her coat, and pointedly looked at the clock, a nonverbal reminder that she, too, had a job to do. She'd have to jog the few blocks to work.

"Maybe," Mrs. Clyde began, and Julia awaited her solution. If Mrs. Clyde didn't give her the other boy's name, she'd demand it. Given the magnitude of the offense, she deserved that much.

"Maybe you should find another"—the director pursed her lips, seeking a word—"*situation* for Calvin."

"Excuse me?"

She assumed a pose Julia knew well, straightening her back, folding her hands before her, dropping her voice an octave. Delivering Bad News. Julia used it herself on clients disinclined to accept a plea agreement.

"Mrs. Sullivan." A thrust of the sword.

"Geary." Parrying, inadequate.

"Mrs. Sullivan, Duck Creek is growing, but in many respects, this is a small town. Many of our pupils are the children of professionals. These are educated people, people who discuss current events. They're aware of your defense of that—that—"

"Boy," Julia supplied. First, her comments to the newspaper on Sami's behalf. Now this. Despite herself, it was getting easier to defend him. "He's a boy. Not that much older than the after-school kids."

"That *predator*." Flung at her with the same unerring aim with which Julia had earlier hurled "cunt." "Calvin is bound to hear more of the same. Given that you chose this route—"

But I didn't choose it! They made me! Julia bit her lip against the words.

"—it might be best that you find a, ah, *private* situation for him. Someone who can watch him in your home."

Julia was on her feet, rushing from the room, scooping up Calvin, slamming the door behind her, too late to block Mrs. Clyde's final hiss:

"If you can."

* * *

Calvin wailed all the way back to the house.

"Want school! Friends!" He tugged at Julia's hand, dug in his feet, finally collapsing altogether onto the sidewalk, on the verge of a meltdown more befitting a two-year-old.

Julia hunched over him, an inadequate shield against all the windows in all the houses, neighbors likely taking in the scene of Beverly

Sullivan's daughter-in-law and grandson in mortal emotional combat. The neighborhood was, as Mrs. Clyde had pointed out, full of professional people, the young parents both working to afford its enviable addresses. But there were plenty of retirees, too, the people with whom in a few short years Beverly had made close friends, insinuating herself so seamlessly into their world that it was as if the grim decades on the farm had never existed.

And now she'd have to face her.

Julia turned on her heel and stalked toward the house, leaving Calvin wailing afresh behind her. "Mom! Moooooooom!" If the neighbors were going to see a scene, she might as well treat them to a good one. Heartless Working Mother Abandons Crying Child.

Calvin caught up with her on Beverly's doorstep, face scarlet, breath coming in gasps, a level of hysteria beyond tears.

The door opened before Julia's hand touched the knob, revealing Beverly clad in coat and hat and buttery leather gloves, heading out to one of her "functions," as she called her various activities.

Her gaze swept the pair before her, Calvin in a state, Julia taut-lipped, freckles standing out against a face gone white. She nodded once, and pulled off the gloves, finger by finger, an elegant move worthy of a black-and-white movie, dropping them into a large ceramic bowl on the table beneath Michael's photo.

"They kicked him out of day care. Because of my job, this case—" Julia began.

Beverly shook her head and stooped, pulling Calvin to her. He hiccupped and sobbed against her shoulder. "You get to spend the day with Gamma and you're crying? Now I'm going to cry." She whimpered until Calvin giggled. She glanced up at Julia and inclined her head in the direction of the courthouse.

"You'd better go do your job."

CHAPTER

19

THE HEAT OF Julia's anger rendered the cold immaterial. But the snow. That was a different matter.

It began in the short walk from the preschool to the house, the small stinging flakes typical of late autumn, a harbinger of the days-long curtains that would soon descend and on which the town's economy depended.

The mountaintop, of course, was already white. In town, shop windows displayed ski gear in kaleidoscope colors. Signs advertising hotel and restaurant specials in advance of the mountain's traditional Thanksgiving opening vied with political posters for the days-away mayoral election.

The wind picked up as Julia hurried to the courthouse, her thoughts swirling, snowflakes melting like tears against cheeks hot with emotion; anger, yes, but also despair. She'd caught Beverly in a rare magnanimous mood. But even before Michael's death, Beverly had made it clear she had no intention of being a full-time babysitter.

She'd call other preschools, but even if she found one that had an opening, it probably wouldn't be within walking distance. Or maybe she'd find a nanny, and God knows what that would cost, and how Beverly would feel about having someone else in her home. Not to mention the fact that Calvin would lose the educational advantage of being in a preschool program.

Ever since Michael's death, Julia had felt herself caged within bars of grief and debt and a serious lack of options. Now the bars pressed

closer. Her breath came short and fast as she ran the last two blocks
to the courthouse, arriving flushed and furious to an empty office.

Claudette had long departed. Pavarotti drooped silent and disconsolate in his cage. The coffee press sat half-full. Julia put her hand
to the glass. It was cold. She poured herself a cup and forced it down,
glaring at the red message light blinking on the phone. She'd deal
with whoever had called later. She'd already lost too much time. The
phone rang a rebuke.

She choked down the last of the coffee and picked it up on the
third ring.

"Julia? It's Chance Larsen over at *The Bulletin*."

Julia swiped the back of her hand across her mouth, trying to rub
away the coffee's bite.

"Hey, Chance." She made her voice flat, cold. She knew Chance
was obligated to include Susan's comments in the story. But that
didn't obligate her to let him think she liked it.

"I'm just calling to find out what you think of the Facebook
post."

For God's sake. Calvin had just been kicked out of school, she
needed to find a new babysitter, she was about to be late to court, and
Chance was pestering her about a Facebook post?

"I have no idea what you're talking about. Listen, Chance, I'm
pretty swamped here. Can I call you later?" She wedged the receiver
between neck and shoulder and scooped an armful of files from her
desk

"I'll text it to you. I think you'll want to call me right back."

"Chance, seriously." She looked at the clock. She had five minutes to get to the courtroom. "It's going to have to wait."

She hung up and hotfooted it down the hallway, only to find out
that her cases had been pushed back in the lineup, her first break
of the day. She took a spot in the gallery's back row and flipped
through her files, half-listening to the litany of drunken misbehavior
and petty drug busts, the familiar routine soothing her into something approaching calm.

Ray Belmar was up for a bail reduction hearing. At his initial
appearance, Judge French had not found the odoriferous damage to

the cop car nearly as amusing as Julia, and set a twenty-thousand-dollar bail, well beyond Ray's ability to come up with even ten per-cent. It was a ridiculous amount for public peeing. Under any other circumstances, it would be a cinch to knock it down. But—a cop car. She'd need a good argument. And Ray would have to convince a judge he was damned sorry. Ray's relentless smartassery made him one of Julia's rare enjoyable clients, but it didn't serve him well in court.

Julia jotted some notes, trying to come up with a strategy, the morning's aggravations moving to the margins as she focused. Her phone vibrated. She ignored it, still preoccupied with Ray. Maybe she'd argue that he was so blind drunk—he'd blown a 0.24, three times the legal limit, after all—that he'd somehow thought himself in a men's room?

The phone vibrated again. She glanced at the text on her screen, her head still full of legal Hail Marys on Ray's behalf. It took a cou-ple of seconds for the words to sink in.

"This has gone viral," Chance texted, pasting in the post below.

It was from Facebook group called Not Here, whose cover image was a photo from one of the anti-refugee demonstrations, a "Terrorist Go Home" poster most prominent.

The post itself was written in the style of a news story, albeit omitting anything resembling fact.

"Muslim rapist goes free in tiny Western town."

Julia scanned the rest of it, phrases jumping out at her: "Young girl repeatedly raped at knifepoint." "Victim in coma." "Muslim terrorist."

"None of that is true," she murmured below her breath. Were they allowed to say that? But it was the internet, where everything was allowed.

Then—oh, God. A whole sentence sank in. "Here's the lawyer defending this scum, the one responsible for turning him loose on the innocent women of Duck Creek." A photo of her face. Beneath it, her office phone number. Her office email address.

"Contact her. Let her know what you think. Demand that this fiend be put back behind bars. We're working to obtain this lawyer's cell number and home address and will post them as soon as possible."

Julia gasped.

Calvin.

Judge French raised her head. Another public defender's case had just been heard; two more remained before her own.

Julia rose on trembling legs. "Your honor. May I approach?"

The judge gave a curt nod. MacArthur peeked around the corner of the bench. A wise attorney came to court equipped with a pocketful of dog treats for just such occasions. MacArthur sniffed the air, scanned Julia's empty fingers, and skulked back into hiding as Julia babbled something about a family emergency, the need to postpone the day's cases, her shaking voice somehow working to convince the judge. The files weighed heavy in her arms. She'd need to leave them in the office. And call Beverly to warn her.

She sprinted up the steps, along the hall, hissing "not now" as Debra, always alert to new developments in interoffice drama, stepped to intercept her. She grabbed the office phone. "You have forty-seven new messages," the automated voice informed her.

Forty-seven? She didn't get that many in a month. Maybe something had already happened, Beverly trying frantically, again and again, to call her. Her hand shook so badly her finger nearly missed the button. The first message began.

"I hope someone rapes you, and that some dumb bitch lawyer gets him out on bail so he can rape you again."

Next message:

"Die, bitch."

Next:

"We'll be waiting for you when you leave work tonight."

Next:

"I'm going to rape you with my gun. And then I'm going to pull the trigger."

She clicked and clicked through them, losing strength with each new diatribe, collapsing onto the floor by the end.

"Bitch."

"Whore."

"Cunt."

The receiver fell from her hand, clattered against the desk, and caromed over the edge, swinging the end of its cord, spewing filth into the too-small office even as Julia backed away, slamming the door behind her and running for the place that, for the first time, she thought of as home.

*   *   *

Beverly yanked the door open as soon as she heard Julia's key in the lock, dragging her in, throwing the deadbolt behind her, face white, mouth a gash. She pointed wordlessly to the coat rack, the shelf atop it. There, well out of Calvin's reach, the shotgun rested.

"I called the police," she mouthed. "They'll be here in a few minutes."

Julia slumped against the door. "They found the home number, then."

Beverly nodded, a sudden tremble in her chin. She clamped her jaw shut.

"That means whoever did it—or the people stirred up by whoever did it—will be here soon. Or at least as soon as they see the police leave." She came away from the wall. "Beverly, where's Calvin?" She ran to the kitchen.

Calvin sat at the table before a half-built Lego structure. "Mom!" He held up his arms. Julia clasped him in a hug so long and tight that he wriggled free.

The landline shrilled. Julia jumped. Beverly reached for it. Julia grabbed her wrist. She lifted the receiver for a brief second, and hung it back up. Then she unplugged the phone.

"Calvin, just let me hang up my coat and I'll come back and help you build—what is that?"

"A fort. It's going to have towers and everything."

Julia thought of thick stone walls, gun slits, a moat. Preferably filled with sharks or crocodiles. A fort sounded just right.

She jerked her head toward Beverly, who followed her back down the hall. Julia hung up her coat, eyeballing the gun above it. "What happened?"

"Just a few minutes ago, I got the most awful call. Somebody saying we should be killed, the house burned down. I called the police
right away. Julia, what's this about? Why are you home?"

"Because I'm getting them at work, too. Almost fifty of them."

"Fifty?"

"Believe me, you got off easy with getting killed and the house
burned down." She glanced up at the coat rack, the gun long and lethal
atop it. "You'd better put that thing away before the cops get here."

Outside, a car door slammed. Beverly snagged a coat from the
rack and tossed it over the gun, tugging it to cover the barrel's pro-
truding tip. Together they looked through the narrow window beside
the door. Two uniformed men stood on the sidewalk. Beverly's hand
went to her mouth.

Julia held herself rigid. Beverly's hand found hers and she reluctantly folded her fingers around it, knowing Beverly was thinking, as
she was, of the day the two soldiers paced in seeming slow motion up
the walk, a pregnant Julia turning and fleeing heavily for a safety that
didn't exist, captured then as now by Beverly's iron grip, the older
woman facing the unbearable with spine straight and chin high.

These were just the police.

Their present torment, just phone calls.

No one was dead.

Whatever this was, it wasn't the worst.

* * *

There was the complicated matter of explaining the presence of the
two police officers, neither of whom she knew, in a way that didn't
frighten Calvin on a day when already, too many things were out of
order.

Beverly made coffee and served it in the living room. Julia stayed
in the kitchen with Calvin, locking brightly colored plastic blocks
into place on the fort. "Higher, I think, Calvin. This fort needs to
be really strong."

Beverly talked with the cops for long minutes. Julia strained but
could not sieve the words from the murmured voices reaching the
kitchen. Finally, Beverly appeared in the doorway. Julia's turn.

The cheerfulness she'd enforced in Calvin's presence vanished as she told them of the phone calls. "They called me a—" She stopped, shocked at the incipient sob.

"Ma'am." The older cop, ma'aming her just like something out of a movie. She didn't know either of them. Not beat cops, then, who sometimes showed up in court to testify against her clients on the rare occasions she hadn't been able to keep them from going to trial. "Walsh," his name tag proclaimed. "I can't imagine anything you heard will be able to shock us." His smile was compassionate, his eyes kind.

Julia took a breath and ran through the litany on a single long exhalation. "That's what I heard before I hung up." But she hadn't hung up. These were cops. This was serious. She had to get everything right. "Actually, I didn't hang up. I dropped the phone."

The younger cop, whose job appeared to be to take notes, raised his head. "Which one was it? Hung up or dropped the phone?"

"You'll have to excuse Robinson here. He's fresh out of the academy." Another of Walsh's easy smiles.

Good cop, bad cop? But what did it matter whether she'd hung up the phone or dropped it? She hadn't done anything wrong. "Can you figure out who it is? Trace the calls?"

Walsh's smile vanished. "From the way you describe it, it was more than one person, right?"

"Definitely. I wasn't paying that close attention to the voices—I was too shocked at what they were saying—but it didn't sound like the same person. Men and even a couple of women. These are felonies, right? Death threats! Felony intimidation."

Walsh and Robinson exchanged glances. "What was that first one again?"

Julia closed her eyes, heard it again. Clasped her hands to stop them from trembling. "I want to rape you with my gun and pull the trigger."

She opened her eyes to see Walsh shaking his head. "You've either got a very smart or very lucky enemy."

The hope that had risen in Julia—they'd find this jerk, arrest him, charge him, make him go away. Along with all the other jerks. The calls would stop. Life would go back to normal—drained away.

"How's that?"

"He only said he wanted to kill you. He didn't say he would. There's a difference."

"Are you freaking kidding me?" Even though she knew, had put forth that very argument herself in a handful of stalking cases.

Robinson stopped his scribbling and looked up again. Julia knew that moment. She'd seen it in court often enough, walking one of her clients through contrite testimony, the performance a thing a beauty, jury eating out of her hand, until her client slipped up and said something so monumentally smartassed and stupid that, no matter how justified, smashed whatever sympathy she'd so carefully crafted.

"Then, harassment at least. It's a misdemeanor, but better than nothing. I mean, fifty calls? More by now, probably."

Walsh still emanated empathy, but Julia thought she saw a shade of reserve, of goodwill squandered. "From fifty different people." She looked at Robinson, he of the hair-splitting distinctions. "Forty-seven."

"You can't mean I've got to put up with this. My office phone— I can't listen through all those calls just to make sure I don't miss any legitimate business. And then the ones coming here. My God. My son might answer the phone. Might hear that. And they said they were going to come to our house. You can arrest them then, right?"

Walsh's head wagged back and forth. "Sidewalk's public. They can walk back and forth in front of your house all day long. Somebody tries to break in, well, that's a different story, ma'am."

So they were back to ma'am.

Walsh leaned forward. "Here's what I'd suggest: Get a new number at work, but leave the old one set up. That way, all the bad calls will go there, but you can just ignore it. And here, either get a new number or go to a cell phone like the rest of the world."

Beverly was going to love that.

"At our own expense. Even though we haven't done anything wrong." A complaint she'd often heard, with full justification, from her clients' victims.

"Here's the problem," Walsh began.

"No." Julia rose and glared down at him. Take deep breaths, she'd tell her clients. Fake a cough. Change the subject. Do whatever it takes, but don't give in to that urge to cuss out a cop. It won't go well for you, and it'll make my job that much harder.

"The problem is," she said, "is that you're sitting here . . ."

But her next words—"in my home, telling me I'm on my own with these imbeciles"—were forestalled by the appearance of Beverly in the doorway, tray in hand.

"The problem is," Beverly said seamlessly, "you've been sitting here all this time with nothing to eat. And look at Julia, on her feet, ready to usher you out, before you've even had a bite of my coffee cake. You'll have to pardon her—pardon both of us. This sort of thing is such a strain."

Julia hoped she was the only one who noticed the tray's slight tremor as Beverly lowered it onto the coffee table.

"Do sit down, Julia. Or maybe you want to help Calvin. He's facing some sort of architectural dilemma with his fort."

Julia clutched at the proffered escape. "Yes." The quiver in her voice matched that of Beverly's hands. "I'll do that. Officers, if you'll excuse me . . ."

As she passed Beverly she caught her mother-in-law's eye and mouthed the first sincere "thank you" of their time together.

*   *   *

Easy to pull herself together in the daylight, in the presence of police, Calvin, her mother-in-law.

Night, though. The ugly voices, slightly distorted by the phone, echoed in her ears; the emails scrolled before her closed eyes. She wondered about the people who'd contacted her.

The phone calls would be easy, a few numbers touched with a forefinger, a few words spewed in a yell or, somehow worse, a whisper. How hard was it to hiss "Die, you fucking cunt" and then ring off?

But the emails. They took some thought. The elaborate scenarios of rape and dismemberment, the more polite using "refugee," others—most—employing racial epithets. Did the writer imagine her terror, her screams, as she writhed beneath the multiple assailants he wished upon her? Did he grow hard as he typed, slide his chair back from the desk to jack off and then resume typing without washing his hands?

Who wrote such things? Easy to dismiss them with the popular depiction of loners in tighty-whities, living in their parents' basements. But what if they were solid citizens? The sheer volume of the abuse argued for that. What if she passed them on the street, said hello in the courthouse hallways, exchanged smiles on the playground? Did such a person hit "send" on such an email and then wander into his kitchen, hug his wife, kiss his kids?

The numbers on the bedside clock flipped inexorably, minutes turning into hours. Julia finally fell into a restless sleep, comforting herself with the knowledge of Beverly's shotgun.

20

"Knock, knock."

Chance Larsen stood in Julia's open office doorway on Election Day, knuckles striking air just short of the jamb.

The paperwork from Sami's case lay spread out before her. She swept it into a single stack, turned it over, and set an empty file folder atop it for insurance. One of the first things she'd learned when she'd started seeing Michael was his trick of dawdling in front of someone's desk so as to decipher the upside-down documents.

"Chance. What are you doing here? Why didn't you just call?"

"I tried to call. But it went straight to voice mail. And your voice mail is full. Then I tried your cell, but that number doesn't seem to be working anymore."

He moved into the office and sat in Claudette's chair. Another trick, based on the theory that it was a lot tougher to throw someone out of an office, or a house, once they were inside. Sit down, make yourself at home, even put your feet up. Which Chance started to do, then perhaps remembering that the desk in question was Claudette's, instead swiveled to face Julia, who was fast trying to figure out the best way to get rid of him.

"I had to get a new phone. That story you wrote about the Facebook post? The whackjobs who hadn't already seen the post read your story, and now they're calling me day and night, threatening—well, you can't imagine. That's off the record, by the way."

"You know the rules. You can't retroactively say something's off the record. But don't worry about it. The police already told me you're getting threats, so I don't need to quote you."

Great. First the police failed to offer her any sort of meaningful protection and now they were spreading her business all over town, or at least to Chance and *The Bulletin*, which amounted to the same thing.

"If you don't need to quote me, then what are you doing here?"

"Killing time before the polls close, mostly."

"Wish we could fast-forward to then." Julia had heard enough of the Candidate's voice in those final frantic days leading up to it to last a lifetime. She said as much to Chance. "I'll be glad when this is over, and we'll never have to hear him again."

The preceding days had involved a flood of invective from radio and television and online as the election moved into its final days, candidates in the verbal equivalent of a bare-knuckle brawl.

Chance sat up and pulled out his notebook.

"So you think he's going to lose?"

Julia wagged a finger at him. "Off the record, of course he's going to lose. What about you? What do you think?"

"Officially, I don't have an opinion."

"Unofficially?"

"Good try. I still don't have an opinion. But I'm supposed to be gathering opinions from every rando on the street so we can post meaningless updates to the web before the returns start coming in. Care to offer yours—for the record?"

"I do not."

He performed a slow-motion rise from the chair, plenty of time for his gaze to sweep the surface of her desk, frowning at the blank backs of the documents there. So she hadn't been paranoid after all.

"Guess I'll throw myself on the mercy of the man on the street. What are you doing here today anyway? Aren't the courts closed?"

She gestured to the concealed—hah!—stack of papers on her desk. "Working on my case. And all of my others, because they didn't magically vanish just because of this one. And then I'm going home to take care of my son, because—"

She stopped. Chance didn't need to know—no one did—about
the latest unwelcome development in her life, which involved another
hallway encounter with Susan Parrish. Julia had reached for her
phone, thinking to mime a call and thus head off Susan's approach,
but Susan called to her so loudly that others in the hall stopped to
watch, forcing Julia to act as though whatever conversation they were
about to have was the most natural thing in the world.

"I'm so glad to have caught you. I've been meaning to call you."
Susan lowered her voice so the hallway watchers couldn't hear.
Deprived of fresh grist for the gossip mill, they moved on. "I'm afraid
Elena can't babysit your son—what's his name? Calvin?—anymore."

"What?"

Julia hadn't found a new preschool yet, mainly because she hadn't
tried, dreading the possibility of more judgmental directors. She'd
hoped to co-opt Elena into watching Calvin after school to relieve
Beverly, who'd proved a less reluctant substitute than she'd thought.
Julia suspected it had something to do with the phone calls that,
she'd gathered from Beverly's end of the conversations on her new
cell phone, canceled two bridge dates in a row. Not that Beverly had
let on. Somehow, she'd constructed a version of events in which she'd
insisted upon watching Calvin herself, underscoring Julia's parental
deficiencies in sending him to day care in the first place.

"I was a teacher when I met Michael's father. Maybe I can dig
out some of my old materials, put them to use, if any of them still
apply."

Now the little heels sat forlorn by the door and Beverly moved
about the house—its curtains pulled tight, doorbell disconnected—
in sturdy slacks and an artist-style smock that withstood smears of
finger paints and the grass stains resulting from backyard games.

Almost, Julia felt sorry for her. Beverly had strived mightily to
remake herself upon moving to town, investing the considerable
proceeds from the sale of the farm in the house in the right part
of town, the new wardrobe, a purring sedan instead of the diesel
pickup. She'd joined the bridge club, wangled invitations to boards.
And now, all her invitations were falling away, still another strike
against Julia.

Chance hesitated in the doorway. "Off the record, I hope you're right."

"About?"

"The election. I hate to say this, but—" He stopped himself. "I don't want to upset you."

"Let's see. In the last few days, I've been threatened with rape, torture, and dismemberment. Oh, and I've lost my day care center and back-up babysitter besides. Go ahead. Give it your best shot. Right here." She lifted her chin and tapped it, inviting a verbal roundhouse.

"I'm almost glad Michael isn't here to see it. I don't want to get all sentimental, but isn't this what he fought for? The right of people to be seen as innocent before proven guilty? All that democracy stuff? He wanted that for Iraq. Bad enough they don't have it there, but that poor Iraqi kid doesn't get it here, either. What must he think of this country? Can you imagine Michael's reaction to something like this? He'd be really proud of you for sticking up for Sami Mohammed."

With a sad wave of his notebook, he was gone, relieving Julia of the fear that he'd been able to tell from her expression that she'd barely given a moment's thought to how any of this might be affecting her client.

*　*　*

Evening brought an ominous sort of silence, akin to the indrawn breath heralding a scream, or a yellow sky presaging a storm of biblical destruction.

"I almost don't care which way it turns out," Claudette said as she gathered her things to leave the office. "There's only one good thing about it all. Come here, baby." She poked a finger into Pavarotti's cage. He skittered over on his perch and tilted his head for a goodnight scratch.

"What's that?"

"I used to wonder if I was crazy, bringing my family to a town so white. Way I saw it, nobody gives a shit about one black family in their midst. It's the masses they're scared of. Now I know it doesn't matter where we live. Whoever wins tonight, those black bandana people are everywhere, and they're not going away. Which I've always known. But living here, I could mostly forget about it, at least until he came along and stirred things up." She zipped her parka. November had ridden in on winds that swept out of the canyons with an emphatic ripping sound, sending temperatures into a vertical plunge and serving as a forceful reminder of what awaited.

"Are you okay?"

Claudette charged through her days, battle flags flying. Even on the rare occasions she lost a case, Julia couldn't remember her sounding so discouraged. On those days Claudette would slam back into the office and start typing up an appeal, pounding the keyboard so hard the letters had long been worn from the keys.

"Oh, hell. We're none of us all right these days. But you know what?" Claudette leaned to one side, then another, removing her heels and sliding her feet into flats. "This right here—my feet being happy—that's one good thing. So I'm going to focus on that."

"Good plan." Julia curled her fingers and extended her fist for a bump. "Good night. Take care of yourself."

"Same."

As always, the office shrank without Claudette. Pavarotti drooped disconsolate. Julia offered a scratch, but he hunched away from her, casting suspicious glances from eyes like polished black seeds. She covered his cage and looked out the window, a scan of the street below now part of her nightly routine. She squinted, trying to discern movement in the shadows beyond the spill of streetlight; saw none.

But a few moments later, despite her precautions, Karl Schmidt scared the hell out of her, stepping from behind an oak's wide trunk and launching a lecture about the peril she'd loosed upon the town's white women, gabbling at her until she whirled on him.

"Shut the hell up, you old crank."

A moment's intense satisfaction, weighed against the rest of her walk home, designing her own defense against the various misdemeanor charges Karl might choose to pursue.

*   *   *

She took the walking path along the creek, no need to hurry straight to Calvin's day care center anymore, trying to make it before the six o'clock closing time and the dollar-a-minute late fee, with a call to Child Protective Services for a parent who failed to show by six fifteen.

"But my job," she'd made the mistake of protesting. Once.

"All of our parents have important jobs," Mrs. Clyde had reminded her, sounding so much like Beverly that Julia had wondered for a brief, crazed moment if they'd coordinated. "Yet they manage to make their children a priority."

"Bitch," she murmured. She took a breath, trying to shake it off. At least, unlike with Karl, her castigation of Jane Clyde was purely theoretical. She slowed her steps, trying to impose a sense of calm before she returned home.

A half-moon hung above the mountain, silvering its peak. In another few weeks, lines of lights would illuminate the runs carved into its surface, the resort maximizing its profits by touting dawn-to-ten PM skiing. But now it stood majestic and seemingly unmarred by man, and Julia tipped her head in appreciation.

Closer at hand, lamps topping decorative wrought iron posts spilled wedges of light across the path at regular intervals and highlighted the creek beyond, half-frozen patches of frazil ice undulating on its surface, hissing winter's approach as they sidled past one another. A shadow moved across them; another pedestrian, approaching her on the path, head down, hatless, collar pulled up around his ears. Julia slid her hand into her pocket, found her key ring and made a fist with the keys poking between her knuckles, a woman's reflexive move. Then laughed to herself when she recognized the thin, slightly stooped figure in the too-big overcoat.

"Mr. Parrish. Dom," she called out when he drew closer. "It's me, Julia." She pushed her hood away from her face so that he could see.

"Julia!" He held out his hand automatically and they smiled together at the awkwardness of their handshake, appropriate for office encounters but feeling foolish under the circumstances.

"I didn't even see you coming," he said. "I was listening to the ice."

"Me, too." Julia suppressed an unexpected glimmer of delight, worthy of one of Dom's high-schoolers. *We're on the same wavelength!*

"It's like a live thing. I always feel sad when it finally freezes all the way over. It's beautiful then, too. But it seems so, oh, I don't know. Imprisoned."

"Exactly."

Instinctively, they moved out of the light and gazed together at the creek. Dom spoke in a whisper that mimicked the shushing sound of the ice. "How goes the case?"

Julia shrugged, her sleeve brushing his with the motion. "Nothing new. How are things at school?"

He exaggerated his own shrug in response. "I've given up trying to figure any of it out. This thing with Sami, this election, everybody so angry all the time. Nothing seems to make sense. That's why I like walking along the creek. These days, it's the only peaceful place I know. And usually there's nobody else here, especially this time of year."

"Same." Again, that long-forgotten sense of being in sync with another person, not so much a jolt as a sigh of relief, the tension of always being on guard dissolving for a welcome moment. Which didn't mean it was mutual. After all, he'd just said he sought solitude on his walks. "I'm sorry to have interrupted your respite."

He swung to face her, grasping her arms for emphasis. "No, no. I didn't mean to imply that at all. It's nice to see you. I'd like to see more of you. I wish the circumstances were different."

Did he pull her to him? Or did she step forward first, press her face into the wool of his coat as his arms slid around her?

They stood that way, his cheek against her hair, comfort given and comfort taken, and just for those few seconds, the weight of Julia's burdens slid away and she thought of nothing at all.

A section of ice scraped against the bank with a jagged, cracking sound. Julia lifted her head, reality flooding back, and with it the awareness that, if she hadn't already crossed an ethical line in terms of the case, she stood wavering on the tightrope, tipping toward a fatal fall.

"But the circumstances aren't different."

She put her hands to his chest and shoved him from her, running down the path, away from his shocked, sorrowful gaze.

21

J ULIA ARRIVED HOME, breath still coming short from exertion and shame, just as Beverly was leaving.

A next-day bridge tournament a couple of counties away beckoned, something for which she'd registered months earlier and so couldn't be uninvited. Beverly was driving over the night before, alone, while the rest of the club carpooled.

"I must admit," she said with a small, tight smile Julia had never seen before, "I'm looking forward to their expressions when I walk in."

"Wish I could see them, too," Julia said, and meant it. She gave Beverly credit for being willing to face the mob head-on, even if the mob in this case comprised a matronly brigade who wielded words— or, more likely, an icy silence—rather than signs and spittle-flecked obscenities.

"I'll be back by dinnertime tomorrow. There's a casserole in the fridge." Beverly drew a breath. "And thank you for taking the day off tomorrow so that I could do this."

Another step toward the hesitant cordiality creeping into their dealings with one another, a bulwark against the daily barrage of malevolence.

"Calvin, let Gamma go." Julia detached her son from her mother-in-law's legs. "We'll be fine. I'm looking forward to playing hooky tomorrow."

It wasn't hooky exactly. She'd sought permission to work from home for a day, a move that reminded Li'l Pecker of her unfortunate

status as a mother and its accompanying reality of that most detri-
mental of characteristics, a personal life.

"Just think," said Beverly, with a nod to the political sign planted
in the next-door neighbor's yard, the Candidate peering from it with
the pursed-lip scowl that made him look like a disapproving dowager. "By the time I get back, this will all be over. I'll be so glad when
life goes back to normal."

"Mm." Julia feared that even the Candidate's defeat wouldn't
result in anything like normal, whatever that was anymore. His campaign had lanced Duck Creek's stolid norms, releasing something
dark and seeping that festered below the surface, undetectable if you
were white and middle class, all too evident if you weren't. As Claudette had been telling Julia for weeks: "Welcome to my world. Even
though for you, this is just an amuse-bouche. Me, I've been force-fed
the whole entree for years."

Beverly opened the car door, then called back down the walk to
Julia. "I can stay. If you don't feel comfortable."

Julia found herself grappling with a wholly unexpected impulse
to accept Beverly's offer. They'd ditched the landline and gotten
new cell phones; in Beverly's case a first. Julia had created new
addresses for both her personal and work email. None of which
would stop anyone from confronting her in person—a possibility
that saw both her and Beverly checking the yard and sidewalk for
potential troublemakers before leaving the house—but that hadn't
happened yet, and she doubted anyone would choose Election
Night to start.

"Everybody's going to be home watching returns. They couldn't
have picked a better time for this tournament. Go on. Have fun."

But fought a pang of regret at the red taillights ribboning into
the distance.

*   *   *

An uneventful evening with Calvin rendered her earlier apprehension foolish. She helped him with the chores Beverly had instituted—
feeding Lyle, scooping the litter box, and picking up every last Lego
that threatened an unwary bare sole.

They washed their faces and brushed their teeth side by side. She read *Goodnight Moon* twice and *Where the Wild Things Are* three times, nodding off during the third, waking to Calvin's chubby fingers prying her eyelids open, and his prompt: "Wild rumpus! Wild rumpus!"

"Buddy, the only wild rumpus that's going to happen now is that I'm going to collapse into bed. And so are you. 'Night, Sweets." She kissed his forehead, quieting his protest with the promise of a surprise in the morning.

Lyle followed her to her own room, purring beside her on the pillow that should have been Michael's. Away from the myriad demands of a four-year-old boy, the memory of her creekside encounter with Dom asserted itself, the solid reassurance of his embrace, the warmth of it, even through their winter layers. And, just as strongly, the rush of fear that even such a momentary and decisively extinguished encounter could shake her ability to objectively handle the case.

"There's no such thing as objectivity." Michael. Alone at night in the room they'd once shared, she squirmed inwardly at the incongruity of falling back on her late husband's words in connection with her incipient feelings toward another man. But Michael had been outspoken on the subject of objectivity, the purported goal in the stories he wrote for the newspaper. "Nobody's objective. Not reporters and definitely not lawyers," he'd said, deftly snagging the dinner roll she'd tossed at his head. "I just do my damnedest to make sure my stories are fair. Same with you and your clients." He broke open the roll, smeared butter across it, and took a triumphant bite.

He was right, of course. But even excluding her encounter with Dom, was she being fair to Sami?

Julia pulled her pillow tight around her head, trying to drown out her thoughts. When that proved unsuccessful, she turned to the more reliable distraction of her phone. Beverly had finally shelled out for a new router, and Julia did a quick scan through the news sites—the returns showed a closer mayoral race than expected—but decided it wasn't worth staying up to watch the foregone conclusion, the reassuring acceptance speech from the Candidate's bland opponent. She finally fell asleep, consoling herself with the delicious thought of a morning that wouldn't involve a rush to the office and would definitely involve golden stacks of pancakes.

*   *   *

A sound.

Lyle stood astride her head, stiff, hissing. She shoved him away and rolled over, still half in a dream. Where had she been? In bed, just like she was now. But not alone. There'd been a man's voice. Michael? Ahhh. She pulled the blankets around her and awaited the dream's resumption.

She'd fallen into a restless sleep, hand still between her legs, a remedy for insomnia only slightly more satisfying than no satisfaction at all. But the heat that suffused her body had carried through into a dream, far more intense than her furtive efforts, a luxurious unfurling of sensation, her body arcing beneath his hands as he gazed down upon her with the smile she craved more each time she saw him . . .

She sat up with a gasp. Not Michael. The man in her dream was Dom. But the voice she'd heard was neither man's, and it was outside the house.

She kicked the covers away and sat up, noting the time as she came fully awake. One in the morning. She sat a moment, listening to be sure. Yes. Someone was there. She tiptoed to the window and pressed herself to the wall beside it, peering through the gap where the curtain met the window frame. A large shadow spilled along the sidewalk, separating and coalescing. Several people, then. She backed away and fumbled around on the end table for her phone.

"9-1-1. What is your emergency?"

"This is Julia Geary." She gave her address—no matter what happened next, they'd know where she was—"and there's a whole bunch of people in front of my house."

"What are they doing?"

She peeked again. "I can't tell. I think they're just standing there."

"Are they on your property?"

Dammit.

"No. The sidewalk. But we've been getting threats."

"Are they threatening you now?"

"No." Julia tried to keep the sarcasm from her voice. "Sorry to have disturbed you." She clicked off and hurled the phone onto the bed.

Outside, a low call, the words indistinguishable, followed by a burst of laughter. Then another, louder.

"You in there?"

She flung herself across the bed, retrieving the phone. But the men remained on the sidewalk. And hollering was a long way from a threat.

"Come on out!"

Creating a disturbance, though. That was a legitimate complaint. Lights blinked on in a few houses along the street. She'd let her neighbors phone the cops. It would only take a couple of calls from this particular neighborhood to get dispatchers' attention.

One shadow detached itself from the rest and moved under a streetlamp. The man unknotted the black bandana from his neck and waved it like a victory flag. More laughter. "That boy's going back to Eye-rack now, and maybe you with him." More laughter, raucous and exuberant.

The gun, the gun, where the hell was the gun? Julia hurried to Beverly's bedroom and yanked open the closet door. She clicked on the light, saw a zippered case the length and shape of a shotgun on a high shelf, just where Beverly said she kept it. But Beverly had said she left it unloaded. Without the shells, it was just a big, heavy stick. And even if Julia found the shells, she wouldn't know how to load it.

Julia ran back to her own room, dragging the gun, and confronted a new development: Beverly's car, pulling up to the curb. "What the—?"

Beverly stepped from the car, regal despite the early-morning hour in her wool coat, her matching beret, her leather gloves, and was immediately surrounded.

To hell with waiting for neighbors. Julia dialed 9-1-1 once more as she ran down the stairs. "It's Julia Geary again. They're assaulting my mother-in-law. And"—she went for broke—"I've got a gun." That would get their attention.

She flung open the front door.

Everyone turned toward Julia, barefoot in the cold, hair a wild red penumbra, T-shirt hanging off one shoulder, Michael's old boxers low on her hips. The shotgun in her hand.

"Hello, Julia." Beverly's voice, cool and contained as though they'd crossed paths at church. Only someone who knew her as well as Julia would have detected the tension reverberating beneath her words. "I was just explaining to these gentlemen that there are more appropriate ways of expressing their displeasure with you."

Around her the men hung their heads and shuffled their feet.

Beverly looked at the gun and inclined her head. Julia tucked it out of sight in the hallway.

"And that while their excitement at their Candidate's victory tonight is understandable . . ."

"He won?" Julia's query drew unwelcome attention.

"Damn straight he did. We've got a mayor who'll finally run this town right. Get ready for a change. A big one."

Beverly cleared her throat and continued, ". . . if he keeps his campaign promises, they'll have no further worries about this case. Isn't that right"—she nodded in turn—"Mr. Adams? Mr. Weiser? Mr. Browne? I'll be sure and tell your wives how kind you were to call on us tonight. Much obliged that you're looking after our safety."

A siren wailed, headed their way.

"Now, if you gentlemen will excuse me, it's late and I've had a long drive." She turned her back on them and proceeded up the walk, step by careful, deliberate step, Julia holding her own breath in appreciation of Beverly's effort to hold herself so rigid and upright.

The men milled about, looking toward Julia. "That's her," someone said. "The lawyer."

The siren moaned closer.

"Aw, hell. Let's go."

They went.

*　　*　　*

"Beverly. You're amazing . . ."

"No time for that. Get that thing out of here before the police come." She didn't wait for Julia but took the gun herself and ran as lightly as a young girl up the stairs, returning barely out of breath as the police arrived.

Julia had seen enough already to let Beverly do the talking. Yes, there had been a group of men outside. "Rowdy? That's a little strong, don't you think, Julia? Excited, I'd say. What with the election results and all. But my daughter-in-law was here alone with her little boy. And, what with the threats lately, you can't blame her for being a little on edge. Gun? Julia, did you tell them you had a gun? The gun is mine, officer. Julia's a city girl. I can't imagine she'd know how to use it."

"I figured you'd come faster if I said that," Julia murmured. Which was true.

A fresh call requiring the officers' attention cut short a lecture.

Beverly closed the door and, for the briefest of moments, she and Julia leaned toward one another. Not a hug—their bodies never made contact—but a sort of bow, acknowledging a challenge shared and met.

* * *

"But Beverly, what are you doing here? What happened to bridge?"

They sat again at the kitchen table, drinks in hand. No Cointreau in dainty glasses this time. Ice cubes tumbled against one another in generous amounts of whiskey.

"I couldn't sleep so I turned on the television right about the time they announced the election results. I just had a feeling." She made a small, helpless motion. "I can't describe it. I left right away."

Julia thought of the foreboding she'd felt when Beverly drove off, after Julia had turned down her offer to stay. Beverly had paid attention to her own instincts. She should have, too.

"The gun. Those guys saw me with it. They'll tell the police. They'll know I lied."

Beverly's laugh threatened to climb out of control. She choked it off with a sip of whiskey. "Not a single one of those men is going to talk to the police. They'll spend the next few days slinking around with their tails between their legs, afraid I've told their wives."

Julia held up her glass. They clinked.

It didn't hit her until she'd gone back to bed, head swirling from the whiskey, that the night had confirmed her darkest imaginings about the people emailing and calling. There hadn't been a Ray Belmar in the bunch outside their door that night. They were solid citizens, people she knew—or at least, Beverly did. People just like her.

22

"**Y**OU SURE ABOUT this one?"

Ray Belmar was back in jail, arrested within days of Julia's superhuman feat of managing to get his bail lowered. He'd allegedly tossed a beer bottle at a cop who asked him to move along from his preferred sidewalk spot. He denied it, and for once Julia believed him. But none of the downtown security cameras was trained on that spot—the reason he chose it—and the cop in question had "forgotten" to turn on his body cam. A cop's word against a frequent flyer's. Both Julia and Ray knew how that would go.

"Sure about your being screwed? Pretty sure. Not that you don't deserve it. You just don't deserve it for this one."

Ray reared back in his chair—the chair itself, of heavy steel, was bolted to the floor to discourage an inmate who might be tempted to bash someone over the head with it—and gave her a long look.

Julia, comfortable with him by now, let him look. He kept his eyes on hers, not dropping his gaze, as so many did, to her chest, letting it roam over her body in ways that felt nearly as offensive as if they'd used their hands.

"You'll get used to jail day," Claudette had reassured her when Julia was still new in the office. "You've just got to nip that shit in the bud. You know how." Of course she did. All women did, even if they'd been conditioned to think it was rude to rebuke a man who was being even ruder. Why, Julia wondered after her first few weeks in the office, was it acceptable to rap her knuckles on the table and remind an inmate that her eyes were up here, thank you, but not do the same with Li'l Pecker? Right. That old story.

Now, parrying Ray's scrutiny with her own, she resorted to the mental exercise she used on most of her clients, imagining him with a haircut, a shave, and a very long shower with very strong soap. Clean, pressed clothes. Some good dental care, and maybe laser those broken veins away. All those things, and Ray wouldn't rate a second glance, and if he did, it would only be because the observer might mistake him for one of the bail bondsmen or private investigators populating the courthouse. There'd be no averted gazes, no quick sidesteps, no cautious hand to the purse or the hip pocket where a wallet resided.

Ray's bloodshot eyes went soft with sympathy.

"I wasn't talking about me. I was talking about you. You sure about this? This new case you've got? You know what they're saying in there." He jerked his head toward the room's back wall, the jail cells just a few yards away.

"What are they saying?"

Inmates who couldn't afford to post bail sometimes languished for weeks and even months while awaiting trial, with nothing to occupy their time but gossip and fighting. Once they were sentenced to the state prison, they could take advantage of the make-work programs there that would keep them occupied and somewhat out of mischief. Until then, they were stuck in the county jail. From her clients' descriptions, she imagined it as a large and menacing high school, with cliques and endless gossip that resulted in its denizens being surprisingly well-informed.

"They're saying it's a good thing you got his ass OR'd. Terrorists rank right up there with baby-rapers. Not that we've had any terrorists yet, but they were ready for him."

"He's not a terrorist." A knee-jerk response, which is just how Ray took it.

"Right. Innocent till proven guilty. Just like all of us in here."

At which point, Julia dropped her gaze, not wanting him to see the agreement there.

*   *   *

She was trying her damnedest to see Sami as innocent, she told herself on the walk to Tibbets' office, where the depositions had been scheduled. Otherwise, why would she be going to all this trouble?

Once she arrived, though, she wished she'd stopped for a coffee along the way, a transition to ease the change from the jail's concrete and steel interview room to the lawyer's office in the restored Victorian home, smelling of furniture polish and a hint of cigar smoke, rather than the jail's pervasive disinfectant mingled the sour reek of alcohol wafting from Ray's pores.

"Dan's suggestion," Susan had said, and Julia dutifully took note of their evident first-name basis. "We thought it best to do them all at once, and there's more room. Given that you've involved so many people in this little exercise." A one-two punch, laying the blame for the inconvenience squarely in Julia's lap, and letting her know, again, that she deemed it a rookie move, gratuitous.

Susan had cited space as the reason for the location, but Tibbits's reception area seemed barely adequate for the crowd within, the players and their lawyers—they were all men—occupying every chair, the sofas, leaning against the walls, air thick with testosterone and resentment. One of the attorneys stood and wordlessly motioned Julia to take his chair, a capacious leather number with brass rivets, a movie version of something in a lawyer's office. She did and wished she hadn't. She was already the shortest person in the room, and seated she was smaller still, diminished. Most of the lawyers sipped from mugs of coffee and stared off into space with a blank expression Julia herself had practiced, if not yet perfected. The boys sat slumped, legs stuck out in front of them, every last one of them in polo shirts and khakis, no doubt the Sunday-dinner-at-grandma's clothes laid out for them this day by parents both fearful and furious. Propriety ended at their feet, enormous in sneakers whose sweeping logos proclaimed price. They folded arms across their chests and sneaked glances at her from beneath beetling brows. She raised her chin and looked from one to the next, catching them at it, suppressing a childish satisfaction when each looked away. She didn't see Cody.

"Mr. Tibbits will be right with you. Coffee?" The receptionist, who in her suit and pumps looked more the lawyer than Julia, emerged from somewhere with a mug on a tray that also held a little pot of cream and a bowl holding packets of sugar—raw as well as white, thank you very much—and artificial sweetener. A spoon lay on a cloth napkin. Julia assessed it as real silver and fought a discomfiting urge to pocket it. She toed the thick carpet with her clog. So this was what life was like on the other side.

She wanted to reject the offer, but her voice betrayed her, murmuring "just black, thanks," as she took the mug. She sipped. Claudette would be glad to hear that, while the presentation may have been superior, Tibbits's coffee was no match for her own morning offerings.

"Good. Shelly got you coffee. Me, I never touch the stuff." Dan Tibbits loomed in a doorway at the far end of the reception area, looming being his particular specialty. He'd been a college basketball player of some renown. The subsequent years of good living had added layers of flesh as solid as bricks to his rangy frame. At sidebar conferences in court, he liked to stand too close to a hapless prosecutor, his stentorian breathing nearly drowning out the whispered arguments to the judge, the prosecutor stepping aside in order to regain a little personal space, only to have Tibbits move closer still. Once Julia had watched that particular dance move all the way down the bench until an exasperated judge raised his voice so that the whole courtroom could hear. "If the prosecution insists upon making its argument from afar, we're never going to be able to get back to the business of testimony." Tibbits smiled cherubically.

The only time she'd seen the tactic fail had involved one of Susan Parrish's cases. Susan had shown up in court that day in stilettos worthy of Claudette. When the inevitable dispute arose and the judge summoned both attorneys to the bench, Tibbits crowded so close that, thought Julia, had they two been strangers in a bar, he'd have merited a slap. Instead, Susan—talking fast and low to the judge—took a seemingly distracted step sideways and brought her heel down on Tibbits's instep.

"Oh!" She gasped and grabbed at his arm as though for support, taking the opportunity to drive her heel even more sharply downward. "I didn't see you there."

Ever since, on the rare times a case brought them together, Tibbits kept his distance, a development so striking as to make Julia consider investing in a pair of stilettos herself. Except that, as defense attorneys—albeit ones separated by six figures of annual earnings—she and Tibbits were unlikely ever to find themselves on opposite sides. Until now.

"Come on in. We've got things all set up for you in a conference room. Let's not keep these boys out of school any longer than necessary. Not that this is necessary. Who wants to go first?"

The lawyer who'd given up his seat to Julia took a step forward and motioned to one of the boys.

"In here," said Tibbits. But he remained in the doorway, forcing her to brush past his bulk. He followed close behind, and she had to force herself not to hurry ahead, run up on the heels of the other lawyer, just to avoid him.

"Third door on the right," he called, so near she felt his breath across the top of her hair. She ducked into the room and shot halfway across it in relief, nearly tripping over the court reporter's steno writer on its little stand.

Susan, sitting at a table with one of her deputies, smirked.

"You're over there." Tibbits pointed to another, smaller table. He rubbed his hands together. "Everything satisfactory? Everybody comfortable? Fine. I'll leave you all to it."

He'd stay for Cody's deposition, of course. But Julia was so happy to see the door close behind him that she had to remind herself that it would be wrong to draw out her questioning of the other boys, just to postpone the inevitable confrontation with Tibbits.

23

STEVEN DALE WAS a redhead, like she was, and his skin mottled patchy and pink just as hers did when she was upset or angry.

The flush crawled up his neck as he raised his hand and swore to tell the truth.

She smiled at him, Tibbits forgotten, hoping to put him at ease. "This won't take long," she said, ignoring Susan's snort. She walked him through the process, telling him all the things his lawyer had already explained to him, speaking in a low, reassuring monotone until his high color subsided.

"First, you'll tell me a little bit about yourself. And then, please just describe what happened that morning. You can start with the time—as much detail as you can remember."

She asked him about all the things she already knew, the things everybody who knew him knew, how to spell his name, and his age and year in high school and position on the soccer team. His lawyer listened, nodding—so far, so rehearsed—and turned his attention to the coffee that had been refreshed on his way in. Susan bent over her legal pad in a diligent approximation of note-taking, but if Julia had to guess, doodles probably looped across the yellow paper. The deputy, closer to Julia's age and less adept at protocol, couldn't resist the occasional eye roll, even once emitting a sigh.

Steven paused in his recital, a staccato series of answers, the briefest possible response to each question. The rehearsal had been thorough.

"You're doing great. This is really helpful."

Susan's pen slid audibly across the page, possibly slashing an emphatic crosspiece for the "t" in "bullshit."

"You were saying . . . ," Julia urged as she continued to elicit fact after useless fact from Steven Dale.

*　*　*

He was sixteen, a junior at Duck Creek High, a midfielder on the team. He hadn't grown up in Duck Creek, but had moved there his freshman year. His parents both worked at the ski resort, his father in public relations and his mother managing one of the restaurants. Sure, he shrugged in response to one of Julia's questions, he skied, too, but he played soccer all summer and fall. On the day in question, he'd gotten to school a little before six thirty. He drove his own car, he said in answer to another question. A Corolla. Used. He tried to get there early because a single minute late by a single team member meant more pushups, more squats, more of everything for the whole team. They worked out indoors for half an hour, weights and floor exercises, before heading out to the pitch for a run and drills in the gray light of morning that came a little later every day.

Then it was back inside, barely time to shower and change into school clothes before homeroom. What time was that?

No hesitation: "About seven forty-five."

Four of them left the locker room together, he and Cody and Cary Sales and Doug Fitzpatrick. The boys' and girls' locker rooms were next to each other, and just as they came out into the hallway, they saw their teammate, Sami Mohammed, going into the girls' room.

Where had Sami been before?

Running some extra laps. He'd gotten on Burkle's bad side again. It happened a lot.

But didn't Burke punish the whole team for a single member's infraction?

Not when it came to Sami. If they all had to suffer for his infractions, they'd spend their whole time in the gym or running laps and never get to drills. Anyway, so he was just coming back in from his laps. But he went into the wrong locker room.

They all laughed about it. He'd be so embarrassed when he realized what he'd done! But then they started to worry. He didn't come
right back out again. What if he'd gone straight to the shower, and
the girls came in and found him there? That'd be even funnier—but
he'd also be in big trouble. So Cody volunteered. And under the
circumstances, nobody was surprised when Sami rushed out, brushing past them, not going into the boys' locker room but flying down
the hall like a bat out of hell—excuse me, ma'am, moving really
fast—trying to outrun mortification, always impossible in high
school, even more so in this electronic age, gone in the second before
they pushed into the locker room he'd just left, bumping against one
another in their haste, to find Cody, yelling at them to go after Sami.
But they hadn't, too dumbstruck by what Cody said next: that he'd
just wrested their teammate off Ana Olsen's naked body.

*   *   *

Then what?

That's what they wondered, too. They returned to the hallway,
confused, no one wanting to go back in after Ana, hoping one of the
girls would come by so they could send her on a reconnaissance mission. But none came, and a few minutes later the door opened and
Ana emerged, fully clothed, hair still wet and face averted, brushing
past them on her way to class like . . . well, pretty much like normal.
His voice rose and cracked on that last word. Because how could she
have looked like nothing had happened if what Cody said was true?

They debated it among themselves the rest of the day: Maybe
she'd wanted it? Maybe she and Sami had arranged to meet there
for a little breakfast bump? For sure, it wouldn't be the first time the
locker rooms had been used for that purpose; along with the audio-
visual room, the music room, and even the tables in chem lab, high
and cold and booby-trapped with that problematic little sink, but
still irresistible to a hormone-addled population accustomed to getting exactly what it wanted.

But Cody was sure. "He was raping her. She was crying."

Julia would ask Cody about that. But from Steve, she needed a
direct account. Was Ana crying when she came out of the locker room?

"I couldn't see. Like I said." He laid a spin of irritation atop the words. "She had her head turned." He turned his own head toward the shoulder of his blue polo shirt, showing her. And for sure, all she could see was the back of his red head, just a bit of ear and jawline.

And then?

"Chewie's mom said we had to call the cops."

"Chewie?"

"Stewart Jones."

Julia checked her file to be sure, already knowing Stewart's name was nowhere in it. He hadn't been among the boys with Cody that morning. The whole team—probably the whole school, and probably a good number of the kids' parents—must have heard about what happened by the time a lone parent urged the boys to do the right thing. Her fingers tightened on her pen.

And?

"We went to the cops and told them everything we just told you. Everything you already know."

Steve's lawyer delicately cleared his throat and his client took the hint. Stopped talking. Waited like the good little client he mostly was.

Julia looked to Susan Parrish. "Any questions?"

Susan invested the single short syllable with depths of disgust. "None."

*   *   *

Cary Sales wore a green polo shirt, and his lawyer was a short fat man whose jowly visage was familiar to Julia from his late-night television commercials in which he posed in front of outdated volumes of the state code, an image of the scales of justice flashing in one corner of the screen as he warned of the dangers of ignoring the aches and pains that followed even a minor fender bender.

Cary was a senior, played forward, and walked to school, but otherwise echoed Steve, not word-for-word, but not enough difference in their accounts to raise a flag of even the faintest red.

Doug Fitzpatrick's lawyer looked like his soccer-playing client, lithe and sinewy even in his suit, knees bouncing beneath the table, betraying his impatience to be elsewhere, probably running trails to get in shape for ski season, Julia guessed.

Doug wore a blue polo shirt and like Steve was a midfielder and said all the same things Steve and Cary had said. By the time he recounted the agitated gathering outside the door of the girls' locker room, even Julia was bored.

"Was she crying when she came out?"

"Bawling like a baby," a bit of unnecessary embellishment that drew a grimace from his lawyer but not an eye-blink's reaction from Susan Parrish.

Julia, who'd raised her head in surprise, looked from Susan to Doug's attorney, who'd resumed his stationary jog, the carpet muffling what otherwise would have been an unbearable distraction. Neither of them seemed surprised by the variance in the narrative, one that hadn't been mentioned in the police report, either. But then, it wasn't unusual for multiple accounts of the same scenario to vary; something that in fact could sometimes lend verisimilitude to the chaotic emotions stirred by such situations. Which Susan damn well knew.

That said, Doug, like his friends, had sworn to tell the truth, the whole truth, all that jazz.

Julia made a notation. Asked Susan if she had any questions. Dismissed Doug before Susan's "none" had faded from the air.

Susan started to stand, but Julia was already on her feet, eager to claim this small bit of initiative.

She went to the door, opened it. Called into the hallway.

"We're ready for Cody Landers."

24

Cody's polo shirt was fuck-you red, and in case she'd missed the message, a toothpick jutted from the corner of his mouth, one that he shifted to the other side with an impertinent waggle each time before he spoke.

He swore truth and sat, flashing an orthodontia-perfected grin her way, the toothpick angling ceilingward.

"Cody, I'm Julia Geary, the defense attorney for Sami Mohammed."

"A public defender." Somehow, even from across the room, Tibbits managed to loom.

Julia ignored the interruption and started in with her questions, age, grade, position on the team, but Tibbits cut her short again.

"Why don't you tell Mrs. Geary what happened? Then we'll be done here."

She wanted to object, but that was the prosecution's job. Besides, beyond the breach in protocol, what was the objection?

"Saw Sami go in the girls' locker room. Waited for him to figure out he'd done something wrong. When he didn't come out, we went in after him. Trying, you know, to save him from embarrassment. Saw him on top of Ana. She didn't have any clothes on. He did, but his pants were down and he was raping her."

"Yes, but." Save some sort of periscope vision, how would he know Ana was actually being raped? She sought words and settled for, "How could you tell?"

He met her eyes with a look so full of knowledge and challenge it felt like an assault of its own, saying, "Because he was moving on her," and for a moment, she was afraid he'd demonstrate, jerking his hips against the chair. The toothpick went up and down, close enough. Even Susan, to her credit, looked momentarily discomfited.

"Can I go back to school now? I've got practice in an hour." He heaved a great sigh and looked at his watch as though its blank black screen showed the time. Julia had been saving up for one of those watches, looking forward to reduced dependence on her phone. Cody didn't look as though he had to save up for anything, instead accepting the watch, the sneakers emblazoned with the name of a multimillionaire athlete, the summer soccer camps, and the car that was almost certainly in the parking lot as his due from parents who wanted only the best for their son.

"I just have a few more questions. You might be a little late for practice"—the toothpick jerked—"but we won't have to do this again. Who was with you when you went into the room?"

"Just me. Steve and Doug and Cary waited outside."

"Full names, please."

Cody's look toward Tibbits needed no interpretation. Save me from this moron.

Julia waited.

"Steven Dale, Doug Fitzpatrick, and Cary Sales." He spelled the names everyone in the room already knew, the letters dropping with exaggerated slowness. Julia wrote them down, something to do with her hands, which kept curling into fists, a visible manifestation of her desire to strike out at the condescension crowding close.

"But they didn't go in with me. Well, they did, but not until they heard me yell. And by then Sami was gone and Ana had run back into the shower room."

Julia tried to picture it, Sami writhing atop the girl, but—"When you first saw them, where were they?"

"I told you. In the girls' locker room." He threw another look to Tibbits, clearly seeking rescue from the utter imbecility of it all.

"On the floor?" Julia murmured.

A tick's hesitation. "A bench."

"A bench where?"

"Jesus! In the girls' locker room! C'mon, Mr. Tibbits. I already told her what happened. I'm missing warm-ups."

"I know, son. Unfortunately, the process allows for this." Tibbits's tone made it perfectly clear what he thought of the process.

"Locker rooms have lots of benches. In the front of the room? The back? If we went there, could you show me exactly which one?"

"I don't know. I was so shocked by what I saw I didn't pay attention." Cody's voice climbed a register. Tibbits shifted in his chair, the slightest of movements, one that nonetheless allowed sudden, expansive breathing room for Julia.

She pursed her lips. "Sometimes, after a shocking event, it takes a few days for memory to settle. Things get all jumbled up."

"Yeah, yeah. What you said. It's all a jumble."

"But you can probably give me a general idea—front of the room? Or back?"

He closed his eyes, thought for a moment, and nodded. "Front."

"Thanks. That's helpful. I think we're almost done here." Which she wasn't, but it seemed to calm him. She spoke her thoughts aloud, musingly. "So. You and your friends see Sami go into the locker room, the wrong one."

"Yeah."

"Maybe you talked to each other about it for a few seconds? A minute or two?"

"Yeah."

She'd hoped to tease some additional remarks out of him that would help her picture the scene, but Tibbits had coached him well. Only yes or no answers. Or, in Cody's case, yeah or no.

"You go in."

"Yeah."

"There's Sami on top of Ana, on a bench."

"Yeah."

"You yell."

"Yeah."

"Loud?"

"Hell, yeah!"

She started to ask another question, then checked herself. She gathered her things, looked to Susan, likewise preparing to leave.

"No questions."

"I guess it's like you said, Cody. It's pretty straightforward. Thanks for your time. Maybe you won't be late after all."

She thought about offering her hand for a shake, but decided to avoid the inevitable hesitation, if not outright rejection.

She backed out of the office, happy that Tibbits chose to stay behind with Cody. She should have cut off her questions earlier. Tibbits and Susan probably had already figured out where she was going with them.

Outside, she walked slowly, taking deep, cleansing breaths of air gone crystalline with cold, running through the scenario in her mind.

Cody, stepping into the locker room, probably laughing, anticipating the look on Sami's face when he realized his mistake. Seeing the moving bodies on the bench—so narrow, so uncomfortable, so prone to pitching bodies to the floor in a struggle—and yelling. But in that split second before they arrived, Sami had time to jump up, pull up his pants, and flee from the bench just within the door, and Ana to run back into the shower room, so that the other boys saw only Cody in an empty room.

Was it possible? So many things happening in just a matter of seconds.

Maybe. Witness accounts of time, like those of facial features, were notoriously unreliable. Seconds slowed and stretched in a crisis. People who were mugged described a struggle that went on for ten, fifteen minutes, when in reality it took mere moments to shove someone, grab a purse, and run away. Sometimes the opposite was true, a drunken argument that escalated throughout the day boiled down to its final moments, a jittery fast-forward through a few final imprecations, the grab for the gun, the scream, the shot.

Cody could have stood frozen—another commonplace occurrence—trying to make sense of what he saw, unable to believe; Sami so intent upon the act that he didn't notice Cody standing there; Ana terrified, maybe her eyes squeezed shut against the reality of the assault, that she failed to see help at hand.

Maybe Cody didn't cry out immediately. Maybe he stirred, some-how called attention to himself, Sami jumping up—or would he and Ana have tumbled to the floor in the ensuing struggle?—offering a quick explanation before Cody yelled for his friends. Maybe Cody, too embarrassed to say he hadn't moved immediately to stop the attack, had left out that part, figuring the basics of the account he'd given were true enough. Maybe.

So many maybes, every last one of them well within the realm of possibility.

Her steps slowed and finally stopped, and she stood in the mid-dle of the sidewalk, pondering the various scenarios, until the curi-ous stares of passersby finally registered, and she moved off toward the courthouse, a three-beat refrain drumming in her head.

Maybe not.

Maybe not.

Maybe not.

25

A ND SO TO Ana.
   Julia had heard through the grapevine—Debra in her ele-
ment, scattering titillating scraps like handfuls of confetti throughout the courthouse—of the towering fury of Ana's parents at her
request to depose their daughter; how their raised voices rattled the
door of Susan Parrish's office, echoing throughout the anteroom.

"Hasn't she been through enough?" The mother, half-screaming,
half-sobbing.

"How could you let that woman do this to her?" The father, all rage.

That woman. As though gender had anything to do with it; as
though her chromosomes turned the very fact of Julia's doing her job
into some sort of betrayal.

Susan insisted the deposition be taken in Julia's office, as though
to further underscore the meanness of it all, everybody squeezing
in, Susan and Ana behind Claudette's reluctantly cleared desk, the
court reporter and her machine barely fitting in the space between
the desks, the warmth of too many bodies in too small a space adding to the discomfort, a cover thrown over Pavarotti's cage because
things already felt unprofessional enough.

The boys had dressed up—at least, what counted for it in teenage male terms—but Ana wore jeans and a gray wool sweater that
enveloped her frame like a storm-threatening cloud, its sloppy hand-
knitted loops raveling here and there, her hands disappearing inside
the sleeves, cowl neck pulled up to her chin.

Julia leaned forward when Ana stood to take the oath, expecting to have to strain to hear her words, so wispy and evanescent did the girl seem, as though Julia might blink and open her eyes to find that Ana had disappeared, her very molecules dissolving within the room's corrosive tension. But her voice startled, low and strong, and at "so help me God," her eyes met Julia's in a challenge that, so help her God, reminded her of the one leveled by Cody only a few days earlier.

*   *   *

Ana said she had timed her arrival at school that morning so she could use the weight room while the boys were on the field. "Because boys. You know."

Before Michael, before Calvin, Julia had put in her time in a gym, had dealt with her share of guys who casually strolled by when she was doing butterflies on the machine, just to watch her breasts—even hers, small though they were—strain forward as she pushed her arms wide apart. Oh, she knew.

"Just you? Not the whole track team?"

Just her. It was off season, but she had her eye on a scholarship. So, the between-season workouts, the usual squats and lunges, but a lot of core work, planks and jackknifes and twists. "You'd be surprised," Ana said with youthful authority, "how important your core is to running."

Julia sucked in her own marshmallowy core and nodded for her to continue.

It was a good workout, one that ran a little longer than usual, muscles burning pleasurably by the time she was through, arms and legs quivering. She shook them out, droplets of sweat flying, and headed to the shower, one eye on the clock. She heard the gym's door open just as she stepped into the locker room's rear entrance, the boys heading back in after their drills, pausing in a great noisy mass at the door to remove their soccer cleats and then thundering in sock feet across the basketball court, wafting a cloud of cold air and sweat that pushed all the way across the gym. She pulled the door closed against it, congratulating herself on her timing.

"Then, in the shower—" She paused.

Julia raised her head. In Cody's account, Ana was already out of the shower.

"Go on."

"I thought I heard something. But I figured it was nothing. Still." She shifted in her chair, uneasy now as she must have been then.

Julia knew the feeling. Every woman did, even Susan, suddenly frozen in place, pen stilled inches above the page. They were all women in this room, harkening to being naked and alone and, no matter how innocuous the environment, the back-of-the-neck, pit-of-the-stomach, eons-of-evolution sensation that warned of something awry.

Julia had felt it herself in the courthouse, that supposedly safest of environments, a building home to the sheriff's office and all its deputies, who prowled the halls, their duty belts bulky with pepper spray, Taser, baton, and service revolver. Even so, she'd had bad moments, working late in the office at the end of the hall, the corridor lights long gone dim, startled by the sound of heavy footsteps approaching. One of the other public defenders, maybe, returning to retrieve some document he intended to work on at home. Or Li'l Pecker—who every so often got it into his head that his appearance in your doorway on a workday that had already gone two hours over would come as a sign that the boss cared, really cared, about your career. "Nothing urgent," he'd say. "Just thought I'd stop by and see how things are going." Fifteen minutes of excruciatingly dull and meaningless conversation would follow, so that by the time he finally left frustration had long since replaced her anxiety.

"I even peeked out past the curtain. But nobody was there." She shrugged, pantomiming her own reaction at the time. "Now, though—I wonder if maybe it was a premonition."

And just like that, there was the voice Julia had expected. She resisted an impulse to cup a hand behind her ear. She looked down at her legal pad. Stilled her face, held her breath, not so much as a twitch to interrupt the flow of words from this girl who, until now, had refused to talk.

"I . . . I got out of the shower." Ragged breath. "Wrapped my towel around me." Another breath. "Walked into the other room to get dressed."

The pause after each sentence excruciating; worse still as it became a pause between words.

"There was . . . a boy . . . He . . . grabbed me . . . Pushed me down . . . I tried . . . to get away . . . couldn't."

Julia wouldn't insult the girl by asking what so many people considered the obvious question. Why hadn't she screamed?

But girls almost never did, not when their assailant was someone they knew, something in their brain flashing "no, no," not just against the *what* of the assault being perpetrated upon unwilling flesh, but against the *who*, because it couldn't be happening; this boy who knew her, he couldn't be doing this . . . this . . . what exactly?

Julia matched her tone so closely to Ana's that the court reporter murmured "louder, please," the clicking of her keys nearly drowning out all of their words.

"Ana, were you raped?"

Ana shook her head.

"I can't record that," the reporter said.

"No."

Julia had to be sure. "I'm sorry, but I have to be very specific. Did Sami Mohammed put his . . . ?"

Ana cut her off. "I don't know."

"But you just said . . ." Julia was confused.

"I know what I said."

The clickety-click halted a moment, the court reporter as surprised as Julia by the strength returning to Ana's voice.

"Nobody put . . . put *that* there."

Which was something. A significant something. Now Julia could argue in favor of a lesser charge. Across the room, a mere few feet away, Susan huffed audibly as Julia requested that Ana use appropriate anatomical terms, and then returned to the issue of identification.

"The boy . . . I couldn't see his face."

"*What?*" Julia and Susan chorused.

"It was too dark."

Julia beat Susan to the punch. "Why didn't you say anything about that before?"

"You don't have to answer that—" Susan began a crap objection, because of course Ana had to answer something so entirely key to the whole case.

"I wanted to be sure." Ana's voice gained confidence by the minute. "I couldn't say anything at first because I couldn't be sure. And I didn't want to talk about it at all. Not to anyone."

So far, so believable. Julia knew of cases with incontrovertible proof—semen, bruises, even sometimes an admission by the man— where women at first refused to acknowledge they'd been raped, the stigma so great it was preferable to let an assailant go free than face up what had been done to them, denying it to themselves as well as to everyone around them.

"And the boys all said they saw Sami. So I figured it had to be him. But the more I think about it, the more I realize I just can't remember. And I can't remember because I couldn't see anything. It was so dark." She looked at Julia and dipped her chin a millimeter: *Yes. You heard right.*

Susan's turn.

"No. Questions."

Said in a tone that made it clear she had plenty. But Ana was her witness and the last thing she needed was to raise any questions about the girl's testimony. Susan's briefcase sat open atop Claudette's desk. She slammed it shut with a snap so loud that Pavarotti objected from deep within his cocooned shelter. Everyone turned to the blanketed cage, as though it held the answer to the question hovering over everyone in the room:

What now?

*   *   *

Nothing, it turned out. Because even though Ana said she couldn't identify her assailant, the other boys could. They'd all seen him; Cody standing aghast as the boy thrust himself against Ana, fortunately falling short of his intended goal; the others as Sami rushed past them out of the room. Susan still had a good case, a little less strong than it had been before, but easily winnable.

But Ana had just handed Julia a weapon, one she had every intention of using, not just in the interest of helping Sami but because it might, even if only for a moment, scrub away the look of utter complacency that suffused Susan's features whenever she looked Julia's way.

Because Julia had stood in that very locker room that very time of day; had wandered along the rows of lockers, easily avoiding the low benches that in darkness would have sent her sprawling. The light at that hour was dim, the big fluorescents running along the ceiling turned off, but a smaller rope of safety LEDs outlined the room, providing plenty of illumination. She'd made her bemused examination of the lockers' decorations, had read the band names from halfway across the room, the lettering clear enough for her to realize that her own musical references were hopelessly outdated. If someone else had been there with her, even across the room, let alone with his face inches from hers, she'd have been able to recognize his features, describe the color of his clothes, whether he wore lace-up shoes or loafers. The light was just fine.

And yet Ana had put her hand on the worn Bible procured by one of the bailiffs, its cover sanitized with a quick swipe of a Handi Wipe, and sworn to tell the truth, then just a few minutes later had turned to Julia with a cool lie on her lips and a plea in her eyes.

"Here," those eyes had said. "I give you this. Use it. Please."

But why?

26

JULIA PAID FOR her latte without looking at the barista and carried it to the farthest corner of the Starbucks beside a highway exit at the edge of town, handy for the skiers stopping for a last jolt before making their way to the mountain, so as to save themselves the wait in the overlong lines in the lodge's cafeteria.

A day earlier Dom Parrish had left her a voice mail: "Ms. Geary?" Points to him for the formality that suggested he was just as eager as she to pretend their creekside encounter had never happened. "You said to call if I remembered anything about Sami that might help. There is something. It's probably not important. But, just in case. Can we meet?"

Julia, still unmoored by Ana's deposition, had left a voice mail of her own, asking to meet the next day, hoping he'd arrive with something that might shed light on Ana's sudden certainty about her own uncertainty. Although, Julia reminded herself, Ana had never said she was uncertain about Sami. She just hadn't said anything at all. Until she had.

It's wasn't enough. Susan would argue that the girl was traumatized, that plenty (although *plenty* would be overstating things by a considerable amount) of other evidence pointed to Sami. Still, if the principal provided something, anything, that added to that uncertainty, maybe Julia had a fighting chance.

She'd suggested to Dom that they meet at the Starbucks, where they'd likely be free of embarrassing stares or, as had actually

happened to her a few days earlier at Colombia Coffee, the humiliation of a patron ostentatiously rising and moving across the room
when Julia sat down at the next table.

Still, Starbucks' cookie-cutter decor provoked a sense of
betrayal to Colombia, where she secretly envied the elaborately tattooed locals in their colorful thrift-store ensembles. What an adven-
ture it must be for them to get dressed, decide which hair color to
flaunt for the week, all of it bespeaking choice, a concept she barely
remembered.

She'd made the mistake of bringing Beverly there once, some
early misguided attempt at detente. Never again, after Beverly leaned
across the table and, cutting her eyes back toward the counter, whispered, "Their poor parents. How do you bring someone looking like
that anywhere with you?"

But Julia admired the skin art, so colorful and intricately drawn,
in contrast to the blurry jail tats sported by her clients. "You should
see what walks into the courtroom every day," she told Beverly.

Julia thought she'd seen every kind of tattoo—too many full
sleeves to count, others that wrapped people's necks or covered their
shaved skulls—until the day she opened a file on a client to see,
among the list of identifying marks, descriptions of dozens of tattoos
including one on his dick reading "Your Name Here." She could just
imagine the fun the guys in intake had with that.

"Those are criminals," Beverly protested. "These are, or could
be, normal kids. Look at the one making our coffee. Rinse that purple out of her hair, lose the nose ring—somewhere under all of that,
she's a very pretty girl. One day she's going to want to get married,
have kids. No child wants a parent who looks like that. Can you
imagine what Calvin would think?"

He might think I was fun. Julia had kept the thought to herself,
even as she imagined Calvin's shout of delight if she came home with
a streak of purple in her hair, a scatter of tattooed stars up her arm,
something to give the freckles a run for their money. Beverly would
have approved of the blonde, scrubbed Starbucks barista in her crisp
green apron, hair dye betrayed only by darkened roots, and nary a
stray bit of ink peering out from beneath a collar or cuff.

A decade-old dark-green Subaru in need of a wash pulled up outside. The town was lousy with Subarus, their all-wheel drive a godsend during the too-long winters that at some point always seemed to surpass the snowplows' ability to keep up. Julia was familiar with Susan Parrish's Lexus and had wondered what Dom drove. But he got out of the Subaru, apparently having shed his wife's expensive tastes as part of the divorce.

He stood a moment in the doorway, scanning the room, brightening when he saw her, and Julia was again struck by the way a smile changed his face, easing the sadness that hardened its angles.

"You're here already." He looked at the mug at her elbow. Disappointment replaced the smile. "I was going to buy you coffee. Maybe even an overpriced, taste-free pastry. It's the least I can do, after—"

She hastened to cut off what she feared might have been an apology for that briefest of hugs, willing him to divine the necessity of denial. "I usually go to Colombia. Their pie—my God. But these days it's difficult."

He hesitated, the slightest shading in his expression as she babbled. Oh, he got it. But then he took the chair across from her and turned it around, folding his arms across the top and resting his chin on them. Looking directly into her eyes, not making it easy. Fair enough.

"Tell me about it. I've taken to doing my food shopping at night when the store's not so crowded. And I use the self-check line for fear the cashiers will charge me double."

She laughed again, savoring the rarest of sensations. "Anyhow, coffee's on me. Given that you called me about the case, I can expense it. So, go for broke on the pastry."

"Coffee, black. And, uh, coffeecake, I guess."

She came back with his coffee, a brick of cake, and two forks. "I hope I'm not being presumptuous. But I can't imagine one person eating something that size."

He poked it with his fork. Crumbs scattered across the plate. "You obviously don't hang around with high school students. They'll show up in the morning with something like this and one of those drink concoctions full of sugar and topped with whipped cream, and then be starving again by lunch period."

Julia forked up a mouthful of the cake and actually felt a tug of longing for Beverly's homemade baked goods. "I've got a few years to prepare myself. Calvin's only four."

Dom lay down his fork. "Elena's sorry about the babysitting. She really likes him." That smile again. "She was going to make it her mission to turn him into a little feminist. I hope that doesn't change your opinion of her."

Another laugh bubbled within her. She suppressed it—good God, he'd think her giddy—but allowed as to how Elena's ambition for her son aligned perfectly with her own.

"Just like his father," she said without thinking. Michael had often contended that, of the two of them, he was the better feminist. Hearing her own words, she waited for the stab of anguish. A twinge, nothing more, but enough to remind her of the painful business at hand.

"You said you had some information that might help Sami?"

He shredded another section of cake with his fork. "I don't know. I can't imagine how it would help him. It seems so trivial. But you said anything."

"And I meant it. It might be nothing. Or it could be something. Better to pass it along now than find out later it could have helped." She sipped at a latte gone lukewarm. The baristas at Colombia knew she liked hers extra-hot.

"Something happened when I was in the drugstore the other day. The checkout clerk recognized me as the principal. Seems like everybody, not just the parents, recognizes me these days."

"Believe me, I feel your pain." She laid an encouraging hand on his arm, then snatched it back. You were supposed to touch clients. Not potential witnesses. "Go on," she said, then sat back and listened, seeing it through his eyes.

*   *   *

He'd gone to the drugstore to pick up tampons for Elena, the ultimate thoughtful dad.

He made a point of keeping the medicine cabinet stocked, checking her side of it for the brand. The first time he'd tried to buy them, he'd had to return home and check again, bewildered by the variety, not just the brands but the types within the brands. He settled for a multipack and hadn't heard any complaints. But then, he wouldn't. He could just imagine her voice climbing in indignation—"I'd rather die!"—if he'd broached the subject with her.

He paused, a blush creeping across his cheeks.

"And she would have," Julia said. "As a former teenage girl myself, I can't imagine ever talking about something like that with my dad. I'm going to have the same sorts of issues in reverse, as a mom dealing with a son. I already dread it."

"Let me know if I can help. Only thing I'd ask in return is advice on the girl stuff."

"Deal." She stuck out her hand and they shook. Again, not the electric, psyche-searing jolt involving every early interaction with Michael, but a stirring within nonetheless, something long dormant rolling over, nudged into wakefulness.

She urged him—and herself—back to his narrative. "Then what?"

He headed for the second aisle and walked straight toward the back of the store to the rows of pastel boxes, nothing to suggest the dark threat of the blood they were designed to stanch. He grabbed a box and started for the front of the store, then went back for a second. Anything to limit his time in public now, no telling whether he'd turn a corner and come face to face with a parent, emotions locked and loaded, ready to fire their anger in his direction. He'd waited until late in the evening, but the store's lights blazed, its interior fairly shimmering with white light.

The clerk stood bored in front of the cash register, surreptitiously checking a phone laid to one side, half-concealed by a roll of receipt paper. He'd feared seeing one of his students at the register, but the clerk was an older woman, gray hair permed into tight curls and shellacked with spray. Maybe one of his students' grandmothers. Or maybe—he lectured himself yet again against paranoia—someone who didn't know him at all.

The woman lifted her eyes from her phone. They widened, taking him in. He gave himself another lecture: Sometimes, paranoia was justified.

"You're that principal." She swiped the tampons. The reader beeped.

"Guilty as charged." He'd meant to crack a joke, but it was the wrong one. Numbers flashed on the register. He held out a bill, but she ignored it.

"That boy, the one who goes to your school. The one they arrested. He was in here that day, you know."

No. I don't know. But she waited, even as he gave the bill a shake, trying to call attention to it. She ignored it, awaiting a response. He sighed. "What day?"

"The day he done it."

Not the time to point out that no one actually knew what had been done, or if anything had been done at all. *Just give me the tampons and let me out of here.*

"He was buying Band-Aids. The big ones, like the kind you use if you really tear up your knee. Suspicious, right? Maybe he knew he was going to hurt that girl."

"What time did he come in?"

"What?" She finally took his money and punched at the screen. "I dunno. Eight, nine in the morning, maybe?"

He glanced toward the door—deliverance, so close! "If he came in then, whatever happened that day was already over. So obviously he wasn't planning anything that needed really big Band-Aids. Whatever that would be. He was probably just running a family errand." By then, he knew better, of course. Sami would have been fleeing the school, whatever had happened in the locker room only minutes behind him.

She sniffed, handed him his change and turned her back, letting him know he was dismissed. He usually asked for a bag for the tampons, not wanting to be seen with them, an old unnecessary embarrassment. But he left without the bag, visible feminine products suddenly the least of his worries.

27

"I WISH I'D SAID something about innocent until proven guilty," he told Julia. "But I just wanted to get out of there. And telling her that Sami buying Band-Aids didn't mean anything, because if he'd come in when she said he did, whatever had happened was already over—should I have said that? Do you think that made it sound like I think he's guilty? Because I don't."

"I know you don't." Julia had a whole stable of such phrases, ones that made people think she agreed with them. If they gave it any thought, they'd realize later she'd done no such thing. But most never examined her words that closely, and if they did, they hadn't let her know.

"Does this help? I can't see how. But you said anything."

"I did say, and I meant it. Off the top of my head, I can't see how, either. But it might. Sometimes I write down all the facts I know about the case on three-by-five cards and spread them out on my desk, shuffle them around." A trick Claudette had taught her. "Once in a while, looking at them like that, something will strike me that I hadn't seen before."

She'd add this to the mix, along with the most recent card she'd added, the one with Ana's declaration it had been too dark to see her assailant's face. More and more, it seemed as though the cards, instead of helping her order her thoughts, were only adding to the confusion. Despite what she'd just told Dom, the Band-Aids seemed barely worth a card at all.

She lifted her empty mug, preparing to go. But Dom leaned back in his chair, giving her a long, thoughtful look.

"That's really interesting. I never thought about how you guys do your jobs. I guess everything I know about it comes from TV. More coffee? My treat this time. What are you drinking?"

"A latte," Julia heard herself say. "Extra hot." Even though she should be getting back to the office, bracing herself for that long walk through courthouse hallways filled with judgmental stares.

The barista steamed milk for her latte. The espresso machine screamed. Julia studied Dom as he paid. Not particularly tall, but then everyone was taller than she. Lean, his shirt drooping off his shoulders. Just a little gray in the curls. And that angular face, its severity disappearing with those rare smiles. She wanted to see another smile.

He returned with her latte and another black coffee for himself. "Where were we? TV lawyers, right?"

"You ever notice how there's no shows about public defenders? That's because none of us can afford to dress like a TV lawyer." The way your ex dresses, she almost said, thinking of Susan's impressive array of suits. She'd had no idea women's suits came in that many colors and styles. "What about TV principals? Any similarities? Is everyone afraid when they come into your office?"

She got the smile she'd sought, evolving into an outright laugh, deep and easy.

"Nobody's afraid of me. But Celia—everyone's scared to death of her. I've often thought she'd make a far better principal than I."

"How is she handling this? What does she think about Sami's involvement?"

Dom studied his coffee as if seeking the answer in its inky depths. "Celia? She's calling bullshit on it, and that woman would know bullshit even if you covered it in whipped cream and plopped a cherry on top."

It was Julia's turn to laugh. "An image that's going to take me a long time to forget."

"Sorry. But it's why I'm so sure he's innocent."

An abrupt reminder as to why they were talking. Julia thought of the files that waited on her desk. "I suppose I should head out; get back to work on this." Said with all the enthusiasm of a condemned inmate lying on the gurney with the line in his vein.

"Me, too. But I'd rather not. This is nice. It's been too long since I've talked with someone who wasn't yelling at me.

"Same here. Thanks for the break."

He took her cup and turned toward the bin for used dishes, tossing a quick question over his shoulder. "Maybe we can do it again sometime?"

"Sure." Said far too quickly. "I mean, if you think of anything else." Under the circumstances, that was the only reason that would justify a meeting with Dom Parrish. Because everything now was about the circumstances.

Her cell phone rang. She wiggled her fingers goodbye to Dom and turned away to take the call. It was from Debra, the office receptionist.

"Julia? I mean, Ms. Geary?" Debra must have gotten another talking-to about professionalism. "That boy. Sami Mohammed. He's here. He wants to see you. Says it's important." She lowered her voice to a whisper. "I put him in your office. I didn't know what else to do. He'll be waiting there for you. Do you want me to call the police?"

"For God's sake, Debra. Ask him if he wants a Coke or some coffee"—if Debra looked half as hostile as she sounded on the phone, Sami would decline and be the better for it—"and tell him I'll be there in a few minutes." She wondered how many people Debra had notified before she'd called her. "And Debra, close the door to my office, please. Give the kid some privacy."

*   *   *

Sami swung in the chair to face her as soon as she pushed open her office door, his face sweaty and flushed, as though he'd run all the way to the courthouse. A cup of office coffee cooled untouched at his elbow.

"What you said," he began without preamble. "The thing you talked about. If I say I did it."

"A guilty plea." Heart in her throat. The case resolved to everyone's satisfaction. Life back to normal, Calvin returning to his day care center, she to her daily pilgrimages to Colombia, Beverly to the biddies in the bridge club.

"Yes. That. I want to make a guilty plea. I did it."

Julia's lips twitched toward a smile, wholly inappropriate. Careful, she warned herself. She had to play this one exactly right. She couldn't afford to make a mistake that might spook him—not with resolution so close at hand.

Another emotion smacked her, so hard and unexpected it nearly took her breath away, sending her whirling on Sami, clutching the arms of his chair, pinning him there, face close to his. "What the hell? After all the work I've done on your behalf? Everything I've been through because of this case?"

The needless goddamn depositions and the knowledge of Li'l Pecker's fury at the amount of the pending bill? The humiliation at the hands of Susan Parrish and Dan Tibbits and Bill Burkle, all of the people who'd looked at her with such disdain, so sure of Sami's guilt? Not to mention the phone calls and texts and emails; the parents hissing and heaping maledictions upon her, even Karl Fucking Schmidt practically jumping out of the bushes to accuse her of betraying the white race. And now here he was, telling her that they'd been right, all of them (well, maybe not Karl Schmidt), all along?

"Dammit all to hell, anyhow." Including herself in that indictment. She'd never once lost her temper with a client, not even Ray Belmar and his Groundhog Day sameness of petty crime. She let go of the chair. Straightened. "Sorry. That was out of line."

He was on his feet in a shot, backing away, fumbling behind him for the door.

"Wait. Wait. Sit down. Please. I'm just . . . surprised. I really am sorry."

She moved toward her desk, praying he wouldn't see the way her knees trembled at each step, grateful for the shield of her desk between them, probably not nearly as grateful as he was. She shuffled some papers and directed her words at them, not looking at Sami, giving both of them time to recover.

"Let's start again. What did you do, Sami?"

"That girl. I did it."

"Did what, exactly?" She slid a quick glance under lowered lids. His hands were clenched, eyes full of tears.

"You know."

"The court has to know exactly what." That way, she wasn't the one asking these mortifying questions, but the court, that amorphous term. "They'll need to know if you raped her." She wondered if he knew the word, but he recoiled, the blood draining from his face.

"No! Never!"

Which explained the inconclusive results of Ana's medical exam, and Ana's more recent explanation, such as it was, about what had happened.

"Did you touch her?"

A miserable, wordless nod.

"Where?"

He shrank into himself. Finally, he raised a hand and made a snatching motion at his chest, so quickly she barely saw it.

"Anywhere else?" She gestured toward her lap. You weren't supposed to ask leading questions, so as to avoid the ugly possibility that a defendant, once confronted with the reality of years in prison, deciding he'd been urged or even coerced into a false confession. But she hadn't asked a direct question and she told herself that there was no way anyone could interpret her vague motion as such.

"No!" Again, such vehemence.

"Didn't she run away when you touched her?"

He hesitated. Julia raised her head.

"I stopped her." He held his hands before him, opening and closing his fingers in a grabbing motion, and again Julia thought of the results of the exam, the photos of Ana's bruised arms. So far, so credible.

"Then what happened?"

"The boys—they shouted at me. I ran away." He extended his arms again. "You arrest me now."

She almost laughed, the soaring feeling back, stronger than ever, anger draining away nearly as fast as it had surged in. She was really, truly going to kiss this case goodbye.

"Oh, Sami. No one is going to put you in handcuffs today. It doesn't work that way. I'll call the prosecutor. If you only fondled her, maybe we can plead it down to a lesser charge, despite the age difference. The penalty will be quite a bit lighter, maybe just a couple of months."

Better for him, better for her. Arguing something down from a felony to a misdemeanor, even when the evidence mandated the move, would count as a win for her. Susan Parrish could likewise tally a victory, and the community would see Sami jailed and forever branded as a sex offender. That, too, should satisfy.

"I'll be back in touch in a couple of days to let you know what comes next. There are several steps yet. This will take a few weeks to work itself out." She practically pushed Sami out the door, ignoring his stammered questions about the process that would follow, and took the steps two at a time to tell Li'l Pecker.

"Nice work!"

She bowed her head, accepting the compliment, trying to ignore the crawling sense that she hadn't done any work at all. And another feeling, darker, that she'd tried to suppress until Claudette spoke it aloud when she returned to the office.

"That's all you've got? And they're running with it? This system is even more fucked up than I thought."

28

IT DIDN'T GO the way she'd thought.

She woke the morning of Sami's change-of-plea hearing in a mental fog so nearly palpable that when she parted her curtains, the morning light startled. At breakfast, Calvin's and Beverly's voices came as if from afar, soft, indistinct. She tilted her head, jamming the heel of her hand against it, almost expecting a bit of water to flow out, something to explain the clogged sensation.

Then, to the courthouse, footsteps silent on the sidewalk, cars passing in a hushed blur. The predictable crowd. Chance Larsen had pounced on her change-of-plea motion the moment she'd filed it—he had the courthouse wired, daily slinging the bull with the clerks and bailiffs who would tip him off to juicy developments—and so Sami's hearing drew even more people than his initial appearance. The anti-immigrant faction lined out along the whole block in front of the courthouse, the remnants of Sami's defenders across the street, a small, sad gaggle, huddling close against the waves of triumph and contempt breaking over them. Cops lined the curb, hurriedly dispatched because you just never knew. Two detached themselves and flanked her as she shouldered through the crowd, past Karl Schmidt, his gun riding prominent on his hip in a tooled leather holster like a lawman of old, brandishing his newest sign: "One down, 50 million to go. Every immigrant out."

Another sign, simply a noose. A cop's words pierced the miasma in which Julia moved. "Is that really necessary?" The response, a diatribe about First Amendment rights, faded back into her auditory haze.

The hearing itself was brief, Susan resplendent in a jewel-blue suit, giving an appropriately dignified nod of acknowledgment at the applause that broke out when Judge Baker accepted the plea, holding up her hands as though she really wanted to quell the jubilation that threatened to drown out Baker's pounding gavel. The tone shifted to full-throated outrage when Baker added that Sami was to remain free on bond until his sentencing hearing.

Cops went to the balls of their feet, hands hovering over the pepper spray and Tasers on their duty belts, reminders of the guns nestling close. An ominous muttering eventually prevailed, broken only by the occasional sob from Sami's mother. The woman in front of her whipped around in her seat. "You *should* cry. You raised a monster," she hissed, only to be swiftly escorted out.

A final bang of the gavel, one that threatened to split its block, the judge's face purpling. For all his colorful reputation, Baker prided himself on clockwork court proceedings, and this one had gone so sideways it was nearly unrecognizable. The police, though, had learned from the first hearing, hustling everyone from the room and clearing the halls before returning to get the lawyers, as well as Sami and his family, safely to their destinations.

Sami's mother rose with the help of her husband and a deputy, body so jellied between them Julia feared she would collapse. But once in the aisle, she steadied herself. Twisted in their grip. Fixed her grief-ravaged face upon Julia. "You were supposed to help him."

Protesting phrases tumbled through Julia's brain—plea agreement, reduced sentence, a matter of months—none of which, she knew, would satisfy. She stood, hands dangling useless against an impulse to go to the woman, clasp her hands, beg her forgiveness. For what? Doing her job? And in this case, doing it well, goddammit.

Hadn't Tibbits himself, passing her in the hallway a couple of days earlier, turned on his heel and boomed so everyone in the next county could hear, bestowing a "nice job" upon her?

Which should have made up for Claudette's near-total absence from the office, Beverly's sardonic raised eyebrows, the voice mail from Dom: "What the hell, Julia?" She'd hung up before listening to the rest of it.

What was wrong with all of them? A guilty plea—not one she'd negotiated after hours of wrangling with a recalcitrant client—but one freely offered, was something of a unicorn in her line of work, and a sop to her conscience besides: Ana, maybe her eyes squeezed shut against the horror of what was happening to her, really hadn't been able to see her assailant's face. Sami really *was* guilty.

She put his file in the drawer with her other closed cases. Topped off Pavarotti's water dish and tucked the cover around his cage. Shut down her computer and closed the door on the empty office, as rare a thing at the end of the day as it was in the morning.

Baker had wisely scheduled Sami's change-of-plea hearing as last on the docket. The demonstrators, their numbers growing ever larger, now approaching one hundred, had departed by the time she left the courthouse, darkness dropping fast. The mountain loomed, a deeper blackness. In a few short weeks, those free of care would disport themselves into the night, far above Duck Creek and her clients' small lives with their small offenses. There'd be one more hearing, for Sami's sentence, and then life would go back to normal. Whatever that was.

She snatched Karl Schmidt's fliers from beneath windshield wipers as she passed parked cars and deposited them in a corner trash can, trying to savor that small satisfaction, to nurture it into the same buoyancy that came with Sami's "I did it."

Instead, her steps dragged apace with her spirits.

Maybe it was Claudette's silence. Jamilah's face. Dom's voice on the phone. All of them telegraphing a sense of betrayal.

"Every year I hear the same questions," one of her first-year law professors had told the class. "How do I defend someone who's really guilty? Or what if I have a client I know is innocent, but I can't get the proof I need? How will I deal with that? Here's your answer: Let the law be your guide. If you work within its strictures, to the utmost of your ability, you can walk out of the courtroom with your head held high, no matter the outcome."

Julia tilted her chin upward. But it dropped to her chest a second later. Because that first-year class, of course, had its share of naysayers. At the time, she'd sneered inwardly at their naïveté. Now, their inevitable quavery protests came back to her.

"Just because it's the law doesn't make it right."

*   *   *

The summons—she couldn't help but think of it that way—from Dan Tibbits came a week later.

Not directly from Tibbits, of course. The secretary called, practically purring into the phone. Mr. Tibbits very much hoped she would meet with him. But he understood the busy schedule of a public defender. So as not to add more stress to her day, perhaps lunch on a Saturday? At the Silver Spoon? The name of the restaurant at the base of the ski hill was a reference to the ore that had been dug from the mountain before its reincarnation, as well as a wink-and-nod to its clientele, the older skiers who preferred craft cocktails and dry-aged steaks at the end of their day rather than the beer-and-burger crowd frequenting the other, cafeteria-style, eateries higher up the hill. Those places were seasonal, but the Silver Spoon stayed open year-round, its patio and glass-walled dining room justifiably famous for its postcard views of Duck Creek nestled in the valley below.

Or so Julia had heard. The Silver Spoon hadn't been on the itinerary the few times Michael had tried to introduce her to skiing. She'd be forever grateful to Calvin, her pregnancy giving her the perfect excuse to beg off from an activity she liked less every time she tried it, her skis prone to slipping out from under her, a glimpse of their tips pointing skyward before she crashed onto her back, floating down through the mountain's famous powder. "Pow," Michael called it. Which is how it felt when her head smacked the packed snow below.

She pointed her car north, the road climbing imperceptibly at first toward the hill standing like a beacon beyond the town. A quick stomp of the accelerator took her past the warehouses and apartment complexes on the edge of Duck Creek where she'd found Sami's home. Beyond, she passed a few scattered gated communities, suburbs of a sort, a concept until recently unknown in the mountain towns of the West, many only recently awakened to the possibility of becoming the next Aspen or Jackson Hole. The road dipped and curved, houses barely glimpsed behind screens of aspen and pine, the occasional Spanish revival or stone French country incongruous among the ubiquitous log mansions, each with its peaked great room, all of them of a size to make Julia wonder at the labor required to clean them. Then shook her head at her own foolishness. People who lived in houses like that hired others for their dirty work— including lawyers to clean up their messes. She thought of Cody slouched in Tibbits's office as though it were his natural habitat, and wondered yet again . . .

Another shake of the head, harder this time. All of that was behind her. Ahead, as the road rose assertively in steep switchbacks, lodgepole pines crowding dark and close, lay a future as glittering as the sunlight that flooded the car when it emerged from the trees into a broad parking area. Julia shielded her eyes and braked.

Dan Tibbits stood at the door of the Silver Spoon, arms spread wide in welcome.

CHAPTER

29

JULIA REFUSED TIBBITS's offer of a martini, and again when he
ordered a second. She'd thought the three-martini lunch was a
figure of speech, until he nodded to the waiter for a third, yet again
urging her to join him.

Yet again, she demurred. Just how stupid did he think she was?
Or maybe it was some kind of test. Was she supposed to match him
drink for drink, show him she had the right stuff? Whatever that was.

She'd expected him to order a steak, red and dripping, but he'd
gone for a salad, sans dressing. Maybe another way to throw her off
guard?

"Watching my cholesterol," he said in response to the look of
surprise she'd failed to conceal. Then he proceeded to nearly empty
the bread basket, waving away the olive oil and balsamic and slather-
ing slices with butter instead. She ordered a lamb burger, and he'd
nodded approval. One test passed, at least.

"I'd have taken you for one of those people who get the vapors at
the thought of eating a cute little lamb."

"They're cute for about five minutes," Julia allowed. She took
another breath. He was pushing her. She thought of Susan Parrish's
stiletto digging into Tibbits's instep and decided the only thing to do
was to push back, no matter how trivial the subject. "Then they grow
up to be assholes."

He dropped his fork. His laugh turned heads, bouncing back off
the windows with their famous view, ending only when he fished a

garlic-stuffed olive from his drink and popped it between fleshy lips slick with butter. "That's a good one. Never thought about it that way. I'll have to remember it."

Julia shrugged. "When I was growing up, my neighbors had sheep. We kids would go over and help out once in a while. Sheep are quite possibly the dumbest creatures on earth."

"A country girl. Not what I would have expected. Not from . . ." He allowed himself a quick, approving glance, pointedly within the bounds of propriety.

Julia took a bite of her burger, pretending not to notice. Beverly had done her job well. A couple of nights earlier, Beverly—padding past Julia's open bedroom door in a new pair of shearling slippers on her way to bed—stopped at the sight of Julia standing before her open closet, hands on hips.

Julia turned. Beverly raised an eyebrow.

"I'm meeting Dan Tibbits at the Silver Spoon for lunch on Saturday. I don't know what to wear." Her wardrobe consisted of weekend jeans, jail-day drab, and the single suit she'd bought for the rare court hearings that went beyond the initial appearances. Which wouldn't do for a Saturday lunch, Beverly agreed.

She looked Julia up and down. "I'm taller," she said. "But otherwise . . . Come with me."

She led Julia to her room and slid open the door to what Julia thought of as the gun closet. Julia checked the top shelf; there it sat, safe in its zippered case. Below it, Beverly's clothing hung in color-coordinated department store sections; blazers, then skirts, then slacks. "These, I think." She held up a pair of camel-colored wool slacks.

"My suit jacket will go with those," Julia offered. But Beverly shook her head. "Too formal for a Saturday." Sweaters lay folded and stacked on a shelf. She selected a black turtleneck shell and cardigan of surpassing softness. Julia stroked them. "But these are cashmere!"

"Yes. Try not to spill anything on them. If you push up the sleeves, you'll be fine."

Julia set the sweaters aside and held the pants to her waist. The cuffs billowed on the floor. Beverly took them from her. "I'll hem them up for you. If I do it Friday night, and let them down again Saturday as soon as you get back, they should be fine." Junior League casual, Julia had thought at the time, trying not to make a face. Except that, as Beverly had known, it had proven perfect.

She'd have to take the sweaters to the cleaners on Monday morning. For all of her calculated flash of boldness, sweat pooled beneath her arms and trickled down the small of her back. She was afraid to lift her water glass for fear her shaking hands would betray her; clutched the burger so tightly her fingertips broke through the bun. Beneath the table, her knees knocked, something she'd always thought of as a figure of speech. When was he going to get to the point?

"You're a surprise, Julia Geary. Like getting that boy to plead guilty. That was truly unexpected."

Now. They were at the point now.

*   *   *

"Well?"

Beverly pounced as soon as Julia opened the door. She must have heard the car pull up.

Julia let her coat fall to the floor and sat heavily on the third step, pressing her fingers to her temples where a headache throbbed hot, a filament of distilled frustration and confusion. "I don't know. He didn't offer me a job. Not exactly."

She'd driven down the mountain in a daze, her thoughts a reflection of the lowering light of late fall. At some point, she'd remembered to switch on the headlights, but all that did was black out everything beyond their twin slices, Tibbits's parting words stabbing at her apace with the headache.

"I'll be in touch. I'm sure we can work something out."

"That's all he said," she told Beverly. "He said he liked how I'd handled the case, and that he'd get back to me. What does that mean?"

Beverly snorted. "It means he's keeping you off balance. Just like he does his wife. My bridge group plays hers sometimes. She's . . ." She hunched her shoulders, ducked her head, sent her gaze darting this way and that, transforming herself into something small and scared.

Julia knew the feeling. It had been all she could do during lunch to hold her back straight, keep her chin up, meet Tibbits's gaze—which, despite his fast-downed martinis, never blurred or wavered—with her own as he quizzed her on her law school years, her time in the public defender's office, and, inevitably, Michael's death. "Such a tragedy."

She'd deliberately cast her mind forward as she gave her rote answers, imagining herself at just such a lunch months hence, maybe with some other junior lawyers in the firm, the ones she'd see occasionally in the courthouse, the men in their suits and those Oxfords with the inexplicably pointed toes, the shine mirrored by briefcases yet unbattered; the women giving Susan Parrish a run for the money in the power-suit department. People whose clients paid and paid and paid, sent fruit baskets on birthdays and bottles of Scotch at the holidays, who spoke of *their* lawyers, not the catch-of-the day according to the jail rotation.

And she'd waited, as Tibbits rose from the table at the end of the meal, for him to venture the only possible reason for such a get-together. The server approached, and Julia realized Tibbits had started to leave without paying. But the server merely shook his hand, and chatted with him briefly about the coming ski season.

"I built this place," Tibbits said in response to her questioning look as he held the door for her. "None of these people would have jobs if it weren't for me." He took her hand, crushed it beyond pain into numbness, and was gone with a promise to be back in touch soon. "Think about what we talked about today."

They hadn't talked about anything of substance. But apparently, she hadn't blown it. At least, she didn't think she had.

"Mommy!"

Calvin, having finally heard her voice, barreled down the hallway and into her arms, knocking her back against the steps, covering her face with kisses, a little more of the headache draining away with each one. Finally, a moment in which she could just *be*.

She held him close. "You have no idea of exactly how much I needed that."

He wriggled away. "I made a volcano. It blows up and everything."

Julia looked at Beverly. Had she really tolerated the mess of a baking soda-and-vinegar volcano in her kitchen?

Beverly nodded, raising her arms to reveal the spattered apron protecting her clothes. "I'm not sure which of us had the rougher day. Come on, Calvin. We'll show your mother how it works. Maybe she'd like to try it for herself."

"Just let me change first." Julia had already done enough damage to Beverly's cashmere without the added indignity of a bubbling science experiment.

But as she turned to go, Beverly laid a hand on her forearm. "He told you to think about it. I'd urge you to do that."

Beverly turned and followed Calvin back toward the kitchen before Julia could ask her, just as she wished she'd been able to query Tibbits, what the hell she meant.

30

S HE UNLOCKED HER office door on Monday, hoping to see the red
message light blinking on the new "safe" office phone, the one
whose number only went to a select few. Despite Sami's guilty plea,
the occasional diatribe still polluted the other line. Maybe there'd be
a new summons from Tibbits, one with details this time.

But the phone sat stubbornly dark beside Sami's fattened file,
shoved to one side of her desk, beside an unopened packet of three-
by-five cards, tied in a festive red ribbon.

They'd appeared in her office the day after her Starbucks sojourn
with Dom Parrish, along with a note: "Something to help in your
search for truth and justice." And, by way of signature, a simple,
sloping D, the initial rather than the full name bespeaking, maybe,
a hoped-for familiarity.

She couldn't accept a gift from someone involved in the case,
even something so inconsequential. But she couldn't bring herself to
return it, either, and so the cards sat unopened in their cellophane
wrapping, the ribbon drooping a little from her inadvertent habit of
touching her fingertips to it several times a day, a talisman of sorts.

The first time Claudette saw it she'd lifted an eyebrow, inviting
explanation. But Julia pretended not to see and so the matter went
unspoken. Which was just as well, given the tenor of her most recent
interaction with Dom.

He'd called and texted her repeatedly in the days since Sami's
guilty plea, and they'd finally met again for coffee, all the good

feeling from that first meeting gone, slouched in chairs shoved back from the table so as to put maximum distance between them, arms identically crossed across chests. Anyone looking twice would have thought they were a couple having a fight. Except they'd never gotten to be a couple.

There was no shared coffeecake this time, forks bumping, mimicking their knees beneath the table. Just Dom's impassioned protest—"How could you?" and her inadequate response.

"I didn't have a choice."

"But he didn't do it."

Just as Dom wanted to believe Sami, she wanted to believe Dom. The man looked like he hadn't slept. She'd seen this same look on the faces of mothers, sisters, girlfriends—almost always women— defending the men Julia was charged with representing. "Miss, you've got to help him. He didn't do it."

Except that, usually, he had. She would lead the women through the evidence, try to make them face reality. And when the time came, she'd do her best to get an appropriate sentence, mitigating the harsh punishment in which Susan Parrish seemingly took such pride.

But Dom Parrish didn't look inclined to hear any talk about a deferred sentence, one that would see Sami's unblemished record restored if he kept out of trouble for a few years. She offered cold comfort.

"You can testify on his behalf at the sentencing hearing. It's a few weeks out; plenty of time to prepare a statement. We owe him that."

"We? Seems like the only one here on his side is me."

Dom arose so abruptly that his chair fell over. He didn't pick it up on his way out.

* * *

A stack of cases of the Ray Belmar variety awaited her attention. She swept them aside, pulled her old stack of note cards from a drawer and laid them out in four lines, one for Cody's bare-bones account of what had happened, one for Sami's even less useful one, a third for Ana's medical report and her belated, opaque statement, and, finally, just a few cards noting discrepancies.

Cody had said he'd seen Sami on top of Ana, on one of the benches, when he came in. But Sami hadn't said anything about lying down, just that he'd grabbed Ana's breast. Julia had tried to press him on that point later, but he thinned his lips and shook his head and said he was done talking about it. "Just put me in jail and get it over with."

The boys had yelled at him, he'd said. Boys, plural. Cody had said that he alone saw Sami and Ana. These things happened fast, a blur, imperfect memory muddying things further. It was possible Cody had seen Sami and Ana spring away from the opening door, and surmised that they'd jumped up. And Sami admitted clutching at Ana: "I grabbed her. Held onto her."

Indeed, her medical examination noted the bruises. Julia reached for the file and slid the photos from it, laying them atop the unhelpful cards.

An image of Ana's slender, pale arm, the smooth little bulge of muscle—all those early mornings in the gym—marred by the five ugly fingerprints, so dark and distinct they could have been painted, thumb on one side, fingers on the other.

Julia could just see it, Ana frantic, gasping, struggling in his grip, Sami's hand wrapping her arm, pressing deep, thumb on one side, fingers . . .

"Oh, my God."

Julia held her own hand before her, fingers spread wide, drawing them slowly closer together.

"My God."

She reached for her phone and punched the speed dial for Claudette, forgetting that they were still barely speaking.

Claudette didn't pick up, although Julia's name was certainly flashing on her screen. Julia gasped a message into Claudette's voice mail, the words surging triumphant, vanquishing even the knowledge that they were damning her nascent chance at a job in Tibbits's firm.

"Claudette, Claudette. Dammit, call me back. He didn't do it. Did you hear me, Claudette? Get back here. Sami didn't do it."

CHAPTER

31

THE COURTROOM WAS jammed to the point of presenting a fire code violation, reporters and hangers-on who'd arrived too late to wedge themselves into seats instead lining the back and side walls of the gallery.

"You're going to have to wait outside," a bailiff murmured to another latecomer, only to be met with "Like hell I will." Those standing inhaled collectively, creating the necessary millimeters of space to accommodate yet another body.

Julia chanced a glance over her shoulder. Chance Larsen was there, in the front row, smart enough to know that the story he'd written would have exactly this result. Julia had leaked her motion of dismissal to him, the one that summarized, "while the identity of the perpetrator or perpetrators remains unknown, the evidence shows one thing is clear: Sami Mohammed did not assault (name redacted)."

Judge Baker swept in. The seated onlookers stood and—at the rap of his gavel—sat, quivering in anticipatory unison, the hiss of the season's first true snowfall against the only sound in the room. Beside Julia, Sami sat motionless as though in a trance, eyes fixed unseeing on some far point.

He'd been like that ever since the single outburst on the day she called him in and handed him the photographs that exonerated him.

"No!" He leapt to his feet, shouting. "I did it. I did it." He snapped his wrist, flipping the photos back at her.

Julia scooted her chair back against the wall, forcing herself not to fling up her hands as though to ward off a blow, trying to project the same sort of calm she tried to maintain in the interview room with volatile clients. She lowered her voice, urging him by example to follow suit.

"No, Mr. Mohammed. You didn't."

He sat, and she let a slow breath of relief escape.

"Please." The first time he'd ever used the word with her. "Forget this. Just send me to jail. Let my family go."

His family? "I don't understand. Nobody's holding your family."

Except that she did understand. His family was as confined as her own, hemmed in on all sides by hatred. She didn't know if the ancient computer she'd seen in the apartment was Wi-Fi enabled, or if the family had a smartphone—how little she knew of them!—but if they did, those devices were surely beset with the same sort of filth that confronted her daily, making it a battle to step outside the front door, straighten her shoulders instead of hunching them protectively, venture into a world seemingly intent upon crushing her.

Yet again, empathy stirred for the youth before her whose anger, she now saw, was not so very different from her own. She held herself stiff against the gut-writhe of shame. How much more quickly would she have accomplished his freedom had she felt that empathy from the beginning?

"Sami." Addressing him familiarly for the first time. "I'm not sure why you saw this as the way to go, but I think I might, just a little, understand." Even as she spoke, she wondered if she could believe her own words. Could jail possibly have felt safer than the taunts and bullying endemic to any high school? "But you're not just out on your own recognizance. It's over. They'll take that thing off your ankle. You'll be totally, truly free."

He rose again, not the furious leap of a few minutes earlier, but a slow unfolding, the motions of an old man bowed by the years. "No," he'd said. "I am not. Not as long as I'm a burden to my family."

Now, in court, he sat immobile as Julia repeated the arguments in her motion, the unlikelihood of Cody's timeline of events, further contradicted by Sami's own abbreviated account. Ana's stated inability to identify her assailant. She tried to ignore the angry rustling from the gallery as she held up the photos of the five fingerprints on Ana's arm. At her request, Sami raised his hand listlessly, showing the corkscrewed middle finger, the one injured in a soccer mishap and forever twisted to one side as a result—the one that had made that long-ago first handshake feel so strange, the one incapable of placing the print flanked by the others.

"So you see, Your Honor, it's impossible that Sami Mohammed assaulted this young woman."

The judge looked to Susan Parrish, on this day in a suit of charcoal gray, straight-skirted and sober. "Prosecutor?"

Susan ran through the evidence she'd outlined in the original charging documents, Cody's statement that morning identifying Sami, backed up by what the other boys said; Ana's admission that she'd been assaulted by someone, even if she didn't know who; underscoring it with Sami's own confession later. Susan turned frequently toward the gallery, packed with high school students and some parents as though they comprised a jury box, one whose members had already made up their minds in her favor. A legally meaningless ploy and a gamble besides, especially in front of Judge Baker. If anyone was going to grandstand in his court, it would be him—and him alone.

Julia watched for the signs, Baker's fingers drumming the bench, an eye roll or two, subtle enough that, should Susan object, he could have claimed an errant contact lens. She was still speaking when he performed a prolonged throat-clearing.

Susan ceased her soliloquy and awaited a pronouncement.

"And we have no further statement from the young lady?"

"No, Your Honor." Susan hurried on. "But the most important thing is, as I said earlier, the defendant"—she fairly snarled the word, swiveling on her heel to glare at Sami—"confessed. 'I did it,' he said. So Ms. Geary's motion is preposterous and should be dismissed."

She sat.

"Preposterous," the judge mused, drawing it out. "Pre-post-er-ous." Enunciating so clearly that a titter ran through the courtroom. "What I find preposterous is that you pursued a case on such flimsy evidence—evidence that now seems to point to someone else entirely.

But who? Ms. Parrish, it seems as though you've got your next case cut out for you. This one"—he banged his gavel—"is dismissed."

He disappeared through the door in the rear of the courtroom as the crowd's mutterings swelled to a full-throated cry of outrage. "Bullshit!" yelled someone, louder than the rest. The bailiffs moved toward the low gallery railing, but not quickly enough to keep Sami's mother from clambering over it and darting to Julia, grabbing her hands, and kissing them. "Thank you. Thank you," she sobbed.

"Mama." The mortification in Sami's voice would have done credit to any native-born American teenager.

"Ma'am." One of the bailiffs tried to pull Jamilah away. Julia shook her head at him. "No thanks necessary," she told Jamilah, offering her a Kleenex from one of the boxes that adorned every desk in the well, and the witness stand too. Tears flowed frequently in courtrooms.

Sami's father pushed his way through the crowd and reached over the gallery railing, tugging at the bailiff's sleeve. He lifted his chin toward Jamilah, then Sami. "My wife. My son." The bailiff opened the gate so he could slip through. He and Sami eyed one another warily. Julia stepped aside. Jamilah gave her husband a little push and the man said something in Arabic. Sami stood stiff.

"English," Jamilah commanded, even for this most personal of communications.

Sami's father glanced shamefaced toward Julia, then reached a hand toward Sami. "My son. I am sorry for—for—" He struggled for the words. "For no belief in you."

Across the room, Susan lifted her unwieldy satchel from the floor and slammed it onto the table. "No belief. His own father," she muttered, just loud enough to be audible to the defense table.

Sami brushed his father's fingers with his own, let his hand fall. His lips moved as though he were going to say something. He didn't, but his face softened before he turned away.

Jamilah tugged at Julia's arm. "Please tell your mother I send my thanks."

"My mother?" Julia's mother had died years earlier and, much as with Michael, Julia had yet to forgive her, as though Mary Ellen Geary were somehow to blame for the breast cancer that claimed her.

Jamilah held her hands high—someone tall—then brought them tight to her head—with short hair—then sucked in her breath and ran them down the sides of her body. Slender, too. She tucked in her chin. Frowned.

Recognition dawning, Julia very nearly laughed. "You must mean Beverly. My mother-in-law. But why are you thanking her?"

"For shopping for food. She takes me." Jamilah's eyes flashed defiant pride. "I pay. For the food and the gas, both. But to bring me, it is so kind."

Julia gaped. For Beverly to take Jamilah to the grocery store was indeed a great kindness. But how had that come about? Then she remembered the day she'd visited the family, stopping by her own home on the way back to work, describing to Beverly their straitened circumstances, the crowd in the parking lot. Maybe Beverly had contacted the refugee resettlement group and volunteered or, more likely, had simply taken it upon herself to do what was necessary. With Beverly at her side, Jamilah could brave the demonstrators, cruise the aisles of Duck Creek's supermarket without fear of facing anything more than a dirty look.

"And your little boy. He is so sweet. Mishmish adores him. And the boys call him 'Little Brother.'"

Beverly had brought Calvin, too? All these weeks she'd felt sorry for him, alone in the house with Beverly instead of romping with his friends at day care, and now it turned out he'd acquired a raft of indulgent sort-of-siblings.

"Ma'am." The bailiff intruded. He spoke to Jamilah, then looked at Susan and Julia and raised his voice. "You, too. I think it might be better if we all went out through the judge's chambers. I'll escort you to your vehicles."

Sami's face relaxed further still, not quite a laugh or even a smile, but a wry acknowledgment of their different worlds. "We don't have a car."

"Oh. Yes. Of course. Then I'll have a sheriff's deputy drive you and your family home. That would be best."

Behind them, the room seethed, anger surging, but now with no clear target. Ana Olsen's hysteria that morning in school, the bruises on her arm and throat, left no doubt: Someone had assaulted her. But if not Sami, who? And that business with the fingerprints— ridiculous! Around the room, people examined their own fingers as though seeking answers in their whorled, neatly aligned tips. One man stood immobile amid the swirl of motion, staring fixedly at Julia, eyes narrowed, full lips pressed tight and white. Dan Tibbits, waiting until she caught his gaze, the long slow shake of his head, confirming what she already knew. Sensation of a door slamming shut.

Then a real door banged as the bailiff hustled his charges from the room, handing Sami and his family off to a pair of sheriff's depu- ties, and offering to walk Susan down the street to her office, an offer she rejected as curtly as she shook off the reporters who swarmed toward her in the hallway.

Julia likewise waved off the reporters and climbed the stairs toward her office, the hallway blessedly empty. She sighed in relief. Too soon. A lone female figure stepped from the shadows in the recess of her office door. Another reporter, probably, more enterpris- ing than the rest, face hidden by a hood pulled forward.

As Julia approached, readying a curt "No comment," the person shoved the hood back. Ana Olsen grasped her hand, much as Jami- lah Mohammed had clutched at her a few moments earlier. She even echoed Jamilah's words.

"Thank you. Thank you. Thank you."

As Julia stood speechless, Ana raised the hood, cinched it tight around her face, and fled back down the hallway.

32

J ULIA PUZZLED OVER Ana's actions—if she was so happy to see Sami exonerated, why hadn't she said anything earlier to stop the proceedings against him? And if Sami hadn't assaulted her, who had?—vowing to follow up, until other concerns pushed past her good intentions.

Leaflets greeted her most mornings now, tucked into the storm door, booted footprints in the skiff of snow on the walk attesting to their early-morning arrival.

"It's like they want us to know we just missed seeing them," she groused to Beverly as she crumpled another sheet touting European Roots = American Greatness, the words printed across a sea of white faces, and lobbed it across the kitchen into the trash can.

Beverly, usually first up, dressed, and pointedly bustling about the kitchen when Julia came down for breakfast, even on a weekend day like this one, sat at the table in her robe, hands wrapped around her coffee mug, exhaustion shadowing her eyes.

"Not just mornings. There was one waiting for me when I took Calvin to the park after lunch yesterday. I opened the door, that . . . that *thing* fell out, and a car took off down the street. It's just as you said. It's not just that they're watching us, they want us to know."

Julia poured herself a bowl of the sugared cereal that Calvin was allowed as a weekend treat and brought it dry to the table, making a quick calculation as she picked out the marshmallow bits, dyed pastel with God knows what sort of chemicals, and popped them in her mouth.

Her success with Sami's case surely spelled emphatic failure for her hopes of a future in a private firm—at least not in Duck Creek and probably not the state. Tibbits's influence reached far, and his death stare the day of the hearing left no doubt that he intended Julia to spend the rest of her natural life in the public defender's office. She was stuck with Beverly for a good long time.

"I'll take Calvin to the park today after you get back from—" She stopped herself, still unable to say "the cemetery."

"Then, maybe we'll drive over to the university, make a day of it. I hear they've got a good planetarium. He'll like that." The university town an hour away was where most Duck Creek residents turned for diversions beyond the ski hill. "If they know we're gone, they'll leave you alone."

The quick uncharacteristic slump of Beverly's shoulders told her she'd made the right move. The stack of work Julia usually brought home on weekends would have to wait.

*   *   *

Instead of their usual playground, she drove Calvin across town.

She was tired of being recognized, of the stares and below-the-breath comments, let alone the ones voiced aloud. It was just cold enough to justify the knit cap that hid her hair, bright enough to demand the sunglasses. Aloft in the distance, the ski hill glittered with alabaster promise, the snow line creeping lower every day, the town's merchants barely able to contain their glee.

Julia filled her lungs with fresh air and congratulated herself on a plan both magnanimous and self-serving. For weeks, her only time outdoors had been the walk from home to courthouse, and she'd been too preoccupied to notice the fast-changing season. Now, she joined Calvin in kicking through a pile of leaves. Maybe, instead of spending a long car ride and then more time indoors in the planetarium, they'd go on a hike instead, taking one of the last opportunities to do so before snow clogged the trails. She'd pick up some deli sandwiches, a couple of pieces of fruit. They'd find a sunny spot out of the wind, make a picnic, forget about work and Beverly and her own dark, yes *dreary* future, and for this one day, live in the god-damn moment.

The moment became whole minutes, fifteen, a half hour. Beckoned by Calvin, Julia swung hand over hand from the monkey bars, making it three-quarters of the way across before her arms gave out and she dropped to the ground, laughing, with an internal vow to create time in her schedule to get back in a gym. Down the slide, repeatedly. And a challenge on the swings as to who could go higher.

All the while, other kids scampered about, mothers chatting on the sidelines, ignoring her but for the occasional nod or smile, no recognition of anything other than her shared mom-ness.

This was how other people—most people—lived, she told herself, pumping her legs to go higher. They didn't lug home briefcases full of work on weekends. Didn't spend their weekdays offering explanations for people whose misbehavior, even when it stopped short of violence, seemed so willfully stupid as to be undeserving of the defense she so carefully crafted, and for what? So they could go right back to doing whatever had brought them to her in the first place?

In addition to their lives of stunning normalcy—lives, she had to admit, she'd once thought stultifying—those other moms most likely went home to husbands at night, husbands who'd stuck around instead of running off to the army and . . .

Her swing's arc slowed, flattening along with her spirits, the old resentments ambushing her. Somewhere, Michael shook his head sadly. And why not? She'd disappointed him enough in life. *At least I'm consistent*, she told him now.

"Mommy?"

As always, Calvin brought her back to the here and now. Without him, how deep would she have sunk?

"I see my friends."

She looked where he was pointing, trying to make sense of what she saw. Kids scattered unsupervised on the swings and slide, out from under the usually watchful eyes of their mothers, who converged at the far end of the playground, voices rising. Maybe he'd spotted some kids from the day care center? But he ignored the children on the playground, looking toward the cluster of adults. Julia hopped down, swung Calvin from the swing's canvas band, took his hand and led him closer, until the words became intelligible.

"Go back where you came from!"

"You're not wanted here!"

A baby wailed, the sound rising and bending like a siren, presaging doom.

Julia stooped and pulled Calvin close, whispering. "Go back to the swings."

"But my friends!"

"I don't know what you mean. Just stay by the swings. And keep in my sight. Don't go anywhere else. I'll be back in a second."

Calvin's face lit up at the unexpected gift of even a few minutes without a hovering adult. Julia grabbed him as he turned to go. "And don't talk to the other kids. If anyone bothers you, yell for me really loud." He rolled his eyes, giving her a glimpse of teenage Calvin, before he ran off.

The day, so full of shiny promise just moments before, seemed to darken with each step Julia took toward the group. Maybe she'd misread the situation. But of course she hadn't, and when she elbowed her way into the group, there stood Jamilah and Sami at its center, Jamilah's face contorted with rage and humiliation, Mishmish shrieking in her mother's arms. Sami's little brothers—Calvin's newly acquired friends, the ones he'd seen from across the playground— had already fled and now stood several yards away, hands twined, chins trembling.

"Good Lord," Julia gasped before she could stop herself. "This is a playground. You're scaring a baby. Children."

The group swayed toward her. Her hat and sunglasses, disguising at a distance, proved useless with proximity.

"And these are our children," cried a woman, features crimped with righteous dudgeon. "Now there's a molester here, and it's all your fault. We've already called the police."

"No need." Sami wrapped an arm around his mother. "We go now."

He made a formal sort of bow to Julia. "Thank you for this"—he paused, waiting as the crowd fell into a menacing, muscle-bunching sort of silence—"freedom."

33

"THOSE WOMEN'S FACES. Just like the men on Election Night. Who turned out to be our neighbors."

Julia's voice shook as she told Dom about the women in the park, the middle-of-the-night visit that seemed so long ago now, but whose effects echoed with every surreptitious leaflet fluttering in the door.

She and Dom sat at a high-top so small their knees rubbed beneath it, which at first made Julia uncomfortable and then, halfway through a glass of wine, she discovered she didn't mind at all.

He'd texted her, suggesting he owed her an apology for his accusations about her acceptance of Sami's guilty plea. "What about wine instead of coffee? Veritas?"

She'd hadn't been to the new wine bar that catered to people wandering down from the ski hill for a change of scenery, its offerings priced with a keen understanding of the desired clientele, counterpart to the microbreweries patronized by the other half of the ski crowd.

She'd flipped her phone face-down upon seeing his text as though someone might materialize in the empty courthouse hallway to peep over her shoulder and read a perfectly innocuous message. Claudette, when she'd told her about it, commanded her to go. "You need to get out more. Is it a date? Even if it isn't, treat it like one. You need the practice. And whatever you do, don't talk about work."

Which so far had been impossible. By way of changing the subject, she lifted her glass and hoped she looked both appreciative,

which she was, and knowledgeable, which she most definitely was
not. Dom followed suit, holding his own glass high, admiring the
color of the contents.

"One of the good things that came out of being married to
Susan, I learned about wine. She considered it"—he raised a pinky—
"essential to her career. Like it?"

She did. Other than the rare beer when the public defenders
gathered to celebrate one of their own who'd snagged a job in private
practice, and the post-traumatic glasses of cordial or whiskey during
the worst days of Sami's case, alcohol had become a rarity in her life.
Beverly never served wine with dinner and Julia, at her limit in terms
of feeling judged and found wanting, had not been inclined to drink
alone. Warmth crept through her. Her shoulders, so long stiffened
against the expectation of insults either implied or outright, relaxed.
She tilted her glass, mesmerized by the slide of liquid.

She caught him studying her, his gaze so intense she had to force
herself not to glance away. Beyond her clients' leers, no one really
looked at her anymore. Beverly, her coworkers, even Calvin—they all
looked past and through her, their flickering glances barely registering the fact of her before their thoughts moved on. Michael—now
he'd looked, that long assessing gaze, the crooked smile. Challenging
her. Oh, he'd been sure of himself, and rightly so.

Dom's gaze was gentler, more curiosity than challenge. And if
it didn't provoke the flash of fire that Michael's had instantaneously
evoked, she couldn't entirely attribute the spreading glow within to
the wine. She was glad they were off the subject of Sami.

Someone walked past, heading for the restrooms, head swiveling for a second glance. Julia turned her face away. Dom touched
his glass to hers. "To human nature, in all of its disappointing
predictability."

She clinked in return. "How long do you think it'll take for this
to be all over town? The principal and the public defender, no doubt
cooking up ways to set more rapists loose on the town?"

"How long have we been in here—a half hour? I'd say it's already
all over town. Guess I should've thought about that. You don't need
any extra attention."

She shrugged. "I keep thinking I'll get used to it. The same way I used to think that the judge dropping the charges would mean an end to it."

"Me, too. Dammit." He drank deep.

The school had proved an accurate microcosm of the town. The populace, once nearly unanimous in its opinion about Sami, pulled apart into factions, a cancerous cell dividing. A not insubstantial portion continued to believe Sami had gotten off due to the efforts of a sly and presumably unethical lawyer. Another, much smaller, group bent over backward to shower the youth with sympathy. Offers poured in: soccer gear, a tablet and cell phone, money for the family. A college fund was established. The most sizable contingent remained uncertain of anything other than that something had happened and somebody needed to pay, their unfocused anger a smoldering fuse.

Dom acknowledged something else.

"Ana. The way they've turned on her. That, I didn't see coming."

Julia emptied her glass and nodded to the server, hovering with a bottle. "I can't believe either of them is still going to school. People are awful."

Trite, stilted phrases, inadequate to describe the horror heaped upon Ana by some members of Team Sami.

"Liar." "Slut." "Bitch." "Lying slut bitch." In some versions, Ana was a privileged white girl who'd thrown herself at the refugee for a little strange, and then cried rape when he rejected her. No matter— how many times did this have to be repeated?—that she hadn't been raped.

"Do you know that some kids are telling her to kill herself? We've tried to put a stop to it, but it's like that game of Whac-a-Mole. You call one kid in and tell him—or her; I've had to speak to more girls than boys—to knock it off, and three more pop up."

Julia's own discomfiting encounters seemed negligible by comparison. "Let's talk about something else."

Silence.

Treat it like a date, Claudette had said. Was it? And if so, what did one do on a date? She hadn't dated, such as it was, since Michael.

Before that, in law school and college, one simply drank one's courage into being and fell into bed with someone. So much simpler. Even if she wanted to fall into bed with Dom—did she?—it would have to be so *intentional*. Somehow, they'd have to end up at one of their houses. Not hers, not with the twin libido-killing factors of Beverly and Calvin. At his, there'd be his daughter, although presumably she spent at least some of her time at her mother's house. It would be like high school, except they'd be avoiding their children instead of their parents, a thought so ridiculous she laughed aloud.

"What in the world are you thinking about?"

Julia jerked. Some wine sloshed onto the white tablecloth.

"I'm thinking we'd better order some food before I have any more wine," she managed.

He signaled again and somehow, through the arrival of crusty sourdough bread and softened butter—"Thank God," Dom sighed. "I am so sick of cheap olive oil and watered-down balsamic"—and then the mussels that each had ordered, she found herself talking about her push and pull with Beverly, her forlorn hope of escaping into a private firm, now dashed.

"So if you'd just kept your mouth shut . . ."

"But I couldn't." It came back to her, the electric thrill of discovery, the fact on which an entire case turned. "It's like a drug, isn't it?" Claudette had said when Julia finally reached her that day. "We all live for it. You should savor it. Might be years before it happens again."

"Besides," Julia said, "somebody else would have seen it eventually." She couldn't help but wonder if Susan Parrish had seen it first and conveniently decided to ignore it. Everything she knew about Susan told her the woman went for the win first and foremost, and damn the inconvenient facts—which in this case, she'd counted on Julia being too inexperienced to notice.

She tried to figure out a way to quiz Dom about Susan—who'd left whom? Did he belatedly recognize that trait in her, and back away? Or did she kick him to the curb as insufficiently impressive as the spouse of a future judge?—and settled instead for asking about his name, which turned out to honor a grandfather. "Born in Italy, came here as a boy, with Parisi changed to Parrish at Ellis Island. Never went back to Italy. Can you imagine? Everything you've ever known, gone forever. Maybe that's why I feel for Sami."

Glasses were filled, quaffed, filled again. They picked through their respective piles of shells, hoping to find a stray mussel that had escaped. Dom held one up.

"I taught at a school on the Oregon coast before I came here. This is what I miss most about it—seafood. Every time I order something like these mussels, I tell myself that they were flown in just this morning. And maybe they were. Because these were pretty good. Or," he rolled his eyes, setting up the cheesiness of the line, "maybe it's the company."

"Cancer."

He blinked. "Come again?"

"I figured you were about to ask me my sign. So I saved you a step. Cancer. Very"—she raised a hand to her forehead and swayed in mock swoon—"emotional."

He rewarded her with a wry smile. "Busted. But give me a pass here. I don't remember how to do this stuff."

Julia didn't either. But it was coming back to her, fast. "Let's get out of here." She nodded to the server for the check, and indulged Dom in a brief back and forth over its division—"You were only in this for a glass of wine, not dinner"—before letting him pick it up.

Outside, emboldened by wine and beset by too much emotion tamped down for too long, she took his gloved hand and pulled him into the recessed doorway of a neighboring business, a gift shop already decked out for Christmas, damn the approach of Thanksgiving. There, she put her hands to Dom's face and pulled it to hers as lights blinked around them, their slow change from red to green failing to keep pace with her quickening pulse, until finally she pulled away, laughing beneath her breath.

"What's so funny?" He clasped her to him again.

"You said you didn't remember how to do this stuff. But I'd say you remember just fine."

34

"*JUST CALL ME angel of the morning, angel*," Julia warbled her way into the office, the dreadful elevator music still in her head, the paper sack in her hand wafting the scent of two slices of pie from Colombia Coffee.

Pavarotti, responsive to anything remotely resembling music, joined in with a high, melodic whistle. Julia whisked two napkins from her pocket, shook out one on each desk, and placed a piece of pie on each, then retrieved two plastic forks from the bag. "Breakfast is the most important meal of the day."

Claudette choked on her coffee. "That is the sappiest song. Got an extra napkin in there? What's wrong with you?"

"Some songs are so bad they're good," Julia handed her the napkin and sang out. "*Baaaaby, baby!*"

Her phone vibrated with an incoming message. She took it from her pocket and laid it face-down on the desk. She hadn't checked her texts or email after getting home the previous night, nor upon awakening. The trolls could wait. She wanted to savor the moment just a little longer. "*Just call me angel . . .*"

"That song's not one of them. It's just plain bad. The only way that song is good is if—" Claudette stopped with a forkful of pie halfway to her mouth. It fell from her hand and back onto the napkin, leaving a vivid berry stain. "You got laid."

"*If morning's echo says we've sinned,*" Julia mumble-sang around a bite of her own pie. She swallowed. "But no. I did not get laid. I did, however, get to first base." She took another bite and contemplated the pie as though the answer lay within its buttery crust. "Maybe. Is kissing first base?"

Claudette shook her head. "Lord help me. Let me think back. Waaaaay back. I can't believe I'm asking this. Was there tongue?"

Julia nodded solemnly. "Tongue there was. Much tongue." She ran her own over her lips, shiny with an application of gloss, something new for her.

Claudette covered her eyes with her hand. "Not even eight in the morning and you're making this black woman blush. And I've got three kids. That shouldn't be possible. So things went well with Teacher Man."

"That's Principal Man, for your information."

"And did he call the Naughty Girl into his office? Never mind, don't answer that. I want to read my paper in peace and you—Debra came by at the crack of dawn with a whole stack of new cases for you."

Somehow, Julia had managed to look right past them. Still high on optimism, she pulled the first file toward her. Maybe Li'l Pecker had decided to start throwing some tastier cases her way.

The office phone—the new one—rang. Julia looked at the clock. Not yet eight. "This early, it's got to be a troll. I wondered how long it would take them to get this number." She lifted the receiver and replaced it, took a sip of her coffee, ate the last bite of pie, and opened the file.

Claudette's newspaper rustled as she unfolded it. Pavarotti trilled softly, warming up.

Julia pushed aside the first file—a minor-in-possession case against a high school student who'd made the mistake of cracking a beer in the park instead of waiting until he got home—and reached for the second. "I should have known. Same old, same old."

Footsteps sounded in the hallway, fast, the telltale click of heels.

"Speaking of same old, same old. I'd know those steps anywhere. Hello, Debra," Claudette sang out, a split second before the receptionist burst into the office, hand pressed to her side.

"Why aren't you guys answering your phone?"

Julia picked up her fork and waved it. "So sorry, Debra. You just missed the pie."

"Then you really don't know." Her gaze darted from one to the other.

Claudette folded her paper. "Give us a break, Debra. Just spill."

"That guy. Your client. Sami"—Sammy—"Mohammed."

"Sami."

"Whatever. Him. Some guys jumped him last night, beat the heck out of him. He's in the hospital. In a coma. For all I know, while you two were sitting here feeding your faces with pie"—oh, Debra, finally some sweet, sweet payback for all those years of diminution—"he's probably already dead."

35

H E WASN'T DEAD.
So a hospital functionary, parked at the door to fend off the throng of reporters who'd beaten Julia to the punch, informed all of them.

"Mr. Mohammed is in critical condition. That's all HIPAA rules permit us to say, as I'm sure you're aware. No one will be allowed in. We can also provide condition reports by phone, so if you all want to go back to your newsrooms . . ."

A broad hint. No one budged.

Someone sidled up next to Julia. "What do you know?" Chance Larsen whispered.

"Nothing."

"Let's get out of here before the rest of them recognize you. I'll meet you in a few minutes at the picnic area around the corner."

The hospital had landscaped an enclosed area with ornamental shrubs, flower beds, and a few picnic tables in an effort to give families and staff a respite from the anxiety pervasive within its walls. This time of year, the beds lay brown beneath a layer of mulch, and the shrubs were collections of so many sticks, black and witchy. But at least the hospital walls provided some protection from the wind—and from the gaze of passersby.

Chance's footsteps crunched on gravel. He sat across from her at one of the tables.

"What do *you* know? And, Chance, before we say another word, this entire conversation is off the record."

"Maybe a statement later?"

Did everything have to be a negotiation? Apparently so.

"Sure. But, please. I just heard about this."

"My story's up online, but it's pretty bare-bones. Most of what I got from the cops was off the record, too—it's that kind of day—but their thought is that whoever did this had been watching the Mohammeds' place for days, learning Sami's routines. Except for the dad going to work at night, the rest of the family usually goes out in groups. Safety—such as it is—in numbers. But Sami's a runner, does it to keep in shape for soccer, I guess. He'd been sneaking out at night for his runs. Last night, they were waiting for him."

"They?"

He shrugged. "That's the assumption, given how bad it is."

"How bad?"

He paused, assessing.

"Chance. Look at what I deal with every day. My clients aren't exactly angels."

"Okay, but don't say I didn't warn you. The cops said it wasn't so much a beating as a stomping. Heavy work boots, probably. Broken ribs, I guess, maybe a limb or two, but it seems they went mostly for his head."

Julia's vision blurred. She closed her eyes. The face that rose before her was not Sami's, but Jamilah's. Her words, too. "You think you're the only one who lost someone?"

She did know, and God help her, she'd once wished loss upon Jamilah, in the form of Sami's jailing. But not this. Never this. Which, in its way, was even worse than what had happened to Michael, whose death came in wartime, an accepted—if unbearable—part of the equation, remote, impersonal, and mercifully instantaneous.

But Sami's assailants had gone after *him*. He'd seen their faces, felt their hot breath before they'd brought him to the ground, had borne the individual blows before something had finally ruptured in his brain.

"I'm going to be sick."

And she was, before Chance could even round the table to hold back her hair as for the second time in her life her body tried to purge itself of her emotions surrounding Sami Mohammed.

* * *

"I'm his lawyer" had the desired effect.

A phrase she used when she'd collected herself, after Chance had disappeared with the statement he'd wrangled from her—"I hope the prosecution will be as relentless in pursuing Sami Mohammed's attackers as they were in pressing a wrongful case against him"—and got through to the hospital switchboard.

Sami's parents had to give permission, but eventually she was allowed to enter the hospital via a back door, in the company of a clearly disapproving member of its public relations department who took her first to a waiting room where Sami's father sat at the edge of a chair, elbows on knees, head in hands. Some consultant, no doubt, had dictated the room's appearance, the walls a soothing aqua tint, hung with images of waterfalls and forests; plush furniture, a coffeemaker and water cooler in one corner, and boxes of Kleenex everywhere, all of it designed for maximum comfort in this place where there was none.

Moheb looked up when they came in, his gaze taking a moment to focus. He gave a small nod of recognition.

Julia nodded back. "But where is Jamilah? Mishmish and the boys?"

"The children are at home. With . . ." She watched him search for the right word. He spread his hands in defeat. "The people." He said it like a curse.

"Ah." The volunteers probably. The ones who helped the refugees; the group that had started the program to bring them to the presumed safety of Duck Creek. And now, this.

"And Jamilah?"

"She is with Sami. I . . ." His head dropped again into his hands, muffling his words. "I cannot."

Julia looked to her reluctant guide. "May I?"

He beckoned her to follow, down a long hallway, everything tile and shiny steel, designed for functionality. He paused outside a half-open door and stood aside.

Julia's gaze went first to the form in the bed and jerked away in shock. She turned to Jamilah, who sat beside the bed, clutching Sami's left wrist, which appeared to be the only undamaged part of his body. Bandages wrapped his head and obscured half his face. The other half bulged purpled and hideous and unrecognizable. His chest jerked up and down in time with the ventilator's hiss and sigh. Tubes ran from his arms, his nose, from under the blanket. Another protruded from the base of his skull.

"A shunt, to drain off fluid. It helps about fifty percent of the time. Without it, his condition would not be compatible with life."

Julia jumped.

The doctor had arrived on silent sneakered feet and he continued his recitation of Sami's injuries, the crushed skull, the broken ribs, as well as left radius and ulna and right tibia, the internal ruptures, until Julia held up her hand. "Stop. Please. His mother is right here. She speaks English."

The doctor gave her a pitying look. "Mrs. Mohammed understands her son's condition all too well. She can stay. But please limit your visits with Sami to ten minutes." He disappeared as soundlessly as he'd arrived.

Julia took a step closer to the bed, her hand hovering over Sami's body. She withdrew it without touching him.

"I told you once." Jamilah's voice, barely audible, emerged like something dragged over gravel. She didn't look at Julia as she spoke, her eyes remaining fixed on the monstrosity that was her son's face. "Asked you. If you thought you were the only one who lost someone in the war."

Julia nodded, then replied in a whisper. "I remember."

"I lost neighbors. Friends. Relatives. Death is part of life. Something you Americans do not seem to know."

"*I* know." Julia could have kicked herself. This was not the time to bring up her own loss.

Jamilah turned to her. "Yes. And now you must tell me. How is this borne? Because it is impossible."

Julia sank into the chair beside her. "Yes. It is impossible." She thought of the days after the soldiers arrived at her door, when she thought the only pain more unbearable would have been the loss of her son. Which Jamilah now faced.

But she thought also of how she'd railed at God. So many soldiers returned maimed, limbs gone, psyches wrecked, brains irrevocably scrambled, but alive. Why couldn't Michael have been one of those? She'd have taken him back, no matter how damaged. Because then there'd have been hope rather than the searing finality of death.

She took Jamilah's free hand, half expecting her to pull away, offended. But Jamilah intertwined her fingers with Julia's, her hand surprisingly warm.

"He's alive, Jamilah. Trust me when I tell you that's a gift."

"The people who did this to him . . ."

"Let me worry about them." Even though that was Susan Parrish's job, not hers. It was even possible, once they were found, that she—or at least someone in her office—would be assigned to defend one of them. But Jamilah didn't need to know that now.

"Your only job is to be with your son. To be his strength."

To sit beside him, hand virtually welded to his forearm, breath rising and falling along with his to the ventilator's stuttering rhythm, to will him to live with a wild fierceness that looked death in the eye and forced it cringing away.

To be for him, she thought, what she was never given the chance to be for Michael.

36

THE HOSPITAL DOOR had barely closed behind her when Julia scrolled through her contacts until she'd found Deputy Sheriff Wayne Peterson's number, tapping it so hard the phone flew from her hand, fortunately landing in the frost-stiffened grass instead of shattering against the walkway.

She dived for it. "Hello, hello, Wayne? Are you there?"

"Where else would I be? And who's this?"

Usually Julia assumed a light, bantering tone with cops and kept the push-and-pull boundaries of their relationship firmly at the forefront. Her job was to extract information; theirs, to determine how much she already knew. She didn't have time for that today.

"Don't screw around with me, Wayne. I know you can see my number. Have you arrested them yet?"

"Them, who?"

She held the phone from her ear and wiped the frost from it, hoping the delay would convey her disgust. "Oh, come on, Wayne. You know who. Karl Schmidt and his goons."

"You must know something I don't. What's Karl up to now?"

Julia nearly dropped the phone again. "I just left that boy's hospital room. It'll be a miracle if he makes it. Karl's been talking smack about Sami ever since this started. Remember that poster with a noose? Why haven't you arrested him before he takes off into the hills, or wherever people like him go?"

It was Wayne's turn to delay, and when he finally spoke, his voice had changed. "None of this comes from me, right?"

"You don't even need to say that."

"Karl's was the first place we went. Understand, with no hard evidence, all we could do is talk with the folks up there—and they were under no obligation to answer any of our questions."

She switched the phone to her left hand, blew on the fingers of her right, and shoved it deep into her pocket.

"So? What did they say?"

"Nothing."

"You mean they wouldn't talk? That's suspicious, right? Are they already lawyered up?" She wondered who Karl Schmidt would hire. No way he could afford the likes of Dan Tibbits.

"No. I'm saying we couldn't talk with him. Not saying this means anything, but you should know that he's gone, along with all of the other guys up there."

*　*　*

Julia typed "Karl Schmidt" and "Real Amerika" and waited for Google to work its instantaneous magic.

It was surprisingly limited.

Chance had written a smattering of stories when Karl arrived with his band of like-minded brothers, wives and children mentioned almost as an afterthought. It looked as though only three families comprised the original group. No photos. Images of Karl and his signs featured prominently in the newspaper's stories about the demonstrations, but when it came to his home, he'd threatened to bodily throw a photographer off his property if she'd so much as removed the cap from her lens. Human rights groups issued predictable statements about the dangers of white supremacy; conservative organizations shot back with equally canned responses about free speech; and the sheriff chimed in, saying that as long as the group followed the law, they were none of his concern. And that was the end of the stories about Little Amerika.

Julia clicked around until she found a few of Karl's writings, touting the region's near-total white population as his reason for settling Little Amerika outside Duck Creek. Julia winced as she clicked through dense paragraphs of rhetoric about blacks as "mud people" and Jews as descendants of Cain, and therefore cursed. Women were the exalted heads of home and family, symbols of purity—"blah-blah-blah," she said to the screen. She knew where that led. She didn't bother scrolling through to Karl's views on Muslims, figuring she could make an educated guess.

She went back to the stories about demonstrations. There was Karl, brandishing the sign depicting a noose. He had to have known he'd be the prime suspect in Sami's beating. No wonder he'd taken off at the sight of the sheriff's black-and-white.

But a civilian car . . . driven by someone who had no arrest powers . . . someone who just wanted to hear him out . . .

Julia pushed back from her desk and paced the office, trying to talk sense into herself, an effort that failed even before she knocked her shin on Claudette's chair trying to make the tight turn. She could either sit in the office staring at her screen or shuffling files or bruising herself on the furniture or go back to the hospital and spend the hours listening to the whoosh-thump of Sami's ventilator.

Action, even clearly ill-advised and almost certainly futile, was infinitely preferable. She went back to her screen, forgoing images in favor of maps.

*　*　*

The blip on the map bespoke the necessity of snow tires; along with serious boots, not the low ones she wore around town; and the region's standard winter emergency pack of food and a sleeping bag in case her car slid off the road.

A dotted line indicated a gravel road, a zigzag of switchbacks foretelling a steady climb not unlike the one to the resort, albeit without the benefit of pavement, daily snowplow sweeps, and the reward at the end of a welcoming lodge with blazing fireplaces and hot toddies arriving upon a nod to the bartender.

Real Amerika was on the mountain's backside, too scarred with mine tailings, adits leading darkly into collapsed tunnels, and swaths of charred trees bespeaking decades-ago wildfires to hold any real estate value other than for the desperately poor or those desperately desiring solitude, not all of them at odds with the government.

"You've got a lot of trappers, live-off-the-land types," the deputy sheriff had once told Julia about the area he patrolled. "There's a few artists who can't afford to live anywhere else. The usual hippie-dippy types, although they tend to come and go. Places like New Mexico look really good to them after a couple of winters here. A lot of them are gentle souls when they start out. But all that cold and isolation works on people. Sometimes I can see it coming, suggest that maybe the mountain isn't the place for them. The ones who don't listen— you know as well as I do how those end up."

She saw them in court when Wayne brought them down off the mountain. But she'd never seen them as he did, on their home turf.

"First time for everything, Pavarotti." The bird cocked his head and sent her off to Karl's lair with a trilling riff on "The Hall of the Mountain King."

Perfect.

*   *   *

Her enthusiasm for what had seemed like a plausible Hail Mary eroded as the road that skirted the mountain rounded its far side and began its climb. Snow coated the gravel surface, posing a slippery challenge. Julia white-knuckled the wheel as the car fishtailed around a curve. The snow tires she'd had put on a week earlier grabbed and held.

An occasional two-track led off into the trees, where one of Wayne's gentle souls likely lived. Or maybe one who'd gone dark and twisty. She passed trailer homes, tires atop roofs as anchors against a grabby wind, dogs leaping and howling at the end of stout chains, glistening ropes of drool swinging beneath bared teeth.

Even when the forest opened into clearings, the road remained in deep shadow, the sun selfish here, spilling its bounty onto the other side of the mountain, turning the ski runs into glittering swaths of guaranteed satisfaction. The snow lay soft on the road, a draping disguise for the deep and frozen ruts below its surface. The road narrowed. The snow deepened. Much farther, and she'd have to worry about high-centering. Like everyone who'd spent more than a single winter in Duck Creek, she'd stowed a shovel in her car but had never used it, thinking of it more as an insurance policy.

The trailers disappeared, along with the side roads. She peered ahead, seeking any sign of human habitation. She wondered what to expect. Nazi flags blazing scarlet defiance against the gray sky? High fences strung with razor wire? Gun slits? Instead, she almost missed the small wooden sign, its crooked letters hand-painted: Little Amerika.

An arrow pointed down a two-track that made the road she'd just left look like a freeway. The track fell away sharply to one side. She took a quick glance at the rocks below poking through the snow like so many jagged, waiting teeth, and then kept her gaze fixed squarely ahead, recalling every commercial she'd ever seen about Subaru's vaunted all-wheel drive and praying that just this once, the hype was real. She hit the brakes as soon as she saw the cluster of cabins, the thought of slogging through snow infinitely preferable to one more minute picturing her imminent death.

There was no fence, no razor wire, no swastika-spidered flags. Just a woman in a puffy blue parka patched with duct tape, hustling toward her through the snow, gloved hand resting on the gun on her hip.

*   *   *

Julia didn't know what to do with her hands. Raise them? But the woman hadn't drawn the gun, wasn't pointing it at her. She let her hands dangle, a little away from her sides, feeling ridiculous. She'd never before had to demonstrate herself unarmed. Was there a protocol?

"I already told you people," the woman shouted as she got closer. "Karl's not here."

Julia took a step away from the car.

"I'm not from the sheriff."

The woman stopped a few paces away. Julia estimated her to be in her sixties, although it was hard to tell. Sun and wind had wreaked unmerciful damage on her skin, turning it blotchy and crinkled, more like a discarded piece of paper than something plumped with lotions and firming creams meant to leave it smooth and glowing.

"Then who the hell are you?"

In her haste to get out of the office, to choose action over endless frustrating inertia, she hadn't thought that one through. Saying she was a public defender would be a sure invitation to leave.

"I'm a lawyer."

The woman studied her with eyes silver and milky as oysters. Cataracts, Julia thought, untreated. No health care, then. She had a wild, hopeful thought that if for whatever reason the woman took a shot at her, she might miss.

But the woman could see well enough. "You're his lawyer. That sand—" She appended the epithet.

"Jesus." Julia turned to go.

The woman's voice stopped her.

"Karl didn't do it. You want coffee?"

The sense of whiplash was so physical Julia put a hand to her neck, rubbing an imaginary crick.

The woman didn't wait for an answer but turned and kicked through several inches of new snow back to one of the cabins, half-hidden in a stand of aspen.

"Um, sure."

Julia followed, stepping carefully in the woman's footsteps so as not to posthole, noting only one other set of fresh tracks, the obvious evidence that beyond the sheriff's deputies, no one had gone in or out for at least the last couple of days.

37

THE COFFEE CAME via the kind of percolator Julia hadn't seen since her grandmother's kitchen, something comforting in its hiss and burble, the brown liquid leaping in the glass insert in its lid. It sat atop a cast-iron stove emanating heat worthy of a blast furnace. Julia peeled out of her coat, and wished she'd worn a T-shirt rather than a sweater.

The woman poured Julia a cup and held out a knobbed hand for a quick, firm shake. "I'm Ada Schmidt."

Tight gray curls topped her head. Karl and his family might have made a point of living off the grid, but Ada had found the time and money for a trip to town for a perm.

"You take milk?"

"Black's fine."

Ada snorted. "Should've known."

This time, Julia kept her "Jesus" to herself, knocked off balance by the combination of hospitality and casual racism. Then, thinking of Claudette, she reminded herself that silence enabled, and tried to ignore the secret shame of the fact that speaking up would be easy under the circumstances. Ada had already told her Karl wasn't around. She wasn't going to provide anything useful, anyway.

"Why do you hate people of color?

"People of color," Ada repeated in a mincing voice. "So politically correct. You want some nut bread? I made it this morning."

Julia rubbed her neck again, so inescapable was the comparison to Beverly, in her cashmere sweater and pearls, cooing graciousness as she offered her own coffeecake to the police officers. Now came this woman in plaid flannel, her hands so rough they'd probably snag on cashmere, dispensing a healthy serving of bigotry alongside her baked goods like a dollop of cream gone bad.

The nut bread, though, its moist dark sweetness hinting at molasses, could give Beverly's coffeecake a run for its money. You had to respect that.

Julia nodded to the other cabins visible through the window, smoke snaking skyward from their chimneys. As she watched, a door opened and a child of about ten ran bareheaded and in shirtsleeves through the snow from one cabin to another. A woman followed him a few steps out of the door, waving a coat, her voice sounding faintly, words indistinguishable but clearly the plaint of mothers everywhere. She shrugged as he disappeared into the other cabin and returned to her own home with the retort of a slamming door.

"How many people live up here?"

"Plenty."

Julia only saw three other cabins, none of any size. Maybe there were more back in the trees. Or maybe Ada just had a liberal definition of plenty. The latter, apparently.

"Someone like you would be surprised how many people want to join us. We get emails every day, from people looking to get away from all the crime, the filth, the ungodliness. A place like this—they come here and can't believe it. They've almost forgotten what it's like to live among their own kind. All that stress goes away."

Julia thought that the coming deep snow and crackling, electric cold—not to mention unemployment and seclusion—might bring its own kind of stress, but Ada was on a roll. Between bites of nut bread and sips of coffee, she launched into the sort of "mud people" philosophy that Julia had already read on the internet.

Julia tried to tune it out, focusing on her surroundings instead. The cabin was small but well-built. Coats in various weights hung on pegs near the door; boots rested in a wooden crate. A couple of paintings hung on the wall, the sort of mass-produced mountain images sold in the box stores on the outskirts of Duck Creek. No framed shrine to Hitler, no copies of *Mein Kampf* lying around. No sign of the contemptible posters that Karl lofted so triumphantly at the demonstrations.

"You understand," Ada said, apparently winding up her soliloquy. "I don't have anything against them personally. Except maybe that pervert that you got sprung from jail. I just don't want to live with them. Don't want them here taking our jobs, having their anchor babies . . ."

"*You* understand," Julia countered, trying to cut Ada off; she'd already heard more than enough, "why people might think Karl had something to do with this."

"But he didn't." Ada's smile was sly, the look of someone who held a secret and wanted you to know it. "So you and that deputy got no reason to come up here bothering us. No one here's done anything wrong."

"Then why the gun?" It lay on a table beside the door, a stubby utilitarian thing, none of the elegance of Beverly's shotgun.

"Coyotes. They're forever after our chickens." That smile again. "And varmints of the two-legged variety. There's people out there— lots of people like you—afraid they'll be left out when the world hears our message and joins us. You never know what they might do to shut us up. You can't be too careful."

Julia tried again. "But Karl . . ."

Ada shook her head so emphatically the curls bounced like springs around her face. "I told the sheriff like I just told you. The ones who did this, they're out there, closer than you know. You could've saved yourself the trip up here. All you got to do is look."

Julia's fork fell from her hand.

"Look where? Who?"

Ada's smile stretched toward smirk. "You think we're the only ones who feel this way?"

Julia knew they weren't. The proof clogged her in box, filled her voice mail to capacity.

"We're just honest enough to say out loud what a lot of people— most people—think."

The bread turned to ashes in Julia's mouth. She choked it down, and pushed the plate away.

"Not most people."

"More than you think. More than you know. People you think are friends. It's our turn now. You want to join us? We could use a lawyer." Goading her.

It took all of Julia's strength to resist the expected reaction, the outrage, the huffy departure.

"You're going to need more than a public defender if Karl had anything to do with this."

"But he didn't."

She wasn't going to get anything out of Ada. She rose.

Ada opened the door for her and stood aside. "I'll be sure to let Karl know you were here."

Julia followed their tracks through the snow back to her car, aware the whole time of Ada's gaze boring through her back, which tingled as though Ada had actually lifted the gun in her hand, crosshairs fixed between her shoulder blades.

What had she expected? That Karl would show himself, say something—not a confession, but something—that would give her an indication she was on the right track?

She imagined Karl in the courtroom, the outrage on his face at finding himself where Sami had so recently stood, pleasurable fantasies that distracted her through the slip-and-slide back down the mountain, until the damnable road finally unkinked her and delivered her onto the sort of straight, smooth pavement she vowed she'd never take for granted again.

CHAPTER

38

"YOU DID *WHAT?*"

Claudette had been on the job a decade longer than Julia and consequently was impervious to shock. Name a seemingly fantastical situation—the guy who'd tried to jack a marked cop car; the schoolteacher who'd adopted a series of large dogs for, ahem, companionship—and Claudette could top it.

So Julia derived some small satisfaction at the look on Claudette's face as she described the visit to Karl's compound, even as she braced for the lecture that followed—"You could have been hurt. Killed!"—one that left Pavarotti trembling and pressed against the bars on the far side of his cage by the time Claudette wound up.

"And besides." Claudette took a long breath, which made Julia fear she was only gearing up for more. "It's Susan's job, not yours, to go after the perps. It'd be just our luck, if it is Karl, for one of us to have to defend him."

"I know, I know." Julia tilted the coffee press over her cup. A drop or two splashed out. "But I'm going stir-crazy here. I want them to get whoever did this to Sami before he—" She stopped. If she didn't say the word *dies* out loud, maybe it wouldn't happen.

"Before?"

Julia moved quickly to change the subject, banish the thought. She held up the press. "We're out of coffee."

"That was the last of it." Claudette looked at the clock. "I've got half an hour before my first case. I'll run over to Colombia and get some more. You want a go-cup, too?"

"Always. Thanks, Claudette."

She sank into her chair as the door closed. Claudette was right, of course. Ada could have pulled that trigger. But she hadn't. "That was a close one, huh, Pavarotti? You okay in there?"

"You talking to a bird?"

Pavarotti proceeded to have the avian version of a near heart attack. By the time he'd quieted, and Julia had swept the mess of scattered seed and feathers from her desk, Karl Schmidt had settled himself in the chair across from her.

"You wanted to see me?"

*   *   *

His wiry whitening beard was stained yellow at the corners of his mouth. A telltale bulge pooched his lower lip. Julia hoped their conversation would be brief, before Karl needed to spit the tobacco juice gathering in his mouth. He wore a flannel-lined canvas coat over his customary buffalo-checked shirt, and knee-high lace-up leather boots that looked impractical for the deepening snow on the mountain and brought with him the fresh scent of cold and pine, cut by a tang of something dank, elemental. It took a moment for her to recognize the scent of blood. Karl's words echoed her thoughts. "You all down here think I went after that boy."

"I think," Julia said carefully, "some of the things you've said have raised the question.'

He jabbed his finger at her and opened his eyes wide.

"Well, I didn't."

He leaned back in the chair and folded his arms across his chest as if to say "That's settled."

Sometimes Julia felt as though men were forever telling her things and expecting her to go along with whatever they were saying. Michael, that he'd enlisted. Li'l Pecker, that he was handing her the "opportunity" of Sami's case. And now Karl, expecting her to swallow the bullshit he'd just offered.

Michael was her husband, Decker her boss. But Karl? Nothing to lose.

"And you expect me to believe that."

Karl grinned, the pointed tip of his tongue showing between his teeth. Julia looked away. He was enjoying himself far too obviously.

"Believe it or don't believe it. It's the truth. I've got proof. I've just been to show the sheriff and figured I'd show you, too, seeing as to how he told me you'd been asking."

He withdrew a phone from the jacket's depths, clicked a few buttons, and slid it across the desk. If Julia had given any thought as to what kind of phone Karl would carry, if he had one at all, she might have expected a flip phone, or something similarly fossilized. But Karl's iPhone was a version newer than hers. Its extra-large screen showed an elk hanging upside-down from a tree, impressive rack scraping the snow below, eyes filmed, tongue lolling fat from its mouth, gut slit and torso propped open with sticks to speed the cooling necessary to keep the meat from spoiling, although the surrounding snow-covered landscape indicated that was unlikely. With difficulty she wrenched her gaze from the gutted elk to the men around it. Yes, there was Karl, cradling the rifle that bespoke pride of the kill.

"Look there." His stubby forefinger hovered over a corner of the screen, the time and date stamp there—the day of the attack on Sami.

"We were up in camp that day, the next mountain over. Were there all week. Every last one of us got a deer or an elk, and every one of us has a picture like this. Not saying that boy didn't deserve it. Just saying I didn't do it. Like you can see."

Julia went out on a limb.

"You know who did, though. Or at least you have an idea."

Karl shrugged. The smile lingered but the tongue tip, thank God, disappeared.

"Could be. All you have to do is look close. Maybe even at your friends. We're not the only ones who aren't sorry about this. Only thing we're sorry about is that they didn't finish the job."

Goading her, just like Ada had. To divert suspicion from himself? He'd already proven he couldn't have been involved; at least he claimed it was proof. Was there a way to alter time and date stamps? She'd have to talk to the sheriff's office.

She sat silent, a dozen replies buzzing wasplike in her brain, eager to deliver their sting.

Karl waited, sneering, expectant. The door opened. A black woman strode in and stood tall over the white supremacist.

Later, Julia would swear she saw Karl flinch, shrink into himself. For sure, the smirk disappeared. His mouth flapped open and shut, wordless, fishlike.

"You were just leaving," Claudette suggested.

He was, with such alacrity the chair overturned in his wake, the bang sending Pavarotti into full screeching crisis mode, necessitating an unheard-of postponement of coffee.

39

COFFEE AT LAST.

Claudette's cup stopped halfway to her lips at Julia's words. "He said what?"

"That all I had to do was look close. That maybe it was even people we think of as friends."

But whose friends? Hers? She hardly had any friends, except for Claudette, and there was no room for a black woman, even as a suspect, in Karl's warped white fantasy world. She took another sip of coffee, hoping the caffeine would jolt her into the same sort of realization she'd had when she viewed the five fingerprints on Ana's arm.

"What's that supposed to mean?"

Her phone buzzed, saving her from an answer.

She looked at the screen. Dom.

This time of day, he was supposed to be at the school. There'd be only one reason for him to call. He'd had news of Sami.

Her hand hovered over the phone. She looked around the room for help. Pavarotti, finally mollified, sat fluffed on his perch, eyes at half-staff, exhausted by the morning and its insults. The clock showed eleven. Weak winter sunshine highlighted the layer of dust on the law books on their shelves. Who died in the middle of a sunny day? Death came in the night, dread inherent in the very silence, everything appropriately shrouded.

Claudette held her own coffee cup frozen in midair. The phone buzzed again and again, quivering like a trapped animal on Julia's blotter. "Just answer it."

Julia tapped it but didn't say anything for a long moment. Postponing the inevitable, the same way she'd tried to run from the soldiers advancing up her walk with the news about Michael. If she didn't hear it, it couldn't be true.

Dom's voice sounded through the tiny speaker, loud enough for Claudette to hear.

"Julia? Julia? Are you there? I just came from the hospital."

The muttered "goddammit" was from Claudette. She swiveled in her chair, turning her back, affording Julia a bit of privacy.

She held the phone to her ear. "I'm here."

"You'd better get over there. Sami's awake. Julia? Did you hear me? He's awake."

But she was already gone, running down the hall, coat half on, stuffing the phone into a pocket without even clicking out of the call, Karl and his clumsy attempts to point blame elsewhere already forgotten.

*　*　*

The hospital sat just a half mile from the courthouse. Even in the cold, Julia usually walked over, looking to the stroll to clear her head, help her focus, gather her strength to deal with the sight of Sami.

On this day she sprinted, lifting her face to the wind, welcoming its slap, cold no match for the sizzling hope of Dom's news. Even the wind, after a single gust, uncharacteristically backed off, relinquishing its power to that of the sun, which bathed the town in the sort of cold sparkling light that sent Chamber of Commerce types scrambling for their cameras to update their websites with the latest come-ons for the "quaint mountain town nestled at the base of a world-famous ski hill."

She slowed to a walk at the sight of the television vans taking up a corner of the hospital's lot, their satellite dishes cranked skyward. The national press, which had departed for the next big story as soon as the charges against Sami were dismissed, had swooped back in at the news of his attack, and this time they'd stayed, loath to repeat their former mistake. Best not to give them any hint that there'd been the kind of change that would provide a reason for breathless new stand-ups, the hospital as their backdrop, faces framed by fur-lined parkas highlighting their mountain locale.

The reporters nonetheless swarmed out of the vans at her approach, boots unlaced, jackets open, jostling to be the first to grab what would certainly be a few seconds of B-roll on yet another uneventful day. Because you never knew. Better to have lousy B-roll than nothing at all.

Julia's cheeks ached from the combination of cold and the effort of holding a poker face. She no longer bothered to cover her hair, duck her head. She'd perfected the chin-up, eyes-straight march to the door, the decisive head shake accompanied by the clear "No comment." She'd gotten used to glimpses of herself on the evening news, something that delighted Calvin and clearly mortified Beverly.

A group of demonstrators, huddled in the far side of the lot, sprang into action at the emergence of the cameras, shouting "Justice for Sami!" Hoping for their own five seconds of B-roll.

The anti-Sami faction had wisely gone underground since the attack, leaving the streets to Team Sami, whose members complained to anyone listening about what they perceived as a lack of enthusiasm for finding Sami's assailants. Which was unfair to Wayne and the rest of law enforcement, Julia thought, although she relished the implicit criticism of Susan.

The hospital door sighed shut behind her, dulling the commotion in the parking lot. She knew that as soon and she turned the hallway corner, no longer visible to the cameras through the glass doors, the reporters would return to the warmth of their vans and the demonstrators to their cars, awaiting the next excuse for action.

Another turn of the hallway brought the sight of Sami's teammates, laughing, hands raised for high fives. They spotted her and fell silent.

"Did you see him? Is he really awake? Did he say anything?"

They stopped, hung back, shuffled their feet, the us-versus-them stances of teens when confronted with adults, no matter what the situation.

"He's awake. But he's not really talking." Cody, as captain, appointed spokesman by tacit agreement. Now that Sami had been proven innocent, the team apparently had accepted him back into the fold. "You should go see for yourself."

She nodded her thanks and waved a goodbye, already jogging again, and heard the burst of laughter behind her, youthful exuberance bursting free.

* * *

Awake!

The news was about Sami, but she thought of Jamilah, the light in her face, its deep lines stretched into a smile, her back—so long held tense against the ultimate blow—finally relaxed into the chair. Maybe, with others there to maintain the vigil, she'd even allow herself to sleep.

Julia's steps slowed as she approached the ICU. Cautioning herself. Lowering expectations. Awake didn't mean . . . *awake*. Sami's eyes might be open, but vacant, important pathways in his brain smashed, nothing connecting. Jamilah might never get her son back.

As if to underscore her thoughts, a doctor rushed past, white coat flapping, breaking into a jog, nearly colliding with Bill Burkle, the soccer coach, heading up the hallway toward Julia. At the sight of her, he stopped.

She didn't bother with a greeting. "What are you doing here?"

She hadn't seen the coach since he'd sat in her office and swatted away her questions about Sami as though they were so many pesky mosquitoes.

"Just checking on Sami. Same as you." Again with the gimlet stare, the challenge.

First Karl, now Burkle. One more man daring her to back down. The thought crossed her mind—Burkle? Could he possibly have had something to do with the attack on Sami? Was showing up at the hospital just a way to deflect suspicion?

She glanced at his hands, looking for the telltale bruising and swelling of a recent fight—nothing—and then his feet, checking for hard-soled boots. But Burkle wore the low rubberized snow boots adopted by most of Duck Creek's population as soon as the first flakes swept in. Still. Julia tossed down a gauntlet of her own.

"I have to say I'm surprised. Given the way you were writing him up all the time. He didn't exactly seem like your favorite player."

"Listen." Burkle took a step toward her, the intensity in his voice so fierce that Julia found herself pressed back against the wall, fighting an urge to raise her arms to ward him off.

"I did everything I could to get him off the team. While the rest of you pussies were taking all the credit, I was the only one really trying to save him. And you, you most of all—you just threw him right back in there, and now this godawful thing has happened. How the hell do you sleep at night?"

He turned and stormed down the hallway. Julia heard the door, the newshounds' shouts, a muffled curse, and almost felt sorry for the television people as she slid down the wall to the floor, where she sat, arms wrapped around her knees, until the shaking stopped.

*　　*　　*

"Ma'am?"

Julia lifted her head.

A nurse crouched before her, speaking in practiced, soothing tones.

"Are you all right? Do you need a place to lie down? Or some privacy? The ICU can be hard on people."

Julia took the proffered hand and let the nurse pull her to her feet. "I'm fine." And she was. Burkle was the one who needed help. She shouldn't have let him get to her. "More than fine. I'm actually here because of good news." She dropped the nurse's hand. "I'm here to see Sami Mohammed. I know where his room is."

The nurse had started to turn away. Now she turned back. "Good news?"

"Yes. He's awake. Didn't you know? Have you seen him?"

"My shift just started. But I think . . . you might want to go to the waiting room first. The doctor is talking to the people there."

Of course. There would be protocols. Julia once represented a client accused in an assault that resulted in brain injury. It went badly. There'd been testimony about the interminable recovery, the steps it took to reroute the brain's pathways, the slow relearning of speech, of mobility. Of personality. The Sami of before, the shy diffident youth, might have vanished. When she'd first met Dom—a few weeks ago, time that now seemed like months—he'd mentioned Sami occasionally lashing out at his tormenters. What if that aggressive Sami now dominated? What if, instead of words, he used fists?

Maybe Burkle had been there for the doctor's cautions. Those would have been more of that damned code they all used, and Cody and the other team members might not have grasped the implications, might have seized on the word "awake," and gone straight to celebration. As had she. She put her hand to the waiting room door. No matter what the doctor said she, like the jubilant soccer players, would focus on the fact that Sami had regained consciousness. All the rest, the things that apparently had so upset Burkle, could be dealt with over time. For now, this was enough.

She pushed open the waiting room door.

A doctor stood over Jamilah and Moheb, sunk side by side in the too-soft sofa in twinned postures of grief.

The doctor turned to Julia. "And you are?"

"A . . . a. . . ." Lawyer seemed strange under the circumstances. "A family friend."

Was she?

Julia looked from Jamilah and Moheb to the doctor's unreadable expression. He must have given them the brain-injury-long-uncertain-recovery speech. Couldn't he have just let them enjoy the fact of Sami's return to consciousness for a single day?

"I understand Sami's awake?" If the doctor wouldn't focus on the positive, she would.

Jamilah looked up. Julia took a step back, Jamilah's face telling her everything she needed to know before the doctor even spoke.

"There's been a setback."

*   *   *

Sami had indeed been awake, fully conscious, eyes open, lips working around the ventilator tube, forming the word, if not the sound. *Mama.* Julia's heart broke a little, imagining it.

Somehow—maybe a nurse with teenage kids at home, texts flying through the night—word of Sami's miraculous improvement had gotten to the high school. His teammates arrived, flowers in hand for Jamilah and a goofy balloon from the hospital's gift shop, a giant inflated upraised thumb. An indulgent ICU nurse. "Five minutes. Not even that. We want his recovery to continue."

Jamilah stepping back, shy in the presence of so much healthy, youthful masculinity, the boys shy themselves at first, all those tubes and weird smells, hacking up stilted phrases—"Glad to have you back, man"—before steeling themselves to approach, whisper encouragement in his ear, no doubt buoyantly off-color, too quickly bidding him goodbye. The tiniest glimpse of a future. The nurse smiling as she ushered the boys out, the room awash in good feeling.

But moments later, as Julia wasted time sparring with Burkle, and precious more minutes sitting in the hallway feeling sorry for herself, Sami's body's arced, hands opening wide, then clenching, strangled sounds nearly drowned out by the sudden beeping craziness of multiple machines. The nurse tugged a screaming Jamilah away: "Please, we have to do our jobs." Doctors arrived in a blizzard of white coats.

One of whom now repeated to Julia the same useless information he'd already delivered to Jamilah and Moheb. An "incident." Likely a small stroke. It happened more often than not in these cases. No way to tell what additional damage it may have caused. Sami's brief return to consciousness, his obvious recognition of his parents, his teammates, had been a good sign. Maybe he would likewise recover from this latest event. "I'd give him even odds." But it was imperative to avoid further visitors, excitement. "Parents only." The doctor trained his eye on Julia.

As did Jamilah, her voice barely audible, the weak counterpart to the force of her hand pushing Julia toward the door. "You go now. You've done enough."

40

"Look at the bright side. If he dies, it's Murder One. Excuse me, *Homicide* One. The guys who did this will go away for a good long time."

Ray Belmar sat across from Julia in the interview room, trying to cheer her up the only way he knew how, even falling back on the correct terminology in the state's legal code.

"Really, Ray? You honestly think a damn thing will happen if that kid dies? Everybody will be so happy to see this case go away once and for all. Oh, they'll throw out some bullshit about continuing the investigation. Chance'll get a few stories out of it. But eventually it'll all just fade away and someone—maybe more than one someone—will be walking around this town having gotten away with murder. Sorry, homicide."

"Hey." Ray made as if to cover her hand with his own, then jerked it back. They sat relaxed in their chairs, more like a couple of friends at a sidewalk café than lawyer and client in a room built for intimidation as well as security. But boundaries remained and Ray was too savvy about the system to want to cross the lines—the physical ones, at least. Emotionally, it was a different story, on this day the client working hard to comfort the lawyer, reassure her that the case would turn out okay.

"I'm the one who's supposed to be the cynic here. Isn't this where you talk up the sanctity of the law? Dish out all that crap about justice? Besides, if they ever haul anyone in on this one, Miss Susan will be all over their ass. I'm not big-time enough for her anymore, but she prosecuted one of my cases early on, and goddamn. Two minutes under her cross, and I told my defender I was pleading guilty. That woman would've had me locked up until hell froze over in a way that even global warming couldn't thaw."

He waited, maybe expecting a smile. She delivered only reality.

"She won't want to prosecute this one. Best thing for her is if this case disappears, just like Sami's case before it. Who wants to go after the guys who took out a sex offender? Because no matter that we got him off on ironclad evidence, half the town still thinks of him that way. Obviously."

"Obviously." Ray lifted a shoulder. It showed bare and scabbed through a tear in his jumpsuit. She wondered if that was the result of a prison scuffle, or just shoddy material, likely to part at the least strain. Not that Ray would put a strain on any clothing. He never spent enough time in jail for the prolonged, strenuous workouts that saw some men go in as stringy, twitching junkies and come out hulking, unrecognizable versions of their previous selves.

"Speaking of obvious. You see any way out of this latest mess of mine? And are you still going to be my lawyer? Word around here is that your office is in for more layoffs."

Julia had heard the same thing two days earlier from Debra, and brushed it off. But when rumors made it all the way into the jail, it was time to take them seriously.

"You guys are amazing. How do you know these things?"

"Maybe because we've got nothing else to do?"

"For what it's worth, we've heard the same thing. But you're stuck with me. They'd never lay the war widow off. So let's see if there's any hope for you today."

Like someone pulling herself hand-over-hand along a taut rope, Julia drew her thoughts back to the matter at hand.

"You ever consider that you could stop screwing up? But since you didn't." She leaned forward, positioned pen over pad, and recited from memory Ray's dwindling series of options given repeat offenses and a stubborn failure to pay fines or show up to court on time, willing the legalese to crowd out the lingering memory of beeping monitors, doctors' urgent voices, a mother's sobs.

* * *

The rest of the day passed in a haze of unanswered calls and voice mails from Dom, and a tactful desertion from the office by Claudette. Even Pavarotti maintained a mournful silence, head tucked under his wing, emerging occasionally to fluff his feathers and test the mood, before ducking back into the safety of warm, downy darkness.

One of the judges was on vacation, meaning a rare clear court calendar for Julia, so she tackled the tower of files on her desk, slotting away the closed cases into drawers, filing the necessary motions and responses on others, updating her calendar, anything she could do on automatic pilot, Jamilah's words lodged with a sickening weight somewhere beneath her heart.

You've done enough.

But she hadn't done anything. Which was the point. She hadn't done shit. Hadn't wanted the case, hadn't had the guts to reject it, hadn't done more than a half-assed job. The only thing she had done—pointing out Sami's inability to have assaulted Ana—came about by the sheer dumb luck of her having taken a second (twentieth, more likely) look at the fingerprint bruises in the photos.

Luck only works if you grab it. Another one of Michael's useless sayings. She'd grabbed, but all it had done was burn her fingers and damn near immolate Sami.

The first tap on the office door was so faint she barely heard it. The second, a bit louder.

"Goddammit." Julia was only halfway through reviewing her notes on the day's jail visits, sipping at coffee long grown cold. Pavarotti lifted his wing and cocked his head quizzically. "If that's Karl Schmidt again," she told him, "so help me God . . ."

"Come in," she barked. Damned if she was getting up for Karl. The door swung open, but no one entered. Julia slid a report back into a file and looked up, registering the person hovering in the doorway. She leapt to her feet, sending the dregs of her coffee cascading across the desk.

"I'm sorry. I'm sorry. I'm so sorry!" Ana Olsen's apology wobbled on the verge of tears.

Julia yanked at the contents of a box of tissues and dumped them atop the spreading pool on her desk, then turned to the girl in the doorway.

"Why are you apologizing? I'm the one who did this." She reached for a tissue and realized the box was empty. Those on her desk had gone brown and sodden, but the one atop the pile was still white, mostly. Julia retrieved it and held it out to Ana, forcing the girl to step into the room. Ana dabbed at her eyes, then blew her nose.

Julia waited through the girl's efforts to maintain a bit of dignity. Ana raised her head, the tissue balled in her hand. Julia reached under her desk, retrieved the trash can, and held it out. Ana took another step forward and deposited it. Julia leaned it against the desk and swept the coffee-soaked mess there into it.

Ana shifted from one foot to the next.

"Please. Sit down." Julia put the trash can back under her desk and sat at her own chair, willing Ana to follow her lead. Anything to reduce the tension wafting from the girl, strong as the scent of spilled coffee. Ana looked to the open door.

"Let's give ourselves some privacy," Julia said as though she'd thought of it herself. She got up, grabbed the Do Not Disturb sign that Claudette had swiped from a motel at some conference or other, hooked it over the knob and closed the door. She and Claudette used the sign as a warning when one or the other was in the midst of a particularly sensitive meeting.

"I'd offer you coffee, but it's cold. I'm sorry I don't have any water or soft drinks."

Ana shook her head.

Julia sat down, started to put her elbows on the desk, considered the dampness there, and changed her mind. "What brings you here?"

Ana took a shuddering breath. "It's about Sami. Is he . . . ?"

"He's alive." Julia repeated a highly edited version of the doctor's explanation for the coma, trying to make it sound like a routine procedure. The fifty-fifty business, the dreadful phrase "not compatible with life"—she left those parts out.

Another shaky breath, longer than the one before. Julia hoped Ana wouldn't cry again. The tissues were gone. She checked the door to ensure it remained closed, scanned its frosted glass window for the telltale shadow of eavesdroppers, someone who might have seen Ana enter the courthouse and, maybe knowing her from school or a track meet, followed her up the two flights of stairs and down the dark hall. Nothing.

"He didn't do it," Ana blurted. "And now he's going to die and it's all my fault." Tears again, in great gusts, gasping so desperately for breath Julia was afraid she'd pass out.

Julia fumbled for her coat, found deep in a pocket the snowy cotton handkerchief Beverly had once pressed upon her, and folded Ana's fingers around it, wishing for a hand towel instead. The girl eventually quieted, twisting the ruined cotton in her hand. "He didn't do it."

"Yes." Julia kept her voice low, flat, hoping for calm. "That's why he was released." She thought of Ana's fervent "thank you" after the charges were dropped. She couldn't figure it out then, and she'd meant to follow up on it. But somehow she'd forgotten about it. Or maybe she was more like Susan than she realized, just wanting everything to go away.

"But no one believes it!" Ana's face went blotchy. Her voice rose. She leaned forward. "And that's probably why this happened. Because people—a lot—still think he did it."

Did it.

It.

Ana had refused to talk with her, or anyone, about that day. All Julia and anyone else involved in the case knew, because of the physical exam, because of her deposition, was that she hadn't been raped. But there were those bruises, the dark and damning prints on her skin.

Julia clutched her mug in both hands and raised it to her face, trying to hide it, afraid her expression would betray the eagerness coursing through her, heartbeat so percussive she feared it was audible.

"Ana," she said, her voice low and soft, inviting confidentiality. Not a question, but a command.

"Tell me about that morning."

41

A SPEECHLESS CLAUDETTE WAS an endangered species. Maybe even nonexistent,

Yet there she sat, not even finishing her morning coffee, mouth open, eyebrows climbing up her forehead as though something were chasing them.

Even as she savored the shock of it, Julia braced herself for the inevitable.

"No. No. No. No. No."

"But it makes sense." Julia started to outline the plan she'd constructed in the sleepless night that had followed Ana's visit, constructing her case for Claudette as though before a jury, each fact a block in an impenetrable wall of evidence.

Which Claudette proceeded to demolish with a single blow.

"You cannot do this. You know that, right? Or were you asleep during—oh, your entire three years of law school? Are there medibles in that muffin?"

Julia inspected her muffin as though expecting she might indeed find flecks of green, although she wasn't sure that's how medibles—an idea newly palatable—looked.

"It's not technically illegal. Not if I do it on my own time."

Claudette rose from her desk and towered over her. Even without her heels, she loomed. Julia likewise started to stand but Claudette sent her back into her chair with a forefinger to chest.

"No. Repeat after me. I am a public defender. I do not file civil cases." Claudette had leveled up from lawyer mode to mom mode. Lawyer mode, as she often reminded Julia, was for amateurs.

Julia, a recalcitrant child, took a bite of muffin.

"Don't you try that trick with me, missy. Either chew that muffin or spit it out."

Julia chose chewing.

"Good. Now swallow. And repeat after me. I am a public defender. And say it so Pavarotti can hear it."

"I am a public defender."

Claudette's glare could burn holes through wood. "I do not file civil cases."

Julia finished her muffin, taking her own damn time about it. Finally:

"I do not file civil cases."

Claudette sat down. Julia relaxed. Too soon.

"Did you tell Ana to go to Susan? That she needs to be talking to a prosecutor?"

"I did." She had. But she hadn't disagreed when Ana protested, saying, "She won't do anything." May even have mumbled, "I'm afraid you're right." *Almost* under her breath.

Claudette lifted her mug toward Julia. "And one more: I am going to stop this shit and get back to my job."

"Yeah, yeah. That, too."

"I'm serious. We're all of us lucky to have jobs. You don't want to be the one on Li'l Pecker's chopping block."

The phone rang. Claudette answered. "We were just talking about you," she drawled into the receiver. She held it out to Julia.

"Li'l Pecker," she mouthed.

*   *   *

Julia wandered through the courthouse doors and stood in a sparkling, still landscape, the snow deposited by the previous day's storm not yet sullied by exhaust, booted feet, peeing dogs.

Its glittering surface bounced the sun's rays back, everything shimmering, imposing cheerfulness in a world where none existed.

"But I'm the widow," Julia said stupidly to no one now, repeating the idiotic phrase that she'd blurted, despite herself, to the last-hired, first-fired news Li'l Pecker delivered.

"I know, I know." He'd nodded that big head in practiced sympathy. "But that makes your situation better than most. You've got that military pension. Your mother-in-law's house. Free babysitting. What am I supposed to do, lay off someone like Claudette, three kids and a husband who just decided he needed to go to grad school?"

Julia squelched the unwelcome *yes*. Of course he wasn't supposed to lay Claudette off. Or anyone in the public defender's office. Jesus H. Christ, everyone was already overburdened.

"This doesn't have anything to do with . . ." She stopped herself before she committed another professional faux pas, suspicious that this was Decker's way of erasing the Sami Mohammed case from public memory. Yes, she'd won a victory for his office, but it remained unpopular, not the sort of thing you wanted brought up during a campaign for judge. Ana's revelation quivered on her own lips, withheld only by superhuman effort. He'd just repeat Claudette's advice: that the girl's accusations made it a case for Susan.

He ignored her half-baked question. "You'll receive a severance, of course. HR will help you get set up with COBRA. We'll pay you as though you've worked the next two weeks, but we've learned it's best for everyone if people leave immediately. You have your personal effects with you? Your coat and such?"

Julia had planned on a Colombia run after her meeting. She had her coat. Her purse—that female accoutrement Decker couldn't bring himself to mention. Probably because it contained scary things like tampons.

She stood. Zipped herself into the parka. Ostentatiously slung the unmentionable purse with its unmentionable contents over her shoulder. Turned her back on Decker's practiced bullshit—"Best of luck . . . Your service has been appreciated . . ."—and walked out of her old life.

CHAPTER

42

Julia did the math on her way to Colombia, a new calculation for each step. Four years of college. Three of law school. Five more in the Public Defender's Office. A dozen years of her life down the drain.

She paid for her latte and did more math—three dollars and fifty cents drawn against a salary that had just vanished. No more lattes for her. She sipped slowly, making it last. Beverly's coffee wasn't quite up to Claudette's standards, but it was close. It would do. It would have to.

As though Julia had conjured her with the thought, Claudette blew through the coffeeshop door, scattering snow and fury like shards of glass. "You know what I drink," she snapped at the cowering barista. "And bring us some pie." She glared at the selections. "None of that custard shit. Something with some damn flavor. Don't even think about bringing it cold."

The barista went into a paroxysm of steaming and pouring and slicing and microwaving, rushing things to their table and backing away, looking as though she'd rather flee the shop entirely rather than rely on the inadequate barrier of the counter.

Claudette dug into her pie, speaking between bites. "What. The. Ever-loving. Fuck."

Your husband. Your kids. More valuable than mine.

Julia used her own pie as an excuse not to speak, afraid the accusing words would escape. Claudette was the closest thing she had to a friend, although they'd rarely spent time together outside work, had never—beyond Claudette's post-funeral visit—been to one another's homes, the job so demanding as to leave little time for things other people regarded as fun.

She'd have time now. But could she bear to be in Claudette's presence, hear her tales of courtroom throwdowns with Susan? Ray Belmar's latest shenanigans? Pavarotti's new song? How long would it take her to start hating Claudette?

Who'd finished her pie, and was staring at her with narrowed eyes, assessing.

Julia put her fork down and studied it, the better to avoid meeting Claudette's gaze. By the purple smears on its tines, she assumed she'd just polished off a slice of huckleberry pie without even tasting it. Which was its own kind of crime.

She spoke to the fork. "What?"

"I'm just thinking." Claudette wet her finger, blotted up a bit of crust from her plate, and touched it to her tongue. "So much butter in this I don't know how it even holds together."

Julia waited. Claudette hunted down more stray crust, humming a little. Forcing Julia's hand.

Julia caved. "What were you just thinking?"

"Your cockamamie plan. The one that was going to get you fired anyway. It's almost like Li'l Pecker knew what you were up to. Moved to pre-empt you. That right there is some kind of genius move."

"Claudette!" How dare she give Decker credit? "Besides, he wouldn't have fired me for it." She paused, thought about it. "If it had worked."

"Exactly." Claudette sat back, face full of satisfaction, as if she'd just finished her closing argument and was waiting on the jury to deliver their inevitable conclusion in her favor.

"Yeah, well. Shame I never even got to try it. Somebody talked me out of it." Bitterness seeped into her words, a hint of the vinegar that through some sort of baking alchemy, paired with butter to make a crust of surpassing flakiness in the pie they'd just consumed.

"You never tried because he would have fired you before it even got a chance to work."

Julia lifted the fork to her mouth and licked it, trying to taste the tang of huckleberry. Still nothing. How long could this sort of numbness possibly last? A few more minutes? An hour? Long enough for her to get home, deliver the news to Beverly in the sort of slow-motion underwater calm that allowed her to sit across from Claudette eating pie and drinking coffee as though her world hadn't just ended? When it wore off, would things ever make sense again? Because, for sure, nothing Claudette was saying made any sense at all. The woman was drawing big verbal circles around her, saying the same thing over and over again, her expression a mix of pity and anticipation, waiting for Julia to get whatever message she was trying to impart.

"Which is why I didn't do it." How many more times would they repeat this pointless back and forth?

"But now that you're fired . . ."

Whoa.

Just like that the numbness was gone, replaced by a rushing fury, a wave mounting and breaking, Julia on her feet, leaning across the table, hand raised to—what? Strike Claudette? Sweep the table free of the plates and mugs for the sheer satisfaction of the resulting shattering of crockery against tile, of the shocked expressions of the other patrons, faces already turning their way?

Claudette sat imperturbable, finishing her sentence as Julia's arm came up.

"Now that you're fired, what's stopping you?"

*   *   *

Later, Claudette would swear Julia had kissed her full on the lips.

"Objection. I did no such thing." Julia was sure of it. She had, however, taken Claudette's face in her hand and planted a big wet one on her cheek, and if in the process her mouth had grazed the corner of Claudette's lips, so the hell what?

"Claudette!" she gasped. "Claudette! Of course! Thank you."

Claudette made a show of wiping her face with her napkin. "You'd have figured it out for yourself. You were just taking way too long about it. Takes a pro like me to see the obvious."

"I was in shock," Julia began, but Claudette made a shooing motion with her hand. "Do I have to tell you everything? Why are you still hanging around here? You've got work to do. Know where you're going first?"

"Yes. Yes, I've got it right here." Her hands shook as she fumbled for her phone, dropped it, retrieved it, swiped through images until she came to the group photo. Took a second to memorize the face, then swiped again until she found the address she'd saved.

"You know where it is? You okay to drive?"

"Yes, and yes again. And, Claudette? Thank you." She leaned toward her friend, but Claudette drew back in mock horror.

"One kiss was enough, thank you very much. Get your ass out of here."

"Right. I'll keep you posted."

Claudette clapped her hands over her ears and shook her head. "No. Don't. I don't want to know any more about this than I already do. You're on your own."

Yes, she was, Julia thought. Had been ever since Michael's death. Funny—for the first time, the knowledge didn't roll over her with the flattening sort of despair to which she'd become accustomed.

Instead, a new emotion propelled her out of Colombia: anticipation.

CHAPTER

43

ONLY A FEW hours earlier, when she'd still thought herself employed, she'd swiped through her phone to those yearbook images she'd snapped of the soccer team, trying to match the faces with the row of youths she'd seen at Sami's court appearances and in the hospital, studying their features, making mental notes besides the names.

She was looking for a certain kind of boy, one in Cody's orbit, a moon revolving around his sun—but maybe one of the remote moons, small, stony, eager for the brief searing flashes of the warmth of reflected glory.

There. Second row of the yearbook photo, just off Cody's shoulder. Most team members stared into the camera, either broad smiles or badass scowls. Sami, in the rear despite his first-string status, studied his feet. But this boy fixed his gaze upon Cody. Had he been in the courtroom, the hospital hall? Julia closed her eyes. Inhaled, exhaled, long slow shallow breaths, tried to empty her brain. Something she'd learned in law school. Clear out the clutter, give the answer room to emerge.

The hospital hallway, the group of boys. One lagging behind, running to catch up. Yes. She committed his name to memory.

Tom Gates.

Karl Schmidt had urged her to look closer to home. Now she would.

* * *

Tom Gates lived in what had once passed for suburbs in Duck Creek, at least before the second-homers swept in and plopped their log mansions atop the foothills. A previous era, though, had seen a hopeful expansion of town farther into the valley, tract homes on cul-de-sacs, the kind of neighborhood announcing itself as a *good place to raise kids*. Apparently nobody gave thought to the fact that once said kids had ridden their new-every-Christmas bikes around the cul-de-sac a few thousand times, there was not a damn thing else to do there, at least not until they grew old enough to smoke weed and have sex in the basement rec rooms while their parents were off working the jobs that maintained their new lifestyle.

The homes, ranchers and split-levels that, with their expansive closets and two-car garages and those soon-to-prove-troublesome basements, must have seemed a delight to the first escapees from the drafty old homes downtown, conspicuously lacking eat-in kitchens and family rooms and separate bathrooms for parents and kids, and always needing some sort of maintenance.

But maintenance on the older homes, so many of them built by Scandinavian immigrants who knew something about construction made to withstand weather, tended toward cosmetics, while the newer ones sagged and faded over the years, developing odd cracks and leaks that betrayed their slapped-together nature.

The first wave of occupants made their money and moved up and out—many of them, oddly, back into town, reclaiming the sorts of homes in which their parents had grown up, stripping woodwork of layers of paint, exclaiming over built-in shelves and roomy fireplaces, knocking out back walls to accommodate the sizable kitchens they now demanded, and insulating the hell out of them.

Tom Gates's parents would have been part of the second wave into the fast-fading suburbs, Julia guessed, arriving as the wall-to-wall carpet had lost its nap, the paint gone dingy, the lawn demanding all-out war on the dandelions.

Julia thought about pulling into the driveway, but opted to park curbside instead, reasoning it would make for a quicker escape if Tom reacted badly. If he were even home. If . . .

"Enough with the ifs," she said aloud, summoning her inner Claudette. "Get your ass in gear."

A thought that propelled her up the walk and to the door, delivering three decisive knocks before she could change her mind.

* * *

"Yeah?"

Tom was indeed home, and apparently was the only one, given the gloom in the room behind him. The door opened directly into the living room, a design flaw apparently inflicted by someone from a warmer clime. All of Duck Creek's older homes, including Beverly's, had the benefit of some sort of entryway to capture and hold the cold before it could seep into the rest of the house.

Tom gave no sign of recognition, his only greeting the single word. He affected the same sort of long-forelock haircut as Cody, but the resemblance ended there, face soft and pale as an undercooked dinner roll, his expression shifting, in contrast to Cody's confident gaze.

"I, uh. I'm Julia. I was hoping to talk with you." This was tougher than she'd thought. When she'd been a lawyer on the case, a mere hour earlier, she'd have had a plausible reason, no matter that it wasn't exactly her case anymore. ("No exactly about it." She imagined Claudette's scowl. "This one's not your case at all.")

But what was she now? Just an interested party? And what were the legalities of a situation like this, a random adult showing up to question a minor? "I'm a lawyer," she added quickly. So no one could say later that Tom Gates didn't know who or what he was dealing with.

The boy blinked twice, slow and uncomprehending. His mouth hung open. "Yeah?" he said again.

"I want to talk about what happened in the locker room."

Slow stupidity fled so quickly as to make Julia wonder at her own first impression, replaced by a narrow-eyed cunning. "What about it?"

"I know what happened there." A bald bluff. "I'm doing a follow-up investigation."

"If you know what happened there, why do you need to do an investigation?"

The little shit, standing there in a T-shirt and workout shorts, barefoot, seemingly oblivious to the cold flowing into the house, had just called her bluff.

"Because your friend Cody could be in big trouble."

Another lightning mood change, a dual blast of fear and anger. "You leave Cody out of this, you fucking bitch!"

"Hey, hey. Take it easy. I just want—"

But she was talking to a slammed door.

*   *   *

It took her all the way back to the center of town to stop shaking; and it wasn't until she pulled up to the house that she realized the error that had doomed her from the start. Until that moment, slapping her head had remained a figure of speech. Now her palm struck her forehead with such force it stung.

She waved to a confused Beverly and Calvin, standing in the doorway, probably wondering what she was doing home in the middle of the day, and pulled away again, heading for the library. The phone photos were too small for her nuanced purposes. She needed larger, clearer images. She made a beeline for the library's reference section. The yearbook fell open to the team pages, probably due to her own recent perusals. Before, she'd looked for a hanger-on, the kind of kid eager to please, reasoning it would be easier to pry the truth from him. But such a kid would be the least likely to betray his idol.

She needed Cody's second in command, his lieutenant, his consigliere. The kind of kid who, like Cody, was so cocksure he couldn't imagine danger—or justice—could touch him. Better yet, maybe the kind of kid who thought himself the rightful heir to power; maybe even not just the heir but deserving of power himself. One who'd be happy to depose the king.

And there he was, chin up, big grin, flashing one of those faux gang signs. Stewart Jones, aka Chewie. The name pinged in her memory. She sat, chewing a hangnail. Oh—the boy who hadn't been with the group that morning, but who'd heard about it from the others and whose parents had insisted they all go to the police and report the assault on Ana, something that could bode well for her mission today. She puzzled over the nickname awhile. It would have made sense had Stewart been a shambling, shaggy-haired guy, but he was wiry in the manner of the rest of the team, and with that same goofy haircut seemingly sported by everyone on the team but Sami. "Stewart . . . Stew . . . oh. Stewie to Chewie. Good grief." Damn shame that Stewie/Chewie had a last name like Jones. She moved to a computer, cursing his thousands-of-a-kind name as she scrolled through Joneses in various sites, finally finding a contact number for Stewart on a team page and then backtracking to an address. Which turned out to be just a few blocks from Beverly's house and clearly was owned by one of the younger couples of means who'd begun repopulating the neighborhood.

The garage had been updated to accommodate two cars and was topped by what appeared to be a studio apartment, probably rented out as an Airbnb during ski season. The owners had popped the top of the main house, a Craftsman-style bungalow, with the sort of expansion that could have been—and frequently was—hideous, but in this case apparently had been designed by an architect with some sensitivity to the neighborhood's history. Beverly, so critical of changes to her adopted neighborhood, would approve.

As soon as Chewie opened the door—painted a glossy scarlet with black trim and a polished brass knocker—Julia knew she'd called this one right. No open-mouthed look of befuddlement. Chewie stood with his arms folded across his chest, legs planted wide, leading with his crotch. Was that meant to impress people or scare them? She'd never been clear and wondered if the guys who adopted that stance ever considered it might simply rouse disgust.

"Tom said you'd been by. Figured you'd show up at Cody's place next. Didn't expect to see you here." Was she imagining the hint of pride in his words? "Doesn't matter, though. Cody's on his way over. I texted him as soon as your car pulled up."

Of course Tom, that craven weasel, would have alerted the whole team. And Chewie, ever the loyal lieutenant, followed up.

"Oh, so you need Cody to stand up for you?" The words were out of her mouth before she'd thought them through. The quick grimace—not quite a flinch, but enough to let her know the remark had hit home—egged her on. "That's fine. I'll wait for him to do the talking. That's how it works, right? Cody calls the shots and you all go along with whatever he says?"

Color climbed fast in Chewie's face. He set his jaw, breathed hard through his nostrils. Julia risked another jab, a hard one. "Just like your friends all did in the locker room? Went along with Cody that day, and then again, putting Sami into a coma? Were you with them for that? I sure hope not, for your sake. Because the whole lot of you will be looking at Murder One if he doesn't make it."

A TV term found nowhere in their state's criminal code, but he didn't need to know that. She shook her head sorrowfully. "Instead of four years in college, you'll be staring down thirty to life. Good thing you're still in high school. Otherwise this'd be a death penalty case for sure. Oh, wait. You're a senior, right? That makes you an adult. So forget what I just said. But look at the bright side. They don't hang people anymore like they used to. Now it's just a needle. Like going to sleep, they say, except when the drugs don't work. From what I've read, it burns like hell while you slowly suffocate."

She'd let the wave of anger at all that privilege carry her away. Had gone too far. She knew that even before he stepped away from her, calling wildly over his shoulder, "Mom? Mom?"

Christ. They'd crucify her for this one. Bad enough she'd been laid off. Now she could kiss her chances for a new job goodbye.

She grabbed his arm and pulled him back toward her, which probably would earn her some sort of assault charge if Chewie were so inclined—and even if he weren't, his lawyer would be.

"Listen to me. It's time for you to stop being stupid. You tell me—and the cops—what really happened, and suddenly you're the hero. Everyone knows Cody was the instigator. But if somebody doesn't talk, you'll all go down with him. Think about it."

"What's going on here?" A slender woman with Chewie's strong, regular features appeared beside her son. She had her son's height, and an unruly cloud of dark hair that would have given credence to her son's nickname, had he not shorn nearly all of it in that militaristic high-and-tight thing. "Stewart, are you all right?" She flicked Julia with a sharp-edged glance. "I'm Laura Jones. Who are you?"

Julia reasoned that she was already in so much trouble it couldn't get any worse. "I'm Julia. I'm a lawyer. I'm worried about your son. I'm afraid he's going to get in trouble because of the people he's been hanging around with."

The woman's mouth tightened. She put an arm around her son and Julia felt an unwanted flicker of sympathy for the boy, so defiant and arrogant moments before, as he leaned into his mother's embrace.

"You mean Cody Landers," the woman said, just as an SUV pulled up to the curb and Cody himself got out.

44

"WHAT THE—"
Cody stood scowling by his car.

Julia scrabbled in her purse for her business card and a pen, scrawled her cell number across the back, and thrust it toward Chewie's mom. "Forget about the front of the card. That's not my job anymore. But call me. Please."

She turned to find Cody advancing up the walk, one menacing step at a time. She glanced back a final time; saw something closed and wary in Chewie's face. Good—maybe.

"I was just leaving." She tried for a smile. Managed a wave. Did a quick sidestep to avoid Cody's attempted shoulder-bump as they passed. Bastard. Drove home with another idea forming in her mind.

* * *

"Even without one of the boys, you've got enough to file. But it's risky."

Claudette's late-night voice was subdued, husky, none of the daytime bombast with which she'd encouraged Julia to pursue a civil case. Julia imagined her under the covers, whispering into the phone to avoid waking the kids or her husband slumbering beside her, just as Julia herself huddled within a blanket fort of sorts, its interior lit by the low glow of her phone.

"I know."

"Does Ana know her name will be out there? That's the down-side of a lawsuit. No anonymity."

Julia thought of the stubborn determination that propelled Ana across the finish line ahead of the other runners. Cross-country, if she remembered correctly. No sprinter, Ana. Now that she'd launched, the girl had staying power.

"I haven't talked to her about it yet. I think she'll be fine."

"Her parents will want to weigh in. They might not be fine at all."

The blanket puffed and fell with Julia's words, soft against her face. "I've scheduled a meeting with them tomorrow."

"When could you file?"

"Few days. A week, maybe." Another silence. Julia waited for the inevitable.

"Who are you going after? The cops? Susan?"

The blanket whooshed away, nearly sliding from her head as Julia blew out a breath. "I wish. Because that's who deserves it. But both of them could make a case that there's not enough evidence to move forward. After all, Ana didn't see anything. She just heard something. And that photo she's so worried about: You can see how that could be interpreted two different ways. Anyway, nobody ever finds against the cops. Look at all the times they've gotten away with shooting black people, and no one's even dead here."

"I'm familiar with that situation," Claudette reminded her drily. Another silence. "You're going after the school district, then."

"It's what makes sense. Failure to protect . . . a history of bullying . . . the usual."

Burkle's words: "I was the only one trying to save him."

She'd have to depose him, see what he meant by that. Had he gone to higher-ups, told them what was going on? Gotten nowhere?

Even in her thoughts, falling back on the generic *higher-ups*. Avoiding the obvious question. Had he gone to Dom? And seen his concerns brushed off? Could Dom have stopped this? Should he have? The question her lawsuit would pose.

"Damn, girl." Claudette's whisper was barely audible. "Kiss teacher-man goodbye, I guess."

Julia guessed so, too. As heartbreak went, it was nothing like the loss of Michael, that wholesale shattering whose effects lingered all these years later, part of her still missing, the empty spaces re-forming in new, unexpected ways. Such as this, her belated willingness to see the case through, no matter the cost.

"Principal man," Julia reminded her, for what was probably the last time.

*   *   *

She put it off as long as possible.

Until she'd talked with Ana and her parents, the latter pale, gripping one another's hands so tightly that Julia's own fingers ached. "You're sure?" they asked their daughter. Over and over again. Ana's reply patient, unvarying. "I'm sure."

Until she'd met with Burkle, who was all too happy—finally—to talk about the way Sami's teammates had indeed nicknamed him The Terrorist, and no, he didn't think they meant it as a compliment. Yes, he'd gone to Dom about it—confirmation that, even though she'd expected it, made Julia's stomach heave so violently she pleaded a twenty-four-hour flu and cut the conversation short.

But the interview she hoped for, prayed for, damn near walked into a church and lit incense for, never materialized. No one in Chewie's household picked up the phone when she called, responded to her texts, appeared in her doorway with the last piece of information she needed—an eyewitness account—that would have let her move the case out of the civil realm and back into the criminal.

"It's been a week," she said, back under the blankets again in another middle-of-the-night conversation with Claudette, the two of them like a couple of teenagers whispering secrets about boys. Which, in a way, they were.

"Then it's time to pull the trigger."

"No. There's one more thing."

"What's that?"

"Wait till tomorrow morning. You'll see."

She clicked off and two-thumbed a text. Then hesitated, the step she was about to take even more decisive in its way than the lawsuit she'd be filing.

Then she hit "send," her words winging through cyberspace to Chance Larsen.

*   *   *

Claudette beckoned Julia to the window at Colombia, filmed with steam from the espresso machine. She ran an elbow across it, clearing a spot.

"Do you think the entire town has come to a halt? Come over here and look at this. Better yet, let's go outside."

"Are you crazy?" Julia, phone to her face, scanning the reaction Ana had told her to expect to Chance's story, didn't look up.

The phone rang. She ignored it.

"Seriously. I want you to see this." The door closed behind Claudette.

Her phone stopped ringing. Then started again.

The door opened.

"*Now.*"

Julia looked up from her phone, took in the annoyed glances of the other patrons, and headed for the door. She handed her phone to Claudette so that she, too, could view the disturbing photo, and crossed her arms against the cold.

Claudette handed the phone back. "We knew this was coming."

"Still. What's so important that I had to come out here to see it?"

Claudette swept her arm, turning one way, then the other. "The whole street. Check it out."

The phone rang and rang. Snow blew sideways along the sidewalk below, swirling as it encountered a number of immobile objects. People, standing still, oblivious to the increasing storm, staring at their screens.

"A million bucks says they're all looking at the same thing." Claudette took Julia's phone again and clicked the volume to mute.

"Way to take a risk. I'll give you a dollar." Julia put a hand to the door, urging Claudette back into the warmth. "What happens now?"

Claudette joined her back at their table, nodding to the barista for refills. "Here's another safe bet. One of those calls is from Dan Tibbits, threatening to sue that girl for defaming Cody Landers's character. Just guessing that a few of the others are from your wannabe boyfriend."

"He doesn't wannabe, not anymore." Julia had thought about emailing, texting, knowing that the adult thing would have been to talk to Dom in person, but in the end opted for the phone, calling him at six thirty in the morning.

"Julia?" The alarm in his voice was palpable. "Is everything okay? Is Sami . . . ?"

"No, no. Sami's fine. I mean, I don't think there's been any change. But a story's going to go up on *The Bulletin*'s website any minute now. Ana and Sami's parents are suing the school district. The superintendent. And you."

"What? *What?* On what grounds?"

"For failing to protect them. From bullying. From assault."

"Dear God." A long silence. She heard a thump and imagined him sitting heavily in a chair at the kitchen table she'd never get to see now, elbows on knees, one hand clutching the phone, the other running through his hair, the sort of meaningless gestures designed to keep shock at bay.

"Dom, I'm so sorry."

A long breath. "Why are you apologizing? You haven't done anything."

Time for a silence of her own.

"Yes, I have. I'm the one who filed it."

* * *

She brought home two pieces of pie, one each for Beverly and Calvin, thinking to bring them out after dinner as a surprise.

But Beverly was still at the kitchen table when she walked in, uncharacteristically lingering over a cup of coffee, her eyes straying immediately to the container in Julia's hand.

Julia opened it. "I thought maybe for dessert tonight."

"For Calvin, certainly. Or maybe this afternoon, after he finishes his assignment. He's taking a big step forward today."

She'd given him a stack of worksheets with simple words—C-A-T next to a cat she'd sketched herself, complete with bobtail, so as to resemble Lyle; D-O-G beside a spotted Dalmation puppy; C-U-P with a drawing of his favorite sippy cup. He was to copy each word five times and bring them to her.

He bent over his task, crayon clutched in chubby fingers, bottom lip caught in his teeth, concentrating so hard he barely looked up when his mother walked in.

Beverly reached for the container. "I'll have mine now, thank you. Would you please turn on the oven? Heating it in the microwave will ruin the texture of the crust."

Julia hurried to comply, popping the pie into the oven, pouring herself a mug of coffee and joining her mother-in-law.

Beverly held up the newspaper, Chance's story bannered across the front page. "It's a day for celebration, don't you think?"

She rose, went to the sideboard, and returned with a bottle of Bailey's, too vilely sweet on its own, perfect in coffee. It swirled in creamy, hypnotic tendrils within Julia's mug.

"This story," Beverly said. "Quite the broadside. Well played, Julia. Michael would be so proud."

Julia decided to attribute the warmth spreading through her to the Bailey's. Whatever the cause, it banished—at least for the time being—the regrets she felt about her lawsuit's inevitable effect upon Dom.

45

CHANCE'S STORY TOOK its narrative directly from the lawsuit, giving the first full account, beyond Cody's abbreviated version, anyone had read about what happened in the locker room that morning—at least, Ana's version of what happened, the story stressed.

Obviously, Sami wasn't talking; nor was Cody, although Dan Tibbits had given Chance an expletive-laden quote before he'd hung up on him.

The necessities dispensed with, the story launched into Ana's recitation, just as she'd told Julia, now part of a publicly available lawsuit.

She'd ducked into the locker room, planning to get in a quick workout in the weight room while the soccer team practiced outdoors. There'd be no one eyeing her ass when she did squats, craning their necks for a glimpse down her sports bra during clean-and-jerks.

She moved through the workout, finishing just as the boys trooped back into the gym, and congratulated herself on her timing, ducking into the locker room before they had time to see her and launch their usual catcalls.

She was toweling off after her shower in the darkened locker room when she heard voices—male voices, prompting the flicker she'd felt just a few moments earlier, a premonition then, full-blown now, the unease that comes from being alone in a place supposedly reserved for girls, but inexplicably filling with boys.

It could have ended then, with Ana hastily pulling on her T-shirt and shorts and singing out "Occupied!" The boys, abashed, backing out, scattering apologies behind them. But as she held her breath, towel clutched tight around her, waiting for them to leave, the next voice she heard was Sami's, high, confused.

"This is room for girls."

"That's right." Cody.

"But we boys."

"No. *We* boys. You—you're a girl. You're a little bitch, Sami."

Low laughter.

Poor Sami. Ana had wondered if schools were the same the world over; if in Iraq and wherever he'd been in between, kids ganged up on each other the same way, always somebody's turn to be the weak one, the rest tingling with mingled excitement at whatever might happen next, and gratitude that, at least on this day, they weren't the target.

"I no bitch." Anger laced Sami's voice. *Good for him*, Ana thought.

"You're a bitch. Because you haven't been initiated."

"In-ish-ate-ed?" Sami sounded out the word.

"It's what shows you're really one of us."

The silence of a collectively held breath, Ana's as well as the boys'. Something clattered onto the floor, followed by a scooping sound as it evidently was retrieved.

"I don't want."

"What's the matter? You a pussy? Terrorist like you, afraid? I don't believe it." Cody's voice again, soft, insinuating.

"No pussy. It's *haram*."

What could *it* be? That ominous clattering sound, something hard, hurtful. Ana had heard stories: JV players afraid to move up to varsity. Dark rites. A boy who'd abruptly quit the team, but couldn't shed the nickname Broomstick Ben, limping for days after what they'd done to him.

"*Har*-what?"

"Forbidden."

"Because of some Islam thing? Well, guess what? You're one of us now. This will prove it."

A scuffle sounded. A strangled cry. Ana reached for her phone; a confused notion that maybe she should call 911—a thought banished as quickly as it arose, the teenage prohibition against snitching so absolute as to be paralyzing.

She peeped around the corner, not knowing what to expect. Thinking she might see anything at all other than the scene unfolding before her, Sami stretched face-down on a bench, the boys bending over him. Pants bunched around his ankles. A whimper slipped between Ana's lips.

"What the hell was that?"

Ana leapt for the rear door in long strides, towel falling away, arm outstretched, fingers actually touching the handle, before they reached her, hands on her shoulders, around her waist, dragging her back into the room, throwing her up against the row of lockers where Sami now stood, sweatpants drawn up, face chalky.

"What are you doing here? How long have you been here? What did you see?"

Cody's words so like a series of slaps that her head snapped back with each question. "Nothing," she stammered, hunched, upper arms across her breasts, hands folded over her crotch. "Nothing. I just got here."

"You going to say anything?"

Her lips went numb, vocal cords frozen. She shook her head.

"Leave her!" Sami's voice half-command, half-plea.

"Shut up. And don't move." As if he could go anywhere, as if either of them could, the four boys a wall of immovable muscle between them and the door. "I want you to see this. Let's get some insurance." Cody stepped forward, phone raised, nodding to the other boys. Two of them grabbed her arms, pulling them wide, her small flat breasts exposed, nipples contracting in the cold. Before she could move, he stood back and clicked a couple of photos.

"You say anything, either of you, and the whole school sees those pictures. Now get out of here." He wrinkled his nose and slid his tongue along the inside of his lower lip as if he tasted something bad. Sami scrambled from the room. But other boys held Ana a few moments more, all of them clustering close, an opportunity not to be missed, fingers exploring, laughing, jostling for a turn, leaving marks on her psyche that no matter how long she stood under scalding water in the innumerable showers she took over the next days and weeks, scrubbing her skin brick-red and sandpapery, would never be erased.

* * *

Footsteps sounded a fusillade across Colombia's warped wooden floor.

"Here comes trouble," breathed Claudette. Unnecessarily.

Susan stood over their table. "I hope you're satisfied."

The phone, its ringer silenced, vibrated against the table.

"Aren't you going to answer that?"

"No. What do you want?"

Susan ignored Claudette and spoke directly to Julia. "You couldn't send her to me, could you?"

"Why?" Julia remembered the time—yesterday? the day before?—when Susan reliably intimidated her. Now, she noticed that Susan's carefully styled hair was oily at the roots, her eyeliner applied a little too heavily, as though in a hurry, and smudged as a result.

"So I could prosecute the boys."

"You would never prosecute this. Not even a misdemeanor charge for what they did to Ana, let alone what happened to Sami." Julia nearly jumped at the sound of her own voice, low and fierce. "In a million years, you weren't going to go up against the Landers family. Because Tibbits would destroy you, and then you'd lose the next election. And you'd never, ever be a judge."

Give Susan credit. She went down fighting. "You're pathetic. As though you wouldn't have done anything to get out of that bullshit job. The job you ended up losing anyway." She drew up, the old Susan reinhabiting herself, raccoon eyes and all.

"You're right. I wouldn't do *anything*."

Susan spoke a beat too late. "Besides, without Sami, the other alleged victim"—investing the words with a sneer—"the only person who could verify her story, there's no case. As you know."

Claudette rose and stood in front of Susan, arms crossed, so close as to nearly touch her, and glared down at her, a move patented by legions of male attorneys. Claudette especially delighted in turning it back on them, but today Susan had earned it.

She raised her voice above the juddering phone.

"Isn't it about time you left?"

46

Cody made good on his threat.

The photo of Ana's breasts flashed through cyberspace, onto phones and iPads and even the old-school monitors that clueless parents set up in kitchens or living rooms or other public spaces as a way of assuring themselves that their children wouldn't get into trouble on the internet. And the photo looked like pure porn, if there was such a thing, Ana's head thrown back, mouth agape in agony that mimicked pleasure. Captions abounded, the printable ones variations on a theme of "She liked it."

Julia felt sorry for her poor phone, that palm-size collection of aluminum and glass, in danger of self-destructing, so continuously did it vibrate with incoming texts and alerts.

"I hope you're happy. You've ruined that girl's life." That message, devoid of profanity, ranked as kindness. The rest, well. She was used to all of it by now. Except the messages from Dom. She swiped past those, the sense of betrayal leaking through the phone in the very letters of his name, unable to bring herself to click on the actual words, to read the things she would have said were the situation reversed.

Nothing to do now but wait. The school had a prescribed amount of time to file its response. At home, she tried to fit herself into Beverly's routine, by now well-established, a daily dance of preparing meals and caring for Calvin, lessons masquerading as games, morning and afternoon breaks out of doors, no matter the weather.

Julia felt like an intruder, always at the margins, hastening to wash up after meals, fold laundry, tagging along on the outings to the park, averting her eyes from the cross streets that led to the center of town, where people headed off to offices and places like Colombia.

Every day, she called the hospital for the report on Sami's condition, the sum total of information it was allowed to release within the strictures of federal HIPAA laws. Every day, she received the same answer. "Critical but stable. No change."

"For heaven's sake, Julia," Beverly said one day when she caught Julia attacking the bookshelves with a feather duster. "Don't you have to file some briefs or whatever sorts of things you do in this case you're pursuing?"

Julia contemplated winging the duster past Beverly's head. No, she didn't have to file any briefs. No way left to defend her case against the response that she was sure would come from the likes of Tibbits, featuring cookie-cutter denials from Cody and his teammates, the word of one awkward loner of a girl (to which words like "hysterical" and "unreliable" inevitably would be applied) no match for that of a half-dozen All-American boys, bolstered by the opinions of the sort of experts Tibbits would be able to afford.

She'd been so taken with her own idea that she'd failed to think it through, guilty of acting on impulse, not much better in that regard in her own way than Ray Belmar was in his. How many times had she berated him: "Jesus, Ray. Couldn't you see where this would end up?"

For sure, she knew how she was going to end up. In virtual shreds on the courtroom floor.

So she was grateful for the sound of the doorbell that put an end to her thoughts, rushing with duster in hand past Beverly to answer it.

47

THEY LOOKED ALMOST like brother and sister, so tall and dark-haired and strong-jawed, the mother youthful in jeans and one of those slouchy sweaters that looked chic on the right person.

Stewart Jones's mother was the right person. She stood, one hand on cocked hip, eyes fierce, determined, in contrast to those of her son, whose gaze stayed firmly fixed on his shoes.

Julia stood aside, the ridiculous duster in her hand. "Come in. I was hoping you'd call." Trying to sound like she'd actually expected it.

Laura Jones practically dragged her son across the doorjamb. "I thought this was better done in person. It's not like you're hard to find. Your address is all over the internet. I think I'm supposed to burn your house down. That's one option, anyway."

Was she making a joke?

Julia looked more closely at her. Despite the insouciant attitude, the woman had the pouchy eyes that betrayed sleepless nights. Her words came fast and flat. No, not joking, just trying to fill the dead air between them.

Julia tried, too. "Come on into the kitchen. There's coffee." She heard a muffled commotion. The back door opened and closed. That would be Beverly, hustling Calvin off to the park early.

"No coffee, thank you. This won't take long. Stewart has some-thing to say to you."

The feather duster fell from Julia's hand. It bounced off the floor in an explosion of motes.

Stewart's mother dropped his arm, and she and Julia turned as one to the boy who finally began to talk, filling in the holes in Ana's story.

*   *   *

"Cody started it," he said. "Calling him Terrorist, I mean. It was just a nickname. You know, kind of like Badass."

Except that no one talked about the 9/11 attackers as badasses. Julia bit her tongue.

"We all thought it was funny. Sami did, too."

Did he really? Julia imagined Sami in yet another new place, yet another new language, uncertain, feeling his way. Of course he went along with it. And of course the other players would tell themselves he liked it. The oldest defense in the world.

"And then there was, you know, other stuff. Fouling him out in practice, seeing how he'd react. To, uh, see how he'd do in a real game."

That was one way of looking at it. *Hazing* might be another way.

"Burkle told Cody to knock it off. I think he even went to the principal. But nobody can touch Cody. Burkle knows that. So he tried to get Sami to quit the team. But Sami—I'll give him this. He's tough. He wouldn't quit." Admiration crept into Stewart's voice. Frustration, too. "He should've just quit!" His voice rose.

"Stewart." Julia couldn't bring herself to use the nickname, Chewie too lighthearted, incongruous for where the conversation was about to go. "What happened in the locker room?"

"Cody decided"—Christ, didn't any of these boys think for themselves?—"that if Sami wasn't going to quit, he had to be one of us, really one of us. He'd need the Triple Threat."

"The what?"

Stewart held out his arm and pushed up the sleeve of his sweatshirt nearly to the shoulder, turning slightly so that Julia could see the three raised X's of scar tissue on his bicep.

"What the . . . ?" She sounded more stupid by the moment.

Laura Jones rescued her with a grimace. "The X's mean triple threat. X-rated, they call it, too. Apparently it's a soccer thing. They all have them. Cutting each other with a razor blade, a penknife. What could go wrong?"

Like what happened in the locker room. Something gone very wrong indeed.

"So they gave Sami one, too."

Julia tried to put herself in Sami's place, the confusion at finding himself in the girls' locker room, the press of his teammates, arms and legs caught in an unbreakable grip, clothing pulled roughly aside. The sudden sharp pain of the blade—all of it to a backdrop of feral laughter. The mix of terror and fury and humiliation.

So that's what the boys had been doing to him. Not the sexual assault that Ana had imagined. No, they'd saved that for her. She fought back her rising nausea, clearing her throat to rid it of the bitter taste. Because there was one more thing.

"What about the beat-down? After the charges were dropped."

"Yeah. Well. That got out of hand."

"So, unlike the locker room, you were there for it."

A shrug. His mother flinched.

"You bastards." The words slipped out. Would she never learn to stop herself?

"That's what I said." Laura Jones again. Julia liked her more by the moment. If, in the years to come, Calvin ventured into unthinkable territory, something hurtful, maybe even illegal, would she rush to his side, in simultaneous defense and insistence that he do the right thing? And would Calvin, like Stewart, go along as nonchalantly as Stewart was trying to appear?

While his mother's face was hot with shame, Stewart's held an expression she couldn't quite read, not quite pride, but a close cousin. Maybe he looked forward to the sort of notoriety this would bring, had rolled the dice on a scenario that could either label him a traitor, forever cast out—or see him assume the king's throne.

With a mother like that, how had Stewart turned out to be such an asshole? On the other hand, he was here now, talking, telling her things that would juice her lawsuit in invaluable ways. She gave herself a moment to salivate over the possibilities and then said the thing she knew she had to say.

"Would you be willing to tell the police what you just told me?"

Because no matter how much Susan Parrish wished the case would go away, there'd be no way she could avoid filing criminal charges against Cody and his crew, not with a direct eyewitness. Julia's lawsuit would have to play second fiddle.

*   *   *

She waited a few minutes after Laura and her son departed, then drove to the police station, scanning the parking lot behind it, making sure the silver Lexus that had deposited Laura and Stewart at her door was really there. She fed a meter across the street, got back into her car and turned the heat on high, slouching down, waiting, wondering. She looked at her watch. It didn't take long.

Dan Tibbits strode up the street, arms swinging, coattails flapping, pedestrians whirling and scattering like a school of fish at the appearance of a shark. He moved so fast the department's automatic door barely had time to fully open before he passed within. Time slowed. People came and went. Solid citizens, tickets in hand, visiting the Parking Authority, which shared office space with the cops. The grievance-prone, bearing fat manila envelopes full of painstakingly collected "evidence," hoping to get an audience with a cop willing to arrest a neighbor, a city councilman, a judge, whoever had unwittingly offended them in ways they were convinced were illegal.

A man in a business suit approached at a dead run, face contorted, grabbing the automatic door and pulling it wider when it failed to open quickly enough. Stewart's father, if she had to guess. At one point, a cop escorted a slight man in cuffs into the building. Julia was pretty sure it was Ray Belmar, which meant the cop in question knew as well as she did the cuffs were unnecessary.

She grew drowsy in the car's blasting heat. She turned it down and cracked the window and worked her fingers through the opening, then touched them to her face, coming fully awake at her own cold touch and the sight of a knot of people leaving the building: a weeping Laura Jones and the man in the suit, followed by Stewart, with a cop on one side and a red-faced, gesticulating Tibbits on the other.

She knew they were on their way to the jail, where Stewart would be booked and processed and—given that he had an attorney at his side and the Joneses clearly had the means to post bond— immediately released to his parents' custody, thus keeping his name off the publicly available jail roster. She didn't bother to trail their vehicles to make sure. Instead, she found her phone and rang up Chance.

"You'll want to check the police reports," she said without preamble.

"Hey, Julia. Sorry about your job. What am I looking for?"

"Stewart-with-an-e-w Jones. Could be problematic. He might be a juvie." Shit. She'd forgotten to check whether he was a junior or senior, and either way, he might not be eighteen yet. On the other hand, given the issue at hand, he might be facing charges as an adult. "And keep an eye out for Cody Landers's name to pop up, along with the other two boys on that godforsaken soccer team."

"Are you saying what I think you're saying?"

She lowered the window all the way. The cold felt like hope, bringing the blood rushing through her veins, banishing the lassitude of the last few weeks. She almost smiled.

"You're the reporter, Chance. You figure it out."

48

CHANCE FIGURED IT out fast, and played it well, waiting until he'd positioned himself and a photographer outside Cody Landers's house, not giving his editor the go-ahead to hit "send" on his initial story about Stewart's arrest until the cop cars pulled up, thus ensuring the exclusive photos of Cody being led from the home in handcuffs.

The wait proved agonizing for Julia, hitting refresh on the paper's website until her thumb went numb, causing Beverly to order her upstairs to her room if she was going to continue ignoring her son like that. Which she was, until the story broke like a rogue storm cell over the town, making memories of previous tempests—the original accusation against Sami and the resulting demonstrations; the charges against him being dropped and still more protests; her own lawsuit—also being dropped, now that criminal charges had been filed against the boys—seem like summer squalls.

The national press returned to town so quickly she wondered if they'd chartered planes—Duck Creek's airport wasn't exactly on the major travel routes—and proved the wisdom of Stewart's strategy.

"The Boy Who Told," read one of the headlines, the laudatory story accompanied by a photo of Stewart, backlit and shot from below, lonely, heroic, his face in shadow. (The better, Julia thought uncharitably, to hide his smirk.) It quoted liberally from the threats on social media, the dead rat tossed on his parents' doorstep, Camp Cody dwindling but its remaining members in full-throated cry.

But it quoted others, too, one person after another praising Stewart's courage, the example he'd set for others, the proof that not all young people were unthinking sycophants. His mother: "I couldn't be more proud of my son."

Still, Cody and the other boys were—like Stewart—out on bail and back in school.

"It's been made painfully clear to me that, legally, I can't suspend or expel them," Dom was quoted as saying.

Julia felt a stab of empathy, uncomfortably tinged with longing. Then reminded herself that if Dom had acted earlier, none of this might have happened. Something Ana reminded her in a despairing phone call. "I'm never going to get away from those jerks."

Julia had successfully applied for, and obtained, a restraining order requiring the boys to keep a certain distance from Ana, a near-impossibility in a school as small as Duck Creek High. Nonetheless, class schedules were juggled, despite Dan Tibbits's very public position that it would have been easier to arrange online classes for Ana.

"I'm not going to treat someone who did nothing wrong like a pariah," Dom shot back in an acerbic exchange caught by local television cameras, his comment almost enough to tug Julia toward forgiveness.

"I just want to hit Cody whenever I see him," Ana told Julia over the phone. "He and his friends know exactly how far they have to stay back. They take a cafeteria table just that far away from me and then they just sit there and look at me. They don't say anything. They don't have to. And the whole cafeteria watches me and watches them. I want to wait until Spaghetti Day and then walk over and throw my tray in their obnoxious faces."

Julia groaned. "Please don't. Dan Tibbits will clean the floor with both of us."

"You mean I'm just supposed to take it? The way Cody wanted me to? I should have told right away. And I would have. The hell with Cody and his stupid pictures. Half the girls in school have put their tits all over Snapchat. But Sami made me promise. He said he'd rather spend the rest of his life in jail than have anyone know. He was so ashamed, not just about what they did to him, but because he ran away and left me there. Even though I told him it didn't matter. But it did to him. It's not fair."

It wasn't fair, Julia agreed. But that's the way it was. If an assault victim acted in a perfectly understandable way by lashing out at her tormenter, she'd be labeled hysterical and thus unreliable, and of course what was "unreliable" but a euphemism for liar?

"It sucks," Julia finished.

"It fucking sucks. And I'm not going to take it."

"Ana!"

But she'd hung up.

*   *   *

By the time Julia caught wind of Ana's decision to take her revenge, the whole town had seen it.

When the knock came at Beverly's front door, she wouldn't have been surprised to see a process server, or even Dan Tibbits himself, although for the life of her she couldn't figure out just how Tibbits would go after Ana. But figuring out just such a move was Tibbits's stock in trade.

She held up a hand to forestall Beverly, who rose partway from her chair at the sound of the doorbell.

"It's probably for me. I'll get it."

"Watch out for flaming paper bags." Beverly's wry attempt at humor, harkening back to what now appeared a more innocent time, when they'd thought burning dogshit was as bad as things would get.

Julia stiffened her spine, opened the door a crack, and stood in utter open-mouthed silence at the sight of Dom holding on for dear life to a bouquet of roses.

The flowers trembled violently in his unsteady grip, throwing off waves of fragrance. He thrust them toward her. "Roses."

"I see that." Her voice surprised her, so level and calm.

"Corny, I know. I maybe should've gotten some other kind. But I don't know anything about flowers."

Somehow the bouquet ended up in her hands, their stems wrapped in some sort of cottony protective covering. The thorns, thus blunted, nonetheless pressed against her palm. She said nothing, seeking to project a frosty disdain. Her face betrayed her, bending automatically toward the flowers, their petals silken against her cheeks.

"I didn't know how else to apologize."

"For what?" The roses stirred at her whispered words.

"You were right to name me in your suit. I'd have brought these even if you hadn't dropped it."

At Ana's parents' urging—and with Ana's permission—Julia had withdrawn her suit as soon as charges had been filed against the boys, with the option to refile if things went south in the criminal case.

"When Burkle came to me and told me the guys were hassling Sami, I brushed it off. I told him we couldn't fight his battles for him. That he'd only lose face. I'm so sorry."

Julia's head jerked up. *Never* apologize. A lawyer's first advice to a client, anytime, anywhere, under any circumstances. No matter how human—and ethical—the impulse, all an apology ever accomplished was a shitstorm of legal liability.

"Chickenshit. That's what I was. If I'd had half the guts—hell, not even half, just the smallest fraction—as Ana, none of this ever would have happened." Part of her resisted his apology. For all his belief in Sami's innocence, he'd failed the boy, and failed him badly. But then, so had she. Maybe it was time to find a way forward.

Julia couldn't help herself. The face she raised from the flowers beamed so brightly she'd later wonder that the flowers hadn't wilted beneath the warmth of her smile. "These are beautiful. And I'd love to talk about it. But not here."

His own smile mirrored hers and she remembered the first time she'd seen it, the two of them standing in the jail parking lot, her startled reaction to the way it transformed his face.

"Veritas?"

The wine bar, where they'd ended up kissing like teenagers in the inadequate shelter of a doorway. Maybe that's not what he had in mind. Or maybe he did.

"Just let me put these in water and get my coat. I'll be right out."

*   *   *

They'd barely taken their seats at Veritas when two glasses of champagne appeared.

"Sorry, wrong table," Dom told the hovering server. "We haven't ordered yet."

The server set down the glasses, shot through with glittering threads of bubbles. "It's because of her." He nodded toward Julia. "Compliments of the owner." Then, in a whisper, "His daughter and Ana are friends. Ana's video—" He shook his head admiringly. "That girl's got some serious stones."

Julia couldn't help herself. She had to see again. She pulled out her phone, turned the sound down low, and pulled up the video that Ana must have arranged for a friend to shoot.

It showed a school hallway in full early-morning bustle, students milling about the lockers, gossiping in groups, waiting for the clanging command for homeroom. But then the hallway cleared, the groups breaking apart, people pressing themselves against the lockers. The soccer team approached in a phalanx, Cody taking point, a bit of a roll in his walk, head dipping and then coming back up, a bull looking to hook something on his horns. He stopped—they all did—presumably within the prescribed distance of Ana, and cupped his hands before his chest, his snigger nearly drowned out by the collective gasp.

"Hey, fuckface." Ana's voice rang out.

The frozen statues came alive, locker denizens fumbling for their phones, holding them high, because God, this was going to be good.

"The only way you got to see these world-class tits was to have your boys hold me down. Anyway, I hear tits aren't really what you were interested in. I hear what you really liked was carving on Sami's ass. You. Sick. Fuck."

Movement far down the hallway, near the front. The video jerked, momentarily focusing on Celia Walks On stepping out of her office, looking down the hall, shielding her eyes against the glare of sun through the windows, trying to figure out what was going on.

The camera swung back to Ana, fumbling at her abdomen. A quick metallic sound, then she was turning around, peeling down her jeans and underwear, calling out a ringing challenge—"Carve on this"—the morning sunshine highlighting the round bright moon she flashed at Cody Landers.

At which point, for all practical purposes, Team Cody went down to defeat.

*   *   *

Julia and Dom clinked glasses.

"I've looked at the numbers," he said. "Her video has way more views than the one he shared of her, uh, chest. I hear stories—kids saying, 'No means no,' when Cody walks by, stuff like that. I suppose I should put a stop to kids tormenting him the way he tormented Sami, but I haven't been able to bring myself to do it yet."

He lifted the empty glass and rolled the stem between his fingers. "Not enough of this stuff in the world to get that image out of my mind of what they did to him. No wonder he wouldn't talk about it."

"I know. Ana said she'd been trying for weeks to get him to tell, but he was afraid they'd do even worse if anyone found out. Which is exactly what happened, except that they didn't even wait for anyone to find out. Remember when you told me about the store clerk saying he'd bought those Band-Aids? It makes sense now. He must have wanted to cover up those Xs. You know, the first time I saw him, when I interviewed him in jail, he was limping. I just didn't make anything of it at the time."

She'd feel guilty forever, she thought, and that seemed appropriate.

He reached for her phone and flipped it face down. "It seems like this is all we ever talk about. Let's try something else. Something cheerful. What about your little boy? What's he up to these days? He's at that age where they seem to change every day, right? What's the latest?"

When was the last time anyone asked her about Calvin in a way that had nothing to do with his daily needs, or school, or scheduling? When she got to talk about who he was?

Ever since Michael's death, she'd composed bitter mental letters, blaming him for what he was missing. What if they'd been celebratory instead? Michael would have delighted in every milestone, would have loved hearing the sarcastic descriptions of Calvin's morning enjoyment of the toast and jam forbidden to Julia, of his unholy alliance with Lyle, and of the way his very presence smoothed even Beverly's jagged edges.

Dom prodded for more details, and still more, not just about Calvin, but about *her*—all the usual things, where she'd grown up, law school—and suddenly she was talking about Michael, how they'd met, the too-soon surprise that was Calvin, Michael's decision to fast-forward their progress toward financial security by enlisting, until she came to the day the officers had arrived at her door. She stopped, hand to her mouth.

"Now I'm the one who needs to apologize. I didn't mean to be a downer."

He touched his hand to hers. "May I?"

She nodded, wordless, as he folded her hands between his.

"Let's make a pact. No more apologizing. By either of us. We've each got enough baggage to get us banned from the airlines for life— although please don't think I'd ever dare to equate my divorce to your own loss."

Julia nodded. "Deal. And, seriously, it's okay." Which—as though speaking the words made it so—it was. She felt light, floaty, an easing of resentments clutched so close for so long that they'd come to seem normal. Sharing the memories of Michael, rather than making her grow cold with anger, had warmed with fondness. Spiky thorns of acrimony still jabbed at her, to be sure, but she sensed softening, shrinking, wearing down; could begin to envision a future where they lay dormant. A future starting now.

A slow smile stretched her lips. Dom smiled back, a little uncertain.

"Are you thinking what I'm thinking?"

"I'm not sure," he said. "But I'll hazard a guess. That we should probably pay up?"

"No probably about it."

And so they reprised their departure from Veritas, more starvation kisses in a doorway until noses froze and dripped unattractively; a quick discussion of the unavailability of either of their domiciles, a decision to continue the discussion in Dom's car, parked in a darkened lot behind the bar, where—heat blasting and windows fogged—the discussion devolved into a tearing removal of just enough layers to enable the sort of thing that saw people ending up on Julia's weekly jail list, and *oh*, the single coherent thought that crossed her mind was that jail would be worth it, yes it would.

CHAPTER

49

Julia slept so late the next morning, indulging in the one benefit of unemployment, that an exasperated Beverly sent Calvin to
wake her, something he accomplished by flinging the cat onto the
bed and then scrambling away from the ensuing pandemonium.

Despite the lateness of the hour, she took her own sweet time in
the shower, running her hands over a body too long neglected and
now reveling in its reawakened powers. "We'll do this better next
time," Dom had said as they'd disentangled themselves, and even
now, so many hours later, she caught her breath at the joy evoked by
the words *next time*.

She ran down the stairs, scooped Calvin into her arms for a hug
so extravagant that he wriggled away with a protesting "yuck," and
dodged Beverly's suspicious gaze by making a great show of donning
coat and hat with an announcement that she was already late for
her daily visit to Sami and she'd just grab a yogurt in the hospital
cafeteria.

At the hospital—perhaps because the universe, apparently bored
with raining disaster upon Duck Creek, had decided to grant it a
day of jubilant sunshine—Jamilah hovered just inside a door marked
"Patients and Families Only." She ran into the cold at Julia's approach.

Julia hesitated. She'd spent too many days enveloped in Jamilah's
icy despair to trust this apparent thaw. And indeed, Jamilah's words,
when she greeted Julia, were tempered with a hard-won caution. Still,
a smile toyed with the corners of her mouth as she spoke.

"He has awoken. Again. A few words. *Mama. Abba.*" Her voice quavered and she pressed her lips together until she regained control. "No visitors this time. They are more careful. But the doctor said the important signs are good. He is going to give—what is it called? When he talks to them?" She pointed to the main entrance.

Julia belatedly noticed the renewed presence of the television vans in the parking lot, a new one rumbling in even as they spoke, the reporters hustling toward a podium set up in front of the large doors, jostling for position, setting their cell phones beside the microphone, photographers and camera people staking out the prime spots, Chance stubbornly planted front and center, bracing himself against the surging pack. Its members stomped their feet against the cold and banged gloved hands together. The unlucky ones cursed with operating equipment blew on bare fingers, the local reporters recognizable by their use of gloves with the fingertips cut away. A cloud of condensation rose above them.

"A news conference?"

"Yes, yes. In just a few minutes."

Julia looked an apology toward Jamilah. "Do you mind?"

The smile won out, Jamilah relaxing into it, able for the first time in weeks to focus, albeit briefly, on someone other than her son, permitting herself the luxury of generosity. She gave Julia a little shove toward the group.

"Go. I will sit with my boy."

Julia shocked herself by pulling Jamilah toward her for a hug. First the kiss on Claudette's cheek, now the embrace with Jamilah. Who next—Beverly?

Laughing at that particular impossibility, she joined the other looky-loos drawn by the commotion just as the doctor emerged from the hospital.

*   *   *

The doctor, hatless, coatless, and gloveless, didn't waste any time.

"This will be our only news conference regarding Sami Moham-med's condition. We're releasing this information with the permis-sion of his parents. Following this, those of you who persist in calling our switchboard three, four, five times a day will be given the same information as before, the only information we're permitted to release under HIPAA regulations: his condition, nothing else.

"I expect that for many weeks hence, that condition will continue to be just as has been reported for the last few, with the exception of that very sobering incident of a couple of weeks ago; that is, stable. However, as of the last twenty-four hours, the word 'stable' represents a marked improvement, one that all signs now indicate will be slow, but steady, recovery.

"Mr. Mohammed suffered grievous injuries, the most serious of which were, of course, the head injuries. A shattered orbital bone—" He touched the ridge defining his eye socket. "A crush injury to the skull with resulting IC—intracranial—bleed.

"Several broken ribs, one of which punctured a lung. Both arms and legs broken from injuries that I would attribute to stomping, probably with heavy Vibram-soled boots of the type that construction workers or wildland firefighters wear. And, of course, the more superficial injuries; the abrasions and deep contusions, and the somewhat older scar on the buttocks in the shape of a swastika . . ."

The scrum surged forward, a wave threatening to capsize the podium, screaming questions in a single incoherent voice. The doctor's hands flew up. He took a step back. Hospital security guards moved in close.

Julia couldn't hear anything over the word roaring in her head. *Swastika.*

No wonder Stewart had been so willing to accept responsibility, had strutted so smug among his peers. He thought he'd gotten away with it; that he and his teammates would be labeled mere schoolboy bullies, their hazing involving a silly soccer symbol, mere Xs, not the obscenely deformed cross.

But it was worse than anybody had thought.

The reporters finally regained the barest semblance of order, the doctor doing his best to answer the machine-gun bursts of questions. Somehow Julia, standing a bit away from the crowd, caught his eye. Maybe his gaze, seeking relief from the horde, strayed her way, alighting on the one person demanding nothing from him.

He could have withheld that bit of information, the scar hardly noteworthy among the grievous injuries that had very nearly taken Sami's life. The same with his remark about the boots. Maybe he'd seen Sami's "friends" during their visit, his teammates grouped around the bed, or swaggering back down the hall in their calf-high black laced boots, the three-hundred-dollar Whites you earned the right to wear only by passing the rigorous firefighting physical. Maybe he viewed the revelation as a bit of preventive medicine, a way of forcing people to face the ugly realities within their community, a bit of editorial comment among the dry recitation of facts. She nodded to him, a salute of sorts, and received the slightest grim nod in return, before he answered another question.

"Yes, I'm absolutely sure. There was no mistaking it for anything else. It was a swastika."

50

IT WAS, IN fact, one of the national reporters, one with a long experience writing about separatist groups, who dug up the same yearbook photo of the soccer team Julia had used, with the damning evidence staring into her unseeing face.

It dominated his paper's website, the caption and accompanying story pointing out that what Julia had interpreted as suburban kids' approximation of gang signs actually signaled white supremacy. Same with the stupid floppy-forelock hairstyle dubbed "fashy," short for fascist, vaguely resembling Hitler's.

"It was right there in front of me all the time."

"Wish you'd showed me that photo. That okay sign"—Claudette made the thumb-and-forefinger circle—"those groups adopted it a while back. Took people a while to catch on what they were about. Same with Pepe the Frog. He was just another innocuous cartoon, until he wasn't."

Julia groaned. "I know. The firefighter boots, too. I can't believe it took the doctor's mentioning it for me to factor it in. Those boys. They must have come to the hospital that day to threaten him one more time not to talk. They came closer to killing him with their words than when they beat him up."

Claudette had joined Julia and Beverly and Calvin at the playground, one of the few places around town that seemed free of reporters demanding Julia's thoughts on the situation. Not just reporters.

Everybody in town seemed to have an opinion, and no one seemed shy about expressing it.

The tussle in the locker room was one thing. A substantial contingent held fast to the boys-will-be-boys version that saw the "XXX" triple-threat scars as distasteful, but no worse than the tattoos and piercings kids inflicted upon their bodies. Maybe the so-called swastika was just a triple-threat marking gone awry? As for Ana's part in it, who knew what had really happened there? It was within the realm of possibility that she'd flashed her breasts at the boys, because you know how bold girls are these days.

The white supremacist business, though. Even if they were just fooling around, that was a different matter.

"Karl Schmidt tried to tell me." Julia lifted a go-cup of coffee to her lips. Claudette had ducked into Colombia on her way to the playground. "All those sly hints. Do you think those boys were in cahoots with him all along?"

Steam wreathed Claudette's face as she sipped at her own coffee. "Maybe. You can see where they might think it was fun, running around in the woods with guns, getting ready for the apocalypse. But I don't think that's what these kids are into. For one thing, there's such a class divide between them and Karl. The only people like him they run into are the school custodians and lunch ladies. For them, I think it's more about that whole aggrieved white male thing. You know, how the likes of you and me are coming along taking their jobs, ruining their futures as movers and shakers."

They sat in silent acknowledgment of the sort of thing they'd heard their whole working lives, the reality that no matter how many cases they won, they'd always be resented as diversity hires, with Claudette facing an extra helping of dismissal as a "twofer."

Calvin waved from the top of the slide, then belly-flopped onto it and zipped down head-first into Beverly's waiting arms, knocking her backward into the dirt. The two arose laughing, brushing dust from their clothes, and Calvin ran to the ladder for another go.

Julia thought of the Beverly of old in her pearls and little heels. Much of that Beverly remained, her back still ruler-straight, makeup carefully applied, and hair waved and sprayed into submission, even for a trip to the playground. But there was a hint of nonchalance about her, her gestures more expansive, her laughter freer. All those years of iron control, making herself over to insinuate herself with the ruling dowagers of Duck Creek—only to see it go to hell when her daughter-in-law had taken over Sami Mohammed's defense. Was life better for Beverly without all that striving? Would it be better for Julia herself when she got over the fact that she was no longer a public defender? She dug deep within, searching for a sense of liberation, and came up dry.

"I'm not taking anybody's job now," she reminded Claudette. "Unless I go after Susan's"—a nod to the fact that Susan Parrish had resigned as county attorney the day after the doctor's press conference.

"My daughter is just entering high school," Susan had said— conveniently glossing over the fact that Elena was already a sophomore—at a brief press conference of her own, no questions taken, to announce her departure. "My job is so demanding. At this stage of both our lives, I feel my time is better spent at home, during these last few years before she goes off to college." The same spending-more-time-with-the-family excuse trotted out by everyone ever pushed out of a job.

The Debra hotline had Susan job-hunting at the big firms on the coast—East or West, it didn't matter—the only sticking point being the custody that she and Dom shared. Julia had gone faint at the thought of Dom's predicament, the possibility that Susan might fight to take Elena with her, but Dom affected a blithe unconcern. "She won't pull Elena out of her school this close to graduation. And once Elena goes to college both of us will lose her anyway. Susan is, above all, a pragmatist. Given everything else she's dealing with now, she's not going to get into a custody fight, too."

Claudette crumpled her cardboard go-cup in her hand, the sound bringing Julia back to the present. "About the job. Or, more to the point, your lack thereof." She raised her hand, took aim, and winged the cup toward the trash can. It sailed in. "Swish!" Claudette pumped her fist, then turned to Julia. "I'm supposed to play emissary today."

"Mom. Mom." Calvin appeared at her knee, out of breath. "Gamma says we can have ice cream."

Julia tried the same trick with her own coffee cup, only to see it land far short of the basket. She got up, retrieved it, deposited in the trash can, and returned to the bench, tucking her hands under her arms. "Ice cream? In this weather? And before dinner?"

Beverly approached. "After everything we've all been through, I think ice cream is the least we can do. Join us, Claudette? I'll go get the car."

"Don't have to convince me," Claudette said. She pulled Calvin into her lap and spoke over his head. "Li'l—um." She put her hands over Calvin's ears. "Li'l Pecker wants to know if you'd be willing to come back."

Beverly's willingness to indulge in midafternoon ice cream cones had been one shock. This new one knocked the wind out of Julia. She blinked, shook her head, blinked again. Yes, that was Claudette sitting beside her, an expectant look on her face. She must have misunderstood.

"What did you just say?"

"You heard right. What do you think?"

Beverly's car drifted to the curb. Calvin leapt from Claudette's lap and ran for it. Julia sat as still and frozen as the clumsily fashioned snowmen scattered throughout the park.

"But they eliminated my position. There's no job to come back to."

"Somebody's leaving. There's an opening." Claudette rose and followed Calvin toward the car. "Forget a cone. I'm going for a banana split. Want to share? And what do you want me to tell him? Want your job back?"

Hell, no. Not in a million years. Go fuck yourself, Li'l Pecker. You don't get to use me to make yourself look good.

"Can I start tomorrow?"

*   *   *

Ray Belmar grinned through a newly split lip and turned his head so that he could see Julia out of his good eye, the other one purple and swollen as a baby eggplant.

"Good morning, gorgeous. What's got you all aglow?"

"Swear to God, Ray, if I didn't know better, I'd say you went out and got yourself beaten up just so you could come harass me." She opened the file, scanning it yet again, looking for the nonexistent detail that could help him.

"You got it. But there's something seriously different about you. And it's not just the hair. Which is good, by the way."

She'd gone to a salon a couple of days earlier, forked over an inexcusable amount of money, and said, "Do something with it." *Something* turned out to be a chin-grazing bob, frizz tamed into sedate waves with the assistance of some goop that nearly doubled the size of her bill. She tucked a strand behind her ear and tried to keep Ray's attention on the matter at hand.

"And there's something seriously screwed up about you. This shit has got to stop. I'm not joking, Ray. You always manage to skate just below a felony, but someday you're going to cross that line and then you'll end up with real time, and there won't be a damn thing I can do about it."

His shoulders lifted in an exaggerated shrug. "Maybe I'm just a lost cause."

You and everybody else I deal with. But her success with Sami, accidental though it may have begun, had whetted an unexpected appetite for lost causes.

"Whoa. What's that?"

"What's what?" She inched her cuff down over wrist, but it was too late.

"Show me."

She sighed and pushed up her sleeve, exposing the wedge-shaped tattoo.

Ray turned his head this way and that, trying to make sense of it. "I give up. Is that . . . a piece of pie?"

"Blueberry." The tattoo artist had done an admirable job of inking in the tiny, detailed berries, and somehow incorporated her freckles into the browned crimping on the edge of the crust.

"But what does it mean?"

She told Ray the same thing she'd told the baffled tattoo artist. "It means I like pie."

She kept to herself the thought that the tattoo would serve as a reminder not to neglect the things she liked. But she'd indulged Ray far too long on the verboten subject of her appearance.

"Look here, Ray." She withdrew a pamphlet from the file. "There's a bed in a treatment center. I got you in. The judge'll have to sign off on it, of course. And you'll have to agree to play by the rules."

"I've never played by the rules in my life." He must have seen something in her face. Stopped. Cleared his throat a couple of times with a phlegmy, strangulated sound that went on far too long, then affected an airy unconcern. "Whatever, Thumbelina. Let's give it a whirl."

Ray didn't ever need to know it, but he'd just articulated her own new outlook on life.

* * *

Claudette at stood at her desk, files in her arms. She dumped them into a box when Julia walked in. "So?" she asked.

"So . . . ?" Julia prompted. Pavarotti whistled a long echoing note.

"When do you move into your new place?"

"What new place?"

"Oh, come on." Claudette yanked open a drawer, scooped out more files, filled the box, and drew a tape gun across the lid with a tearing sound. "You've been trying to get out from under your mother-in-law ever since I've known you. New hair, new guy—I figure a new place is next." She picked up a flat sheet of cardboard and fit notches and tabs together, assembling another box.

Julia chose a sliver of carrot from the vegetable dish and poked it through the bars of Pavarotti's cage. He extended one of his legs, grabbed it in his claw and pulled it into the cage, then nibbled delicately along its length, making little chirps of approval.

"About that."

Claudette stacked one box atop another and began filling a third. "What about it?"

"I'm saving a lot of money by staying with Beverly. And she seems to like babysitting Calvin. Given that he starts kindergarten next year, she says he won't be too much of a burden on her for too much longer. And she's—"

What *was* Beverly, exactly? Julia thought of all the words she'd mentally applied to her mother-in-law over the months. Pain in the ass. Stiff. Self-righteous. Oh, hell, she'd labeled the woman a stone-cold bitch.

Now, though . . . *stalwart*, maybe. Her unyielding nature had demonstrated its advantages. They might never be friends. But they'd come to a wary, circling sort of mutual appreciation.

Only the previous morning, Beverly had delivered the usual plate of slippery eggs and flabby strips of bacon. But, when Julia sat, Beverly joined her at the table, placing between them a plate stacked high with slices of toast, their surfaces soft with butter.

"I can't eat it all myself," she said at the look on Julia's face.

Julia luxuriated for a single instant in the thought of lofty rejection, of letting the toast go cold and limp. The moment passed. She snatched a piece, then another.

Beverly waited until her mouth was full before suggesting that Julia and Calvin stay on awhile.

"Financially, it makes sense," she said. As though that were the only reason.

Julia chewed frantically, trying to swallow her way to a reply.

"And now that I've quit bridge for good, I have so much time on my hands. Without Calvin, and with you working so many hours, I'd just rattle around the house by myself all day."

"You'll do that anyway, once he starts school." Julia spoke without thinking, then wished she could recall her unthinking cruelty. So many times, she'd wanted to slash back at Beverly. But the one time she hadn't meant to, she'd cut her anyway. She apologized the only way she could—"It's a lovely offer, Beverly"—and watched her mother-in-law stiffen in anticipation of the "but" to follow.

"And I'm happy to take you up on it."

She wasn't sure who was more surprised at the words, herself or Beverly, both of them now shifting uncomfortably in their seats, struggling to maintain their chilly formality. "As you said, it makes sense. And Calvin doesn't need any more disruption in his life."

"Exactly." Beverly latched onto the excuse as eagerly as Julia had claimed the toast, each of them turning her face away to hide a secret, satisfied smile.

Julia offered Claudette an inadequate summation. "It's better than it was."

The tape gun dropped from Claudette's hand and clattered across the floor. "Well, I'll be . . . I'll be . . . I don't know what I'll be. Surprised, I guess. Which is an understatement."

Julia retrieved the tape gun and held it out.

"What are you doing, anyway? Clearing space for new files?"

Claudette hemmed. She hawed. She fiddled with the tape gun, pulling out some tape, tearing it off, balling it up, tossing it toward the trash can. Nailed it, as usual.

"Out with it, Claudette. Whatever it is."

"You'd better sit down."

"Drama queen," Julia accused. Nonetheless, she sat.

"I'm taking Susan's job."

The shovel hadn't been invented that was capable of scraping Julia's jaw from the floor. She finally managed to close her mouth, only to have it flop open again.

"Wha—?" Even a single syllable was beyond her. She gulped, and miraculously achieved four.

"*Prosecutor?*"

Claudette shrugged. "Change of pace." She smiled. "And a big-ass raise. Not to mention that sweet office down the street."

"But." Claudette as foe, rather than friend? Claudette facing her across the well, towering in her stilettos, wiping up the floor with her because that's what Claudette did with her opponents.

"That's right," Claudette said, divining her thoughts. "I'm going to kick your ass every chance I get. But I won't be turning my back on you."

"Why's that?" Julia could barely speak past the tightness in her throat. After Sami's case, she'd envisioned them working more closely than ever before, not quite peers, but a step up from the mentor–baby lawyer relationship they'd had before. Claudette fitted Pavarotti's cover over his cage. "Because I know you'll be trying to kick mine right back. And the way you've come along, you might just land a few." Julia knew that was as close as Claudette would ever come to an embrace.

Claudette hooked an index finger through the metal ring atop Pavarotti's cage and swung it free from its stand.

"Got a sheriff's deputy waiting downstairs in a nice warm van to drive us the two blocks to my new office so Pavarotti doesn't catch cold."

She raised a hand as she walked away, waving without looking back, her big voice booming a farewell and a promise.

"See you in court."

CHAPTER

51

By February, everyone in Duck Creek—even the ski crowd—
was sick of the necessary layering.

Julia pulled on tights, long johns over the tights, and then pants.
Thin socks, heavy wool ones on top of them. On the worst days, she
wore glove liners and wool gloves inside heavy mittens. The walk to
work became a waddle, although her arrival inside the overheated
old courthouse, its radiators gasping and clanging, required a sort
of striptease, if one imagined flinging away bulky woolen sweaters
instead of flimsy bits of satin.

The darkness, of course, was its own sort of layer, reluctantly
peeling back at around nine in the morning, enfolding the town
again by four. Daytime showed as brief glimpses of gray through the
courthouse windows. Julia, along with everyone else in Duck Creek,
craved the lightness of summer, not just the sun, but its physical
aspects, the delicious freedom of stepping outside with arms and legs
bare, feet in sandals rather than heavy boots that dragged at every
step, movement easy and free rather than being restricted by layer
after layer of fabric.

Which Julia nonetheless pulled on, smiling, one Saturday morning. Because if nothing else, the sun had emerged from hibernation,
yawning and stretching as it were, spilling into long-dark crevices
and hearts. It laid a path across her bedroom floor to the door, beckoning her up and out. Lyle sprawled in the middle, his entire body
rumbling in a contented purr.

Julia stepped over him and moved awkwardly down the stairs that in less restrictive clothing she'd have taken two at a time.

Beverly stood at the stove, although a pair of eggs sat uncracked in a bowl on the counter, rather than already sliding around on a plate being thrust toward Julia. They'd each given some ground.

"Calvin and I have already eaten. You?"

Julia shook her head and ducked into the breakfast nook for a good-morning kiss to Calvin. "I have to go out for a while. But when I come back, we'll . . . we'll . . ." She tried to think of some fun indoors activity, although she was sure they'd exhausted all the obvious possibilities in the preceding weeks. Beverly would already have taken him to the park by the time she returned. "We'll figure out something."

She took her heavy down parka from the coat closet with a sigh. The sun, while delightful, had a nasty trick of shining without appreciable warmth.

"You won't need that." Beverly pointed to the bay window and its view of the sparkling, snow-covered yard. "Look at the thermometer. There's a chinook."

"What?" The coat dropped to the floor. Julia turned to the window and looked toward the thermometer fastened to a tree limb, a few feet above a birdbath's frozen surface. It read forty degrees—forty *above*—virtually tropical, compared to the mini–Ice Age of the previous few weeks.

Julia started shucking layers. The fleece vest fell atop the parka, followed by the turtleneck. She wriggled out of her pants, peeled away the long underwear, and added it to the pile. The thick wool socks followed with a flourish.

Even Beverly laughed, though unable to stop herself from issuing a command to scoop it all up and put things back where they belonged because the kitchen had not become an extension of the laundry room, no, it had not.

When Julia came back downstairs again, moving considerably more easily, Beverly performed her patented head-to-toe scan and posed her routine question, albeit with a slight variation.

"Is that what you're going to wear?" A pause so brief as to be nearly unnoticeable, if you didn't know Beverly and didn't know what it cost her to continue in an exaggeratedly casual tone. "To see your fella?"

It was the term she apparently found acceptable for the man who appeared to be moving into the position once occupied by her son; *boyfriend* a little too juvenile, and suggestive besides of romance; *lover*, unthinkable.

So, fella.

Julia, too, hesitated.

"Yes," she said. "Going to see my fella."

*   *   *

Dom lived a few blocks to the south, on the farthest reaches of Beverly's neighborhood—her neighborhood now, too, Julia reminded herself—having stayed behind in what had been his and Susan's starter home.

But Julia drove west toward the foothills that closed in on the long valley, past a swath of fields, stubble poking through snow, where a few farmers somehow hung on, their land too far from the ski hill for the kind of outlandish sales price that would allow a retirement complete with winters in sunny desert climes.

Her destination bumped up hard against the foothills, a last stretch of level land ringed by cottonwoods that in the summer would provide deep shade and the soothing sort of quiet enforced by the shushing of the breeze through their leaves. Now, their bare branches scratched at the sky. She parked in an otherwise empty lot nonetheless scraped free of snow, got out of the car, pushed open a wrought-iron gate, and walked down a path she hadn't trod for nearly four years.

She'd cursed herself for being unable to forget that day, its memory raking at her with bloodied claws, yet it turned out she actually had misplaced some of the details, enough that she'd needed to consult a website for the precise location she sought. She paced the rows, counting as she went, comparing the number against the directions she'd memorized. One. Two. Three. Four. Turn right at five. Slower now, looking to the right, ignoring the left, ticking off the individual sites. Stopping at the seventh.

"Hey, fella," she said to the simple white gravestone.

*   *   *

Michael, who'd been taunting her for months—*Fake it till you make it. Be the bigger bitch*, all those things—chose this moment to clam up.

She listened hard, just in case. But all she heard was the tinkling drip of melting snow, punctuated by the occasional trill of birdsong, the earth luxuriating in this briefest of breaks, yearning toward the spring that lay still so many weeks away.

She knelt and laid the single rose she'd brought atop the stone. As she'd long suspected, Beverly and Calvin's weekly offerings had been cleared away. She glanced around first to make sure she was alone. The stones stretched away in so many identical rows, narrow, white, and rounded, most with a simple cross carved above a name, a few with Stars of David. She wondered if a single stone sported the crescent moon of Islam.

"I'm sorry I haven't come around. But"—but what? "I've been busy."

She could imagine his retort. *Suck it up. I've been dead.*

She forced the words out before she lost her nerve.

"I fucked up, Michael. I fucked up big time. I had this case. A kid. I didn't want to deal with it. I used you as an excuse. I didn't want to do it because of you. You'd have been so mad."

She took a breath, awaited judgment. Nothing.

She could just see him, waiting patiently, hearing out her latest confession of inadequacy, detailing her fears, her failings, the way he had so many times in their too-few years together. He'd nod occasionally, holding her hand, nothing more. No enveloping hugs, no soothing "there-there" pats, no soliloquies about how she could fix things. He'd just . . . listen. It was so little. It was the world.

"I wasted so much time. I let that kid twist in the wind before I finally got my act together. I ignored Calvin. Was mean to your mom. To be fair"—Julia scrubbed the back of her hand across her eyes; it came away wet—"she was mean to me, too."

Clash of the titans, you two. Always.

So he hadn't completely abandoned her.

"And I used you as an excuse for everything. For my own assholery."

Is that a word?

"It should be." She drew a deep, rattling breath. She'd stood so still for so long a patch of snow had melted, puddling around her boots. She lifted her head, straightened her shoulders. For so long, she'd walked with them rounded, chin tucked toward her chest, hunching her way through an existence she'd narrowed to nearly nothing. She let her gaze wander, across the rows and rows and rows of stone, past them to the foothills, lifting inexorably to the mountain, on this day topped triumphantly by a slyly teasing sun. *There's more where this came from*, it seemed to say, as it shone down upon her. *But you won't get it by hiding away.*

Was that the sun? Or Michael again?

"Now what?" she whispered. Grief, she'd known how to do that. Hadn't asked for it, but once it descended she'd pulled it to her, swaddled herself in it, made it her whole goddamn identity.

You know this part.

Did she?

But it's so hard, she started say. Then stopped. She knew what he'd say to *that*. He'd play the dead card again, and the only way to compete with that was to be dead herself, or at least locked in the nearest emotional equivalent. She'd tried that. It hadn't worked. Only one thing to do now.

She ran her hands over the stone's smooth surface, warmed by the sun.

Traced the words and numbers:

Sgt. Michael John Sullivan, 1982–2011.

Leaned in and touched her lips to stone, a real kiss this time, not the perfunctory, dismissive peck, sour with resentment, she'd administered the hallway portrait.

"Goodbye, sweetheart."

She turned and walked back up the path, steps quickening, heading into her future. She didn't look back.

ACKNOWLEDGMENTS

Tʜᴀɴᴋs ᴛᴏ ᴍʏ stalwart agent Richard Curtis, who took an unwieldy manuscript and gently helped me extract the parts that worked. I'm thrilled to be working again with editor Terri Bischoff, and so thankful for the support of the Crooked Lane crew shepherding this book to publication—Matt Martz, Melissa Rechter and Madeline Rathle.

Dan Weinberg and Michelle Tafoya Weinberg generously provided writing space and solitude in a hushed, snowy locale so beautiful it worked its way into the novel.

Jim Taylor graciously answered questions—almost certainly not nearly enough—about legal processes. Any mistakes are my own.

Then-Missoulian editor Kathy Best helped me carve out writing time from the crazy, adrenaline-soaked hours demanded by a daily newspaper. Along those lines, I'm indebted to the baristas at Black Coffee Roasting, Break Espresso and Clyde Coffee who kept the java coming during those predawn writing sessions.

I've benefited immeasurably over the years from the friends and mentors I've found via membership in International Thriller Writers, Mystery Writers of America, Sisters in Crime and Rocky Mountain Fiction Writers. I'm especially grateful to the Creel crew and those in

The Thrill Begins—still can't believe my good fortune in being included.

Tip of the hat to Lyle, my brother Roger's sweet chocolate Labrador, whose name I unforgivably gave to a cat.

And always and forever, profound gratitude for Scott's unwavering support.